The Gravedigger's

Volun

Sam Feuerbach is a bestselling fantasy author. His series *The Krosann Saga* and *The Gravedigger's Son* garnered more than 30,000 enthusiastic reviews (Audible/Amazon) in Germany. In October 2018, *The Gravedigger's Son and the Waif Girl* was awarded the **German Fantasy Prize** for German fantasy prize for the best German-language audiobook 2018.

His humorous fantasies, set in the middle-ages, are full of riveting action and captivating dialogue. Even when he is not writing, Sam is thinking about what to write and always looking for the magic in the everyday.

Fantasy is as much a part of Sam's life as brushing his teeth and waiting to cross when the pedestrian light is red.

The Saga of the Gravedigger's Son
Volume 1
Volume 2
Volume 3
Volume 4

Sam Feuerbach

The Gravedigger's Son
and the Waif Girl

Volume One

Translator: Tim Casey – with thanks to Erika Casey
for all her inspirational help over the years

Proof-Reader: Neil McCourt

Special thanks to my valiant helpers
Benedikt, Jasmin, Dagi and Johanna

Cover design: Johanna Benden, bene
Photo: @wingnutdesigns, depositphoto

Illustrations: Iga Żywicka

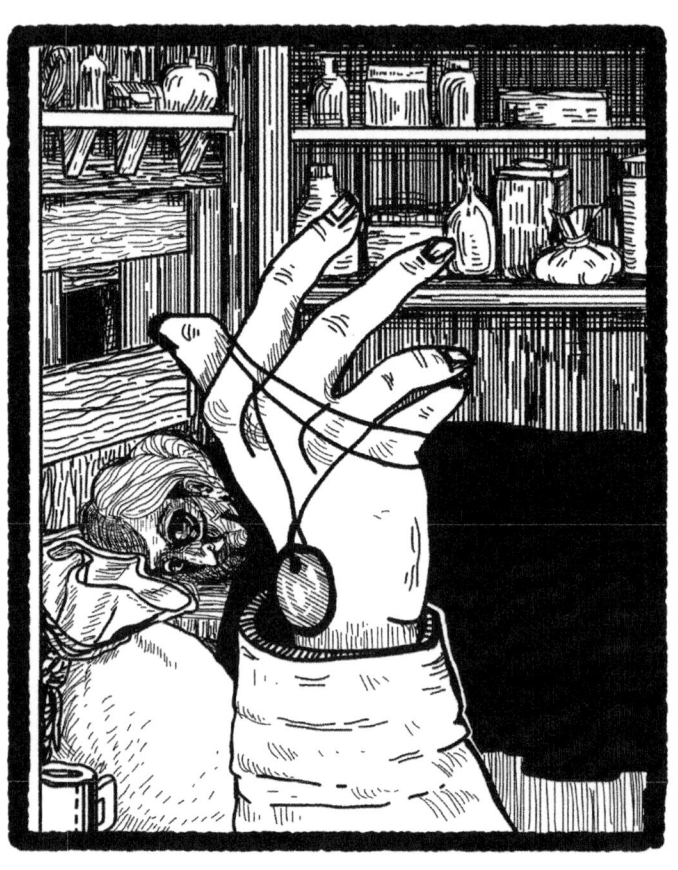

the preparer of poisons

Farin shoved the woman's tongue back into her gaping mouth with two of his fingers. A clout of flesh, dark-blue and fissured, its appearance would doubtless have been too much for sensitive souls. The left one of the two remaining brown-stained teeth in her upper-jaw jiggled as he worked, while the sole occupant of her lower-jaw peered up from below. Her masticatory organs were undoubtedly in poor condition, but there was another reason why Farin busied himself blithely in the woman's mouth: the dead don't bite.

He tied her chin up with a hemp cord. The old woman had closed her mouth for the last time. The cord helped to keep it in place. Her pale eyes looked accusingly at him although he'd had nothing to do with her passing. At least, not until this afternoon when the alderman had turned up in his horse and cart with the dead body. He had ordered him to unload the woman and have her ready for burial tomor-row evening. A wondrous occurrence – why would the head of the village be bothered with the woman, especially as he wasn't related to her? It went completely against his notoriously stingy nature.

Farin splayed his thumb and index finger, gently covering her eyeballs with her lids, which he glued shut with a few drops of sugar water from a small bowl. The old woman had closed her eyes for the last time. He knew her only in passing, had seen her a few times in the distance, usually frantically doing a runner. Dark rumours had grown around the woman – her life had been shrouded in mystery. Yes, shrouded in mystery – that's what was always said about people who didn't keep to the straight and narrow, who went off on their own strange way. But it made no difference what odyssey the old woman had been on – death is always the final destination; it brings everything to a predictable end. What was her name again? He rattled his brains in vain – the name just wouldn't come to him.

He took her chin firmly in his hand, turning her head, first one way, then the other. He had to remember to disguise the dark marks on her throat, one on the left and several on the right.

The smell, the condition of her skin and the dissipating rigor mortis all suggested to him that the old woman had been dead for roughly two days. Farin sighed – it was going to be a long evening. Father would be raging if the body wasn't immaculate and ready for the graveyard the next morning, which meant there was no time to waste. He grasped the hem of the coarse linen dress from below her knees and gingerly pulled it over her hips, chest and head. The material was caked in dirt, particularly the bottom third, on account of the bodily discharges. Although the stench of death stuck to her garment like pitch, he couldn't just throw it onto the fire. As she had no other clothing, he would have to wash the dress and put it on the woman again. He folded it once and placed it at her feet.

The rain began pattering on the roof of the small canopy. Father and he had prudently repaired it during the summer. Now he was standing in the three-sided hut and was dry. The old woman was lying at the gable end, in front of him and on the long workbench. He stepped back and looked at her. What was he dealing with here? A body – was that all? A piece of dead meat that nature had given, only to take it away again? It could also be an empty body that God had given, only to take away again, one whose soul had departed from it, in order to float away to a better world. Regardless of with or without body, the Lord must have set down strict rules, otherwise there would be an unseemly scramble over there. The Plague had carried off three-quarters of the villagers seven years previously. His mother too had been one of its victims. First there was the fever, then the terrible boils all over the body and two days later, the Black Death. It had all happened so quickly, not even time to say goodbye. Mother was burned along with twenty other plague victims, all piled together. Father and he had dealt with the bodies, day in, day out, but neither had been infected.

"Even the Plague gives the gravedigger and his son a wide berth," was the conclusion the villagers reached.

How could Farin define it? Luck? That wasn't right, for the loss of his mother was the worst thing that had ever happened to him. None of the healer's measures had been effective. On the contrary – Farin had noticed that the excessive bloodletting especially had only weakened the people further. Hoping against hope for recovery had been totally useless.

It had been several years since he'd stopped paying attention to the village priest's sermons. A certain pragmatism had crept up on him, a bitter, practical orientation that hardly harmonised with the religious digressions on heaven and earth. Was he in danger of becoming a disbeliever? He blessed himself quickly just in case. Whatever the case, there was one thing he knew: every birth led to a corpse.

It was only a matter of time.

Farin pressed his lips together. He would never forget the first time he had to prepare the body of a child. A three-year-old girl, an innocent thing, who'd kicked the bucket on account of some mysterious bug. The tears had streamed down his face as he'd cleaned the child. And then there were her relatives, praying and praying and praying. Luckily, the priest had a comforting explanation at the ready during the funeral service: "The Lord moves in mysterious ways."

Oh, right!

Instead of doing his work, he was thinking of God only knows – at this rate he wouldn't be finished by midnight. He took a cloth from the hook, dunked it in the big water-bowl beside him and wrung it out. "Washing of the body begins with the arms", his father had taught him. Farin took hold of the woman's right arm. He slowly wiped upwards along the withered skin of her forearm and stopped suddenly. He stared at the old woman's chest in disbelief. A perpendicular line, encrusted with blood, ran from her bellybutton to the base of her neck, a crossbeam stretched across under her breasts. It was the shape of a large cross made up of ridged scars caused by countless cuts and wounds. Most of them old, a few fresh. He ran his fingertips along the bulges and craters. She really had taken her signs of the cross too literally. She must have been cutting the Sign of the Lord into her body with a crude knife for years.

"Never speculate about the deceased while you're working." That was another thing his father had taught him. Farin shook his head and set to work. He'd make sure that she'd meet her Maker clean, and her nearest and dearest would remember their last viewing of the deceased fondly. People never forget the last viewing.

When he was finished with her arms and legs, he carefully cleaned her upper and lower body. He rinsed the cloth in the bowl several times, the water becoming grey as the skies above. It was still raining, but he urgently needed to get fresh water from the stream because the rotten base of the rain barrel was no longer watertight. His father and he lived at the end of the world – or so the little homestead where Farin worked was referred to by the villagers. It was apt really – at the end of the stream, at the end of the village, at the end of the world. Anyone who made themselves comfortable on the workbench in this open shed really had reached the end. From here on there was nothing – except for a heavy heart, undrinkable water downstream, and contaminated air all around.

The autumn wind drove the low clouds before it in the failing light; it didn't look as if the rain would stop before nightfall. And so Farin took his washbowl, left the protection of the canopy, and stomped a few yards out into the yard. Some of the stinking brew splashed onto his trousers in the process.

"Oh, shit!" cursed Farin. This wasn't the first time it had happened to him. Once again, he'd carelessly overfilled the bowl. A bucket would be much more practical, but father couldn't add it to the bill – in contrast to the traditional washbowl. He threw the dirty water, as always, into the bushes a few yards away from his workplace. It didn't seem to bother the pink hawthorn. On the contrary: the plant would bloom and flourish like no other in the surroundings – the branches had grown taller than his head long ago. Farin ran to the stream with the empty bowl. He was still annoyed at himself because he was going to have to wash his trousers and dry them over the fire, as they were the only ones he possessed. What *did* he possess, anyway? Nothing, if he thought about it. Nothing except his name. He was one up on God in that respect.

"Farin!" he said loudly.

That was something, anyway.

Farin loved the stream for many reasons. Its gurgling sounded friendly and calming, its cool water was always refreshing, and he always fund it easiest to think about things when sitting on one of the enormous boulders scattered around in the stream. His thoughts would float longingly downstream. The current would wind its way around bend after bend in the forest, plummet down a sudden waterfall, run across a meadow until if finally flowed into a large river. It would get bigger and bigger, making its inexorable way through the Worldly Kingdom in its constant search for the sea.

The sea! They said it consisted of an endless supply of water, and that its waves crashed against the shore, never growing tired.

Is there somebody trying to carry a gigantic bowl there too? I want to see the sea. Just once, dreamed Farin.

He carried the bowl, filled to the brim, carefully back to the shed. Why don't I bring the water in a bucket and then pour it into the bowl? Farin asked himself, not for the first time. Because father taught me differently and that's the way he wanted it, was the all-explaining answer.

He set to work again with the fresh water. Having finished with the body, he started preparing the head. He washed her hair with a concoction of egg-yolk, camomile, nettle-juice, burdock-root stock and plenty of water. Then he cut it – a tedious undertaking, which was more down to the clunky scissors than to the woman's thin strands of hair.

"The hands are very important", his father always stressed. After all, they lay respectfully folded on the chest of the deceased person during the ceremony. Or, to be more precise, his father would beat these rules into him with his cane – his preferred teaching method. Then Farin took care of her fingernails. He didn't need to use the heavy scissors for this, thanks be to God, but he could cut the nails with a small pliers.

His father had bought the pliers two years previously, after Farin's mishap with the big scissors. That time he had cut off a deceased person's finger by mistake. It hadn't bothered the corpse, but the relatives were quite put out, unimpressed by the peacefully crossed nine fingers on the chest, accompanied by a bloody stump. Unfortunately, all the relatives had been convinced that the deceased had worn an expensive ring on the missing finger – after all, that was why it was called the ring finger. The piece of jewellery was nowhere to be found. The mourning relatives had made a serious complaint, not at the graveside, but before the alderman, and then everyone got their just deserts – his father got no payment for his work and Farin was paid double in the form of an extra sound beating.

Thanks to the pliers, all the fingers were safe this time. Then he cleaned the nails with a short knife. He got rid of the black behind the fingernails, but also some bits of skin that were stuck behind the nails of her right hand.

"Nobody looks at the feet," his father had taught him, drumming it in with an encouraging slap on the face. Still, Farin attended to the ten toenails with as much diligence as he had to her fingernails.

Maybe God looks at the feet.

Just like every other evening, the daylight disappeared slowly but surely. Farin lit an oil-lamp and placed it on a board positioned on the workbench. Yes indeed, this contraption was called a workbench. Once, when he was a little boy, he had used it as a table by mistake, which had made father livid.

"THAT'S THE WORKBENCH!" he'd roared. "You don't put dead people on tables!"

Overwhelmed by so much piety, and strengthened by a sound educational beating, Farin had never forgotten his lesson.

Shit, he should have taken and washed the filthy dress when he'd collected the fresh water. Now he'd have to make do with the remaining water in the bowl because he really didn't fancy going to the stream again in the dark. Still, the material looked dirtier than the water so it might get a little bit cleaner. He soaked the linen garment in the bowl with both hands, then squeezed the brown water out of it. Limited success. No, that wasn't going to work. He'd bring the dress to the flowing water the next morning and wash it a second time. He turned to the dead woman again with a sigh. There was a blinding flash of lightning, and the accompanying clap of thunder made him shiver.

Don't be afraid, you idiot! It's only a thunderstorm.

He hung the dress from a beam and turned his attention to the old woman's face.

"The face is even more important than the hands", his father had drummed into him. Farin had known that already. Dead or not, people always first sought out the eyes of their fellows, and when it came to dead people, their eyes were still in the middle of their faces. He examined the woman's cheeks and nose. The blood had had settled at the back of her head and so her skin looked as pale as goat's milk. The wrinkled skin over her cheekbones and chin hung down in folds. Sorrow, care and affliction had chiselled a grimace into her features. As if paralysed, Farin stared at her face. What was it that was bothering him? There was something else in the features of the dead woman. Something intangible, something evil, scornful. He shivered again.

An unfamiliar sound made him spin around. It had become completely dark behind him and it took his eyes some time to become accustomed to the blackness. Was that a shadow moving there? There were goose pimples on his arms, he felt he was being watched.

"Is there anybody there?" he called out and was shocked by the thinness in his voice.

Nobody answered – what had he expected? He chided himself for being so chicken-hearted, but still had a queasy feeling as he turned back to the workbench.

Don't let yourself be distracted, Farin. Nobody comes here of their own free-will, stands out there in the darkness and watches as you wash a corpse.

His new-found courage didn't last long. He felt as if a bucket of freezing water was being thrown over him. Her eyes – wide-open – were staring at him. He let out a short scream. He could have sworn that the eyes were alive. Hadn't he just seen a glimmer of light in the pupils, as if somebody with a lantern had just run past a window? Dumbstruck, he stared at the dead woman's face.

If she blinks now, I'm going to collapse. He had only just gently closed the eyes of the old woman and glued them. His heart was pounding as he repeated the procedure. It's not unusual for the lids to spring open again as the rigor mortis disappears, he reassured himself.

He turned around abruptly – nothing but darkness behind him, everything as normal. His body slowly began to warm up again. What was wrong with him at all?

A washer of corpses who gets the creeps, he thought with a crooked grin, is like a butcher who's afraid of the sight of blood. Come on, Farin, do your work professionally.

"Now, my dear...eh, what's your name again?" he asked the deceased, but she didn't answer.

Something with "G" or "K" at the start. Farin looked again at the deceased's body. He leaped backwards a yard as if somebody was yanking him with a rope.

There was something else on the old woman's chest. Something shiny, something round. Anyway, something that hadn't been there a moment ago. He glanced around him, his heart hammering. Nobody apart from himself could have been close to the corpse. So where did this thing come from? He slowly tiptoed closer. He pressed his lips as closely together as possible so he wouldn't scream. Unable to blink, he stared at the dead woman's chest, just where her heart had once beaten. A pendant was lying there, or an amulet. Very carefully, as if he feared his hands might turn to dust at any moment, he reached out to the jewel with his fingers and grasped it. It felt warm and it looked like a coin without an impression: round, plain, and smooth on both sides. Only a hole near the edge, obviously for attaching a chain. It had a yellowish sheen in the lamplight. He felt its weight with his outstretched arm – too light for gold. He carefully bit into it. His teeth left no marks. He'd never seen a metal like that. Was he imagining things, or did he get the faint taste of garlic in his mouth? What should he do with his find? Not having a box, he threaded a length of hemp cord through it and lifted it over his head, the amulet disappearing like a necklace under his linen shirt. He would give the piece of jewellery to her family before the funeral, but he would have to keep it safe from his father in the meantime. His old man would be guaranteed to hold onto it until a bit of grass had grown over the grave. Then he'd sell it in a village far away and get drunk on the money. His father had all too often cashed in the contents of dead people's pockets, thereby confirming the prejudices towards, as well as the poor reputation of, the gravediggers' guild. His old man was good – at nursing his bad reputation. Farin did not want to be like his father. On no account. Was that why he was honest? How would he have turned out if his father had always behaved righteously and impeccably? Would Farin now be a scoundrel, one who never missed an opportunity of enriching himself at the expense of others?

These thoughts weren't really getting him anywhere although they did help to normalise his heart rate.

Where does this amulet come from, though? Stop asking questions, concentrate on your work, Farin!

The old woman's face was the personification of inno-cence. He stopped short again. Really? It certainly looked more relaxed, or was he just imagining things? He took a cleanish cloth from the hook and dipped it in diluted brandy, liberally rubbing it into the forehead, cheeks, chin and neck. This slowed down the decomposition process.

Be careful not to use too much. Or waste it, as father would say. No wonder – he preferred to drink the cheap booze.

Next, he added a little colour to the deceased's cheeks. For this, Farin used a thin paste of ochre and oil – an old, secret family recipe for enhancing the appearance. He blackened the lids and eyebrows with a stick of charcoal and added a little shine with a touch of sheep-grease. Then he combed the corpse's hair.

He took a step back and looked at his handiwork. Miraculously, the woman looked a few years younger, around eighty maybe. It still didn't make her more alive. Damn it, what was her name – it was on the tip of his tongue.

Farin yawned. It was late and he decided to go to bed. He'd wash the dress a second time in the morning – that would leave enough time for it to dry. Perfuming was tomorrow's job anyway – the aroma would only dissipate overnight. The old woman wasn't going to run away, and so he went to the cottage where his father was.

Such was his life, and such was his home. Simple. The little hut consisted mostly of clay. A firmly trampled clay floor, wattle walls plastered in clay, the roof covered in flat clay shingles. There was only one room. He smelled and heard his old man before he saw him. He was lying in the corner behind the stove, grunting and farting and sleeping off his inebriation. His mouth was open, and his lips glistened with dribbling drool. An old man, bowed down by life, eaten up by hatred and embittered by jealousy towards those who were better off. More or less the whole village then.

Farin took off his dirty trousers, lay down on the straw mat opposite, and fell asleep immediately.

"Lazy good-for nothing!" His father's loving voice, accompanied by an encouraging kick, woke him up.

"The cock has finished crowing and you're still asleep."

There was something about this tradition. Father always

claimed the cock had finished crowing. Because Farin was still sleeping at that time, he could never put that claim to the test. Maybe he should just stay awake one night and keep his ears peeled.

"What's the story with ugly Gerlunda – she's still lying naked in the hut, kindly get her done, son."

Farin sat up. It was still dark outside. "Gerlunda! Of course, that's her name. Why couldn't I remember?"

"Because you're stupid, lad," his father explained.

Oh, right!

A few moments later and he was standing in front of the body in the shed, dressed only in his shirt. She was lying there, just as he had left her, and her dress was hanging from the beam. In the light of day Farin questioned the fears he'd had the evening before. Had he been dreaming? Instinctively, his hand went to his chest and immediately rejected that possibility. An amulet was hanging on a hemp cord around his neck.

How did this peculiar piece of jewellery end up on Gerlunda's body, and what did it mean?

He peered at the body with a mixture of suspicion and wonder. Gerlunda – the preparer of poisons – that's what the villagers called her. He grabbed the dress, ran back into the house, picked up his trousers from beside the door and hurried to the stream. First, he washed the two pieces of clothing thoroughly, and then himself. Farin rubbed his forefinger across both rows of teeth and then washed his mouth out. He cleaned the gaps between them with one of the little pointed sticks that he kept safe here. His reflection thanked him with a white grin. Mother had shown him how to do it, while father just had laughed at the idea. He looked at his dark, unkempt hair in the stream. He liked it like that –

he'd comb his hair when he was dead.

When he arrived home, father was standing beside the corpse with his hands on his hips.

"Where have you been hiding yourself?" he snorted. Then he pointed at Gerlunda. "We'll add the bowl, the comb, the cord and the make-up to the bill. Is that clear?"

"And what about the water for washing?"

"Don't be getting greedy, lad. We won't charge for that." He gave a wheezy laugh.

Farin took little pleasure in such business acumen. All of the objects he'd used in preparing Gerlunda were now considered unclean and no longer usable – especially the washbowl. This was traditionally destroyed after the procedure and added to the bill for the bereaved. Farin looked at the bowl and frowned. A truly amazing implement, because it must have been destroyed and added to the bill at least thirty times. The same was true for the comb.

"The burial is this afternoon, so get cracking, lad."

"What happened to her?" asked Farin.

His father cocked his head and stared at him. He couldn't stand questions. Especially questions like that. He growled: "The priest found her in her hut, dead. He came into "The Warm Beer" yesterday afternoon and told me. After that he sent the old woman here with the alderman."

"The Warm Beer" was the name of the village tavern opposite the church – a very enticing and appealing name. Presumably the innkeeper would have had the same number of regulars if he'd called his pub "The Warm Piss" – for the simple reason that it was the only tavern in the village.

"How did she die?"

Father scowled. The tip of his tongue darted through the gap between his upper teeth like a snake – it sashayed in and out beautifully, thanks to the two incisors having fallen out.

He aped Farin: "*How did she die?*" This particular question always annoyed him – but Farin kept on asking it. "Her heart stopped, what else, son."

"Oh, right!"

He knew well that his father knew much more, and that he knew that Farin knew. But dear daddy didn't give a damn. "Dead is dead", father regularly said, and like many of his pearls of wisdom, it was hard to contradict. "Questions only damage business." At the end of the day everybody died because their hearts stopped. Period! Even though Farin had been looking for reasons of late that might at least make a mockery out of this particular insight of his father's, he had to admit that the phrase did contain a grain of truth. People's hearts stopped sometime. That applied equally to everyone, whether it was a seventy-year-old succumbing to age, or a warrior stabbed through by his enemy, or even a ten-year-old boy, falling from a tree and breaking his neck.

"I'll go dig, you finish off the old woman. And remember: Dead is dead. Questions only damage business."

Farin didn't reply.

Father grabbed the pickaxe and shovel and headed off towards the graveyard. Not bad, considering there were days when he generously left this work to his son too.

Farin wouldn't see his old man until early evening. After digging out the grave, the old man would retire to the village tavern opposite the church and get drunk, just like yesterday and the day-before-yesterday and every day before that. At that hour he would generally drink alone with the innkeeper, while the other regulars would turn up considerably later. That was fine by father – he had to sit at a corner table behind the door anyway, far away from the other villagers, who wanted to have as little to do with the gravedigger as possible. That made no odds so long as the tavern was empty.

Farin watched his father leave. He yawned.

I'll catch up on some sleep later, he thought.

the village

The clatter of hooves woke Farin at around noon. He quickly slipped into his still-damp trousers and stepped out of the hut. The village alderman pulled up with horse and cart in the middle of the yard.

"Come on, you scoundrel! Load up the old woman!" was his greeting.

"And good day to you too!" He gave Hamak a friendly smile.

There was no smile in response. "Stop talking! Get on with it!"

"Wait, I'll bring her to you."

"Hurry up!"

The alderman was always in a hurry, nobody knew why. His name was Hamak, but for some reason Farin never addressed him by that name.

He shrugged his shoulders and went to the shed. He carefully straightened out Gerlunda's dress one last time and looked at his handiwork. All in all, he'd prepared her pretty well, he thought to himself with satisfaction. As was his practice, he shoved his arms under the woman's body and carried her to the cart. Being eighteen and having a powerful build, this wasn't a problem for him. Farin was used to dealing with considerably heavier people. That, along with countless digging of graves, had resulted in powerful arm and back muscles. He gently laid Gerlunda onto the bed of the cart.

The alderman glanced at the corpse and smirked joylessly. "The old one never looked that good before." Hamak clicked his tongue and tapped the horse with his reins. The animal turned the cart around in the yard.

"When is the burial?"

"When the bells ring, scoundrel."

His name was Farin, but for some reason Hamak never addressed him by that name.

The horse, the cart, Hamak and Gerlunda left the yard with a clatter of hooves.

Shit, he'd forgotten to cover Gerlunda with a burial shroud. He looked up at the cloudy sky. Not fatal – as long as it didn't rain.

Father arrived home in the early evening with empty hands and a stomach full of beer. He staggered and shouted and shouted and staggered around the place, aimlessly and pointlessly as so often before, listlessly chewing on a crust of bread before sinking down peacefully onto his mattress. Father had left his pickaxe and shovel in the tavern as was his custom. If he woke up at the crack of dawn the next day and two of his most important implements were missing, he would angrily place all the blame on his wayward son. And because Farin knew no other ne'er-do-well he in turn could stick the boot into, he headed back to the village himself.

It was raining – an unpleasant, grey drizzle. He pulled the hood of his cloak further over his face. The bell in the church tower had stubbornly refused to chime, but if the funeral was to take place today, then it would need to be happening soon. The journey to the village took three-quarters of an hour if you were fast; it took Farin half an hour. The red-tiled church steeple rose in the distance above the tree-tops – the proud high-point of the little town. He trudged through the mud in his bare feet. Winter was bearing inexorably down, and he urgently needed a new pair of shoes. A pair of simple clogs from the village turner would do. That was a job he'd have loved to have trained in and practised. He loved the smell of new wood and sawdust; he loved the implements, the merry lathe, and the pole lathe. He'd spent many days in the workshop as a boy and had always lent a hand. Until father had got wind of it.

The first huts of his home village of Heap appeared right and left in front of him. Gerlunda had lived on the very edge of the forest, in one of the further houses. Hardly anyone in the village could stand the preparer of poisons – they had all steered well clear of her.

It's not much different for the gravedigger, thought Farin.

No wonder! Father reminded people of the inevitable, the uninvited, the unrelenting. And he was the grave-digger's son, the inheritor of this unpopularity. The villagers might as well despise and avoid him: Death was God's broomstick. And Farin liked things to be tidy.

He could hear it in the distance already: the faded sign with the warm tankard of beer swinging wantonly in the wind. The mounting, two rusty chains hanging on two rusty nails, squeaked gently and guided the ears towards the village tavern. A cunning move on the innkeeper's part.

Now he could see his destination too. A simple, half-timbered building with a taproom and four guestrooms above. The innkeeper, his wife and two sons lived in the annex to the rear.

When it came down to it, Farin didn't like being

among people. But he plucked up courage, stepped onto the broad wooden step and forcefully pushed open the door. The latch slipped out of his rain-soaked hand and when the door crashed into the inner wall, it rattled for what seemed like an eternity. What an entrance! All of the regulars in the pub turned to look at him. Farin smiled apologetically. Nobody smiled back. About a dozen men were sitting there, including Alderman Hamak. He turned away with a bored expression. None of the others showed any reaction when they recognised the gravedigger's son. He wasn't worth it. They turned back to their beers and their pipes.

"It's only the gravedigger's son," grunted the inn-keeper.

"I can see that myself, Georig," replied the man with the rat face, whose name Farin had forgotten.

Everyone in the village had a name – with a few exceptions. His father, for example – he was simply called gravedigger. And then Farin was gravedigger's son.

It smelled of alcohol, sweat and pipe-smoke. Each of the men was puffing away at his own individual sucking-device – long, short, thin, fat, high or flat, each pipe was discussed, disputed over, or spun yarns about. This was the raison d'être of these village champions. On the table lay an array of pipe-bowls, mouthpieces, pipe tools and tobacco tampers.

"My new briar has to be smoked in yet. First, I'll fill her loosely up to a third," explained ratface, dramatically holding up his churchwarden pipe.

The others nodded appreciatively and honoured his expertise with a moment's silence. Then half of them stuffed their pipes with earnest devotion, the others cleaned their pipes with unshakeable meticulousness.

Farin didn't give a damn about their pipe blather, but he'd never have said so out loud. He wasn't allowed to join in the men's conversation anyway. In the village pecking order he came somewhere between the mangy street mutts and the goats. Knackers, whores, executioners and grave-diggers had to sit in a corner to the left of the front door. They got their beer in separate tankards at a separate table. Which was exactly where Farin found both pickaxe and shovel – he could always rely on father.

He took the tools and stepped into the middle of the room.

"Alderman, please say when the burial is."

The men disliked being spoken to during their smoking sessions, especially by the gravedigger's son.

"Don't be so pushy – your father is never satisfied, is he?"

"What do you mean?"

"You two can't wait to cash in, can you, scoundrel?" grunted Hamak. He tugged at one end of his tousled handlebar moustache. "And anyway, it's raining – does anyone here want to put the old preparer of poisons six foot under in this weather?"

A collective groan came from the group, not least because rain was the natural enemy to any delicious pipe.

"Now piss off, gravedigger's son. Don't you see I've just lit my pipe?"

It was a sacred ritual in the village of Heap, and one couldn't be disturbed after the packing and lighting of a pipe. It was, after all, the gentlemen's most fervent desire to follow the tradition of dedicating oneself to the enjoyment and fraternity that was kindled by smoking.

And so, with the pickaxe on his left shoulder and the

shovel on his right, Farin stood there none the wiser, like the village idiot, in the middle of the tavern and knew neither what to do nor what to say. In fact, his plan had been simply to return the amulet to the deceased's family. The men turned their attention back to their pipes, clearly intending to ignore him, not just for now, but for all eternity. With a lump in his throat, Farin wondered if it might just be best to give the amulet to the alderman – then he'd be done with it.

One last shot: "Did...did...", what was her name again? "...the preparer of poisons have family?"

He could have passed the hat around considering the uproarious laughter his question provoked.

One of the men snorted: "That takes the biscuit! Does Gerlunda have family? Did you ever hear the like?"

Once the men had stopped laughing, Hamak grunted: "The old one had no living relatives. Nobody visited her over the last few decades either. Now, get lost, gravedigger's son."

What else had he expected? Farin slowly turned to the door and left the tavern. Hardly was he outside when the innkeeper's son came around the corner. The gaunt lad's name was Blossak.

"Hey, Farin. I heard the news. Did you really prepare the preparer of poisons for the grave?"

They'd known each other since they were nippers. They'd been good pals when they were children, but they'd hardly met each other in the last few years. The innkeeper's son avoided the gravedigger's son too.

"Hey, Bloss. Yes, I did. And she really was quite dead."

That was clearly what Blossak had wanted to hear, for his face took on an ominous expression. Farin knew this face – usually it was accompanied by some absurd plan, which meant a lot of trouble if it was implemented.

"People are saying the maddest things about the preparer of poisons. Some people are convinced she was possessed by evil spirits." He was whispering as if he were afraid that she might hear his words.

"If that's true, then they're dead too. I haven't heard much of the gossip going round."

"That's because your customers usually don't chat to you much."

"True enough," nodded Farin. He was used to people seeing the deceased as his customers.

"A wayfarer told my father over a beer years ago that Gerlunda had once been a lady-in-waiting at the court of the king."

"After how many beers?" Farin associated ladies-in-waiting with beautiful, gentle creatures – qualities which were as far from the preparer of poisons as the king's court was.

Bloss now had his hand over his mouth as he whispered: "Let's have a gawk in the old one's house."

"What? Why do you want to go there?"

The innkeeper's son whispered even more quietly. "Keep this to yourself now. Gerlunda is supposed to have concocted drinks – love-potions too, which are guaranteed to win over any girl."

Farin looked wide-eyed at him. "Are you serious? How's that supposed to work?"

"Let's go there, pick up the drinks and check them out." Blossak winked at him.

"Hmm, I'm not so sure." Farin sucked his upper lip.

"C'mon now! What's going to happen? The old dear is dead!"

"But isn't that theft?"

"You've just heard my old man and his cronies. There is no family. So, nobody is going to notice if we take a few things before they rot. It would be such a shame if we didn't..." He winked again. His voice sounded oily, lewd and conspiratorial. "Just imagine, you put a few drops of the elixir of love into the drinking mugs, and the women will be all over you."

No matter how hard he tried not to, Farin couldn't help thinking of Annietta, the blacksmith's daughter. A wonderful girl. They had been playmates from the age of four. He had saved her countless times with his sword *Windswipe* from the clutches of an unseemly dragon or an even more unseemly kidnapper.

He remembered wistfully back to the time when the adults' reservations towards children hadn't yet applied. In those days Farin had been Annietta's favourite rescuer and favourite knight. It hadn't taken much, just children with imagination who liked each other. Added to that, a knotty branch with a little stick tied on with hemp cord as a cross-guard. A sword couldn't be more magical. *Windswipe's* hiding place was always in the undergrowth behind the privy. He closed his eyes nostalgically. He had loved this girl all these years, something he had never shared with anybody. Especially not with Annietta herself. A few months earlier at the midsummer festival he hadn't been able to take his eyes off her: Her nimble turns at the dance, her spinning dress, her wavy hair, her smile. She, on the other hand, had hardly noticed him at all during the festivities – the gravedigger's son. Farin had summoned up every ounce of courage, had walked up to her and was about to ask her for a dance, when her father's stare hit him like a hammer on the anvil. At which point he'd reconsidered his plan. Or had he just bottled it?

"What's wrong now, Farin? Don't be a wet blanket!" Bloss prodded him on the shoulder in a comradely fashion. No villager had touched him in years – after all, touching the gravedigger or the hangman brought bad luck. Whether he wanted to or not, he was grateful for this gesture, even if Bloss was just trying to win him around.

He thought for a moment. Even if this absurdity with the elixir of love were to work, Farin couldn't see himself satisfying his frustrated yearning through deceit. "That's not my cup of tea."

"Were you not listening? It's not you who's going to drink it." He winked again; clearly, his brain was in his trousers.

"Just come with me."

Farin swallowed hard. "Now, you mean?"

Blossak snorted. "Of course, now – while it's raining, and before the funeral starts."

A final attempt to talk Bloss out of it. "Aren't we a bit too old for that sort of thing?"

"I'm not too old for shagging. C'mon, let's go!"

Was it curiosity, was it boredom, was it stupidity? Was he just happy that somebody was sharing secrets with him? Already Farin heard himself utter the two fateful words: "Right, then!"

The three greatest catastrophes of his youth had begun with "Right, then!": The dare of running between the windmill sails as quickly as possible, the scheme for luring the wood sprite out of the sinister forest with a live piglet and locking him in a chicken cage, and the attempt to spy on the village girls as they bathed in the lake.

Wasn't it time to forget these "Right, then!" escapades

once and for all? After all, he was now eighteen years old, an adult, rational and cautious. Well then, just one last time.

The two young men started walking. When they reached the small crossroads, they took the narrow path towards the forest, and it wasn't long before they were standing in front of Gerlunda's property, which was surrounded by thick hedges and a rotten picket-fence. The tall shrubs hid most of the hut – only a narrow, hardly trodden path led through the thick blackberry bushes towards the inside.

Farin sucked on his lower lip. When he was younger, he had never dared go near the place for fear that the preparer of poisons would come storming out, cursing and waving her broom.

It was raining heavily, one reason why they had come across nobody up until now. Just as the church had been standing in the middle of the village since time immemorial, so too had the preparer of poisons always lived in the lopsided cottage behind the hedge. Farin looked sceptically through the narrow gap between the blackberry bushes. He squinted over at the innkeeper's son just as sceptically, in the silent hope he might be having second thoughts.

Blossak noticed his expression. "Don't chicken out now. But leave the stupid pickaxe and shovel down somewhere."

"No way, I'm holding onto them, they're our most important tools."

Blossak grunted. "Whatever." He actually managed to move briskly towards the old woman's house even though his face was telling a different story. "Come on!" he whispered.

A quick glance behind. Nobody to be seen. Farin ducked and slipped through the opening in the hedge too. The path to the front door led through an overgrown herb garden.

Baffled, Blossak looked down to the ground, left and right. "What *are* those horrible flowers. What was the old one going to do with them?"

"Dunno." Farin inhaled deeply – a comfortable feeling, it eased some of the pressure he was feeling. And it definitely smelled better here than at home. He looked at the "horrible" flowers – Blossak really was an idiot – the rain strengthened the scent of sage, thyme, sweet woodruff, rosemary, dill and chives.

The grey entrance door had been painted green long before Farin's birth, as the remaining flakes in the cracks revealed. The door had neither a handle nor a bolt. Nobody in Heap locked their doors, which had less to do with the excessive trust of the residents but owed more to the fact that they didn't have much worth stealing.

What were they doing here anyway? Oh yes, to steal some kind of a love potion – what utter nonsense. Bloss pulled open the door and went in. He really must have been desperate; there was no other explanation for his new-found determination. In the past he'd always sent Farin ahead. Quietly, as if he might wake somebody, the gravedigger's son pushed his way into the hut. He leaned the pickaxe and the shovel on the wall behind the door, then surveyed the scene. He gasped. There was only one room, yet it took him what seemed like an eternity to take in half of what he was looking at. Hundreds of garlic heads, branches and animal skins were hanging from the ceiling. This was enough to send anyone packing, and yet both Blossak and Farin bravely held their ground. Broken containers, items of clothing, boxes, plants, shards of glass, ripped volumes lay scattered on the clay floor, along with lumps of animal – or so he hoped – flesh. Bloody crosses had been painted onto the walls, and on a shelf were little crucibles with powder, ampoules and vials filled with various liquids. Underneath was a row of glasses with spiders, worms and beetles, some appeared dead, while others were still twitching their legs or other body parts.

The stench in the room could knock you for six. Farin's nose was undoubtedly tougher than Blossak's, but the innkeeper's son was holding up well and was breathing through his mouth, pale faced.

"Holy mother of God! What happened here?"

Farin gave a start, then realised it was Blossak he had heard. His mind was racing. Somebody had turned the place upside down, looking for something. But what? There was one thing that was crystal clear: Her name, Gerlunda, the preparer of poisons, wasn't created out of thin air – and she was much more than that – a member of the circle of black or red witches. Father said the priest had found her dead in her hut. What had he made of it all?

Farin walked forward gingerly; he didn't want to step on a glass shard in his bare feet. The glass crunched under Blossak's leather boots as he peered at the shelf with the powders. Finely ground to coarse-grained and in all the colours of the rainbow – plenty to choose from.

"There's nothing labelled," he concluded in disappointment. "How am I supposed to know which of them are the shag-drinks?"

"Don't think I'm going to test them out for you," said Farin emphatically. "Anyway, I'm passionate enough as it is."

Bloss gave a half-hearted smirk. "Well, I definitely don't want to sleep with *you*."

The gravedigger's son gestured to a low door at the back of the hut. "Let's get out of here – best if we go this way."

He stooped down low and slipped out through the back

door. Now he was standing in another herb garden, directly at the edge of the forest. Bloss struggled out into the open air too. The rain had stopped and the last of the daylight fell on the plant-beds. Various types of mushroom were growing in a secluded corner – hardly surprising in this damp autumn.

"The red ones with the white spots, I know them. They're fly agarics," said Blossak proudly. "Those ones are poisonous. The others look edible."

Farin's eyes narrowed. He recognised clouded agarics, deadly skullcaps, death caps, destroying angels, and slippery jacks. Exclusively toadstools, all deadly. Mother had taught him a lot about plants and animals – quite casually, and always without beatings. Thirsting for knowledge, he had soaked up every word.

He looked at Gerlunda's collection of offshoots. How the devil – he stopped himself from instinctively blessing himself – did the old woman manage that? Another example of her witchy activities, for only women who had fallen into evil ways grew toadstools. Flabbergasted, he looked at the dark earth.

"We'd better get out of here, through the forest would be best so nobody will see us," suggested Farin, turning away. The star-shaped leaves of a plant with withered yellow blossoms caught his eye as he was about to make a move. He stood there dumbstruck. He found it comforting that at last he'd got a real fright.

Blossak followed his gaze. "Why are you staring at that weed?"

"That…that's a mandrake."

The innkeeper's son's face went as white as Gerlunda's this morning when she was lying on the workbench.

"*Whaaa?* Are you sure?"

"Of course, I am! Nobody jokes about mandrakes."

As if by command, they both looked upwards. A beam stretched from the roof until over the plant.

"Old…old Gerlunda must have hanged someone here," stuttered Bloss. "There can't…can't be any other explanation. Somebody swung from these gallows and passed water when they were dying."

Farin nodded, horrified. After all, mandrakes only grew in ground sprayed with urine from the hanged. Every child knew that. It followed that Gerlunda wasn't just a black witch, but probably a murderess as well.

The two young men gawped at the mandrake with a mixture of fascination and disgust, their fingers shaking. Anyone who grasped this plant and pulled it out would die. The mandrake's dreadful yelping and groaning would travel directly through the auditory canal and into the person's head, destroying everything within.

"That's worth a fortune," whispered Blossak.

"And why did the intruder, who turned everything upside down, not take it with them?"

"Probably there at the wrong time – you know how hard it is to pluck a mandrake. Maybe he'll come again soon."

Of course, Farin knew the stories about the most magical of plants. If you wanted to grasp one, you had to stop your ears with wax or pitch, and you had to pick your time carefully – either on a Sunday after sunset, or on a Friday before sunrise. On Sunday you needed a black dog, and on Friday a white one without other colours on the body. You had to tie the mandrake to the dog's tail with a noose and chase the animal away so that it would pull the plant out of the ground. The poor mutt would kick the bucket in a most painful way on account of the mandrake's screams.

By this point it was all too much for Blossak. "Let's skedaddle. I'll...I'll have to think of another way of winning Annietta round."

A hot shudder ran down Farin's spine like lightning, and it had nothing to do with the persistent drizzle, nor with the toadstools, nor with the state of the hut, nor with the mandrake. Had he heard correctly? Had Blossak actually mentioned Annietta? Annietta of all people. Unable to respond, he let on that his head was full of noxious thoughts.

"What's wrong with you? Let's get out of here." Blossak raced to the remains of the rear fence and disappeared into the forest.

Slowly, Farin's spirits revived. Gritting his teeth, he followed the innkeeper's son.

Reason

Good-for-nothing ne'er-do-well!" Father's loving voice woke him. "Where are the pickaxe and shovel? Stupid idiot!"

His endearing visage loomed over him – creased, shot through with grey stubble, red nose, droopy eyes. And, last but not least, the old familiar smell – of warm beer and sweat.

"Good-for-nothing ne'er-do-well" was a phrase Farin knew well. It was the standard wake-up call. But what did good old dad mean by pickaxe and shovel?

Farin sat up with a start. With sudden terror the image of the two tools flashed through his mind – in Gerlunda's hut behind the door. The sheer horror of bloody crosses, toadstools, mandrakes and Annietta's admirer had meant he had clean forgotten them.

Farin, you're nothing but a moron.

"Are they still in Georig's tavern? I thought you were getting them. Didn't you head off to the village yesterday? I'm taking that from your wages," father grumbled.

Oh, right!

Taking it from his wages was new, especially as he'd never received a wage. And it was probably best not to completely forget either, who had left them behind in the first place.

His father started shaving himself with the kitchen knife.

It wouldn't make much of a difference – he still always managed to appear unshaven.

"Why don't we just leave the shovel in the graveyard? Then it's there where it's needed," suggested Farin.

"Are you mad? With all the dishonesty in the world? It'll be nicked in no time. I paid the blacksmith twelve coppers for it."

As much as his father would spend on booze over two days in Georig's, thought Farin. "I'll get them."

He swallowed hard at the thought of having to go into the witch's house again, but the thought of what the other villagers would think if they found the gravedigger's pickaxe and shovel was too much to contemplate. They certainly wouldn't look too kindly on this knavery – at the very least they would suspect him of theft.

Blossak would be of no help, he knew the coward all too well. He'd probably deny having been there at all. His ire rose when he remembered what the innkeeper's son had said about Annietta.

His heart pounding, he ran towards the village and took the turn to Gerlunda's hut. The fat miller's wife was coming along with her handcart and looked after him in surprise as he ran past. His dark thoughts increased the speed of his legs.

Suddenly he stumbled over something that had appeared out of nowhere. He fell to the ground, pulling his arms forward at the last moment so his face didn't crash into the dirt. His palms burned terribly, the path being covered in sharp pebbles.

Laughter above him.

"Hey, corpse-digger. Why are you stumbling around here and not at the graveyard?"

Farin recognised the voice immediately. Peat, the alderman's son, and his three bored cronies. What were their names again? Blunt, Dull and Dense – something like that. They were all two or three years older than him and were notorious ruffians. They were standing on the edge of the path, and Farin hadn't spotted them in his hurry. One of them had stuck his leg out, probably the beanpole – over six feet tall and skinny as a rake. The four were always on the hunt – for a fight, that is.

Farin pulled himself up and rubbed his stinging hands.

"He walked right into my leg. Just like that," grumbled the long one.

Laughter all around him. The four were surrounding Farin now.

"Why did you hurt my friend?" said Peat, the ringleader, in an enraged voice.

Oh yes – beanpole's name was Kaal. And he was as stupid as he was long.

Farin forced himself to get the words out: "Oh, I'm so sorry. I never saw your leg, or I'd never have fallen over it." He looked at his bleeding knee with gritted teeth.

Shit, I really need to get going.

Peat turned to his cronies. "Ah now, this is all a bit fast for me. And you know, I don't think it really came from the heart. What do you think, lads?"

The three shook their heads sadly.

"It sounded just too trite. It sounded too phlegelmatic."

"Phlegmatic?" suggested Farin.

"Exactly, arsehole. You said it. There's the proof!"

Laughter again. They were really having a good laugh at him. Which took nothing away from the fact that the situation was becoming more dangerous by the second.

What should he do? He could spend the day apologising – it wouldn't make a blind bit of difference. Should he make a run for it or let himself be beaten up by the four wretches. Not a good option, either way. He was in a real bind. He was the master of binds. His whole life was nothing more than one incomparable, magnificent, abominable bind. He really should change his job: Farin, the binder! Whenever he had a choice, then it was always between pretty awful, really awful and unbeatably awful.

Why be in a bind, Farin? The solution is simple. Turn around and run away. Then wait a while until the idiots have disappeared and go into Gerlunda's house.

With a sigh he decided to leave that strategy to the next life, assuming there was one, that is.

One desperate attempt to use an old tactic to make progress, a tactic that hadn't worked successfully in the village for centuries, namely the tactic of reason. "I really don't have much time. I'm sure you've heard that old Gerlunda has died. Your father brought her to me."

Not a bad idea to mention Peat's father, the village alderman, that might get him a modicum of respect.

"I heard that alright, gravedigger's son. And no doubt you stripped the old dear and played around with her. Was it fun?" asked Peat.

His three cronies roared with laughter and slapped their thighs with glee.

So much for respect and reason. Neither were traditional in Heap.

The next breath took longer than normal.

Don't let yourself be provoked. There are four of them: ruthless, hard-bitten and much better when it comes to fist-fighting. You probably wouldn't stand a chance against one of them.

And so Farin knew what his best move would be: keep his hand in his pockets, clench his fist, and then really try to get as much distance between him and them as possible. What to do with his fist? He thought of a good place for it. He took a step forward and slammed it into the middle of Peat's face. Yes, that's where it belonged.

Peat merely shook his head for a moment – he could absorb a lot. In the next instant the four of them were on top of him. Farin felt the full force of their fists everywhere – his nose cracked, warm blood ran down his lips. He collapsed to the ground, only a minor mercy that his enemies' fists weren't raining down on him. The tips of their boots had taken over the role. He curled up in an effort to protect his lower body, held his hands in front of his face. The kicks hurt unmercifully. They kicked and kicked, his entire body was hurting now, and he was beginning to accept the fact that they were going to beat him to death.

A moment later and they stopped.

"That's enough!" ascertained Kaal with satisfaction.

"Crawl back into your mud-hole. See you later, grave-digger's son," said Peat, bidding farewell.

They left Farin, groaning behind them. He listened to his body. How many ribs had he broken? Where did it hurt the most? What should he do now? Maybe just lie here and die. Naw, he wasn't good enough for that. He couldn't even manage a decent death.

It took a while, but finally he managed to pull himself up. He couldn't walk properly anymore, his knee hurt when he bent his leg, so he had to drag it behind him. He gingerly felt his ribs. What was the point? Everything seemed pointless to him. He stood there for an eternity, absorbing all the pain like a sponge absorbs dirty water, and tried to get rid of some of it through breathing.

For some unknown reason he proceeded towards Gerlunda's hut. Was it obedience, custom, habit? Part of his aim in life, retrieving pickaxe and shovel from the witch's hut? He had to laugh. Clearly, it *was* – what else could it be? He couldn't think of any better reason.

Get the tools, Farin, and then home like the wind to father.

He slipped through the gap in the blackberry bushes with a groan. Everything looked the same as yesterday, except the door was half-open. Had they forgotten to close it? He hobbled into the house and looked behind the door. Pickaxe and shovel, the gravedigger's tools, his symbols of fate, gawked back at him. Instead of feeling relief, he was filled with rage – rage at the injustice of it all and his inability to change it. He'd already toyed with the idea of leaving the village several times. And then? How would he live? Gravedigging was the only thing he knew. And he was under no illusions – his skills would only earn him contempt and repulsion in other places too. For how much longer could he put up with his fellow human-beings' haughtiness?

The shocking state of the hut, which had appalled him so much yesterday, seemed almost normal to him in the light of day. Farin looked around at the chaos dispassionately – the bloody crosses on the walls and the garlic hanging from the ceiling. Was the old woman scared stiff of vampires? She seemed to have lost all grip on reality. He didn't believe in vampires. Or in werewolves or other shape-changers – all rubbish. Figments of people's imaginations, so they could find something worse, more horrible and bloodthirsty than themselves.

The rage in his stomach outweighed Farin's aches and pains. He looked around. His eye was caught by a sight in the corner of the room – like a sausage is caught hanging from a hook. There was a cold hand on the nape of his neck – at least, that's what it felt like. The shelf with the crucibles filled with powder, ampoules and vials had been emptied, the glasses with the spiders, worms and beetles were smashed on the floor. Somebody had frequented the hut after he and Blossak had been there. And they must certainly have wondered at the pickaxe and shovel behind the door.

His first thought was: Just get out of here. But then he felt the rage again. What exactly he was enraged at, he couldn't say. Enraged at Peat? At himself? Why should he be afraid anyway? Afraid of what? What did he have to lose?

Shaking his head, Farin went out of the hut through the low back door. His eyes fell on the mandrake, this magical plant with its roots full of mystery, poison and danger. His rage and bitterness boiled over.

Then let's see what this superstitious crap all means. He groaned, his maltreated body made bending difficult; he ignored the pain, dug his fingers deep into the earth and yanked the mandrake out with one pull. Easy as pie, like plucking a daisy.

Ha! No wailing, no howling, no nothing. Just what I thought! As if plants could scream the place down! Only people scream like that. No vampires, no werewolves, no magic, no howling flowers, no devils, no angels... for a moment he stopped in silent shock. And no God? He didn't want to think about that too closely, not now, because his doubts concerning His omnipotence were pinching him all over, as if he were rolling in nettles.

And what do I do now with the mythical mandrake?

He shook off the remaining earth from the plant and with a little crack broke the root off, whose forked shape reminded him of a miniature person. The mandrake had made no other sound apart from this crack. Farin stuffed the root into his belt pouch. He tossed the star-shaped leaves behind a clump of thistles at the edge of the fence.

Just as yesterday he left the property by the back. The stream flowed nearby, and so he washed the blood from his face and cooled his wounds. And his temper.

The church bells rang at half-volume and half-speed – Gerlunda, the preparer of poisons, was making her final journey.

Whether he wanted to or not, Farin listened to the music of his guild of craftsmen: a percussive, resonating song of complaint, consisting of two tones. Not merely the ding, but also the dong, asked for his presence. What now? Should he answer the call and head for the graveyard, or shuffle home and spend a week lying on his straw mat. His body ached, his soul asked for peace, his obligation demanded work. It was his job to cover the grave again afterwards. Moving loose earth, a task simply and quickly done – at least, if he were in his normal bodily condition. At that moment he remembered the amulet on his chest. He had intended giving it to Gerlunda's family. But no-one had turned up until now. Would he manage to get to the graveyard in time with his damaged knee? He had nothing else to do, and before he could succumb to self-pity again, he decided to make his way there. And anyway, he had the shovel – father would be standing there uselessly if he didn't turn up. He hobbled towards the church with its adjacent graveyard, the pickaxe across his shoulder, and the shovel more a crutch than a walking stick. Groaning, Farin limped over the grass behind the house of God towards the graveyard. He could hardly bend his knee. From afar he could see only four people standing at Gerlunda's grave: Alderman Hamak, the priest, the gravedigger of Heap – his distinguished father – and also a man he didn't recognise, wearing a black cloak.

The village priest, whom everybody simply called Amen, had already begun the funeral oration. The dark robe with the white collar really suited him. His voice boomed in Farin's direction. "And so once again a warm-hearted, goodly member of our village community has departed from us."

The first thing Farin got was a fright. Had somebody else died? The next moment he was ashamed of his own naivety.

Silly fool, of course Amen was talking about old Gerlunda. He'd never talk like that if the preparer of poisons could hear him. He belonged to the tradition where the dearly departed were practically canonised after their death.

"About time you came. And be glad you brought the shovel, you good-for-nothing," his father hissed in greeting. "Have you been beaten up?" he looked at his son's face with a scowl.

But Farin's eyes were glued to the stranger. There was something unnerving emanating from this figure – involuntarily he sensed the smell of burned earth in his nostrils. The cloaked man was staring into the grave; now he seemed to sense he was being watched, so firmly were Farin's eyes fixed on him. The stranger slowly raised his head. Their looks clashed together like two swords. The stranger's eyes swallowed an endless amount of light, his pupils were as big as lumps of coal, no hair peeked out from under his hood, and his nose hooked from its centre, so that its tip almost divided his thin upper lip in two.

Questions raced through Farin's head. Where does the stranger come from? What does he want? Is he related to Gerlunda? Why is there such a morbid coldness all around him?

"Why is he only coming now?" asked the man in black hoarsely, staring at the pickaxe and shovel in Farin's hand as if he wanted to bite through their shafts. He looked Farin up and down with the same destructive fury.

The village priest paused and scratched his double chin which perfectly reflected his two functions. He couldn't stand being interrupted during his sermon or when he was passing sentence. Whether by coincidence or design the priest also acted as the village judge. Therefore, he sealed every judicial verdict with a cheerful "amen", which only God could refute – and that had never happened yet. This position in the village presented many advantages, particularly for Amen himself. It made him mightily mighty and almightily self-confident. And rich and gluttonous. Farin wondered if the upper or lower chin belonged to the judge part of the priest. Probably the lower one, serving the earthly laws, while the upper one followed the heavenly commandments.

Pater Amen pragmatically took up God's thread again. "And so, we bid farewell and praise the uniqueness of the Lord's creation." He threw a glance over at Farin and preached on with a reproachful undertone. "The grave-digger's son too has joined our funeral congregation."

The blackness in the stranger's eyes widened. "You...prepared the deceased's body!" Even his voice sounded black – an ominous whispering, which nevertheless sounded as clearly as if he had spoken loudly.

"We wish to pay our beloved Gerlunda our last respects,

and so I would ask you to wait until the end of my sermon before clarifying this matter." There was one thing Amen hated more than being interrupted once during his speeches. Being interrupted twice.

"Then hurry up and finish, priest – or I'll give you a hand." The stranger bared a couple of black teeth, pushed his cloak backwards a little and placed his left hand on the handle of the dagger hanging from his belt. Black sparks spewed from his eyes.

"Are you threatening me?" Pater Amen's double chin wobbled.

"Of course, I'm threatening you, man of the cloth. You'd want to get on with things because it's only me standing between you and your dear God." The man in black sneered liplessly. "You're closer to Him than you've ever been before."

Amen was clearly considering how to react to this provocation. On the one hand, he couldn't allow himself to be spoken to in this way, especially as other villagers were standing around and watching what was going on. On the other hand… The moment he could have flown into a rage passed. He had elegantly evaded this potential problem. Farin could see it written on Amen's face. He relished his too pleasant, too comfortable, too satiated existence, to risk it all on account of a cockroach who'd just crawled out of the woodwork.

And so, he concentrated fully on his devotions. He abandoned any attempt at making his voice sound compassionate. "That which is sown – turns to dust – rises again – incorruptible. And so, we give Gerlunda's body to the earth and her soul to the mercy of God. Amen."

This was the first time Farin had time to look at the dead

woman. The burial shroud had been pulled back, revealing her face. Dear God! Yesterday's rain had caused the charcoal to run down from her eyebrows and lashes and into her eye-sockets, so that they looked deeper, darker and bigger. The rouge on her cheeks had run too. A grim skull sneered out of the hole in the ground into the faces of the living. Scornful and truculent, embittered and care-worn, with a hint of triumph as if it wished to say: It's all behind me now – but not you, you who are doomed. Farin didn't have much time left. He looked away from Gerlunda as the stranger walked around the grave and positioned himself directly beside the gravedigger's son. The man's hooked nose neared his face in a dangerous manner, as if it were about to hack out his eyes. The man's stare weighed at least as much as the church bell. He grasped Farin's upper arm with his spindly fingers, and immediately ice-cold water streamed through the gravedigger son's veins.

He spat the words out: "Give it to me, boy!"

The world slowed down. Farin felt his heart stopping – this universal cause of death – but amazingly he was able to remain upright. And as long as he could use his own strength to stay standing, he was still alive, he was certain of that.

The stranger's grip continued to suck the heat out of his body as a tick sucks blood.

"What…what do you mean, sir?"

"What you found at the witch's place, damn it."

Had he really said witch's? Had he really said damn it?

The amulet was burning on his chest. The amulet on his chest twitched. The amulet on his chest bit. He felt it digging into his skin, he felt the hemp cord tightening around his neck like a hangman's noose.

The pressure on Farin threatened to squash him. He was

about to say "Oh, you mean this here" and pull out the piece of jewellery when he noticed the make-up on the stranger's left cheek. And particularly the gouge underneath it. Farin bit his lower lip, he could hardly feel it for it was numbed through the cold – it was colder than Gerlunda lying in her bed of earth at his feet. But the last scintilla of resistance rebelled. Madness was controlling the man in black, an unmistakable villain, one who had come directly from the sagas and fairy tales. A sorcerer, a conjurer of black magic, an evil magician – almost too weird to be real. And it was just this superstitious mumbo-jumbo he was using as his trump card.

You're not going to frighten me. I've just plucked a mandrake – with my bare hands. Me, the gravedigger's son. So, have some respect. And I know what you've done – you can't fool me.

"What do you want from me? I don't have anything! The alderman brought Gerlunda to me, she was just wearing a dress." Farin spread out his hands in front of him innocently, shaking off the ice-cold grip as he did so.

"That's right, sir," said Hamak in confirmation. "She was wearing a dress without pockets. And no jewellery, not even a hair clip. I don't think the deceased deserves any closer attention."

The man in black's thin lips became even thinner. No, they disappeared, completely. Obviously, he'd paid enough attention to Gerlunda's appearance for now; at least he didn't bother looking into the grave again. And strewing the earth three times into the coffin didn't interest him either, his black eyes were focussed completely on the gravedigger's son.

Farin felt scorn and suspicion being strewn on him by the man.

He doesn't believe me.

"Who found the body?" The stranger's voice sounded grating.

"That was me," explained Pater Amen. "She had nothing with her."

With a jerk, the sinister man's mouth shot up again, remaining closed, nonetheless. Even his silence was threatening.

"Have you any more questions?" It sounded like an accusation, and that had been the intention. Pater Amen didn't bother hiding his distaste for the stranger standing opposite him.

This didn't put the latter out one iota – he was undoubtedly used to the reaction. "Who else had contact with her after her death?"

"The alderman, the gravedigger's son and my humble self – and nobody else," explained Amen.

The stranger's nose almost imperceptibly hacked the air three times.

The gravedigger asked: "May we close up the grave now, Pater?"

Farin noticed immediately that this didn't suit the man in black one little bit. The murderous look in his eyes made Farin shiver. With a slow movement the stranger's hand moved towards his hip, his cloak, his dagger. Just at that moment all the members of the esteemed pipe smokers' society came loudly around the corner of the church, bearing down on the graveyard – fifteen of them, give or take. After the funeral there was generally a funeral meal or at least drinks in honour of the deceased, and even more importantly, at the priest's expense. With cheerful merriment they had come to pay their respects.

Pastor Amen was acutely aware that something was troubling the man in black. Now he took the opportunity to show the stranger who was in charge here. With a triumphant undertone and a commanding hand gesture he announced: "Close up the grave!"

The man in black paused in silence, his lower jaw grinding the upper one liplessly until the picture he presented was that of a leering skull. The similarity to the deceased woman at his feet was remarkable.

Father jumped into the grave and closed the burial shroud over Gerlunda's face. She was being tucked in for the last time in her life. The gravedigger scrambled out of the grave with a groan and gave a similar commanding hand gesture to Farin. The work had arrived at the final link in the chain of command. And so, the gravedigger's son dug the shovel into the earth and began closing up the grave. The preparer of poison's body slowly disappeared under the dark soil. Farin continued to dig in a strangely stiff manner; he didn't want to bend over too much for fear of the amulet slipping out above the neckline of his linen shirt – and added to that, his back was aching from the beating he had suffered.

His father asked immediately: "What's wrong with you? You're moving so strangely."

"I stumbled and fell." Farin pointed at his bloody knee and his battered face.

The onlookers looked down at the diggers without pity, but with plenty of contempt.

"You're lying," breathed the stranger in a hoarse voice.

Only Farin could hear him. The members of the celebratory pipe smokers' society were slapping the priest heartily on the back in expectation of their drinks.

Farin was glad he could concentrate on his gravedigging as if he had heard nothing. What did the stranger mean? Lying about the piece of jewellery or lying about his injuries? Amen felt safe and sound surrounded by his flock, and so he raised his arms high into the air. "My dear people, before we drink to Gerlunda and treasure her beauty in our memories, just as she was, we must go through the bureaucratic formalities."

Somebody shouted: "But make it snappy, my throat is dry from mourning!" The others cheered sorrowfully.

Pater Amen spread out his arms. "As there is no last will and testament, the land and house now pass into the ownership of the village community, and thereby into the safe hands of mother church, who will know how to administer these worldly goods in a way that is best for the general good. Amen." Blinded by his own sanctimonious sanctimony, Pater Amen closed his eyes in satisfaction.

Farin was deeply impressed by Amen's ability to bear the double loads of priest and judge.

The man in black seemed impressed too. "Son of a bitch. You're almost as unscrupulous a bastard as I am. But only almost. And I never forget!"

The rain was easing off, although the shivering on Farin's spine was increasing. They were all standing very close together now. Hamak, Amen, father and the man in black.

The priest turned to the stranger. "I already asked you before the funeral service what your relationship to Gerlunda is. You stressed that there is no family relationship, and you laid no claims. May I enquire precisely after your wishes?"

"You may enquire." The stranger's mood was plumbing new depths. His face left no doubt, but that Amen would spend the rest of his opulent life waiting for an answer.

The man in black ground his teeth. "The gravedigger was in her hut!" It was as if Farin had been stabbed with the stranger's dagger. How could an accusation be so calm and cold and yet sound so wrathful? Having heard these words, there was nothing Farin wanted more than to lie beside Gerlunda and ask father to quickly cover the grave.

Pater Amen turned to father. "What were you doing in the old woman's hut, gravedigger?"

"Huh?" his father stared back, his glassy eyes uncomprehending, and he scratched his head.

Keep your mouth shut, father, Farin prayed silently.

It all seemed a bit too much for the old man, having already consumed a few too many warm beers.

"Not him! Him!" The man in black pointed at Farin.

The wrath of God, manifested through Pater Amen, bore down now on the correct person. "What have you to say for yourself, gravedigger's son?" Only the thunder and lightning were missing – at least it was beginning to rain again.

Farin stopped his work and leaned on his shovel. He needed to come up with a good explanation, calmly and self-confidently. A credible, reasonable explanation. When it came down to it, he wasn't an idiot, he was bound to come up with something. His mouth opened and he began to blurt. "Um…well…" and he stopped. The only thing swirling around in his head was the truth: I wanted to steal a love potion. One of those "c'mon then" escapades with Blossak. I mean – I'm still only eighteen.

Oh boy!

A voice spoke: "I sent him there. He was to collect a nice clean dress for Gerlunda. You can't imagine the pitiful state of the clothing she was wearing when the Lord called her home."

These words of salvation, this simple and ingenious explanation came from the gravedigger. Perplexed, Farin glanced at father, who was looking steadfastly and with tremendous righteousness at the man in black. This event was among the very few moments when Farin could sense why his mother had made an honest man of the gravedigger many years ago.

The alderman too came to his aid. "Her dress stank unmercifully, full of faeces and urine." He dramatically scowled to the point of being unrecognisable.

The priest spoke soothingly: "That's that clarified, then! The gravedigger's son is a good lad. A little slow in the head, but he does his work diligently." Amen pursed his lips in a Godly manner. "Esteemed sir, can I help you in any other way?" Amen looked as if the last thing he wanted was to dedicate another second of his life to the stranger.

"I know she carried it on her body," snarled the man. Aggression was blazing from his eyes.

The members of the Heap pipe smokers' society were standing in the rain getting wetter and wetter.

"What happens now, Amen?" pressed ratface.

"We'll go in now. The first three rounds are on me," called out the priest.

"And what about the other ten?" another one wanted to know.

The man in black suppressed his rage. "We'll talk again, priest." Then he turned to Farin and whispered: "I watched you yesterday evening when you were washing the old one. You were afraid of something. Of what?"

"Oh, that was you. I felt that somebody was watching me."

The dark eyes of the stranger didn't blink. Had the man

even blinked once during the funeral?

"And I don't believe you called into Gerlunda's house looking for a dress. There's something not right about you, lad. You're hiding things." The stranger's smoky voice was positively smouldering.

"I don't know what you're talking about." Farin attempted to put on an innocent expression. The amulet hanging from his neck was heavier than a millstone.

The man in black leaned forward, his mouth nearing Farin's ear. "First, I'll take care of the son-of-a-bitch-priest, then the village alderman. And guess who's next on the list after that, my friend?"

The goose bumps made Farin shiver. The man in black left without another look or another word.

Pater Amen was looking after him ruefully too. Thoroughly irritated, he turned around to Farin's father and gave his order smugly:

"Gravedigger, deal with that grave. And tell your son not to be late the next time."

The indignation had a warming effect. He wasn't being treated like scum now, but even worse – like air. And the air had no idea of how it should respond.

Pater Amen remembered that he had to fulfil his promise of booze at the bar. "Then let us mourn." He called his little sheep together and they disappeared in the direction of "The Warm Beer".

Hardly was Farin alone with his father again when he began to feel better. He could still feel the injuries inflicted on him by Peat and his friends, but the coldness was gone. Lost in thought, he continued digging.

"That's some arsehole!" scolded his father.

"Who?" asked Farin. That distinction was a toss-up between the stranger and Amen.

"The stranger, of course." Father spat. Just beside Gerlunda's grave. Then he reached forward and struck Farin on the face with the flat of his hand. "You're even more stupid than I thought."

It wasn't just his burning cheek that turned red. He really had to suffer a lot of beating today – his father hadn't dared to beat him for at least the last two years.

Too perplexed to get angry, Farin asked: "Because…because I went to Gerlunda's hut?

"Ah, not at all. I couldn't care less about that. Because you never thought of a convincing explanation beforehand in case you were caught. That's why!"

When it came to cunning worldly wisdom, father was way ahead of him. Farin felt pathetic; he was ashamed of his naivety.

It was nice when a son could look up to his father – or had to.

The gravedigger looked at him. "Keep digging and don't forget to tramp down the earth. Then off home with you. I'm going to drop into Georig's. And don't forget the tools."

Farin's sigh was deeper than any grave he had ever dug.

What a day.

the mole

Hey, Farin. You know I fancy Annietta," said Blossak.

Sure. How could I forget it? And I fancy punching you in the face, thought Farin, sitting opposite the innkeeper's son.

Still, Bloss had gone over to him at the outcasts' table. And so, they were socialising together in "The Warm Beer", drinking warm beer and talking about women. In the main taproom the Heap society of pipe smokers were practising their art.

Shrouded in a cloud of smoke, Farin forced out a wimpish "and, what about it?" through his constricted throat.

"Can you help me to get the message through to her?"

"Whaat? I...I..." He, of all people, was to deliver a message from Bloss to the goddess Annietta?

Outside was the clattering of something heavy, powerful. It stamped onto the wooden step, which creaked in protest, threatening to snap in the middle. Instinctively, Farin mentally closed his ears. Not a moment too soon, for in the next instant the door flew open, was lifted straight out of its hinges, and crashed against the wall before landing with a clatter on the floor. All eyes focussed on the doorway as if through a burning lens. An enormous silhouette prevented all daylight from getting in. The new arrival had to duck his head as he stepped over the threshold. Struggling to regain his composure, Farin slid his chair backwards until it could go no further – he pressed its back against the wall, his back against its back, top lip pressed against bottom.

What in the name of God is that? Or rather: *Who* is that?

The wooden planks creaked piteously under the stranger's steps. The plate boots suited the rest of the armour: the plate greaves, the plate gloves, the plate chest armour, the plate gorget, the plate helmet.

Farin's eyes were like plates as he stared at the visitor: it was a knight, a real knight.

Farin's eyes couldn't open any wider. He'd only ever seen a knight once before – in the distance, riding by on his charger. Just then he heard a horse snorting loudly outside. Not that it meant much – after all, the door lay wide open on the floor.

A knight and his warhorse.

Farin had dreamed of being a knight himself more than ten years ago, serving his king and performing countless heroic deeds. He had dreamed of rescuing virgins in distress from the claws of murderous dragons, just as he had freed Annietta from the most impossible of situations, always in time and always with his trusty sword, *Windswipe*. Father had laughed him out of it. "Finding a dragon – that's possible", he'd opined. "But a virgin?!" His father had been doubled over with laughter all day. At the start he had laughed too without knowing why.

Until now Farin had never imagined that the smashing in of doors was considered another example of knightly heroic deeds.

The knight pushed up his visor with the same nonchalance as he had knocked down the door. His eyes took in the two young men in the corner as well as the pipe-smoking villagers and the innkeeper behind the counter. It all took no longer than the blink of an eye. The hinges on his full-fingered gloves clanked quietly as his forefinger pointed at Hamak. The knight's other hand rested lightly on the handle of his belted sword.

Farin had completely forgotten to breathe. What a hilt! You could easily fit five hands between the pommel and the cross guard.

"YOU!" roared the knight to Hamak.

The clay jugs rattled on the wooden shelf.

The colour drained from the village alderman's face. He bowed, then knelt, then bowed again, his head almost hitting the floor.

Impressively flexible, this alderman, when necessary.

"What…what can I do for you, sir?" Hamak bowed and scraped like crazy. He looked like a cat, there on the floor and would be meowing in no time.

"WHERE IS SHE?" The deep voice caused the floor-boards to vibrate.

"Eh..what? Who…do you mean, sir?" asked Hamak, his lowered pate towards the wooden tavern floor.

And what a ridiculous question. It was obvious who the knight was looking for. Obviously. Gar…Gir…God above, what was the preparer of poison's name again?

"GERLUNDA!" roared through the tavern, extinguishing the tobacco in the pipes.

Exactly, that was her name.

Strangely, none of those present made a complaint about this disruption. With their finer instincts the villagers sensed that the new arrival didn't hide within him a contemplative pipe smoker and might be miffed were he to be criticised regarding their quenched instruments.

"Ah, you mean Gerlunda sir. But of course. Yes of

course, sir. She died and I…eh…took care of the matter, sir. I organised a dignified burial, sir. Her grave – a really wonderful grave – is directly behind the church, sir."

Farin had counted "sir" five times there.

And the sir stood there, quite alone, and seemed decidedly unimpressed.

"Take me there, beadle."

Beadle was really not a very pleasant title for the village alderman, who reacted, however, as though the knight had said "Your Majesty" to him.

Admittedly, respect towards the newcomer was certainly advisable – after all, knights served the king, functioned as his right hand and executive power. Consequently, Hamak nodded vigorously and answered almost euphorically: "But, of course, but immediately."

He had forgotten "sir" through sheer excitement; Farin hoped the knight would let that pass. Although it was raining, Hamak left the tavern without a mantle, turned around and said cravingly: "If you would be so good as to follow me, sir."

The knight stamped over the door and outside. Silent, pale men watched him leave. Farin was still sitting stock-still on his chair, slowly absorbing what he had just experienced. Blossak looked just as stunned with his mouth gaping.

The elemental steel-plated force turned around once more. "Pipes, come with, all of you."

The men jumped to their feet, one of them calling: "Of course, sir!"

The innkeeper Georig asked: "Me too, sir?"

"How much room for interpretation is there in the word *all*?" asked the knight, his voice sounding like a war drum.

The innkeeper hesitated for a brief moment, then joined the procession.

When Farin left the tavern, he stared at the charger as if it were a unicorn. Never before had he seen such an enormous horse. Its nostrils were steaming, its mighty chest rose and fell under the broad straps that held the jousting saddle. Farin's gaze travelled in amazement from the mighty rump armour to the embroidered saddle cloth with its royal coat of arms. He could easily fit his head into the enormous hanging stirrups. Unfortunately, there was barely time to give the charger its proper attention as the group walked over towards the church.

"We miss her already, the good Gerlunda," said Hamak sorrowfully.

"Nobody misses that ugly toad!" roared the knight.

Such demeanour was not at all to Farin's taste. He had always thought until now that knights exhibited the best of manners and treated ladies with politeness and respect. Although, if he were honest, ugly toad described Gerlunda better than fair maid.

"Yes, she wasn't particularly beloved." In the blink of an eye Hamak had learned how to adjust in the most flexible manner to the higher echelons of society, and how to handle them. He had rediscovered his courage, after all – when it came down to it, he *was* the village alderman. He strode onwards manfully. "We have to go behind the church, sir."

Within a few moments the group was standing in mourning around the preparer of poisons' grave. On a crooked wooden sign written in charcoal with ungainly lettering was "Gerlunda".

"This is where she lies interred – a lovely grave." Hamak's enthusiastic, encouraging nodding made the resting place almost more beautiful.

The knight stood in front of the grave, his legs apart and planted firmly in the ground, looking monumental – an impressive statue with a commanding charisma. His stony demeanour was suggestive of a gravestone.

The rain was coming down harder and there was a flash of lightning.

The knight slammed down his visor. "When did you bury her?"

"Five days ago, sir."

"Who was in attendance?"

"Me and eh…" The alderman thought hard. He pointed to the gravedigger's son. "…and him and…eh…" There was a momentary delay before the Godly insight manifested itself. "…our Pastor Amen, of course."

For a moment Farin could only see the whites of the knight's eyes through the slit in his helmet.

"It's been brought to my attention that it was the priest who found the dead woman, is that right?"

"Very true, sir."

What the knight said was not only true, but *very* true, noted Farin to himself.

"Let the priest be brought here immediately!"

Hamak stammered: "That…that's not possible, sir. The priest is nowhere to be found. He…he left the village three days ago."

"Your priest has disappeared then." The tone and urgency in the knight's voice had sharpened.

"We…we believe he's on some sort of business trip."

"You believe." This new information too, didn't seem to improve the knight's first impression of the village and its inhabitants to any great extent. The patience of the exalted visitor was wearing thin.

"EXHUME!" thundered across the graveyard, causing Farin to duck.

"Sir, you mean...?" Hamak bowed his head and his face looked as obsequious as possible.

"Dig'er up, muttonhead."

Everyone turned their heads towards him.

"Exhuhu...eh...dig'er up, you...scoundrel" said the alderman to the gravedigger's son.

"Eh...!" What Farin wanted to say was that he needed a shovel, but he didn't manage to even get one comprehensible word out. Instead of which, he spread out his arms helplessly so that everyone could see he didn't have any suitable equipment to hand.

The alderman lavished him with praise. "Idiot!" he said. "Then go and get a shovel and make it snappy!"

Even if he ran, it would take almost an hour to get there and back. Would the knight be happy about waiting so long?

"Father has one in the tool shed," said Blossak, tuning in with unusual quick-wittedness.

Georig nodded to him, and Bloss ran off.

Why am I standing here stammering? Even the innkeeper's son is coming up with good ideas and has raised his game.

Farin was unhappy with himself. He looked up. Never before had he imagined a fresh mound of earth could be of such interest, the congregation of mourners staring at it with complete reverence. The world stopped – only the thunder clouds were moving, the rain was easing off.

The alderman could bear the silence no longer. "We feel truly honoured that Sir Knight has granted upon our modest little village the honour of his visit", he said in an oily voice.

He has it down pat, thought Farin.

"Beadle, the only thing that interests me in this shithole Heap is Gerlunda."

If there was anything at all lacking in the legendary knight it was a certain finesse in his way of expressing himself. Although – any deficit in high-flown language and pathos was compensated for eloquently by clarity and directness.

This was how the alderman saw it too. "Of course, sir."

In the meantime, Blossak had run back with the shovel. "Here!" He shoved it into Farin's hands with a look of disdain. "Dig'er up!"

It had to be clear to even the most menial of knights where Farin stood in the village pecking order. Not to worry, he wasn't ashamed. Farin set to work like a rabid mole. The earth was loose but lumpy and heavy due to the rain. Notwithstanding that, he swung the shovel skilfully and elegantly. His work had never had such a large audience before. Everyone looked at the hollow in the earth, gaping deeper and deeper, while the pile of earth beside it grew higher and higher. He was hardly down a yard when he hit something soft. He carefully dug around it.

"The lad can dig most delicately, can't he, sir?" Hamak was trying to present the village community and its alderman in the most positive light.

Farin could hear furrowed brows crackling underneath the plate helmet. "What's delicate about that earth-poker? Spare me your drivel."

These words struck home with Farin too. He immediately stopped making such an effort – nobody valued his handiwork. What had he expected anyway? His place at the butt-end of society was carved in gravestone. He hit the burial shroud and gently exposed its outlines.

"Can't you go faster?" grumbled the knight.

"Hurry up, you scoundrel!" said the alderman, motivating him.

Farin wondered if he should take a break first and yawn loudly, but his respect for the knight caused him to reject the idea. And so, he bent down and pulled the cloth along with the rest of the earth from the body. That was the plan – but Gerlunda of all people had put a spoke in his wheel. She had been gone. There was no body under the cloth.

Stunned, Farin looked up out of the grave and into the faces of his equally dumbstruck audience.

The knight's voice thundered across the graveyard. "WHERE IS THE BODY OF THE OLD TOAD? I'll flatten this village, you losers, if you don't show me Gerlunda's corpse!"

Farin began digging more furiously, but he noticed that the earth was only getting hard. There was more chance of finding gold here than Gerlunda.

The knight slammed his visor up. "What have you done with the old woman?" His voice sounded like a tensed catapult.

"She…she has left us," stammered ratface, holding on firmly to his new, expertly broken-in pipe. He never saw the back of the hand coming. The thorns on the upper part of the plate gloves ripped his right cheek and nose. There was a cracking sound as his cheekbone broke.

"Living people leave, the dead stay lying where they've been put." The knight was on a roll now. "You are complete idiots. A disgrace that such a collection of suckers are breathing the same air as me. But I can change that."

The knight slammed his visor down. He pulled out his sword wrathfully. The metal made an unholy hum as it slipped out of the scabbard. "YOU THERE!" He pointed the tip of the sword at Georig. "WHAT HAPPENED HERE?"

Farin had never seen the innkeeper look so helpless. He stammered in a hoarse voice: "I...I...don't know."

Everyone was arguing amongst themselves, protesting their innocence, coming up with wild theories, muttering about desecration of graves and body-snatching, apologising again and again for their own inadequacies, kneeling down and pissing in their pants.

Farin remained silent. He clambered out of the grave and observed the tumult. He too had proper respect for the knight, but it never crossed his mind to crawl about on the ground. Now, as he saw the fear written on the faces of the men around him, he understood how serious and dangerous the situation was. And so, he prepared to become afraid. Only the fear didn't come. Quite the contrary. He enjoyed standing up straight in the midst of the bowing and scraping villagers.

"You!" The sword-tip wandered to under the point of the alderman's chin and left a little spot as if from a red paintbrush. The knight swung his mighty sword as dexterously as he would a dagger.

Hamak's eyes bulged forward – he stared like a flatulent frog.

"Let's start at the beginning. Were you present at the burial?"

Hamak couldn't nod unless he wanted to plunge his chin directly into the sword. "Yes, yes, yes, sir."

"Who else was present?"

"I..." The alderman rolled his eyes. "eh, the gravedigger and the gravedigger's son." He pointed to Farin, delighted to divert attention away from himself. "There! Him there!"

The helmet turned mercilessly with a little squeak in his direction. The knight observed him as if he were a well filled chamber pot. His face bruised, sweaty and grimy, his legs and arms caked in the remains of the dark earth, Farin stood beside the empty grave, leaning on the shaft of the shovel. One enormous step and the giant was standing directly in front of him, his sword pointing directly up at the grave-digger's son's nose. Farin could well and truly smell the steel, the blood groove of the flashing blade was two fingers wide. But he never even thought of flinching back, instead he went into gravedigger mode – slow, sad, stubborn. After all, what did he have to lose?

The knight mistook his unwavering courage for unwavering stupidity. "BEADLE! You're presumably the chief of this village. Why did you refer me to this moronic mole?" thundered the knight.

Too true, thought Farin. At the same time, he was annoyed – and his annoyance increased, the longer he thought about the "moronic mole".

"But…he was there," said Hamak defensively, wiping away the blood from his neck with his sleeve.

The knight snorted like his horse had done earlier. "He's the only one of you lot who hasn't said a word yet. Can he talk at all?"

It took a while for Farin to realise that "he" referred to himself. Of course, he could talk, and as far as he was concerned, he was remarkably articulate for a gravedigger's son. That was thanks mainly to mum. But Farin was still mulling over the derogatory word "mole". He decided to swallow his pride regarding the mole and show the knight what he was made of.

He pluckily opened his mouth. "Eh! Ehmmm! Aah!"

He didn't sound like a moronic mole, more like a silly sheep. Unfortunately, he hadn't impressed. Against Farin's will, all his blood was rising up to his head.

The knight looked at him in disgust and sighed at so much simple-mindedness and stupor. He became increasingly enraged. "I'm going to stick all your stupid pipes up your arses – and the wrong way around to boot!"

Farin failed miserably in his attempt *not* to imagine that.

"I'm going to cut the brainless skull off each and every one of you if you don't tell me what happened here. AND I MEAN IT!"

A shudder ran through the crowd. For the first time the knight was speaking at his normal volume, and they sensed he was being blood-thirstily serious. "AND I MEAN IT!" left little room for interpretation.

"You first, beadle! On your knees – don't worry, I only need to slice once."

"No! Sir! I'll do whatever you want." Hamak's bloodless face glistened with sweat.

"ON YOUR KNEES!" The giant raised his sword. The alderman's life wasn't worth much now.

"Wait, Sir Knight!" Farin's voice croaked a little but it rang loud and clear.

"Mole?"

"There was a stranger present at the burial. In a black cloak with a hood. Dark eyes, hooked nose. He wore a dagger on his belt. This stranger is the…murderer."

Alderman Hamak interrupted him. "Yes, exactly, sir, a stranger with a hook nose and…"

"Shut your trap and let mole finish what he's saying."

"But, sir, he's only the gravedi..."

There was a horrible crack as the knight's iron fist connected with the alderman's temple. Farin gawked down at him in shock. He was reassured when he saw Hamak's chest moving up and down.

"So, the mole can speak. What else do you know? Go on!" demanded the knight.

"The…the stranger is Gerlunda's murderer. He strangled her."

Deathly silence! As was befitting a graveyard. Every pair of eyes was boring into the gravedigger's son.

An unnerving hissing whisper emanated from the plate helmet. "How do you know that? Were you there when it happened?" The knight was focused only on him – he and his sword were threateningly close to Farin again.

He was in too far to bottle it now – there was no going back. "Gerlunda had bits of skin under her fingernails. And I spotted scratches on the stranger's face that were concealed with make-up." And suddenly Farin's submerged self-confidence dug itself free – after all, when it came down to it, the gravedigger's son knew what he was talking about. "Also, Gerlunda had strangulation marks with a thumbprint on the left side of her throat, so obviously caused by a left-handed person – the stranger wore his dagger on the right, like all left-handers. He pushed the larynx towards the spine with only one hand."

For a moment nothing moved; not the leaves on the trees, not the villagers standing around the grave, the very clouds themselves remained still. But, yes – there *was* movement. Slowly, almost lovingly, the knight slid his sword back into its scabbard. With a movement of his arm he took off his helmet. He had dark-brown hair and bright blue eyes with bushy eyebrows peering over them which almost had a life of their own. His wide chin moved from side to side like a ruminant's. With an expression as inscrutable as heaven and earth he looked at Farin. Then something happened which nobody had expected. The knight laughed. A resounding laugh like an army on horseback.

"What's your name, mole?"

He almost replied: gravedigger's son. "Farin."

The knight looked at him steadfastly with his bright eyes. "Where are you from?"

"Heap is my home village, sir," he said and was annoyed at his feeble voice. Now he was almost sounding like the alderman.

"Alright, then!" Suddenly, the knight seemed mollified, especially as he was showing no inclination to chop off any heads.

Farin glanced around at the villagers. The alderman, who was still lying in Gerlunda's grave, opened his eyes. Blood was running down his temple over his ear. Although Farin had just saved his life, he threw him an accusing look, as if the gravedigger's son was the cause of all his misery.

"With the exception of him over there…" the knight's index finger clanked again as he pointed at Farin, "…the rest of you are exceptionally dim-witted." He snorted in disgust. "Now I believe you that you didn't hide the old toad from me." He thought for a moment: "Who found her body?"

Hamak scrabbled out of the open grave with a groan. "That was me, sir. She was lying dead on the floor of her hut."

"Did you find anything near the dead woman? On her body, I mean – a ring, a bracelet or a chain?"

"No, definitely nothing, sir. She was only wearing a simple dress without pockets. No jewellery, nothing."

"That would have surprised me anyway." His voice was

sounding edgier again. "If the man in black killed her and found it, then God have mercy on us all."

Overwhelmed, the villagers looked at each other. This enchanted amulet was spinning around inside Farin's head again like a carousel. Should he mention it, or was there too great a risk of provoking the unpredictable knight again?

At that moment the knight turned around and stamped over the meadow back to his charger. The horse greeted him with a friendly whinny. It was the gravedigger's son, of all people, who ran after him.

"Sir Knight – one more question, please."

The giant affixed his heavy plate helmet to the saddle with a familiar movement. "What do you want?" he growled.

"You know who the man in black with the hooked nose is, don't you?"

The knight's blue eyes looked him up and down. "Believe you me, the less you know about that guy, the better."

"He was looking for something Gerlunda had on her or had in the hut – twice. Who is he?" asked Farin, with a just a tad too much enthusiasm.

"And didn't find it, or he wouldn't have dug the corpse up and taken it with him. Which gives me some hope."

"Who is he?"

At first Farin thought the knight was going to strike him dead as the giant's powerful armour-plated hands bore down on his head.

"Pull! Help me get these gloves off."

Farin grasped the metal edge of the right glove using all his fingers and pulled it off the man's hand. The knight took the other one off himself.

"Uncomfortable pieces of shit. And as for these damned boots", he grunted and looked down at them.

"Why do you wear them then?" asked Farin without thinking.

"Because of their effect on clodhoppers like you lot."

A yearning Farin had never felt before overcame him. This man fascinated him, stirred something in him, gave him an insight into the world beyond Heap. He stammered: "Sir Knight, I…could you imagine, having me as…"

"Spare me your babbling. I have to go."

Tight-lipped, Farin swallowed his disappointment. If the knight thought that he was going to cave in or eat humble pie just because of his standing in society and the constant insults he endured, he had another thing coming to him. He folded his arms in front of his chest and said in a firm voice: "You still haven't answered my question. Who is the man in black?"

The knight put his hands on his hips. "You're the most impertinent mole I know. Haven't you noticed that I don't want to answer the question?"

This knight was still calling him a mole, and his terribly dismissive tone did for the rest. Farin exploded: "You are a knight. I thought knights stood up for justice. I helped you, and you won't even tell me who this man is."

The other villagers were standing in front of the church looking over suspiciously, but nobody dared come closer.

Silence for a moment.

"You're more annoying than a wife," stated the man. "Scram."

Farin stood there with his arms folded, looking accusingly. The knight ignored him at first and continued preparing for his journey. His brow was furrowed. Their silence spoke volumes.

With a swift movement he took Farin's chin between his

thumb and forefinger. "Listen here, gravedigger. You're almost too chipper." His voice was becoming more threatening. "You didn't happen to find anything on Gerlunda? A piece of jewellery like a ring, a bracelet or a pendant?"

Farin felt again the amulet on its hemp cord burning a hole into his chest. He thought he could already get the smell of charred skin. For a moment he actually considered confessing everything and handing over the necklace with its pendant. But something rebelled inside him. Anger at the ungrateful knight? Instinct? Or stubbornness, truculence, obstinacy?

"No, I didn't discover anything like that", he uttered, and it even sounded halfway believable.

The man looked at him severely, shook his head and fastened his plate gloves to his saddle. Then he loosened his leg armour and stored that too.

"Farewell, mole." The knight swung up onto his horse and looked down at him. "You're interested in the black lad. Very well, then. You had the honour of meeting the raven, one of the leading lights of the Necorers. An unscrupulous murderer, which means the next time you meet him, don't talk but run for your life. I'm surprised that he actually spared you lot. Presumably he didn't want to leave any obvious evidence behind."

"What do these Necorers want?" asked Farin.

"Your curiosity is only outstripped by your audacity, boy", muttered the knight, but then continued: "They're a well-organised cult, dedicated to death. These fanatics have already razed a number of villages to the ground in the south of the kingdom because the people refused to renounce God. The Necorers drive men, women and children into the church, barricade the door and burn down the house of God."

"There must be something behind it all," suggested Farin.

"I think so too. Forget about it – it's out of your league."

The knight spurred his horse. Without looking back, he rode out of the village towards the south.

Farin stared after him, open-mouthed. What did he mean by the raven? A murderer? Of course – the man in black had transmitted danger and shiftiness through every pore of his body. He had threatened Farin – he remembered the words of the man in black only too well: "First I'll take care of the priest and the village alderman. Then I'll come after you."

Amen had disappeared three days ago. Coincidence? Farin prayed that the priest really was gone on a business trip. From time to time he would travel in his carriage, the only one in the village, to the nearest big town.

Now that the knight was no more to be seen, the Heap society of pipe smokers retired back to the tavern. They swaggered past Farin without giving him a second glance. They walked through the empty doorframe into "The Warm Beer" as if nothing had happened.

Only his father and the alderman remained standing there, the latter holding his hand to his bloody temple. "I think you deliberately held back with your conclusions so you could put us in a bad light, gravedigger's son", grumbled Hamak, obviously grateful that Farin had saved his life. "I won't forget that."

Threats instead of thanks. Hamak really was petty-minded. Farin was almost shocked at this realisation. After all, next to the priest that bloke was the most important man in the village.

The alderman followed the others into the tavern.

His father shook his head wearily but said nothing.

The silence hit Farin with more force than a roar or a clip across the ear.

I know, father, dead is dead. Questions only hurt business. Everybody dies because their heart stops.

Without knowing any better, Farin had broken the grave-digger's code, and played the smart aleck. Father was pissed off. Hamak was pissed off. The latter had forgotten in no time how his life had been in great danger.

Farin sighed.

the hayloft

ARROSsssssssssss!!"

It was exactly the same spluttering sound as when the disgusting gruel boiled over on the hearth. No wonder – the matron herself was boiling with rage. "If I catch you, I'll rip your ears off!"

That sounded dangerous. Faster than a fleeing fox Aross flitted out the back door of the kitchen and into the yard. Without her ears she'd look like a pumpkin with her round head and short hair – like a reddish-brown pumpkin if she were to wash it. But without ears her old felt cap would lose its practical stoppers left and right, which naturally prevented it from slipping down and over her eyes. And who knows what other uses her lugs had. The matron would have calmed down by the evening and would proceed to her favourite routine. She would flog Aross on her hands and fingers with the cane. Not pleasant either, especially as the back of her right hand was still black and blue from the last time.

"Stay there, you damn rat!"

"Wouldn't you just love that, you damn torturer," she muttered to herself in a low voice, not wishing to provoke her persecutor any further.

The rat reached the dilapidated barn with impressive speed. It served as a henhouse now and was situated opposite the orphanage. Up to a few months ago a donkey and two goats had also been resident here. The birds clucked irately as Aross stormed in like a fury, passing a haystack on her right before throwing herself at the rails of an old ladder. Fleet-footed and at a speed which suggested she had four legs, she climbed upwards, shoved open the hatch into the loft, and slipped through it before finding at least temporary refuge at an altitude of four yards or so. The matron wouldn't follow her up here, not least because the brittle rungs wouldn't bear her weight. The fat, greedy quail only had herself to blame.

"Nothing to eat for you tonight, you good-for-nothing. Twenty of the best instead. I'll be expecting you in my room," she cursed after the girl, before turning away from the barn door empty-handed and disappearing back into the kitchen, where she proceeded to hurl commands at the two maids.

"Woah!" gasped Aross, sitting on her knees. The loft was so low that not even Aross could stand upright. She leaned against one of the crossbeams and buried her bare feet deep into the extra straw that was still stored up here.

The orphanage in the town of Hubstone had been her home for as long as she could remember. And for as long as she could remember she had been the target of regular beatings by the matron. An arrangement that was both simple and predictable.

It had all started barely fourteen years ago. An infant, only a few weeks old, was discovered by a maid on the steps before the front door of the orphanage. Half-starved, half-frozen, half-covered by rags in a half-rotten wooden box, it lay there conspicuously inconspicuous. And it refused to do what infants normally do so well and do so frequently in such a situation – it refused to cry. Not a peep did the little waif utter. Instead, she stared defiantly up at the heavens. The word AROSS was branded on one of the crate boards. And so that was what she had been called ever since.

Consequently, Aross knew neither her birthday, nor exactly what age she was. That wasn't really the point, though. What was more important to her was how much longer she would stay alive. A strange thought for a young girl, but recently almost every new day had been crashing in on top of her with increasing force, bruising not only her body but also her soul, to the point that she was asking herself how much longer it could go on like this. There were only two options: either the day would get damaged or the young girl. And today's beating had already been on the cards since early morning. Just because she'd wanted to steal a slice of bread. She'd earned the beating, not because of the bread, but because she'd allowed herself to be caught by the matron. And she wouldn't cry, no matter what happened. The thing with the meal wasn't really that annoying, seeing as how the portions in the orphanage were little bigger than a small heap of mouse droppings. And tasted no better. In the mornings you got gruel with water, and in the evenings, water with gruel. That was both cheap and quick to prepare. Watery gruel would have been on the menu in the middle of the day too were it not for the fact that the matron had thought up an even cheaper menu – nothing.

Which was why Aross was constantly on the lookout for additional sustenance; otherwise she'd have starved to death in the old house long ago. It was only up here that she had stashed a few secret provisions, and she was sure there was a wrinkly old apple on one of the roof beams. While her eyes were squinting upwards into the gable in search of the wizened fruit, her attention was drawn to a noise coming from below. She lay down in the straw on her stomach and peered down into the barn through the gaps between the boards. All she could make out was Wolf, the old hunting dog, who had made himself comfortable in his corner. The mutt's best days were long behind him; his hips had become stiff and he could only move with difficulty.

"Hey, Aross! What have you been up to? Pilfering food as usual? Or did you piss in the matron's wine again?" A young boy appeared at the foot of the ladder; he was peering in all directions in a halting, awkward manner. It was Grim of all people, the matron's pet, looking up at her with his sticky-out ears and his brown locks of hair – not brave enough to climb up to her. The boy was one of the most repulsive people in the orphanage. He had actually managed in all these years not to give the matron even a single reason to give him a beating. What shame!

"None of your business, Grim. Piss off! And be quick about it!" she ordered him brusquely. If he as much as dared to enter into her kingdom, she would slam the hatch down on his head or push him off the ladder, something she'd done once before. She'd been happy to pay the price of twenty of the best that time. Grim was at least two years older and two heads higher than Aross but she still had no respect for the little shit. Because of her state of destitution there were some things she simply didn't have. Shoes and respect were two of them.

"You're going to come to a bad end."

She thought she was hearing things. Grim sounded like the matron, only a hundred years older. Wow, did he sound sensible!

"Spare me your stupid talk. Now piss off and go wash your feet!" That was Grim's speciality. His feet always looked as pink and as fresh as a new-born baby's. His buckskin boots helped, of course, and she had no idea how he'd come by them.

He looked up at her scornfully. "You are reprehensible and...and contemptible".

The words he knew – she really couldn't keep up with him. "And you're a little shit, Grim. Piss off".

"I hope the matron gives you a right beating."

"She'll have to catch me first, dimwit."

"I should catch you and bring you to her. Then maybe I'll get a reward."

"You'll have to get me first, dimwit."

"Really? Why? You'll have to go to her this evening and pay for it anyway. Otherwise she won't let you into the dormitory anymore, and then see where you'll end up."

Unfortunately, he was right. Aross clenched her little fists. She knew that Grim had to be taken seriously when it came to close combat. No conscience, but broad shoulders and strong arms with hands like vices that wouldn't let go once they had you in their grip. The swine had more than enough strength – no wonder, as he seemed to be the only child in the orphanage who always got enough to eat. Another reason for hating him.

Grim's face twisted itself into a sly and vicious grimace.

"I've just thought of how I can tempt you down."

The boy went over to the old hound and kicked against his long muzzle, which the tired animal had placed between his forepaws. Wolf yelped loudly. Partly because of the shock and partly in pain. Crouched, and wagging his tail furiously, as if he had done something wrong himself, he stood in front of Grim, licking his bloody nose. And to cap it all, Aross could see that his hips were hurting him terribly.

The mutt was even more stupid than Grim.

He prepared his right boot for a second kick. "Come down or I'll kick him to death!"

The hatred in his voice was unnecessary. Aross screamed loudly, slid through the hatchway and in one leap jumped down the ladder and landed on top of Grim. She'd often leaped down here onto the big pile of hay, but always for fun and not filled with hate nor onto a person. With her arms stretched in front of her, her fingers bent like claws, and her eyes and mouth opened wide in rage she landed on top of him. The sheer force of the impact knocked him backward and she managed to ram her knee forcefully under his chin. Grim's lower jaw crunched, his teeth slammed together, and his eyes rolled backwards. It was clear he had never expected an aerial attack from a height of over two yards, in which Aross could have broken her neck. Her little fists pounded away at Grim's face until bright red blood was flowing from his mouth and nose. Aross knew that every surprise attack was over just as swiftly. She disengaged from him quickly and climbed up the ladder again. Her knee was hurting a little, but the feeling of having been hammering into the bully's gormless head gave the pain a sweet taste.

When it came down to it, nothing had changed. She was still up high, and he was still down low. Except that Grim was now lying on his back, groaning and bleeding. Wolf, terrified, had retreated as far as possible into his corner.

As if asking Grim for a favour, Aross said in a sweet voice, "Now, listen to me Grim. If you ever hurt Wolf again, I'm going to kill you".

The dog pounded the floor with his tail when he heard his name.

"You're crazy. Totally crazy," whined the boy. He slowly

got up to his feet and wiped the blood from his face with his sleeve.

Aross was pretty certain he wasn't going to snitch on her by going to the matron or anybody else. It would be very embarrassing if it ever came out that the small, skinny and worthless girl had beaten up the powerful Grim. A bloodied face was looking up at her. His eyes were blazing hatred towards her, but another emotion had won the upper hand. Fear! The powerful Grim was afraid. Not of Aross, but of her incalculable self-sacrifice. Aross didn't know if she could *really* kill him. She had never killed anyone up to this point and she had no desire to do so. She hated weapons like daggers and swords. But Grim didn't know that – and that was the point. The idiot straightened himself with a groan and looked at Aross out of the corner of his eye, with his lower lip protruding. Slowly and trying to maintain some last semblance of dignity he shook the dirt and straw off his clothing and left the barn without saying another word.

Once Gram was out of sight, Aross leaned her upper body down through the hatch. "Now listen to me, Wolf. The next time don't just accept everything that happens but give the swine a good bite in his leg."

Wolf wagged his tail and licked his grey snout as if in agreement.

But Aross wasn't convinced. "Believe me, wagging your tail isn't enough in this world. You have to bite, bite, bite", she grumbled at the dog. Her strong conviction more than made up for her high-pitched girl's voice. Wolf seemed quite impressed anyway and crouched behind his forepaws.

Happy with her victory over Grim, Aross stretched out in the straw. She would gladly spend the rest of her life up here, but her experience told her she would have to pee sometime and get herself some more food supplies. And anyway, the matron had threatened that one day she would set fire to the ground floor of the barn under the girl's backside. The two fat spiders who were busily spinning their webs between the roof beams wouldn't be too happy about that either. Aross had christened them Tip and Tap because they were constantly tipping and tapping with their many legs.

She stuck a piece of straw in her mouth, tilting it alternatively up to between her eyes and then down until it slapped her chin. The old bag of a matron would even complain about that. "Women don't chew straw!" Aross stuck her tongue out scornfully, artfully keeping the straw stuck to it. Women could only do things that were no fun. Women didn't climb up into haylofts – but rats were allowed. As if to confirm this, there was a rustling behind her in the straw. Aross peeled her eyes in search of a pointy nose, beady eyes and a long tail but could see nothing. Aross would never be able to do right by the matron, not in a hundred years; not so long as her tormentor seemed to enjoy walloping her.

What now? She could go to the harbour and steal fish scraps. And she'd heard that Mattilda was now working on pier four. Aross considered the girl to be something like her friend. At least they'd grown up together in the orphanage until about a year ago when the matron had given Mattilda and another girl called Jennie to the whorehouse. A man had arrived that time with a fat stomach and a fat moneybag and then he'd left again with a fat stomach and a thin moneybag. He'd used the occasion to cart the two girls off like hens. Jennie and Mattilda were one or two years older than Aross, and so she reckoned that she would suffer the same fate next year at the latest. The prospect of an overflowing purse as well as the money from the town coffers for every child in the orphanage were the only reasons the matron hadn't beaten Aross into an early grave long ago or sent her packing. Although the latter would probably have been a better fate.

Slimefoot

Aross decided to check if everything was alright down at the harbour. She pulled herself up onto a beam, pushed her way through a hole in the rotten roof shingles, skipped along the ledge to the branch of an old beech tree, and Bob's your uncle, a long branch bent under her weight onto the ground, and she jumped off lightly. Aross ran off – rats always ran. Just keep going? How would that work out? Aross knew every street and every gutter – the narrower, the more despicable, the better. After all, the town orphanage was situated in the middle of the old town – a term which suggested tradition and the preservation of the tried and tested. This was what the unexperienced traveller coming from afar might think, but nothing could be further from the truth. Lowlife, filth and sewers were the only things to be found in the old town. It made no difference if the chamber pots were emptied out from the houses onto the streets or not. It mattered not a jot if all types of rubbish landed in the gutters or not, or in the town moat, or in the town streams. Mouldy wooden boards crossed over stinking rivulets. Dirt attracted dirt, and so tanners, dyers and knackers had established themselves in the old town. It smelled abominably to strangers, homely to Aross. Here, in the middle of filth and lowlife, was where Aross had grown up, up to nearly five feet tall – without shoes. She always ran barefoot through the dross. Did rats wear shoes? Feet black to her ankles –

dirt was the best protection. Aross Slimefoot, queen of the rats, one of the nameless boys called her once. A name like that had to be earned. She took it as recognition. After all, it wasn't the king who ruled the town, but the rats. They scampered everywhere – in the gutters, in the cellars, the canals, the ditches. There were a hundred rats to every person, and the crawling creatures were unspeakably tough. It takes thirteen blows to kill a rat, so they said. The sewers had no effect on the animals, as opposed to the people, who perished in their own filth. Aross didn't know how many people had fallen victim to the polluted state of the old town. A good many anyway. Lots of her fellow-orphans constantly had diarrhoea and were always throwing up. Bitter experience had taught her early on never to drink from the well in the old town. How could it be in any way clean if it was pumped up through the middle of excrement? The ultimate proof lay with the genteel matron: she wouldn't touch water from the old town's well. For these reasons Aross hid her water-skin in the back corner of the barn under the straw. She'd nicked it barely two years ago from the market. Here she had water from the upper town, right beside the artisans' district.

It wasn't long before she reached the harbour area. The large market hall was snug against the castle wall; it was a rectangular tented structure of planks and waxed canvas. The fishing boats had moored earlier in the day and now their catch was being sold. Aross loved the deafening shouts of the stallholders. This was when the fish was fatter, fresher and cheaper than any time until tomorrow at the same time. Aross pulled her old felt cap further down her face, making her look older. She pushed her way through the mass of people with many small but sharp digs of her elbows, occasionally knocking people sideways, even some who were twice as big and heavy as she was. All a matter of momentum, of technique, and most importantly, strength of mind.

"Brazen hussy!" cursed a woman behind her.

Exactly – brazenness was part of it too.

"The fattest Northern Sea eels!" a fisherman touted his catch; rusty eel pots were stacked up behind him. "My good lady, only five coppers for four – just for you."

A woman with a colourful plumed hat, clearly a noble-woman, examined the display. For some inexplicable reason she hadn't sent one of her servants, making her own way here instead. She seemed undecided and inexperienced – the ideal victim for the streetwise fishmonger.

"My dear man, I fear your offer may not be commensurate to the value."

Aross rolled her eyes. Did she really say, "my dear man'? There was no such thing here. And what did she mean by, "not be commensurate'?

These thoughts didn't prevent her from going up on her tiptoes and whispering into the woman's ear: "You give me one copper and I'll lower the price by two."

The lady turned and looked questioningly at Aross, her nose puckering, her eyes too.

No, she never chewed on a piece of straw or jumped from the loft onto the hay. Not to worry. Aross could smell a copper earned through honest work. "Right, then – a deal? Just watch…"

The woman looked her up and down with a mixture of fascination and disgust before nodding nervously.

"Only five coppers for four," repeated the fishmonger.

This was the moment – Aross roared: "WHAAAT? That's extortion! Those eels are smaller than your dick. I'll give you two coppers for five of your runts."

Impressed by such eloquent negotiating skills, the lady grimaced. Suddenly, it looked as if she'd lost her appetite for eel. Blushing deeply, she disappeared into the crowd, and Aross, saying nothing, was relieved of her negotiating mandate.

Which was how the eel-seller saw it too: "Vamoose! If I catch you near my stall again, there'll be trouble," he threatened.

"Offer reasonable prices for your half-starved blind-worms, then you might sell something." Aross wasn't going to be intimidated by somebody like him. She stuck her tongue out at the dimwit and strolled on. Just as she was about to shove a bulky person out of the way with a swing of her hips, she heard a strange voice call out her name: "Aross!"

The girl turned around; only a few people knew her name. An old woman was sitting cross-legged on the ground. She was holding a bowl with a few cheese rinds in her gaunt, trembling hands. She was wearing a headscarf, a faded dress and sandals that were far too big for her. They fixed their eyes on each other. The old woman's hands stopped shaking, her back straightened up, and the girl felt how the woman was pulling her in like a whirlpool. She continued to stare into Aross's eyes, snapped the fingers on her right hand, before hooking her forefinger repeatedly, indicating to the girl that she should sit down beside her.

"Come to me." The wrinkles and valleys on the old wom-an's face took on a friendly demeanour and she wiped away a stray strand of grey hair. "You're the girl from the orphan-age. You're the waif-girl, Aross."

Brilliant! What amazing news! Was the woman paying her

a compliment or making an accusation? Hmm, it sounded like neither one nor the other. Something made Aross hesitate, and she asked suspiciously: "And if that were the case, who would want to know?"

"She, who knows."

Evasive trickery and humbug. The type of thing Aross couldn't stand. "If you knew anything, you wouldn't be mooching about on the ground begging for a few rinds of cheese. Only people who have no clue, no money and no nothing do that. And don't know their arse from their elbow."

Ha, a good speech, thought Aross. Let's see what Shewhoknows has to say to that.

Instead of becoming enraged, the old woman smiled. "You're strong, just as I expected, girl. Trust me, I've got something that you need – just so you know."

"Oh, right! And that would be?"

A man interrupted their discussion in no uncertain terms. "Get out of my way, hussy!" He shoved Aross aside, almost causing her to lose balance.

The girl squeezed in beside Shewhoknows on the ground – after all, rats were fundamentally very curious. Now she was no longer in anyone's way, and the two of them could carry on their conversation among the market noises without fear of being overheard. In fact, the old woman had stirred something in the girl which she had thought couldn't be stirred. It had something to do with the word "future".

"Tell me then, what do I need?" Aross made her rat-face by making her nose, lips and ears go pointy.

"Child! It's cost me five years of my life tracking down. Now, listen carefully and take the matter seriously. You don't know who you are." The old woman's voice sounded neither faltering nor self-pitying, but clear and emphatic; her eyes shone green.

The girl thought aloud: "I am Aross Slimefoot, queen of the rats. And it's taken you five years to find me? And yet I live in the orphanage in the old town – hardly a good hiding place."

"The first tasks were to find out who you are and where you are. Now we have to figure out what you are."

Aross's eyes rolled quite automatically. "Very simple. I know exactly what I am. Hungry! In fact, I'm always hungry. And your idle chatter doesn't fill any stomach."

"The future is the key."

Aross didn't need to think for long. "The present is shitty."

"Without the present, no future."

Shewhoknows had a fancy answer to everything.

"Aross! You're only missing a little something. And when you find it, you will see." Red sparks danced in the old woman's green eyes. "Collect it in the burning night. And only then! Have no fear and no shame – all is well."

"What do you mean: 'a little something'?" Aross was becoming impatient. She had no time for this convoluted pussyfooting around.

"Child, the tooth of time will show you when the moment is right."

The old woman continued to smile. A friendly smile. Something you could never take for granted when it came to adults. Aross was generally mistrustful of smiles, for the joy on the lips seldom made the journey as far as the eyes.

The girl had the feeling she was treading water – not a pleasant feeling for a rat, who was otherwise always running. "And when will I know that the moment is right?" she asked impatiently.

"Listen out for the..." the old woman's voice grew softer. "For the witch's peal."

Aross had heard enough. In all the filth, among all the crackpots around her, she had already experienced a lot in her young life. But the old woman was teaching the concept of the creeps in a totally new way: On the one hand, she was surrounded by an aura that churned Aross up, yet on the other hand she was talking gibberish. The tooth of time and witch's peals. Too crazed, too vague, too ludicrous.

She crawled away and stood up. "I have to go."

The old woman smiled again. "You'll understand then that the time is right. Pardon my metaphors."

"Exactly! Your meta...force won't feed me. So, spare me your riddles. It's enough for me to know where I can get something to eat."

"Nourishment you will not be lacking in. But you have other challenges ahead of you." She rolled a silver coin in her fingers and flicked it to Aross.

The girl caught the coin in her hand and held it firmly in her fist. Now she was talking! A language that Aross and the traders with all their delicious wares that filled your stomach understood.

Why is Shewhoknows begging on the ground, with nothing more than a few rinds of cheese, throwing money around?

Where was the catch? What was the deal? Did she have to listen to more of the old woman's mumbo-jumbo? Things like: "Don't believe everything you see" or "always listen to your heart, my child'? Aross didn't believe in anything but her stomach, otherwise she'd have died of starvation in this hellhole long ago. Her world consisted of filth. Perfumed claptrap, on the other hand, belonged up in the castle with the nobility.

She thought for a moment. She could put up with a lot for a silverling. She also felt the need to chip in herself. "I have a metaforce for you too: I don't waggle my tail – I bite, bite, bite. To the very end!" She leaped up.

The smile disappeared off the old woman's face. "I know. You have a thousand teeth, more than any shark, Aross. You are the next one after me. Do not forget my words – my death should not be in vain."

The girl could think of nothing to top that.

"I understand I'm demanding too much of you." The furrows on the woman's brow became thinner and deeper. "So, you call yourself Aross Slimefoot, queen of the rats, and you bite and bite. Then I will ensure that you think of me in your hour of greatest need on the day of the thousand bites. I can only help you once, and then you are on your own. Remember everything we have spoken about."

She placed her hand briefly on Aross's breastbone. It tickled, and Aross had to stop herself from instinctively shaking her off. She didn't like any physical contact. The old woman raised her bony forefinger. "And another important piece of advice – find the bone reader."

Wow – that really took the biscuit, even for all that money. Aross's legs were itching to go; she just wanted to get away and forget the old woman. "Thanks for the silverling. I have to go."

The expression on the woman's face changed momentarily. A shadow flickered across her face as she closed her eyes. First enraptured, then beguiled. The old woman raised her eyelids; Aross blinked – for a moment all she could see was a yellow shimmer. Perhaps it was the diffuse light under the canopy. The next moment the eyes were sparkling green as before, and the old woman smiled happily, as though someone had taken a great weight off her shoulders. She spread out her arms and whispered: "Now I am ready."

Just get me away from the madwoman, thought Aross. She crawled on all fours between two pairs of legs, the silverling clenched firmly in her fist. Ignoring the enraged looks of the legs' owners, the girl reached the exit. Here too, the masses of people were pushing and shoving as they walked along the quay. The harbour was always jam-packed at this time of day. The sailing boats bobbed up and down on the piers, the seagulls swooping hither and yon among the masts in a constant search for food.

Like me. Rats with wings, thought Aross and looked longingly at one of the large birds, flying in an elegant curve through the air.

Aross liked the smell of fish, thick smoke, sweat and salt. There was something fresh, foreign and faraway in it, compared to the sewers around the orphanage.

A whole silverling – she could buy food for a week. She was in a good mood now and remembered she wanted to look for Mattilda. In spite of the crisp autumn wind, the whores were skimpily dressed, standing on pier 4, the main trading point for transactions of a bodily nature in Hubstone. Aross had a good idea of all the goings-on here, even if she didn't want to. She craned her neck in search of Matilda.

A fat woman with a long scar on her cheek snarled at Aross. "What do you want here? Pier four belongs to the reapers. And anyway, no man wants to touch a greasy, skinny bag of bones like yourself."

Should she waste anger and time on this fat ferret? Aross

decided against it and left her standing there. Why should the queen of the rats be bothered by what some dung beetle was saying about her? She was already past the fat woman and had forgotten the incident when she finally spotted Mattilda at the end of the pier.

"Matt, you look like shit," said Aross by way of greeting. Mattilda's small face brightened up a little, apart from her right eye, which was beaten black and blue. The girl's once lively eyes were as dull as the water from the well in the old town. Welts and bruises decorated her arms and legs.

The two embraced each other.

"Hello, Aross," whispered Mattilda. "Better you go quickly. Or we'll both be in trouble."

"Who did that to you?" asked Aross, pretending not to hear her.

"The protector I've been assigned to – you know that the protectors control everything here. And above all they cash the money."

Aross looked at her friend and frowned. She had aged years in the last few months, and a crooked, insincere adult smile distorted her face even more. At their last meeting she had explained to Aross that she always had to have a friendly smile so that the men would take her to the dive nearby.

"And who protects you from the protectors?"

Mattilda looked at her sadly. "Aross, get away while you still can. Just run away – away from the crazy matron before she sells you into this hellhole. Away from the town. Once the protectors have you in their grasp, you're done for – then you're better off dead." Her last words ended in a sobbing whimper.

Aross wasn't really surprised; she knew the laws of the old town and of the skulduggery in the harbour. But

Mattilda's pitiful appearance and her drastic words hit her harder than she'd expected.

"I have a bit of money – shall I give you some?" she asked.

Mattilda's eyes became even wetter after hearing this. She whispered to Aross in a voice she had never heard before: "You just don't have enough money. It's like the story of the bleeding giant – it's always too little and never enough." She wiped her face, smearing the heavy makeup around her eyes. "Just like the giant – I don't have enough blood...it's...not enough."

A thickset guy in a jingling chainmail shirt strode towards them. His gait was ostentatious and powerful, as though he were wading knee-deep through water.

Horror was bursting in Mattilda's eyes. "Leave me in peace, Aross! Scram! Here comes my protector, Chain Dog."

A sword, a club and a whip were swinging from the man's belt. "You there, you're supposed to be working, not gossiping." Without hesitating, he slapped her with the flat of his hand, making a cracking sound. Mattilda uttered a cry of pain.

Chain Dog turned to Aross. "And you, pipsqueak, get lost. You're still too young and...too ugly; you'll just get us into trouble with the authorities." He aimed a kick towards Aross with his right foot, but she evaded him skilfully. The guy pulled the whip from his belt. She had no other option but to run back along the pier. She could do nothing for Mattilda at the moment, but she swore that she would keep Chain Dog in her heart for the future, and not release him again until he had paid his dues.

"The bleeding giant". Mattilda's ominous whisper stuck in

Aross's mind, just like the thick spiders' web in the hayloft. She felt goose bumps on her skinny back, and she shivered. Every year the matron told the children of the orphanage the story of the bleeding giant: Once upon a time there was a giant who lived in the mountains of Groanpeaks. Aross hadn't the foggiest where Groanpeaks was, but that wasn't so important for the story. The matron would begin with a description of the giant. He was enormous of course, over six yards tall and as strong as twenty-one bears. Why twenty-one bears exactly, she never explained, but that wasn't so important for the story. The giant lived happily in his mountain cave and, on account of his friendly manner, he never touched a hair of anybody's head but was always friendly.

A sweet giant then, Aross had thought at that point in the story the first time she'd heard it. Lovely!

The matron slowly came to the meat of the matter. One day the giant saw the king's daughter being driven through the valley. She looked out the window of her carriage, and then it happened. The giant fell madly in love with the young woman at first sight.

How anyone could fall in love with somebody being driven past at high speed in a carriage was a mystery to Aross, but that wasn't so important for the story either.

The giant could do nothing else the livelong day but think about the king's daughter. He wanted nothing more than to be with her, to look at her and admire her. And marry her. And so, he told the king of his wish. The latter wasn't overjoyed at the prospect of having a giant as his son-in-law but didn't want to alienate himself from him under any circumstances. Who knew how dangerous a furious giant might be? So, the king made a proposal to him. "Fill the top tower-room in my castle-keep to the windowsill with your blood – then I shall give you my daughter for your wife."

The giant looked in bafflement at the king and then at the castle-keep, a tower not much bigger than himself and not much thicker than his thigh; and the room at the top looked laughably small. "I'll do it", he decided. Without further ado he cut his wrist with his enormous knife and held it at the highest window of the castle-keep, so that his blood flowed in. With one eye he examined the scene through the other window as the room began to fill. The blood slowly advanced, and it wouldn't be long before it was dripping out of the windows. But then it stopped, just under the window-sill. The giant squinted with effort into the room until he discovered that the door had been opened by the king's servants. "Oh, the king has lured me into a trap. My blood is flowing down into the lower rooms of the tower. Then I'll just fill them too." And so, the giant put his hand further through the window and dreamed of the beautiful king's daughter. The whole tower was filling with his blood, and the level continued to rise. The king observed what was happening in horror and ordered the doors to the dungeons be opened. And that was damned important for the story.

The giant couldn't see the open doors to the dungeon. He bled and bled, he became dizzy, he squinted into the little room, there wasn't much more blood needed. He bled on until finally the castle dungeons were filled with his blood. When he dropped dead after two days, there was a small earthquake.

What a shitty story! Five times over the previous few years they had been forced to listen to the story, and each time they had cheered the giant on and hoped he'd manage it this time, but the dimwit kipped over and died every time. Aross had noticed the last time that the matron got pleasure from seeing the looks of horror on the children's faces – the old torturer had really revelled in it.

What lessons had Aross drawn from this story? Firstly, giants are stupid. Secondly, kings are nasty liars. Thirdly: fool me once, shame on you; fool me twice, shame on me.

And I shouldn't forget the fourth lesson, thought the girl. The matron is a bad person.

Her concern for Mattilda was growing. Chain Dog was worse, it seemed to her, than the king in the story of the giant. Unfortunately, there were quite a few of these characters in the capital of the Worldly Kingdom. Hubstone prided itself on having the largest sea harbours, the largest cathedral and the greatest buildings in the Worldly Kingdom. Aross couldn't judge if this was indeed the case, but it was certainly true that the largest arseholes of the Worldly Kingdom were running around Hubstone.

The old town, which the harbour was part of, was controlled by two clans: the turners and the reapers. The men in these fine organisations divvied up all the lucrative businesses between them. Obviously not peacefully, there was constant fighting over control of the whorehouses and bordellos at the harbour, as well as of the gambling joints; then there was the blackmailing, not to mention the protection rackets. The turners' speciality was the noose fixed around the victim's neck from behind and twisted tight by means of a stick – as slowly as possible. The reapers on the other hand, used a more traditional method. Always armed to the teeth with knives and daggers, they preferred to slit their victims as they walked past. A two-week war had raged between the two parties a year ago, which had cost twenty people their lives. A pity they hadn't all killed each other.

Aross changed her silverling at a stand into fourteen coppers and a pickled herring. She then purchased a pastry at pier two. She swallowed both ravenously and for the first time in days she felt half-way satiated. Hubstone was more bearable on a full stomach.

Aross's experiences at the harbour were enough for one day. Here might was right, and by might was meant brutality and unscrupulousness. She had to go back to the orphanage. She would present herself to the matron there. That was the only way she could get to her bed in the dormitory where she slept with fifteen other girls. The price for entry was twenty of the best on the back of her hand. She wouldn't flinch and she wouldn't complain. Her feet flitted through the alleyways, and strange words through her head: Chain Dog, witches' peal, bone reader. What a world. She decided to forget this nonsense.

She arrived at the orphanage and headed straight for the matron's room. There she sat, in her rocking chair, reading a hefty tome. Doubtless more stories about dim-witted giants and rotten kings. The matron looked up and smiled. Not the embracing smile of Shewhoknows, but rather a typical adult's smile. Lip service, singular and fake!

"Ah yes, it's always much better when the little rat comes crawling to pussy cat. Twenty of the best! Give me your hand." The matron stood up.

With teeth clenched, but standing up straight and without hesitation, Aross reached out her left hand to the matron.

She shook her head and said in a disconsolate voice: "The other hand, my child."

How Aross hated those lips describing her as "my child". The back of her right hand was still swollen and beaten black and blue from yesterday's flogging. The girl changed arms without batting an eyelid. The matron had a special contraption for her disciplining. She tied the girl's wrist to a small wooden block which was screwed to the table by means of a leather strap. That way her victims could not pull away their hand.

The matron went over to a shelf which had five canes, all of varying lengths and thicknesses. Aross blinked. Five? Up to now only four canes had hung there.

She wasn't long waiting for an explanation. "Today I am going to christen my new darling in your honour," beamed the matron as she reached for number five.

"Best willow wood," she said, singing its praises and clicking her tongue.

Aross gritted her teeth. The rod was longer than all the others, and the very sight of it was painful. Savouring the moment, the torturer raised the cane high before slamming it hard against the tabletop, just beside Aross's hand. The whizzing through the air and the ensuing thwack on the wood was enough to make the other children scream and whimper. Aross, on the other hand, remained stiff, silent and still. This attitude enraged the matron no end, the girl knew that much at least. The woman raised the cane for the first proper blow, the cane whipped down, landing with precision on an already swollen part. Aross almost fainted with the pain. She swayed momentarily but didn't even let out a groan.

"It's always a particular pleasure with you, child. You're very special. I shall break you, rest assured. I'm going to start with your fingers."

Then came the second whack; a vein burst, and blood splattered onto the matron's face. Her eyes and cheeks had become rosy, making the blood almost imperceptible, and she was breathing more quickly and seemed to be enjoying every moment. No sound passed through the girl's lips. Another eighteen whacks to go. It became clear to Aross that the woman would turn her hand into pulp, she would destroy her fingers, her knuckles, the back of her hand. Tears poured down the girl's face – tears of pain, of helplessness, of rage. She tasted the salt in her mouth. Should she scream? Surely, she had to scream now? Maybe that would change things.

No! I don't bark, I bite.

After the fourth or fifth blow Aross toppled over, the pain simply pushing her into a deep hole. A hole without light, without feeling, without agony. She barely sensed how she'd almost wrenched her arm out, which was still tied to the tabletop. Then the hole closed over.

champion

My champion! You must come and help your king."

"Must I? I see, I see." Vigo relaxed.

The king's messenger shifted awkwardly from one foot to the other. "The enemy is before the castle. The outer city wall has already fallen. It's only a matter of time before the barbarians from the south will force their way into the castle." His champion not exactly reacting in sheer horror, he added: "And into your bedroom."

The king had indeed sent his most cunning errand-boy.

"Is that all?" asked Vigo.

"The…the king commands…uh…he asks you to help. It will be a fight to the death."

The naked woman's head lay on the champion's chest, her long legs wrapped around his. It had never occurred to her to hide her nakedness. "Do I have to go then, my love?" she murmured in a lascivious voice.

"Don't you dare, Orelia. We've only just started," he said with a smile. "Wait here for me – I'll be quick."

Vigo swung out of the bed; he knew when it was time for action. After all, it was all a question of compromising – which then allowed him to live it up afterwards. A sense of duty had nothing to do with goodness. Not even the sensuous pouting of his playmate could change his mind.

"Stringing a king along is dangerous. Even more indecent

to let the enemy wait for a fight to the death. It's a question of upbringing," he explained to her.

Vigo enjoyed her "you-look-so-wonderful" gaze as he pulled up his trousers.

The messenger stood in the doorway all the while, sweating. It couldn't have been easy for him to invade the bedchamber unannounced. There had been times when Vigo would have killed him for doing just that. The messenger justified himself swiftly. "I thank you, sir. The king will tear my head from my shoulders if I return without you at my side."

"Then I would avoid him if at all possible if I didn't have my champion at my side."

The servant considered that for a moment. "Even better to return to him with my champion. I'll wait."

Vigo grinned as he pulled on his studded armour – his breastplate consisting of three layers of hardened leather, and his thigh armour, which attached to his waist armour. He strapped on his broadsword and looked at himself in the man-sized mirror. He didn't look genuinely terrifying. He was, though. An opponent to be taken seriously by the enemy. He resolutely reached for his leather helmet, put it on with the eye slit facing backwards, waved around his arms helplessly and whined in consternation: "I'm blind, everything is dark, I can't see anymore!"

His beloved giggled, impressed. "Are you the king's court jester or the king's principal knight?"

"What's the difference, my precious?"

She nodded, as if she were the last person capable of answering this philosophical question. "Take care of yourself, principal court jester."

A joyful roar rang out when Vigo stepped out of the palace and into the inner courtyard. The soldiers, artisans, vassals and citizens, who made up the throng, all loved their champion Vigo, first knight of the Northern Kingdom, who had remained loyal to his king, Ekarius the Fifth.

No wonder! If he were a normal citizen, he'd also love himself – hadn't he already saved the town and its castle no less than five times from siege, destruction or worse by winning in single combat. Decisive duels that were fights to the death. This was what Vigo lived for; this was why he served his king; this was why he always got what he wanted.

The attacks on the capital of the Northern Kingdom had become fewer in recent years. Word had spread about Vigo's fighting skills – after five glorious victories the enemies knew what they had to expect before these walls. They prepared for either an unbelievably demanding fight to the death, or a siege that would last for years, by the end of which they would have lost countless men and conquered a city which would have little in common with how it looked today. Supplies would be used up, the people dead or on the point of starvation, the wells poisoned, the city treasures buried. All this unpleasantness could be simply avoided – by a duel for control of the city, which would of course require the permission of its defenders. If the fighter representing the attacking army lost, then that army would withdraw empty-handed. If he won, however, the city would submit to the enemy leader without further combat. The victor would receive the key to the castle, and so the authority over the city. The previous leader, generally a prince or, as in this case, a king, would then abdicate. The conqueror gained control over the city and all its resources without significant losses, generally including the citizens, who had to accept the outcome of the fight for good or ill. Of course, there was a certain hidden risk; the conqueror might not adhere to tradition but instead, having entered the city, he might execute the conquered king first and then all of the citizens, but this rarely happened.

With a spring in his step Vigo climbed the wooden defensive corridor. He raised his eyebrows heavenwards when he saw the enemy army. Fierce-looking soldiers as far as his eyes could see. On all sides he could see the yellow and black banners adorned with their peregrine falcon on the coat-of-arms of King Grachus. A dangerous enemy who already controlled the south. His domicile was Hubstone, the most important harbour city of the Worldly Kingdom, which had made him rich and powerful. Grachus had been extending his claws northwards since time immemorial too; this man wouldn't rest easy until he had the entire Worldly Kingdom under his wing. This endless striving for power and yet more power was a mystery to Vigo.

The enemy army had overcome the first hurdle in the twinkling of an eye – there were impressive holes gaping in the outer wall. In the background the houses were burning, sending up clouds of black smoke. Too black. Grachus's soldiers had clearly helped things along with oil-soaked rags. Which merely emphasised the need for a duel. Ekarius simply couldn't afford to reject the offer.

He spotted his king on the balustrade directly over the castle gate. The show-off had put on his pageant armour. A mixture of gold and silver. Although gold was, of course, a totally unsuitable metal for armoured plates. Soft and heavy. As befitted its wearer. Beside him stood the chancellor, Tarian Wineview, the king's closest advisor. What the man did all day remained a mystery to Vigo. Oh yes – he advised the king closely. Vigo imagined to himself how this had manifested itself up to now. Presumably, the king had asked: "The enemy is outside our gates. What do we do now, my dear Wineview?" Vigo could literally see it before him, Wineview swaying his head left and right with gravitas. "Let me think, your majesty. Give me a little time. I will gladly advise you closely." His head continued to sway. "I have found the solution. Send for Vigo, the principal knight."

"A splendid suggestion, Wineview", praised the king. His work being done, the resourceful advisor leaned proudly, if a little wearily, against the wall.

With a little shake of his head, the champion marched towards his ruler and nodded respectfully. "My king."

"You're here, Vigo."

The king's chancellor ignored him completely. Vigo didn't like rudeness. "Hail, unto thee, Chancellor Wisenot."

"You're not going to fight back the enemy from the south with your clownish tomfoolery", snarled Wineview back at him.

"Now, now, don't battle," intervened Ekarius magisterially. "Vigo, can you imagine, King Grachus desires my head yet again."

"Your majesty, forgive me, but my head is top of his list, ahead of yours."

"By all means, you go first." King Ekarius could be extremely generous at times.

"For variety, we could allow the closest advisors to step into the arena," suggested Vigo, throwing Wineview an encouraging look.

The latter declined the offer. "It is precisely for this purpose that we can afford your good self, Cavalier Vigo."

How he hated this cowardly smart aleck. And to top it all,

Wineview had clearly been ogling Vigo's beloved, Orelia. No wonder – there was no woman more enchanting at court.

"Could we set aside this squabbling and concentrate on the enemy?" asked King Ekarius.

"Right then, let's move onto our familiar acquaintance, King Grachus. It hasn't even been a year since his last visit," declared the champion. "And he was hopping mad when he had to turn around last time. I wouldn't put it past him that he'll go against tradition and make an example of us by flattening the whole city."

The fine shimmer on the king's forehead suggested to Vigo that he wasn't far off the mark with his prediction.

"Grachus has a new principal knight. He's a true master of his arts and is said to be the most dangerous duellist of all time. His king is so enthusiastic about him that he's been named head of the army."

"Stop trying to frighten me – that will only make me up my price." Vigo wiggled his eyebrow, but his all-conquering smirk put the lie to his words. Fear played no role in his life. "And the most dangerous duellist of all time is standing beside you."

There was movement within the enemy ranks. A group of men broke away and briskly approached them – King Grachus leading the way; Vigo easily recognised him on account of his long, two-stranded beard. Beside him strutted a bloke so big that he could look over the castle wall on tiptoes. As he came closer, he performed obscene gestures towards the defenders.

"Who's that baby?" asked Vigo in amusement.

"Like master, like man. That's your enemy. Don't under-estimate him – you're not in a competition of poets and muses, but a swordfight to the death."

Vigo looked at his king in amazement. "Thanks for reminding me."

The king sighed. "If I didn't like you so much…"

"If you didn't *need* me so much. Our fates are intertwined, Your Excellency. What do you know about the giant?"

"He's won two fights already, which means Raktardom and Settland are under Grachus's control," explained the king. "Both enemies fell faster than you can utter your impertinences. People have considered him to be invincible since then."

"Just because somebody's plopped into the water twice is a long way from saying they can swim," said Vigo dismissively. "Did he stick to the rules and spare the city retainers and population?"

Ekarius nodded. "He did. But now Grachus is in front of my city a second time. I don't trust him."

I wouldn't trust somebody who wanted to take away my gold, my people and my kingdom either, thought Vigo to himself.

By now King Grachus and his entourage had reached the city gate. His principal knight looked even taller and broader up close.

"He's going to have to squeeze his way through the gate." Vigo looked him up and down – the man was wearing a lot of armour – a mixture of leather studs and panels – solid protection allied with maximum freedom of movement. A two-handed sword was hanging on his back; strapped, the mighty weapon would plow the ground.

"Where do our enemies always get such giants from?" complained the king.

"*Your* enemies, Your Majesty. I could imagine inviting

the big lad out for a mouthful of beer on a different occasion. We'd drink to the great rulers of the world."

His Excellency was spared a retort by a bellow from below: "HERE STANDS KING GRACHUS!"

"Indeed!" responded Vigo light-heartedly.

"Be quiet now!" hissed Ekarius. The king leaned over the parapet and stretched to peer down. No mean undertaking on account of his fat stomach and short neck. He called out in a firm voice: "Hail to thee, King Grachus. What brings you here, this fine day, before our castle walls?"

"What does it look like?"

The men around Grachus laughed merrily – except for the hulk; not a single muscle on his face disturbed his battle-ready features.

"I'd like to hear it out of your own mouth, Grachus. I'd like to hear that you're abiding by the traditions of our beloved Worldly Kingdom."

"But, of course, honoured Ekarius, the what-number-again? Was it the third or fourth? – I've lost count."

Ha-ha, thought Vigo to himself. Grachus is provoking Ekarius the Fifth brilliantly.

His Majesty remained relaxed. "Perhaps you are not capable of counting so far, Grachus. And so, I forgive you that. Say loudly and clearly what your desire is."

Not a bad riposte at all.

Grachus called out in a firm voice: "My desire is your title, your city, your kingdom. And so, I challenge the principal knight of the stone dragons to come out for a duel to the death in the tradition of the old Worldly Kingdom. Should my champion lose, I shall command a retreat. Should he win, I expect the surrender of the city and your abdication."

Or your extinction. Vigo would prefer not to find out.

It was now up to the defenders if they wanted to accept the challenge to the duel or not. Otherwise, a potential conqueror would be knocking on the city gate every Sunday. King Grachus undoubtedly had good reason for throwing down the gauntlet. The thousands of soldiers behind him also exerted a certain pressure.

"Let it be so!" replied Ekarius.

A deafening roar rang out. Attackers and defenders welcomed this strategy – both sides would end up with nothing more than a bloody nose. No, not even that. Only for the two participants in the duel to the death would the reckoning be different.

"Who will fight on behalf of the house of the stone dragons?" asked Grachus despite knowing the answer already – after all, he was familiar with Vigo from the last encounter.

Yes, tradition meant people always did the same things again and again. Which is why it was called tradition. They'd be stuck in the loop for ten thousand years.

The king prodded him on the shoulder; he'd almost forgotten his mission. "Oh, Grachy, me of course, Vigo, the principal knight of the House of the stone dragons." He gave a friendly wave to down below.

The castle residents cheered encouragingly while the opposing champion's ferocious glare left no doubt as to the carnage he had already inflicted.

"Who will step into the ring on behalf of your house?" asked Ekarius.

"Aaargh! I am Torrremmm, the principal knight of the house of…er.."

Grachus whispered something.

"...the house of the peregrines!" he thundered persuasively.

"So shall it happen," shouted Ekarius joyfully. "Tomorrow at the tenth hour before the gates of the citadel the fate of the city and its inhabitants will be decided by the combat between the champions of the houses of the peregrines and the stone dragons."

Another tumultuous cheer. What, precisely, were the people cheering about? Oh yes, some fool had volunteered to gut the fish for them.

Another question was bugging Vigo. "What else do we need to find out about the principal knight down there? Do we know his fighting style?"

King Ekarius turned to his principal advisor. "You yourself travelled to his last duel, the one for the city of Crossford, and you watched him. Tell our champion what you discovered."

Wineview's chest swelled up like a bellows. "The principal knight of the peregrine house is an enemy to be reckoned with. His tried and tested weapon is the two-handed sword, and so he fights without a shield. He does, however, generally wear chainmail for protection. He fights in the classical style, nothing spectacular, nothing you can't handle."

Vigo had picked up all this information already with one glance at his opponent; nevertheless, the king seemed satisfied. This advisor served his own interests principally and did so magnificently.

King Ekarius, Wineview and Vigo strolled back to the main building. The king's consort approached them in the courtyard.

Vigo bowed graciously before her and kissed her outstretched hand. "You become more beautiful every time I see you, Your Majesty."

"I get fatter every time you see me, principal knight."

The queen was expecting, and it could only be a matter of days before the house of the stone dragons would announce a new princess or prince.

As if being able to mindread, the queen continued: "Of course we are hoping for a son, an heir to the throne. Guess what his name could be."

"Your Majesty, it is a privilege for your humble principal knight to be honoured with such a question." He struggled to think for a moment. "I...I would hazard to guess: Ekarius, the sixth."

She turned to her husband in surprise. "My dear king, have you been slipping him information?"

Vigo hurriedly tried to dampen her suspicions. "My dear queen, I merely made a lucky guess, Your Majesty."

She smiled with satisfaction.

That was enough courtly drama for one day as far as Vigo was concerned. "With your permission, Your Majesty, I shall now withdraw!" It was more of a statement than a question.

"Where do you want to go?" asked His Majesty.

"To bed! I must rest before tomorrow's combat," answered the champion, failing completely to hide a mischievous grin.

Undoubtedly, King Ekarius was thinking the same thought. Vigo saw, out of the corner of his eye, the king give an order to the captain of the watch. From now on he would be under increased protection – or under heightened surveillance. It had happened on more than one occasion that the principal knight of a kingdom had done a runner at the eleventh hour before a duel. In such cases the coward would be ostracised and hunted to the end of his days – and duel, castle and honour were invariably lost.

It was very decent of King Ekarius the Fifth that he wanted to protect Vigo from the fates of banishment and persecution. Completely unnecessary, of course! As if he would flee from someone like "Torrremmm". There was nothing and nobody he would ever run away from.

He entered his bed chamber in high spirits.

His beloved was waiting for him with pouted lips. Had she been pulling that face the whole time he was gone? "You were gone a long while, Vigo."

He kissed her pursed lips. "But I have time now until the tenth hour tomorrow, my love." With nimble fingers he loosened his armour and disrobed.

He heard soldiers marching up to the door outside.

This will be the safest place in the Worldly Kingdom until tomorrow, thought Vigo.

the Anvil

D ays passed by in Farin's life as did the dark autumn clouds above his head. He found it hard to keep track of the hours; it was the same repetitive monotony, the same greyness when he woke up in the morning and the same vapid grey aftertaste before he went to sleep at night. The man in black and the knight slowly disappeared from the villagers' conversations and so from their heads. They were replaced by their growing concern regarding their priest Amen, as not even his attendants had news of his whereabouts. Farin's mood was darkened by other matters. He constantly thought about Gerlunda, especially as the peculiar amulet he wore about his neck reminded him of the preparer of poisons every time he washed himself in the mornings. The jewel tugged at his nerves – there was the never-ending danger that father or somebody else would spot it and ask awkward questions. His thoughts concerning the murderous man in black were even more disturbing – the raven, as the knight had called him. Were the stranger and the knight really both on the hunt for the same unremarkable piece of jewellery? His thoughts went round in circles, and in the middle was always the amulet. Holding it between thumb and forefinger, he rubbed its smooth metal surface. Completely innocuous, a coin without an impression. He shoved it back under his shirt.

I'll just bury it behind the house – this was his plan for

the afternoon, once father had retired to "The Warm Beer".

The highlight of the day was the fact that father had left the shovel at innkeeper Georig's and had sent the forgetful Farin off to get it post-haste. Father placed great value on tradition. And so, the gravedigger's son made his way to the tavern.

The autumn sun was strong and cheerful for a change, as though it wanted to make a good impression before wilting in the winter months. Farin particularly liked looking across the wheat fields at this time of year, the ripened ears swaying gently in the breeze. Like a gentle golden sea. A yearning came over him. Or was it wanderlust?

Halfway along his journey he saw the village ropemaker approaching with his dog. The ropemaker wasn't a member of the society of pipe smokers, which in Farin's eyes was something in his favour. He was approaching fifty, had friendly eyes and not a single hair left on his head. Farin envied the man a little because of his trade. He was respected in the village and regarded highly as a craftsman. Using horsehair, hog's bristles, flax and hemp, he made ropes for tillage, nets for fishing, lines for washing and hemp cord for tying up chins or for threading into dubious amulets that hung around your neck.

What was the ropemaker's name again?

The dog consisted purely of hair, in contrast to his owner, which made him seem even bigger than he really was. The enormous mop stormed towards Farin, letting out deep barks and jumping up at him.

"Growler, you old mop," said Farin in greeting and went down on his knees to stop himself from being knocked backwards.

The mop swept his enthusiastic, rough tongue all over

the boy's face, and whipped his tail against his leg. The dog loved him and didn't give a hoot about his profession. If Growler had his way, Farin would be village alderman at the very least.

"Good morning, ropemaker," said Farin and smiled as the dog licked his hands. Luckily, you could address anybody in the village by their trade, no bother.

"Good morning, gravedigger's son," answered the ropemaker in a halfway friendly manner, without returning the smile.

Farin ruffled the animal's fur with both hands. The dog was now wagging his whole hindquarters gratefully.

"Has our priest turned up again?"

"He's still missing as far as I know." The ropemaker called his animal to heel. "Come on, Growler. We need to get something to eat."

"Good luck with the fishing," he said to the ropemaker, who was carrying a long fishing rod on his shoulder and was taking the path to the great lake.

He bade farewell to the dog by tickling him between the ears and received a final lick right across his face before Growler stormed after his master.

Farin strode on towards the village. When he reached the little wooden bridge, he heard voices echoing from the riverbank, but could see nothing on account of the bend in the river. There were much more suitable places than this part of the stream for washing clothes or bathing. He crossed the bridge and, curious, he made his way through the vegetation on the riverbank until he spotted two people sitting on a rock beyond the bushes. They were facing away from him, but he knew who they were immediately. Blossak and Annietta. He scowled in spite of himself.

Uncontrollable rage towards the innkeeper's son filled Farin. Jealousy tortured his already battered self-esteem, shovelling salt and pepper into the wound. Reason meekly tried to intervene, attempted to explain that he really wasn't entitled to these feelings of rage and jealousy — after all, Blossak knew nothing of his fervent veneration of the girl. Not to mention Annietta herself being completely oblivious to it.

So what! Such trivialities were tossed aside by his overwhelming emotions. Their bright laughter echoed in his ears — every giggle felt like a knife wound. There was nothing amusing about Bloss — he was boring and ugly. How could Farin's goddess stoop so low?

Unaware of his own movements, he crept closer along the embankment towards them. They didn't hear him, being so wrapped up in each other's attention, and now he could hear what Blossak was saying.

"Just imagine, the knight ordered Gerlunda's grave to be opened. And the two gravediggers were standing there without a shovel between them. Luckily, I remembered the spade in father's tool shed."

Annietta chortled quietly.

Were they laughing about that "gravedigger halfwit"? His heart was ready to burst out of his chest, it was shaking and pounding so much. Incapable of rational thought, he stood there dumbstruck although he really didn't want to hear anymore. It took a while until he absorbed more of Blossak's words.

"Anni, just imagine. It was such a dangerous situation. Just as the knight was about to behead the village alderman — I could do nothing else."

Then I just let it out, pissed in my pants so much that my

feet were completely clean afterwards – only my pants stank. That was just how Farin remembered it, and that was exactly how he expected the story to continue.

Blossak nonchalantly revealed a different version of events. He began speaking in a somewhat deeper voice than was his norm. "I had to step in. I called out loudly: Stop, Sir Knight! I know what you want." He paused dramatically.

"Tell me more, Blossi."

"Everybody looked at me, awestruck. And I explained: Sir Knight! There was a stranger present at the burial. In a black cloak with a hood. Dark eyes, hooked nose. He wore a dagger on his belt. I actually managed to distract the knight from killing Hamak."

"Are you sure that's how it happened?"

"Of course I am. How else?"

"Then you're a hero", announced Annietta.

"Come on now. I couldn't allow our village alderman to be beheaded." He clicked his tongue. "It got even better, because from then on the knight was only interested in me. I said this to him: The stranger is Gerlunda's murderer. He strangled her with only one hand."

"Dreadful." Annietta put her hand before her mouth. "How did you know that?"

"Powers of observation and ability and deductive reasoning, Anni. Gerlunda had strangulation marks on her throat. Right…or…left? Hang on, let me think." The hero was faltering. "Eh...the man in black carried a weapon...eh...and...eh...the marks were…"

"You were clever and brave, Blossi."

Oh. I see. Farin's intellectual capacity was suspended momentarily and dark desires rose up within him. His hands became sweaty with rage. There was a roaring and pounding in his head. Would he be able to strangle a person with one hand too? The innkeeper's son was very inviting just now. Why had he bothered to eavesdrop?

Anni leaned over to the clever and brave Blossi and kissed him on the cheek.

Farin died a little death at that moment. There was nothing left of his fury against this injustice. He retreated with his last remaining strength. The two were too engrossed in their billing and cooing to notice anything.

"You were clever and brave," she had said. It was *he* who had earned those accolades, not the lying good-for-nothing Blossak. He felt robbed, undervalued and cheated. The innkeeper's son had basked in *his* words and *his* deeds. Farin slowly gathered himself together. Should he turn around and take Blossak to task? Would Annietta believe him? Would she *want* to believe him? All these thoughts weighed heavily on him. Farin's head hung low like the branches of a weeping willow. What did he himself think? The blacksmith's daughter would never accept him anyway, never think of him as a real man. Him, the gravedigger's son. The sheer pointlessness of his existence was clearer to him now than ever before. Why was he going to the village anyway? Oh yes, to collect the shovel. Why was he collecting the shovel anyway? The shovel could go hang. He didn't want to see another human being – ever again.

Farin left the road. He battled his way through bushes and boulders towards the Anvil. That was the name of the only mountain far and wide, whose outlines in the distance gave the impression of an anvil. There was no path to its summit – you needed a certain dexterity to be able to snake your way between the rocky spurs, holding onto the correct stones or branches and hauling yourself up. As a child he'd climbed up here a hundred times and the route was still familiar to him. He reached the peak of the Anvil, which was far from peak-like, hardly losing breath. An airy plateau with an impressive panoramic view was the reward for his efforts, but this wasn't why Farin was up here. He was swimming in a sea of self-pity up on top of the mountain. Swimming was something he did well – his mother had taught him.

"Mother!" he sobbed into the wind. He missed her terribly – even still, despite long having become a young man. She was gone for more than seven years now.

How can you be thinking of your mother in your melancholy mood?

Farin slowly approached the Cleft. That was what the chasm was called, which dropped to a depth of thirty yards. A myth had grown up around this place. Long, long ago, a giant supposedly had an argument with his wife and swung his axe mightily, creating an enormous fissure in the rock. He really must have been annoyed at her.

Farin's feet kicked against some small pebbles that clinked and tumbled over the edge and into the abyss. Misty-eyed, he watched their journey until they disappeared out of sight in the depths below. One more step and he'd be following them. Then it would be over – at least with this life, who knows, maybe every life would be over.

He leaned forward, becoming lost in reverie at the maw of the chasm. Below were only rocks, which ensured that anyone who jumped here would certainly be dead when they hit the bottom.

One more step. Then only air...and rocks – the thoughts raced through his head.

What was he doing here? Farin noticed he was feeling dizzy. He, who had climbed every tree to the very top, who had stood at the edge of the chasm on the Anvil countless times before. What was happening to him? Were fear or temptation infecting his mind? One more step? No more steps! Gripped by rapture, he inched defiantly towards the drop.

Just so I can look down properly.

Again, he thought of his mother. And the promise he had made to her as a little boy. Or had she with foresight wisely drawn it from him?

"Promise me that you'll never give up on yourself", she had said. "No matter what happens."

"Of course, mama. I'll never give up on myself", he'd answered light-heartedly, without fully understanding what she'd meant.

And now he found himself here, standing on the edge of death again.

The wind was strengthening, and Farin spread out his arms like a scarecrow.

"Of course, mama. I'll never give up on myself. And I'd really love to see the ocean."

Come on now, jump!

Behind him he heard the scratchy voice of a man. And Farin jumped. With fright. Not forwards, but backwards, spinning around on his own axis at the same time. Although this was his only movement, he landed on both feet in a squatting position, gasping for air and with burning lungs just one yard away from the fatal drop. He stood up straight and peered around. But there was nobody there except for a totally confused gravedigger's son.

You're a loser. You've already let go of your soul for a moment. Give it to me – completely! commanded the voice.

The plateau on top of the Anvil was just about the most open area Farin could imagine. There were no trees, no hollows, no rocks, nowhere for hiding. Who was talking to him?

Come on, jump! And bequeath me your damn soul, you pathetic worm!

Farin rubbed his temples with both hands. Was it possible? Was this voice coming from inside his head?

Hahahaha!

The booming voice made him stumble, leaving him sprawling on the ground. He quickly sat up, pressed his ears between his hands, wrapping his legs in his arms. He listened tentatively. It reminded him of the tall amphora outside the church. He'd often stuck his head into it as a child and laughed loudly. The voice he'd heard a moment ago was just as loud and powerful.

It was all too late now – madness had afflicted the grave-digger's son. It was cold comfort that it would hardly bother anyone. Time passed. Farin sat huddled in the autumn wind on top of the Anvil plateau and only slowly calmed down. His sobs tasted of bile. He sought to explain the inexplicable. Had his mental derangement led him to imagine everything? A terrible daydream in the midst of his despair?

Just as he was beginning to accept these unlikely yet comforting thoughts, it came again.

Come on! Jump, you loser! Do the right thing for once – just this once!

His head was pulsating like the veins on his neck. Overcome again, he closed his ears. He was close to tears.

Bawl away! And then…JUMP! I can feel your pathetic soul in my hands already. It despises you. It wants to get away from you! The Cleft is calling you!

Closing his ears didn't help a whit. After all, it was happening *inside* his head. The voice was scolding him. Or was he scolding himself?

Farin heard a faraway whisper: "What's happening to me?" He recognised it with a shiver. The thin, self-pitying, shaky little voice was his own. Who was he asking? Himself?

He continued to sit there, shivering, as if frozen on the plateau, his chin on his knees, terrified of invoking the voice again through the tiniest movement. It was quiet for a while, enabling Farin to gather together all his strength, his thoughts and his courage. The horrible voice had called him a loser. He couldn't accept that.

God, give me the strength to object.

GOD?

It boomed in his head again.

Oh my God! Oh my God! First, he cries for his mama and now for his Lord Almighty. Pshaw! A crumb from the table has more worth than him.

"Who are you?" asked Farin loudly into the wind.

I'm not going to tell a crumby worm who I am. My name bespeaks might, magic and mystery. A person must earn the right to learn my name.

Farin was startled. He could have a conversation with the voice.

"What do you want from me?"

Your soul, you wormy loser. Your pathetic soul.

"It…it belongs to me", squeaked Farin.

How could this lousy day, when he'd been forced to watch Annietta fall for the phony braggart Blossak hook, line and sinker, and even kiss him, get any worse?

He summoned up all his courage. "I'm not going to give you my soul. Get out of my head."

If it weren't for his voice sounding whiny, Farin could even be a little proud of his clearly expressed message.

Sad! But only a matter of time when all's said and done. You were so close to doing it, mama's boy.

"Why are you scolding me all the time?"

Because you're the most pathetic worm I've ever had to slip into.

"How? You mean, you "had to" slip into me!" He emphasised "had to" – that felt good somehow.

Yes, you hardly think I'd willingly seek out a wimp like yourself, do you?

"I don't understand…"

Exactly, you don't understand. One of your main problems.

The thoughts behind Farin's closed eyes were swinging like a pendulum in his head.

Have I gone totally mad? Who am I letting myself be insulted by?

In a low but firm voice he concluded: "If somebody is forcing you to slip into a loser like me then you're not all you're cracked up to be."

Oho! Not bad. A cheeky crumby worm.

"What are you? Where do you come from?"

Think about it. I'm sick of having to explain everything. People are always looking for explanations. Why? How come? Wherefore? Sickening! Just act – then no explanation is needed!

As if pulled by puppet strings, his right hand wandered towards his chest. With two fingers he fished the simple amulet out from under his shirt, held it close to his eyes and squinted at it. It had to be connected to this. A strange explanation to be sure, but the only possible one. Who knew where the enchanted trinket came from?

And about time.

A scornful snort confirmed that he should have thought of this a long time ago.

The gravedigger's son asked in a whisper: "You're hiding in the damn amulet. And judging by what you're saying, you're not human."

Almost right. And thank you for the praise.

Farin leaped up. He had no idea where he got the strength from. He yanked the hemp cord and amulet forcefully from his neck and strode towards the abyss, his lips pressed firmly together.

Oh, you do want to jump? Good lad.

"I'm sick of having to explain everything – to whomever. Right then. This unadorned adornment wants to jump."

First a short silence, then: *Oh no. Don't do it.*

For the first time this insulting, patronising, arrogant voice sounded uncertain, almost pleading.

"Oh, yes. Who's the whiner now? I don't want you! Whoever or whatever you are."

He'd let so many opportunities for getting rid of the amulet slip through his fingers already. He could simply have given it to the priest, the alderman, the knight, but no, an inner voice had stopped him every time. And now he wanted to get rid of this different inner voice as quickly as possible.

If you're heading for the Cleft anyway, why don't we all jump together?

"No! Out of the question!"

Just one little hop, that's all.

Farin stepped towards the abyss, the amulet held tightly in his fist.

"Good riddance to bad rubbish, you creep". He raised his closed hand in preparation.

Don't throw it away. Please!

It was wailing woefully in his head.

"Find yourself somebody else – whoever or whatever you are." With an almighty throw of his arm, Farin flung the amulet into the chasm.

NOOOOoooooooooo.

The whoever-or-whatever-it-is-you-are's voice caused Farin's body to shudder violently with its ear-splitting sound, which gradually faded away to nothing.

He was suddenly possessed with a new clarity – he felt better. Nobody would believe this story. And who could he tell, anyway? Relieved, and unburdened of this load, his thoughts became more carefree. How did that piece of jewellery end up on Gerlunda's body? Why did the man in black and the knight desire it so much? Great that he was able to get rid of it so easily. He looked into the depths again. It was lying down there somewhere and would eventually rot.

Stop dawdling and jump, you worm!

He heard the rough voice behind him.

Hahahaha!

The laughter almost pushed him over the edge, but instead he fell backwards onto his backside.

Did you really believe you could get rid of me just by throwing the amulet away, you birdbrain?

"But...but..." Farin remembered the voice's woeful wailing only too well. Then the penny dropped. "You fooled me."

That's one of my favourite activities – fooling people.

The voice sounded pleased with itself.

"PISS OFF AND LEAVE ME ALONE!"

"Alo-alo-alo-alone" echoed the chasm gleefully in all directions.

There's nothing I'd rather do, worm. You're even more useless than the old toad. But we're going around in circles. There's nothing I'd like to do more than to rip out your gullet, but my hands are your hands for the time being. And I'm afraid you wouldn't do that for me now, would you? That would be even better than jumping. I couldn't leave you alone even if I wanted to.

Losing his mind, Farin stood before the Cleft and was completely at a loss, not knowing which way to turn.

Now that we have neared the wonderful abyss again – you're not thinking after all of...? The voice sounded unashamedly hopeful.

"NO! ARSEHOLE!"

"Hole, hole, hole", sang the echo.

The voice groaned dustily. *Even the Cleft is mocking you. Now that we're both enjoying the view together, turn your attention to the east, down below to the very left, there where the three birch trees are growing between the two boulders.*

Farin didn't want to, but his eyes began travelling obediently in the direction described. "I don't see anything. What's supposed to..." He became silent – he really had to look more closely. He looked down the Cleft to the indicated location and stared. Two people were lying there. They looked as small as thumbs from up here. But even from this distance he could tell – they were dead. A shapeless dark shadow surrounded the bodies – he couldn't make out what is was. If he climbed down to them, they would be as big as him, but still dead.

Two bodies are there already. Come on now, jump, worm. Another one will hardly make a difference. Death is a righteous friend. The great leveller.

That unashamedly hopeful undertone again. Then he heard the question in his head: *What do you think now? Whose corpses do you reckon are lying there?*

Farin's brain did its duty through gritted teeth. "Gerlunda's and our Pater Amen's."

Those are the first words you've uttered that, with a lot of benevolence on my part, might lead one to conclude that there is indeed a lifeform, whose intelligence may be enough, after many thousands of years, to enable it to shit into a ditch.

Farin could only ask: "How can I be free of you?"

Jump.

"Absolutely not."

Do it.

His rebellious streak was giving him strength. With a scowl he decided to simply ignore the chatter in future. A difficult undertaking, because the voice echoed insolently and relentlessly in his head.

He blurted it out: "YOU PATHETIC SOMETHING! Can you not just leave me in peace? Can't you just manage that? And if you get bored, just piss off. You don't even need to ask. Don't let the door hit your arse on your way out."

No answer. With furrowed brow Farin cocked his head in the wind – ready to hear at any moment the words of a total stranger drone in his skull. Silence. He slowly began to move. Silence. He had lost his mind. Silence.

After a few moments he began heading back. Which meant he had a challenging descent and the path to the village ahead of him. He was starving and parched – no wonder – it was early afternoon now. The red-tiled church steeple ahead offered some comfort – perhaps it was the familiarity it radiated. Farin yearned for familiarity, for something he could hang onto. Now more than ever, now that the voice in his head had made him lose his mind.

Should he tell the alderman of his experiences? Instinctively he listened to himself, but this time he only sensed the gravedigger's son. A feeling of relief came over him.

I am the gravedigger's son and I never give up.

a lot of lugging about

With the image of the two bodies in his head, Farin entered the village of Heap. The man in black wasn't just behind Gerlunda's murder, he also had Pater Amen on his conscience. Farin had played in the Cleft as a child with the village children. Very few people strayed into the almost impassable terrain, which was clearly the reason the bodies hadn't been discovered. Whether for good or ill, Gerlunda had already been dead; the priest however had been in the best of physical and business health. Was that really Amen lying there? Farin couldn't be absolutely certain from that distance away.

He was sweating in spite of the cool autumn evening. The alderman's house lay near the marketplace and not far from the church. A cast-iron ring served as the door knocker. He hesitated before using it. He would tell Hamak about the two bodies. Then they would be able to bring a stretcher on Hamak's horse and cart as close as possible to the chasm, go the rest of the way on foot and then carry Pater Amen and Gerlunda back.

What will I do if the sinister voice pops up in my head again?

He thought of something. It had called the preparer of poisons an old toad, just as the knight had done. Coincidence? Anyway, the voice hadn't made an appearance since leaving the plateau – maybe its dubious owner had fallen asleep, maybe it was just gone. Maybe it was only able to talk to him on top of the Anvil, the mountain shrouded in myths. Or maybe throwing the amulet into the chasm had really worked. The last thing in the world Farin wanted to do was to listen in on himself and make further enquiries. Let sleeping, impudent dogs lie, he thought. A quiet head – that was the main thing.

Have I gone out of my mind? Should I wait a bit? No, I have to inform the alderman.

Determined, he knocked on the door.

Peat, of all people, opened. The lad looked straight past Farin and murmured: "Who could have knocked? There's nobody here." He chuckled sleazily at his own corny joke.

"Who's there?" asked the lady of the house gruffly, as she pottered around at the hearth.

"Gravedigger's son," answered Peat.

"What does he want? Send him away, he'll only bring trouble!" bawled Peat's mother, a large woman with fat arms and legs.

"I have to speak to the alderman," said Farin.

"FATHER!" shouted Peat over his shoulder. "The grave-digger's son is standing here. Didn't he put you in a pretty bad light when the knight was here? Shall I beat him up?"

"Leave it!" The alderman came to the door and shoved his son aside.

"What do you want, you scoundrel?" asked Hamak in an unfriendly voice. "I already paid your father for the witch."

"There are two bodies in the Cleft. Probably Gerlunda and…Pater Amen."

"What are you telling me?" Hamak's eyes opened wide with fear. "Show me the spot. Quick, before it gets dark. Peat, you're coming too."

They had ridden as closely up to the chasm as possible on the horse and cart. Now the alderman was following Farin on foot, Peat marching behind with the stretcher. It was basically two long poles made from ash wood connected lengthways by a sheet of strong linen. It probably wouldn't have taken Hamak much effort to lift Gerlunda, but Pater Amen on the other hand was a man of the church, God's messenger, not to mention the judge, and – which carried just as much weight – the richest man in the village.

"The gravedigger's son can haul the stretcher too," grumbled Peat.

Farin didn't like the idea at all, but his opinion wouldn't count.

"Take over, you scoundrel!" ordered Hamak.

Peat grinned.

And so, Farin shouldered the long poles – a wonder he hadn't been forced to carry them from the start. They would only manage the journey to and from the chasm once before darkness. The rock faces narrowed towards each other. At one point the men had to really squeeze between them, then the chasm broadened again and in the middle there were even a few trees growing. Three sparse birch trees gripped the stony ground with their roots, just as the last few colourful leaves clung to their branches. The men could already see the scene from a distance – a sight they wouldn't forget for the rest of their lives. Nobody spoke a word at first – words were hard to find that could express their horror. Suddenly Farin understood what had created the dark shadows he had seen surrounding the bodies when he'd looked from up high. Blood. And yet more blood.

The body of the preparer of poisons, Gerlunda, lay on a rocky elevation, almost like his workbench. Ribcage and stomach had been cut open lengthways. Heart, lungs and some of her intestines were scattered around near her body. Her skullcap was missing, and her brain hung crookedly over her forehead, as if it were trying to crawl out of her head. A few yards away they discovered the village priest in a similar state, gutted like a goose. His stomach, fat once, hung down in loose folds, left and right. His arms disappeared behind his back – presumably he had been tied at the wrists. His skull had been opened by a single blow, and its insides resembled a bloody pulp. In recent years Farin had not only seen many dead bodies, but he had also prepared them for burial – bloated drowning victims, half-decayed human remains, crushed bodies, for example – but this opened up a new dimension, even for him. Only people did this to people. The alderman, glassy-eyed, did his best to avoid looking at the corpses, his puckered nose betraying his futile attempt at breathing though his mouth. Peat's face took on the greenish-white colour of Gerlunda's brain.

Something about this place irritated Farin; he glanced around but couldn't figure out what.

"What the devil happened here?" The alderman was the first to speak.

The three of them were standing by the body of the priest. Amen had never tolerated the devil being spoken of – now, he was silent. The gravedigger's son placed his forefinger under Amen's chin and raised it gently. A deep cut had almost completely severed his head from his neck, an almost perfect job. Only the neck ligaments held the skull and cervical spine together. The cut ran along the neck from bottom-right to top-left. The manner and depth of the wound provided important evidence. The blade of a left-hander, of a murderer, of a leading light in the cult of the

Necorers. And what else had the knight said: "The next time you meet him run for your life." The man in black must have succumbed totally to madness.

The gravedigger's son studied his surroundings again. If he ignored the corpses, the stench, the unspeakable crime, what else irritated him? His comprehension began to take shape – he had to think the other way around. What *didn't* irritate him? What had the knight immediately called the man in black? The raven. The ravens, the crows and the flies were missing from this blood-soaked spot. What is too sinister here for even the birds and insects? Farin refrained from sharing any of his thoughts with the others. Hamak and his son Peat were so much cleverer and would draw their own ingenious conclusions.

"I could puke", said Hamak just then, sharing *his* conclusion.

As if he'd been waiting for the magic words, Peat turned away suddenly and bent over a rock. The splattering sound was accentuated by violent gasping, retching and spitting. He wiped his mouth with his sleeve when he was finished and mumbled: "It was just the smell, it's such a horrible stink."

"We'll carry Amen's body back to the horse and cart and ride back to the village", was Hamak's response.

"What will we do with Gerlunda?" asked Farin, placing the stretcher beside the priest's corpse.

"We'll pick her up tomorrow – it'll be dark soon."

The three of them rolled Amen's body onto the frame.

"You at the front, us behind", ordered Hamak and grasped the right rod.

Well, that's a surprise, thought Farin, as he bent down and grasped both poles.

Father and son shared the load at the other end. Even

though Pater Amen had lost pints of blood and an organ here and there, he still weighed as much as an old nag. It didn't take long before Farin's arms and back were aching.

Peat asked: "Should we swap?"

What was wrong with him? A streak of humanity? In his confusion Farin almost forgot his exhaustion.

"Agreed," answered his father.

Gasping, they set down the stretcher, only nobody came forward to lend a hand. Peat and Hamak swopped poles at the back.

"Go on!" grunted the alderman to the gravedigger's son.

Everything in best order – normal service has been resumed, thought Farin as he bent down and grasped the stretcher with both hands.

"Boy, he's heavy," groaned Peat.

"Gerlunda and Amen couldn't have been brought there at the same time if it was only the man in black. Unless we're dealing with more than one perpetrator," ruminated Hamak aloud.

The stretcher poles almost slipped out of Farin's hands. He had successfully suppressed the raven's words until now. "First, I'll take care of the fat pig-priest, then the alderman. And guess who's next on the list, my friend."

Is Hamak next? And then…

His simple life threatened to be turned upside down by murder and strange voices. He gritted his teeth. He shouldn't waste his strength on such thoughts while his arms were burning under the stretcher's heavy weight. They reached the horse and cart and heaved the body of the priest onto the load bed.

A public position in the village demanded a public funeral, and Farin was under no illusion: the job would end up on his workbench, and piecing this tattered body back together again meant a lot of work. Only now did it hit Farin that he should have looked for and brought back the skullcap with him. You couldn't expect the residents of Heap to tolerate the rain falling into their priest's head during his funeral. I'll mask the missing skullcap with a headpiece, thought Farin. And I'll stuff his sliced stomach with wood shavings and sew it up with thick yarn.

"You're going to pay for this, gravedigger's son," hissed Peat quietly so that his father couldn't overhear him. The two of them were standing behind the cart while Hamak was taking his place on the box.

"What do you mean?"

"For dragging me into this shit."

Farin could hardly believe his ears – did everybody in the village really have to blame him for every depravity and trouble? "Puke your guts out, scaredy-cat. You're good at that", he whispered back.

Hamak glanced over his shoulder. "You get up in the front, Peat. And you at the back, you scoundrel."

Peat fired a look of revulsion and repulsion at Farin, before clambering up beside his father. The episode in the Cleft had certainly not improved their relations. Still, at least he could sit on the cart bed and keep Amen company. Off they set towards the yard of the gravedigger and undertaker.

the arena

D ecision day. Vigo was putting on his leather armour. Each part carefully went into its place, tailor-made, countless fins of hardened leather covering him – they offered sufficient protection while still allowing freedom of movement. If Torem caught him with his mighty weapon, panels wouldn't help him anyway. The leather helmet would protect him from a closed fist or a headbutt at most. Agility and adroitness were what helped most in a duel with the champion of the house of the peregrines. Vigo's strategy: don't get caught – especially not by a mighty two-hander.

When principal knights fought to the death just about anything went. Throwing sand in the eyes, kicks in the abdomen, biting off ears and ripping buttocks. There were a few rules, the most important being: only one weapon and it had to be a sword. If one of the competitors pulled out another weapon, for example a throwing knife, then he'd be executed by the archers, and officially lose the fight. The sword would be examined and cleaned before the fight. This measure was necessary because some particularly valorous principal knights had dabbed up to fifteen different poisons on their blade although it was forbidden. Always fascinating to consider what things people dreamed up in their efforts to gain an advantage. The competitors were allowed recourse to the complete arsenal of armouring and shields to defend and protect themselves.

Torem will wear chain and swing his long two-hander. I'll choose my bastard-sword and the oak buckler with the large steel stud.

He could only use the round-shield once to head off a blow from his enemy, at least if Torem's blow was a direct hit. Although the wood had been hardened three times, the buckler would split. So, he would avoid getting hit at all costs.

His beloved observed his ritual. "I prefer it when you *un*dress yourself."

"I prefer it when I undress *you*," said Vigo, wiggling his eyebrows.

"I'm being serious, my bold principal knight. I'd hate to become the principal widow", said Orelia.

"We'd have to be married for that."

"But we are – spiritually at least."

A man had to know when it was best to change the subject.

Vigo changed the subject. "Are you going to be at the fight?"

"You know I can't. It's…it's just not possible for me."

"Then I'll tell you afterwards what it was like. I'll be gone a little longer than yesterday."

Bleary-eyed and sobbing a little she said: "Take your time. The important thing is you come back."

"I'll be a little dirtier and bloodier."

"So long as it's not your blood…"

A pounding at the door. "Principal Knight! The time has come!"

"Till later, my precious!" Vigo rolled his shoulders forward and back, turned his head left and right. The vertebrae in his neck cracked, battle-ready. Without turning back, Vigo strode out of the principal knight's chamber.

The roar of approval that greeted him put all previous roars in the shade. Ten thousand people greeted their champion. Five clear victories had made him a legend, and the people fervently believed in him.

Don't lose your concentration, the only thing that matters is that *you* believe in yourself. When it comes down to it none of these idolaters and exalters are actually going to help you. Surrounded by twenty thousand people, you're going to face the principal knight of the house of the peregrines, lonely and alone.

He raised his buckler in salute, the roar of the enthusiastic crowd grew louder, a thunder like the flood waves of the Northern Sea. They were standing everywhere – on the defensive corridor, on the walls, even on the rooftops – waving and shouting at him.

"VIGO! FOR THE STONE DRAGONS!"

"FOR THE KING!"

"OUR CHAMPION! FOR VICTORY!"

This time Vigo's path didn't lead him to the defensive corridor, but instead over the lowered drawbridge to an area in front of the castle. A scramble of people accompanied him, he was their principal knight, they loved him, and everyone wanted to be near him.

Now he saw it – the arena. An oval hollow in the middle of a field offered seats to over ten thousand spectators with its twenty-two stone-tiered rows. The crowd was divided into two zones – after all, there were two hostile fractions in close proximity to each other, and there was only one reason they weren't all butchering each other: they were leaving that to the principal knights.

He was grateful for the protection his leather helmet

offered: his eardrums were insulated from the noise of the people in the tightly packed oval; they were louder than any thunderstorm. Although it was already a tight squeeze, many of the spectators shared their narrow seats with another onlooker. Wooden tribunes made of precious timber had been constructed on both the north and south side. Here the officers, the nobility and of course the royal families made themselves comfortable. His liege, King Ekarius the Fifth, was already sitting in position. Was that a tankard of red wine in his hand? His principal advisor, Chancellor Tarian Wineview was sitting to his left. His consort was tarrying to his right.

Vigo's opponent was waiting for him in the northern half, under King Grachus's tribune. Torem stood there motionless, legs apart, waiting for the inevitable. His two-hander was behind his back as it had been the day before.

The booing and whistling, the shouting and cheering grew louder, and a peculiar sport developed. The mission of the kings was identical to that of their peoples, who expressed their support through delirious shouting.

King Ekarius the Fifth stood up. The south side abruptly went silent. At which point King Grachus stood up in the north tribune – his vassals, mainly soldiers, went silent too.

King Ekarius greeted Vigo with a fashionable hand gesture. A true benefactor. With a powerful voice he opened the ceremonies. "Hear ye, my principal knight, Cavalier Vigo. An adversary lusts after our city, our castle, our homeland. My title, my honour, my power I place in your hands for the duration of this duel of the champions. Defend your people and extend the fame of the stone dragons. Cavalier Vigo, my principal knight, I am your servant this very day."

Defenders had been using these words for generations.

Now it was the challenger's turn to speak, and King Grachus didn't waste time. "My principal knight, Cavalier Torem – a rival resists my will. My title, my honour, my power I place in your hands for the duration of this duel of the champions. Conquer these people and extend the fame of the peregrines. Cavalier Torem, my principal knight, I am your servant this very day." His eyes smouldered as he spoke these words.

The two servants could get down to fighting now, thought Vigo.

The principal knight of the peregrines reacted neither by word nor gesture; he was mentally preparing for the fight.

It was getting serious now. Vigo positioned himself opposite his opponent at a distance of about ten yards. Slowly the giant began to come alive. He reached behind his shoulder, pulled his two-hander out of its clasp, shaking off the latter so that it clattered to the ground. Both hands were clasping the sword-hilt. His body was protected by impressive chainmail. Impressive, because no part of it matched the next. Vanity was something you couldn't accuse Torem of. How many suits of armour had he used in creating this patchwork? His neck guard consisted of chain mesh hanging from his helmet and over his shoulders like long hair. His mail shirt was made from thousands of intertwined steel rings. Getting through this armour would require a strong horizontal thrust of the sword-tip. More important than the enemy's armour was his weapon. The two-handed sword boasted no decoration. Smooth blue steel bereft of a blood groove, of engravings, of jewellery. Both hands still gripped the hilt and held the sword perpendicularly upwards before his chest. What did that mean? Torem wore a chain gauntlet on his left hand and a heavy, metal-plated one on his right.

Ten fanfare blasts gave of their best and signalled the

beginning of the fight. Only one of the champions would leave the arena alive. A moment ago, you could hear a pin drop, now the stadium shuddered to the cheers, jeers and whistles emanating from the stands. Torem came back to life, he stretched out a long arm and pointed his sword-tip at Vigo. The mountain of muscles in his upper arm flexed. Vigo cautiously drew his sword from its scabbard. It probably didn't weigh a third of his opponent's. With every exchange of blows Vigo would have to watch carefully where the swords met, because if his blade broke, he was a goner.

Vigo held his buckler chest-high with his left hand, he held his sword like a walking-stick with his right. The principal knight of the house of the peregrines wasn't into long introductions. He stormed towards Vigo, his right hand letting go of the hilt, and he used his considerable reach to sweep his blade at neck height. Vigo ducked away at the last moment, his eyelashes trembling in the rush of air. He straightened up immediately and sought the opportunity of a counterattack. But he took too long, and the blade was aiming at him again.

To the ordinary layman or woman nothing much had happened yet apart from a missed blow, but Vigo blinked as a realisation dawned on him.

His opponent was quick in spite of his size, his chainmail was only restricting his movements marginally. He'd expected all this beforehand, but another discovery surprised him. Torem was manipulating the two-hander with only *one* hand, and moreover it was with his left one. The other hand was thereby free. Alongside enormous strength in his arm and hand he was also using a sophisticated technique. Vigo had only heard of such fighters up until now. Torem had sacrificed a shield in favour of a particularly powerful plate-glove. He was basically fighting with two weapons, because a belt of the steel-reinforced fist resembled the blow of a cudgel.

And only the day before Chancellor Wineview had assured him there was nothing unusual to report regarding Torem's fighting technique. A wave of anger radiated in his head – not a good sign. Heightened concentration was in order now. The principal advisor hadn't even mentioned he was a southpaw. Sloppiness?

I'll deal with Wineview later, decided Vigo.

Mind you, he'd have to make sure he was in a position to investigate the matter later. Otherwise, things would take care of themselves.

Vigo hoofed it back three steps towards the middle of the arena. Neither two-hander nor plated gauntlet must hit him; he had to be quick or his fight and his life would be over.

His deadly enemy charged forward again, unfortunately not furiously and unbridled like a bull, but at a controlled tempo with well-managed, practised movements. The giant was performing circular movements of his weapon, all with his left hand. Vigo stayed where he was this time and deflected Torem's sword with the tip of his own, so that it slid by him. Just as he was about to deftly stab with his own weapon, he saw the right fist flying towards his temple. Vigo yanked his head backward, but he wasn't quick enough – the metal glove grazed his leather helmet at cheek-height. A loud crack echoed through his head. That's how broken bones in the area of the ear sound. He would have to dedicate time and attention to it after the fight. The blow had foiled another planned counterattack. Vigo didn't want to be in the position of only reacting. Again, he footed it backward a few paces in the hope that Torem would make another charge toward him. His opponent just stood there however, cool as a cucumber, five yards away.

The spectators were screaming their lungs out; Vigo could hear nothing but could see it in their distorted faces. Mouths and eyes wide open, grotesque visages vacillating between hope and fear and bloodlust. Concentrate on the eyes of your enemy – that's what it all came down to. Do the right thing at the right time. It all boiled down to killing when it came to it. Now the principal knight of the house of the stone dragons was being proactive. He approached Torem's right hand using a semi-circular approach. He wanted to provoke a backhanded sword strike. His opponent had no intention of falling for that one. On the contrary, he turned on his own axis and swung his mighty weapon towards Vigo's hip. His longer reach would ensure he would hit Vigo before the latter's own blade would hit its target. There were two possibilities left: either Vigo would abandon his attack, elude the sword-strike and make a backward movement for the third time in a row, or he would deflect the blow with his buckler and make a thrust himself. Well, there wasn't much time to think things through – roughly the time it takes to blink. The latter! He pushed his small round buckler forward, placed it at an angle so that the broadside of the blade would hit the metal stud in the middle. This, apparently, was exactly what Torem was expecting, because just before contact he twisted his sword a couple of degrees so that it slammed obliquely into the wood and split the buckler in two. Pretty evenly too, pretty much in the middle. Two or three of Vigo's fingers on his left hand were probably broken too, so forcefully had the blow connected. The numbed fingers shook the useless remains of the buckler off. So far, the battle had not been running to plan or in his favour. Once again, he had merely reacted.

Torem was now holding the sword above his head, which made the show-off look even more enormous. Vigo realised instinctively that his opponent had no intention of simply hacking down violently on him from above. Soon he was in reach. The giant directed the sword with one hand once again; he simply let it drop from above and spun himself around at the same time. A murderous carousel! Vigo dived in a twinkling, before the attack could slice him in half. He felt the clay soil, rolled away and completed a thrust towards Torem's right leg. A hit! But his blade couldn't penetrate deeply enough, being prevented by the forged chain rings. Vigo was up on both feet in one move, made a lunge and stabbed at stomach height. This was exactly what the cursed giant was anticipating – he turned to the side. The two-hander was still some distance away and wasn't a danger; the steel fist of the right hand, however, smashed into Vigo's shoulder. Another crack, and the pain forced tears into his eyes. Everything seemed as if under water – the sounds dull and muffled and the view washed-out, foggy and indefinable. Torem had caught his shoulder joint. Vigo couldn't move his weapon arm anymore. The bone, the joint, the muscle, whatever, refused to cooperate. His weapon-arm! Nobody could suggest that Vigo was leading in this duel to the death.

Don't lose your nerve. Despite the excruciating pain, he still held his weapon in his right hand. He'd learned never to drop his sword from when he was a child – never, ever. The weapon was useless there now, he would have to fight on with his left hand. Although his middle finger was broken there too – at the very least.

Torem aired his views concerning the spectacle for the

first time. "We're the playthings of the corrupt juggler, little man. And you're the one he's abandoning. True power determines truth, which neither of us can contend with."

Vigo looked at him, dumbstruck. And he also knew he needed a miraculous wonder; no wonder – for it certainly didn't look good for him at all. Once more the two-hander flew towards him. As fast as he could, Vigo turned to the right, the pain in his shoulder causing him to flinch. Since his earliest childhood he had learned to suppress pain, to ignore it, but he'd never experienced the agony he was suffering now. His body was rebelling, his muscles and sinews were refusing to serve. A knee gave way, Vigo landed on the clay. Torem was already above him and preparing for the coup de grâce.

Wow, Vigo, that was your worst fight ever. Small comfort that there wouldn't be any worse ones to follow. Let go, Vigo. There's no point. Let go!

who is he?

Lazy good-for-nothing!" Father's loving voice woke him. "Where's the shovel, moron?"

His endearing visage loomed over Farin, punctuated by grey stubble, red nose, droopy eyes, the ubiquitous smell of warm beer.

Seldom had the gravedigger's son been so happy to see this familiar face, to smell the familiar smell, to hear the familiar words. What horrible things he had dreamed about. Of blood, murder, voices in his head, and of the most melancholic thoughts a person could think of. Sleepily he straightened himself up on his straw mat. Arms and back complained of considerable stiffness.

Did the aching not spring from considerable lugging?

His right hand felt along his neck of its own volition. His fingertips felt a hemp cord and then touched the smooth circular metal of the amulet. Relieved, the gravedigger's son sat upright. He had plainly and simply dreamed he'd thrown it from the Anvil deep into the Cleft. Ha-ha. What nonsense! It got even better – on that occasion he'd discovered the bodies of Gerlunda and Pater Amen lying at the foot of the chasm. No, it had been the terrible voice in his head that had made him aware of the dead bodies. What a horror – even the memory of the whoever-or-whatever-you-are wiped the smile off his face.

"Amen is lying in the shed waiting to be treated."

"What?" Farin was now standing wide-awake on his straw mat. "Amen is dead?"

His father looked him up and down indignantly. "What are you asking, muttonhead? Didn't you get him out of the chasm yesterday and bring him here. The alderman, his son and yourself."

Holy shit – where did the dream stop, and reality begin? He clasped his head with a sigh. The longer he thought about it, the less he knew which was worse and more real: the nightmare or the life he had just woken up to. He pulled on his linen trousers awkwardly. His shirt was stinking of sweat, he pulled a fresh one over it. To be precise, his other linen shirt, ripped in several places, for he only possessed two, an old one and a new one. As soon as he stepped outside the house, he smelled him too – the dead priest on the workbench. A white, floppy figure consisting of dead meat. His right arm hung twisted downwards as if Amen wanted to touch the ground. Farin was struck by the two glittering rings on his fingers.

His morning routine always led him to the stream. Once there he would piss against his favourite beech tree, then he would wash his torso, face and shirt, and clean his teeth as usual.

Why actually? There hadn't been much to chew yesterday.

He urgently needed to get his thoughts in order. What had really happened the previous day, what had he imagined, what had he dreamed? He studied his image intently in the stream. A young man with high cheekbones, round eyes and sharp teeth was examining him studiously. Should he smile at him? Naw, better not, he wouldn't be able to bear it if he didn't smile back. But he could talk to his mirror image – he mustered up all his courage. "Are you still living in my head, you whoever-or-whatever-you-are?"

Silence – the best answer of all. He must have imagined that bit, especially as the amulet wasn't lying somewhere deep in the Cleft but was still hanging around his neck.

Halfway reassured Farin stood up from the water's edge and trotted back home. Doubts were still gnawing at him – was the incident on the plateau nothing more than a figment of his imagination? Even if that were the case, it didn't bode well for his state of mind.

Getting Pater Amen ready for a decent funeral was going to take him half the day. Before he started there was breakfast – two chunks of old bread and a sliver of old bacon, as wide as his little finger. Farin thought over what he should do as he chewed. The biggest problem facing him was the open skull – nobody likes having their heads looked into, especially not when everyone is standing around you.

His father came shuffling out of the cottage with his usual hangover and held his hand over his eyes to protect them from the blinding daylight. He joined Farin at the workbench and commented expertly on Amen's condition: "Nice mess."

"We're going to need a headpiece," said Farin.

"Hm!" The gravedigger stepped towards his son. "I'll bring his tasselled hat later, the one he often used when he was giving sermons."

A surprisingly constructive idea – his old man's day had clearly got off to a good start. Farin felt emboldened to share his thoughts with his father. "I…I had wild dreams. Of a strange voice in my head, yesterday on the Anvil plateau. A mean, nasty…"

"You should have gone and got the shovel and not

climbed up the mountain. What did you want up there? Do what you're told and then nothing like that will happen."

The old gravedigger continued in a more conciliatory tone: "Don't worry about it. I experience the same thing every night when I'm coming home from Georig's." His father laughed wheezily. "Don't talk now but get down to work. We'll take the coarse flax yarn for sewing up the chest, nothing else is strong enough. We'll do it together, because one of us is going to have to hold the abdominal wall together."

"Yes, father. We also need to stabilise the neck and head before we sew up the cut on his throat."

"Right. It won't be nice if he loses his head in the middle of the funeral ceremony." Father rummaged through the firewood and pulled out a stick almost half a yard long. "We'll stick that into his gullet with a nail as a barbed hook at the top."

"Why was he so brutally mauled?"

"Son, don't you worry about that. The priest died because his heart stopped. Full stop! Our guild isn't interested in anything else. If somebody wants to clear up what happened, be my guest. We, on the other hand, don't uncover. Quite the contrary, we cover up and put them under the earth." His short laugh turned into a long coughing episode. The gravedigger soothed his throat with a draught of water. "I'll be going to Georig's later anyway, then I'll bring the shovel back."

Farin was almost suspicious of all this understanding and willingness to help coming from his old man. Would today actually turn out to be halfway peaceable for a change?

"Come on, now, we have to stitch him up before washing him." The gravedigger gathered up the requisite utensils.

Father and son spent the whole morning preparing the body of the priest for burial. It took a masterful performance to get him looking reasonably presentable again. The gravedigger even whistled a song as he worked away. They had the donkey work done by midday. Washing and make-up were left to do. Amen lay peacefully on the work bench, his double chin alone pushed his mouth shut, his hands lay prayerfully on his chest. A golden ring glistened merrily. Only one? Farin sucked at his upper lip. Where was the other one? He squinted over at his cheerful father.

"Where's the other ring?" Farin asked forcefully.

If he'd expected his father to feign ignorance, he was to be sorely disappointed. "Don't go on as if you don't know full well. We'll be able to live well of it for six weeks. At least."

You can booze well of it for six weeks, thought Farin. He wondered why he was disappointed in his father – after all, it was far from the first time.

"Nobody's going to notice", snorted the gravedigger.

"Apart from the fact that even the alderman can count to two, it's not a question of whether anyone will notice it or not. It's not…right, it's theft. They can chop off your hand for that, father."

"Now don't you take the high moral ground, Your Majes-ty. What do you mean by talking to me like that? It doesn't suit you. You're a nothing, just like me."

"Put the ring back on him."

"Since when do you boss me around? I will in my arse. We need the money to live, to feed and dress ourselves. It's late autumn now and you're still running around in bare feet. I'm buying us boots tomorrow at the market, and that'll be the end of our money. Then we'll need to stock up our coffers. Get that into your thick skull."

Pointless. Of course, Farin was in urgent need of boots and a fur coat. Still, he refused to become a thief in the process. He turned away with a sigh, a gesture that clearly provoked his father. "You think you're something better, don't you? Listen to me: You're a gravedigger and nothing else. Nobody in the village gives a toss about you, just like me. Just do your work." With a fierce look he pointed at Amen and then disappeared into the hut, only to come out a moment later. "I'm going into the village. I'll collect the body with the alderman's horse and cart in the late afternoon. He'd better look alive by then. Preferably very alive."

Farin didn't utter a word.

"He just has to be washed still", his father opined patronisingly. A short time later and he'd disappeared around the bend in the path.

Well, hallelujah. *Just* has to be washed…

Farin examined the body with furrowed brows. The face was barely recognisable with the sheer volume of dried blood, cerebral matter and dirt. Not a shred of naked skin on the body; arms and legs that didn't look like arms and legs. Farin decided to collect two buckets of water from the stream first and trotted listlessly to his favourite place. This time, however, he couldn't bring himself to enjoy it. He knelt down, filled the buckets and then slowly carried the heavy loads back towards the yard.

Life consists of nothing but lugging things.

Halfway back he put down the buckets with a groan; exhaustion was threatening to overcome him.

You can't go on like this, he scolded himself. It's all a matter of attitude, he encouraged himself. He forced his back into action, still weary from its exertions of yesterday.

I'm not hauling, I'm carrying, he comforted himself. Now just deal professionally with Amen and then you can have a rest.

Filled with fresh joie-de vivre, he bent down to the water buckets and as if by a miracle they actually felt a little lighter.

And I'll get more muscles this way, he thought, sugar-coating his situation even more.

Reaching the shed, the gravedigger's son put the water down in front of the workbench. He heard hooves in the distance. Were the alderman and his father coming already? No, he heard the galloping hooves of a few horses approaching. His experiences over the last few days, not to mention the dormant fears within him enabled Farin to act without giving things too much thought. He ducked down, crawled on all fours under the workbench and waited. From where he was, he had a good view of the yard, at least up to knee-high. Three riders came into view as they brought their horses to a stop. Two of them jumped off, and four legs stretched and shook themselves off. They clearly had a long ride behind them.

"Anyone home?" a voice called out.

What do they want in our yard? Maybe just to place an order?

The two men in brown leather trousers stepped towards the shed.

"HELLO! Gravedigger!"

Farin didn't recognise the voice. What now?

Act like a man, crawl out from under the workbench and enquire after the gentlemen's wishes.

Embarrassing – how was he going to explain why he'd crawled into a hole like…like a mole.

The third rider dismounted his horse, so that Farin could

see his black leathered legs. His black cloak didn't completely hide them.

It became just as black in front of Farin's eyes. Please no! Could that be the raven? He felt a rising sense of panic. If so, why exactly did the murderer come to *their* yard? They wanted to collect him, just like Pater Amen.

Stay calm, Farin. Black trousers aren't that rare. Maybe it isn't the raven at all.

He was filled with hope.

The dark legs came directly towards him. The scabbard of his dagger clattered against the edge of the workbench.

"The fat priest is really lying here. They found him faster than we expected."

His hope evaporated. Leave naïve hoping well alone in future, he scolded himself.

The unmistakable smell of soot and scorched earth filled the gravedigger's son's nostrils. If he stretched out his hand, he'd be able to touch the man's feet.

"The man of the cloth knew nothing and wasn't carrying anything in him. Either the alderman or the gravedigger's son must have the object of desire", the voice wheezed, "either through the medium or already in the body."

What in the name of all that was holy did "object of desire" mean?

"Why must? Couldn't it be anywhere?" asked one of his companions.

"Only three people had contact with Gerlunda's body after her regrettable demise: the priest, the alderman and the gravedigger's son."

"And what about you?"

The raven laughed humourlessly. "Yes, me too, it was me who strangled her after all." The hoarse voice became more aggressive. "Only I don't have it, you moron. Because if that were the case, we'd possess it now and we wouldn't have to be looking for it."

This clearly enlightened the moron.

The gravedigger's son could make out the sound of hands being rubbed together. "We'll take a closer look at the alderman and the gravedigger's son then."

"We will indeed!" answered the raven. "More at their inside than their outside."

Sweat was dripping from Farin's forehead, his whole body itched. If they caught him now, they'd open up his head and slit open his chest and stomach – while he was living – he could feel it already.

Oh God, please make the murderers go away. Preferably, without looking under the workbench first.

God? God yet again? Whining and whimpering. If only you'd jumped, you worm.

The terrible shock caused Farin to flinch, almost slamming his head off the underside of the workbench. His head was booming appropriately. The loud voice had surely revealed him.

The six legs carried on as if they'd heard nothing.

They haven't heard anything, so the voice is only in my head, Farin clarified to himself. The voice! No! Yes! It's there again! At this impossible time. I have the choice: go mad or die.

"You look in the house! According to my information the old man goes into the village in order to booze at this time; his son must be hiding here somewhere," opined the raven.

Two legs disappeared in the direction of the cottage.

They're going to slice me open, they're going to slice me open, hammered in Farin's head.

Pshaw! Stop taking yourself so seriously! The slicers are only doing that because they want me.

Oh, right. Well then.

Is the voice able to read my thoughts?

That had never occurred to Farin up on the plateau.

Only when you're in a panic and are thinking particularly loudly and slowly. So, almost always. A merry grunting laugh followed.

I'm allowed to panic a little when I'm in fear for my life, explained Farin to himself as quietly and as unobtrusively as he could.

"Two years it's taken us to track down this witch, Gerlunda. This time we have to get hold of it – once we have it, our rage will be boundless and our cult unconquerable. You've seen what the unutterable is capable of. Imagine what both daemons together can achieve."

Did he really say, "the unutterable"?

Be quiet, voice! Farin pressed his shaking body against the wall behind him, his fear of being caught nibbling away at every bone in his body like a worm nibbles its way through an apple. Hm, he should really cross the word "worm" out of his vocabulary.

The third man stepped out of the hut. "Looks like a pigsty in there, but there's no pig in there. I'll go look in the privy."

The legs disappeared again. "No-one here!" shouted a voice in the distance.

The raven ground his teeth: "My instinct is telling me that the gravedigger's son knows more than he let on. And this more will help us significantly."

Can that really be true? The unutterable is here? rumbled in his head.

Be quiet, thought Farin loudly. He kept feeling the whole world could hear the voice.

"Should we go check out the alderman?" suggested the third chap.

"I think we'll deal with the gravedigger's son first. Pity we missed him. You realise we have to be careful for the time being and we should avoid attracting too much attention. Emicho turned up here a few days ago."

"So what? What's so special about this Emicho?"

The raven responded impatiently. "The fact that nothing is special about him. A man of his abilities should have become principal knight a long time ago. He isn't though, and that's what makes him dangerous."

"Don't get you."

The raven's voice lost its hoarseness and cracked like a whip. "Which is why I do the understanding. And the thinking. We'll pull back for a few days, especially as I'll involve the boss. We'll nick this little snip of a delver eventually. Right then, off to Hubstone!"

The black leather-legs returned to their hooved four-legger and disappeared. The two other men mounted their horses too and galloped away.

Farin remained frozen under the workbench as if dead, although silence had been reigning for some time now.

Are you going to stay lying here to the end of your days?

Beat by beat his heartrate slowly returned to normal. The men were hunting the object of desire. And that was to be found in his head. But why?

"What will happen if I give them the amulet? Will they leave me in peace afterwards?" he whispered.

That won't satisfy them, they want me. The amulet is only my medium. They'll rummage around in little Farin in order to be sure.

"I don't understand a word. Why would they do all that?

Because I'm inside you, pure and simple. You needn't worry — they're going to frisk you and turn you on your head, before opening you up.

"If I give them the good-for-nothing piece of jewellery, I won't have anything left expect empty pockets. What are they hoping to find?

Are you really that stupid? They're going to search through your head and the inside of your body. After which you'll resemble the fat one lying over us, before your father and you sewed him up. The voice chuckled cheerfully.

"I thought you'd gone. I'm going completely mad."

Farin would only too happily follow the voice's advice and stay lying here for the rest of his days. Why should he bother coming out into all this shit?

Every worm crawls out of his hole sometime.

Just as the day before he yanked the amulet from his neck and squeezed it in his fist. He crawled out from under the workbench with steely calmness. This time he was going to get rid of it once and for all. The work on the priest would have to wait, the salvation of his soul was his primary concern now. Salvation of his soul? Hadn't the voice demanded his soul yesterday?

"You want my soul? Isn't that what you said?" Farin strode out of the shed and marched off – not towards Heap but towards the great lake.

I know what you're planning – I know, it smirked in his head.

With lips pressed firmly together Farin increased speed, he was almost running now.

I'll save the bother of pretending to be shocked, we went through all that yesterday.

Now the gravedigger's son was running along the path at

a gallop. He saw the surface of the water glistening in the distance.

Listen to me, worm. What you're planning is going to be useless. It'll be hanging around your neck again tomorrow.

"I don't believe a word of anyone I can't see in the eye."

But you believe in your God?

"He never spoke to me before."

No surprise there.

Gasping, Farin arrived at the side of the great lake. The name was an enormous exaggeration because great it certainly wasn't; however it compensated by being deep and muddy. First, he ripped the hemp cord off the amulet and threw it on the ground. With his toes already in the cold water he placed one foot forward, wound himself back and then flung the purveyor of misfortune with his outstretched arm towards the centre of the lake. An unremarkable splash…and the amulet sank to the bottom.

Do you feel better now?

"Just leave me in peace." His fear of the man in black and his two companions, his concern about the events, about the future, even about the alderman were preoccupying him. And then the outrageous phantom in his brain. Or phantasm. Or whatever you liked to call it. He trudged back, his head hanging.

What a dog's dinner. Where to now? Should he return to the gravedigger's yard and wash Amen in preparation for burial? Or run to Heap and tell the alderman everything? No, better not. Hamak was in danger himself and might hand him over to the man in black in order to save his own skin. The men wanted to ride to Hubstone – to this "boss". Hubstone, the capital of the kingdom, lay at the very south of the Worldly Kingdom. Mother had told Farin of the city.

He couldn't hear enough stories about it, especially about the royal castle, the harbour and the sea. Ten thousand people supposedly lived there – he could hardly imagine it. Mother had assured him that one day he would see the capital city with his own eyes. His father had intervened with a grunt. "Don't be putting wild ideas into the boy's head. Hubstone is more than twenty days away on foot, even a rider would need nearly ten days."

Which meant that the men wouldn't be back for three weeks at least. That's how much time he had then – before they would chase him down, catch him and slice him open.

hundred years

Farin spent the rest of the afternoon washing and making up the body. He carefully rubbed all of the priest's body parts clean using plenty of water. The activity soothed him – it provided him with meaning and an objective for a brief moment. How would his life go on once he had finished this work? He couldn't just ignore the threat of the man in black and his accomplices. Should he flee? Where to? What did he want to achieve in his life anyway? To survive was the first thing he needed to do, he thought. But why?

I'd like to rise in the villagers' estimation – just a little. I want to kiss Annietta. I want to see the sea for the first time. Maybe I should be wishing for things that are easier to achieve – flying through the air like a falcon, for example.

The obnoxious voice in his head remained silent. But this time Farin sensed that it was still there, skulking and waiting for the opportunity to break forth and mock him. When did it foist itself on him and make itself important? When he was agitated and thought aloud. So, the best thing to do would be not to get agitated and to think silently. Easier said than done since Gerlunda's death. A little agitation was in order if he was hiding a few inches away from men who wanted to kill him. A little tincture of deadly danger certainly invited a certain liveliness and vigour – not to mention the voice. It wanted his death, seemingly. Or his soul? Something bad had slipped into him. Shit, shit, shit! If only he'd never found that damned amulet. Farin didn't know much about body, spirit, soul – but decided it would be best to investigate them further.

As the gravedigger's son cleaned the priest's feet and marvelled at his long, unkempt toenails (God, it seemed, didn't look too closely at feet after all), he asked himself whom in the village he could trust. There were only very few villagers who would listen to him at all reasonably.

The sun was already touching the forest treetops when he washed his hands in a bucket of fresh water and the alderman rode into the yard on his horse and cart. The gravedigger was sitting beside him and looking remarkably sober. Before jumping off the cart he flung a tasselled hat to his son, and Farin ran to the priest with it, before pressing the headpiece down on the open skull.

Hamak stood before the workbench, his legs as widely splayed as his nose was fat. Having been aware of the body's sorry state before the extensive work carried out by the gravedigger and his son, he seemed genuinely impressed by the expert reconstruction done. "Good work", he said despite himself.

Hamak's gaze ran the length of the priest's body. Farin held his breath. Father stood there calmly with arms folded.

If he remembers the missing ring, things are going to get difficult.

It took an eternity before the alderman completed his expert examination of the body. "Let's load him up!" he said.

Using all their combined strength, the men lifted Pater Amen onto the bed of the cart for his final earthly journey. "We'll inter him tomorrow at the eleventh hour. Be punctual!" Without another word Hamak tapped the reins, clicked his tongue, and horse and cart moved off.

Father's self-satisfied grin annoyed Farin no end. He looked ugly when greed and malice distorted his features. A common thief and proud of it too. Farin began tidying the shed to distract himself. He decided against another try at explaining the voice in his head to his father.

That night Farin tossed and turned for hours on his straw mat. The multitude of unpleasant events and future prospects prevented him from sleeping – they lurked in the background only to prod him awake every time he was about to fall asleep. He realised with mixed feelings that it was his father's snoring of all things that calmed him down. He simply counted the snores and when he got to one hundred and twenty-four, he dropped off.

Farin's body snapped upward like a hinge. Something fell from his chest onto his lap. He instinctively felt for it and touched circular metal. The amulet, this time without a hemp cord, was sitting in his palm.

Shit – how can it be? Throwing it away doesn't work then – I'll have to destroy it.

The village blacksmith could put it on his anvil and smash it to pieces. And he might bump into Annietta. But then he'd be showered with questions. Especially regarding the origin of the piece of jewellery, and above all, why he wanted to destroy it.

What other possibilities were there? Throwing it into water was useless – what about fire? Exactly – the next chance he got, he'd surrender it to an inferno. For the moment he'd store it in his belt pouch beside the mandrake.

A cursed, bewitched amulet is what I'm carrying around

with me, which the cult of the Necorers and an imposing knight called Emicho are hunting down. And let's not forget the most sorcerous root of the Worldly Kingdom. You really are something special, gravedigger's son.

Half dead because of the raven and half maddened because of the voice, but never mind. How boring life would be without these things. He clung to his plan – the amulet must burn.

Farin decided to get up. The grey shadows of the waking morning pushed their way through the window. His father was still snoring. Should he wake him with the motto: "The cock has finished crowing and you're still asleep"?

Better not – father never understood jokes at his own expense. Naw, he didn't get jokes at all. The last time he laughed was probably when he was still in his mother's tummy. As though aware of his son looking at him, the old man's eyes opened. "You're awake already?" He sat up with a struggle.

Farin became aware for the first time of the certainty that there would come a point when his father would never stand up again. A man stooped from years of digging and drinking who had forgotten the point of his existence many years ago.

"Rest for a bit longer, father. We have plenty of time until the eleventh hour."

Farin ignored the gravedigger's bemused look.

His father said nothing, just collapsed again in the corner. "Just another bit", he grunted quietly.

So far, the funeral was going without a hitch, it wasn't even raining. All bar a few of the Heapers had gathered in the little graveyard behind the church to honour Pater Amen.

The alderman gave an unforgettable eulogy. Unforgettable because he'd only managed about eight sentences and it had taken him half the afternoon. "And...so as the Lord...um, well...giveth, and..uh" Hamak faltered and considered if the Lord also tooketh, "...um, welllll..."

Don't say *welllll*, just get to Amen, thought Farin.

The gravedigger's son stood in the third row and sensed the amulet in the pouch on his hip. Had the preparer of poisons infected him with her black magic just as the pestilence seven years ago had galloped from one person to the next? As soon as the funeral ceremony was over, he'd turn his attention to the piece of jewellery. He spotted Annietta in the row in front of him. Farin slowly pushed himself forward, perhaps he could stand beside her. And then? Somebody was pushing his way forward from behind. Blossak shoved him roughly aside and planted himself beside Annietta. Right, that was all he needed. The innkeeper's son's hand, down by his hip, unobtrusively stroked Annietta's fingers, and she returned his little gesture of endearment. Farin couldn't look any longer – jealousy again burned in him like a fever.

If only I were an innkeeper's son!

The villagers were throwing handfuls of earth into the grave, one by one. How fast things could change: the wealthiest and most important man in the village one minute, in the grave the next. Heap would be needing a new priest now, not to mention a new judge.

Father and son closed up the grave in the early afternoon. A dark mound of loose earth remained; the stonemason would deliver the gravestone in the next few days. Farin gently pressed the earth down with his feet – it was disrespectful to stamp heavily on a grave.

"Hurry up!" ordered his father, who was leaning on his shovel looking on. "No-one's looking."

"I'm looking." Farin said no more.

His father was silent but threw him an angry look.

When he was finished, the gravedigger headed for Georig in the tavern. Farin headed for home with the shovel. His steps became quicker. At last he was going to rid himself of this burden, this millstone, this sorcery. Once he arrived in the cottage, he filled the stove with twigs. It was basically a cast-iron basin for wood or coal with a vent. Farin created sparks with the flintstone. Dried mushroom served as tinder, and soon he had a cheerful fire burning. He added two logs and watched the greedy tongues of flame.

Yes, I like your appetite. Gobble up the cursed amulet.

He took it out of his belt pouch and turned it around in his hand. Innocuous and innocent it looked, just a simple little thing, no engraving, no flaw, no scratch. He almost dropped it in shock. He saw something in the light of the fire – the outline of a pentagram appearing on its surface. He turned it over. Shapes were appearing on this side too, outlines of…flames, the picture of a fire. In amazement Farin turned the amulet towards the daylight, the pictures disappeared on both sides. The firelight ensured they reappeared.

Ha, proof! Fire is the answer to the puzzle. I'll get rid of it for ever by burning it, he rejoiced.

No, don't do it! You can't reverse it again. On no account throw it into the oven!

I see! Either the voice is having a laugh at my expense like on the Anvil, or it's really worried this time. It made no difference – both possibilities strengthened Farin's determination. Without giving it another thought, he flung the amulet onto the flames. It hissed quietly, like water on the hob. The piece of jewellery now lay in the oven, the pentagram was brighter than the flames around it. He stared into the fire as if hypnotised, then sensed how his head began to expand, as if it were going to burst. The heat was drawing his eyeballs into the flames, his eyes were smouldering, his skull burning, he'd be unconscious in no time. Molten metal was flowing through his veins, his heart was blazing in his chest.

Noooooooo! You pathetic, unworthy worm, you!

The voice sounded distraught, but hadn't it said once its favourite pastime was tricking people? Farin crawled away from the oven, he could bear the heat no longer. He made his way out into the yard on all fours and lay on the ground on his stomach.

Done! I was right to throw the amulet into the fire.

Man! You've sealed the deal. You should never, ever have thrown it into the fire.

The palms of both his hands were pressing hard against his temples, something he only noticed when his arms began to ache.

"Oh, come off it! Just leave me in peace!" he gasped.

It took a while for the voice to calm down. *It's too late for that now. Flames work as a catalyst for the amulet. Why do you think they were pictured on it? It penetrates your body by means of heat. We're united now until you die. Congratulations.*

It echoed like in one of the caves at the foot of the Anvil. The ground was turning even though he was lying flat on top of it. Then everything went black.

The smell of damp earth revived him. He was lying on the ground between the shed and the cottage. What had he gone and done now?

Now you've gone and done it, worm! It took Gerlunda twenty-five years to come up with such a pathetic idea. The voice in his head was struggling to regain its composure: *Man, you're going to regret that.*

"Man" sounded like a curse word, coming from the voice.

"Man" is the most shameful, disgusting, insulting curse word I know. There's nothing worse.

At least the smug tone was gone. It took a while for Farin to recover enough to say something. "Explain to me who you are and what you want."

No answer.

"Are you the devil?"

Devil? You human imbeciles believe in good and evil, in God and the devil, heaven and hell. The voice cracked, it was so enraged. *Of course not. Your limited understanding can't comprehend who I am. Call it chimera or daemon for all I care.*

"How about arsehole?" asked Farin. He was getting sick of this performance in his head.

Oh, yes, please let's fight! I feed on strife, draw pleasure from conflict, lust after war. I lock horns with martial men, but not with a worm who gives up the contest before it even begins.

"What sort of mumbo-jumbo are you spouting? What contest are you on about?"

Don't you see?!

"Explain that to me about the fire. What's a cata...?"

A sigh in his head. *Fire is the catalyst. Have a look in the oven — the amulet is gone because you're carrying it in your body now, and it will only materialise again after your death. So, what do you think of climbing up the Anvil and throwing yourself into the chasm?*

"Forget it! I'm not going to do that!"

The raven is going to visit you again in three or four weeks. Let's see how old you'll get to be.

Was it chuckling with gleeful anticipation in his head? How he hated this gloating, amused noise.

"Can't you just leave me in peace until then?"

You're making it difficult for me to pull back. You attract misfortune like a corpse attracts flies. Your life is a vale of tears, but the man in black will help you get out of it.

"I didn't do anything. You and that stupid amulet are responsible for my plight."

Wrong, worm. Don't push the responsibility for your life away from yourself. Nobody asked you to hang the amulet around your neck, to hide it, and — to crown it all — to toss it onto the fire. You slunk into Gerlunda's hut of your own volition, of your own volition you're chasing this Annietta girl, and…

And now for the killer blow. Farin could sense the enjoyment growing in the voice.

…of your own volition you dig graves and wash corpses.

"Somebody has to do it! And I can do it well!" Frustration filled him.

I'll give you that. And there's nothing wrong with it. But do it then and be satisfied. And stop the moaning and groaning!

That was the limit. Farin felt he was being unfairly treated — it was simply too easy to have a laugh at him.

"What must I do to get rid of you?" he asked through gritted teeth.

Jump!

"Out of the question."

Die!

"Out of the question."

Come on — just the once.

"That would suit you just fine. I'm going to live to be a hundred so I am, just to spite you."

Why? Have a look at your pathetic existence. If I were capable of feeling something like pity, I'd be bawling the whole day long. Look at yourself, a lad who can dig most delicately.

His mouth pinched, Farin still sat there on the ground in front of the cottage and talked to himself. Or with that which was hiding inside him. If the son of a bitch could quote the alderman, then he'd witnessed everything that had happened over the previous few days. This unbearable thought fuelled his rage. "I DON'T WANT YOU! What's the possibility that you'll disappear, and quickly?"

Just listen! I'm in your spirit, in your head, in your body. A mighty power trapped inside a worm. That is my fate – until I find it. it's not you who is the victim…

"Rubbish!" Farin leaped up and hopped scornfully here and there. "Who are you? What do you want?"

The laughter reverberated between his ears. Then there was silence. Farin too kept his mouth shut – he no longer wanted to talk, wanted to hear neither insults nor lectures. He walked quickly into the hut and examined the oven. He couldn't see the amulet among the embers – had it melted perhaps? He couldn't make out any remnants of metal – had it really penetrated inside him? The voice's observations sounded convincing. They explained the sudden appearance of the piece of jewellery on the preparer of poison's chest. It had been in her body, in some form or other. And the raven and his two friends had simply slit open Gerlunda and Pater Amen in their quest to find it.

How were things to go on? He squeezed his hands into fists. I'm not going to give up. Hundred years old, yes sire! I have to find out more about this chimera. About daemons, evil spirits, black magic.

the sea

L ying prone on a little jetty, Aross enjoyed the gentle lapping of the waves. Hubstone was somewhat quieter during the late afternoons, especially towards the rear of the harbour where only rowing boats and small single masters were moored. Lost in thought, she held her right hand in the seawater and tickled it with her fingers – caressing it almost tenderly. The saltwater thanked her with its healing powers. The wounds hadn't become infected, the swellings had gone down, and no bones seemed to have been broken. The dear old torturer must have stopped beating her once Aross had lost consciousness. Clearly, the matron took less pleasure out of tearing strips off an insensible girl.

Twenty of the best with number five is close enough to butchery, thought Aross as she continued to move her hand in the water. Her forefinger hurt particularly badly – she couldn't bend it fully yet.

Dear day, let's call a truce for a short while.

For the past while Aross had gone out of her way to avoid beatings. Stolen no food, given no smart answers, performed all her chores dutifully and not scuffled or argued with the other children. Dead boring, then.

Pure survival instincts had determined Aross's actions ever since she'd become acquainted with the ecstatic, lecherous look in the matron's eyes. The woman would thrash her to death some day. As tragic as it was traumatic, nobody would be particularly concerned. One waif girl less in the world. So what? Jennie and Mattilda had disappeared too. So what? Aross had searched the harbour, especially pier four, in vain every day.

She drew her hand out of the water with a sigh and dried it off on her linen dress. She had to go back to the orphanage. Today it was her turn to serve at table, it would be wise not to be late.

Even at some remove, when she saw the grey silhouette in the distance, she sensed that something was wrong. True, the silhouette was always grey, even in the bright spring sunshine, but today the grey was swallowing everything good – venomous and vindictive it lay in wait like a snake before its lethal lunge. Aross approached carefully, looking all around her as well as up and down, because the unease was pressing in on her from all sides.

What was wrong?

The sun was already sinking behind the horizon – was that why the shadows seemed endlessly long to her? As if being drawn by a string, the first thing she did was look in the chicken coop, just a quick glance. She smelled it, heard it before she saw it. Her eyes misted over with tears. It took her a moment to fully comprehend what she was looking at.

Wolf was lying in his usual place in the corner. Normally a rusty, three-pronged pitchfork hung on the wall opposite. But not today. The fork was stuck into the body of the dog, so deeply that the animal was skewered right through. His tongue was lolling, and his eyes bulged in their sockets. Fat flies were buzzing and scrabbling everywhere. Everything smelled of blood and wickedness.

Aross staggered. Who could do something like that? The

answer came to her, short and simple: Grim.

The girl wiped a solitary tear from her cheek with her sleeve. Only one – what good was this shitty sobbing anyway? It never changed a single thing.

She ruffled the dog's fur one last time. You never bit, Wolf. Now you'll never even wag your tail again.

Noises from outside the barn.

"There she is! She just stabbed the poor dog to death!"

The words echoed across the yard. Aross couldn't make sense of it but it sounded like Grim's voice. Rage and pain made her feel sluggish, her head had the same jellyfish texture as the orphanage gruel.

Grim stormed into the barn, followed by the matron. "The poor animal never did anyone a bit of harm!" The unhappy lad struggled to fight back the tears. "Why did you kill him, Aross?" he sobbed. His chest was heaving with anguish.

"You're going to pay for this, rat!" The matron waited for neither an explanation nor an answer. She started laying into Aross with a cane like someone possessed. With number five!

The girl held her arms protectively over her head and cried out: "IT WASN'T ME! I'd never ever hurt Wolf!"

"And she's lying!" called out Grim, outraged. "I saw it with my own eyes, how she...with the pitchfork..." Now round tears were really rolling down the boy's round cheeks.

Stunned, Aross realised that she'd lost already, she just didn't want to believe it. Lost comprehensively.

"Admit it at least, Aross." Grim was bending down towards her. And with a furtive wink and a grin, which only she could see, he confirmed to her the nature of her total defeat.

The matron believed what she wanted to believe, and Grim had done the groundwork for her. The cane whipped through the air, catching her with a zing on her throat, on her ear, on her temple. *So this is the day, then. The matron is going to beat me to death. I have to save myself. I have to escape!*

Aross scrambled to the ladder up to the hayloft. *Clamber up, then over the roof, onto the beech tree and run away. Only death awaited her in the orphanage. She had to do it. It wasn't far. Two paces exactly.* But, to her misfortune, the damned Grim had anticipated her move. *Crocodile tears dry quickly.* Just as she was about to grasp the ladder, Grim grabbed her right wrist. "You're not going to just run away. First, you're going to get your rightful punishment, you animal torturer."

How had she got herself into such a hopeless situation? Very simple – she'd made a simple, naïve mistake – she'd underestimated Grim. The boy's fear of her had only made him more dangerous, more unscrupulous and deceitful. He was getting his revenge so rigorously and systematically that she would never hit back again – and that was by destroying her.

He held Aross firmly in his vice-like grip while the matron laid into her, her eyes sparkling. A lascivious expression played around her mouth. Aross collapsed helplessly at the foot of the ladder and curled into a ball. Grim let go of her wrist – there was no more possibility of escape. She shielded her face with both arms, but what was the point in that? Her body provided enough surface for assaulting, beating and whipping, ensuring that number five always found its target.

She didn't scream – pressed her teeth and lips together. Not a sound. Out of the corner of her eye Aross saw the cane, glowing hot. Everything hurt, but not so badly as a few days earlier in the matron's room. Clearly her torturer wasn't hitting quite so hard so that Aross wouldn't lose consciousness, and the enjoyment of all involved would last longer. Or maybe it was simply that Aross was coming to terms with her life ending shortly.

Congratulations, day. You've had your victory. Once and for all.

The long cane continued whipping Aross. It almost smashed her forearm.

Not a word!

"Harder!" called Grim, merrily.

Thirteen strikes to kill a rat. How many then for a queen?

Suddenly she shrieked. Shrilly and hysterically.

It took all her final strength for Aross to pose the question. Had she really fulfilled her torturer's desire and screamed? No, she hadn't! Only now did the penny drop.

It wasn't Aross who was screaming, but the matron. And her screaming had turned into a bestial shriek. The blows stopped. Aross could only see out of one eye – her other socket was full of blood. She sensed it. A thousand little feet were scrabbling over her body, over the ground, over the hay. Yellow teeth were attacking the matron from all sides. Rats, countless rats. They disappeared under her long skirt, ran up her legs, over her stomach, onto her shoulders. And yet more rats. One of them jumped down from the hayloft directly into her hair.

"GET AWAY! MAKE THEM STOP, AROSS!"

The rats were biting and biting! They were really good at doing that – after all, their teeth could nibble their way through wood, stone and even metal. And the rats knew that their teeth, unlike people's, grew back again. Which was why they bit unscrupulously, recklessly and mercilessly, although it had to be said that the soft matron-flesh really didn't present much of a challenge.

"AROSS, IT WAS ME THAT RAISED YOU! I LIKE YOU VERY MUCH! MERCYYYYY"

Wow – all of a sudden.

Aross had never heard such sounds before. Cracking, gnawing and nibbling on all sides. She didn't avert her eyes – calmly observed the proceedings. The matron's screams grew louder and higher.

"NOOOOOooo!" The voice died away with a gurgle.

Trying to hit the rats in her panic, she was whipping herself with cane number five – on her head, her arm, her chest. Blood ran down her face and saturated her skirt. The rats ran over the body of the girl again and again, but she wasn't bitten. Aross sat herself up with a groan and leaned against the ladder. Grim stood stock-still beside her. A look of horror had spread across his face, his eyes were threatening to fall out of their sockets. Then Grim simply fell over, just as Aross had done in the matron's room during the last flogging. The rats spared him too, they were only interested in the matron. The woman wasn't defending herself anymore but now she was clawing with both hands at a rung of the ladder. Her knees gave way, her legs hit the floor, her head cracking against one of the ladder rails. The next instant her tormentor was buried under a sea of rats. A deluge of pink feet, long tails and yellow teeth. The sea became red, the little feet and the tails became red, the ground became red. The matron's puddle of blood intermingled with that of Wolf. Thousands of teeth tore the woman to ribbons, even partially gorging on her.

A few minutes later and it was all over, the rats disappearing as fast as they had arrived. Aross was still sitting with her back against the ladder, groaning and observing the mess in front of her. It was almost impossible to distinguish clothing from human flesh; bloody bones were jutting in every direction. The matron's face was completely gone, and enormous holes gaped on her arms. Cane number five lay beside her right hand, which was missing two fingers.

Aross had outlived the matron, at least for the moment. Laboriously getting up onto her legs, her back against the ladder, she slowly pressed herself up, rung by rung. Grim lay on the ground, unscathed and motionless.

This swine is to blame for everything, which is why I'm going to kill him now, thought Aross.

She looked at the three-pronged pitchfork in Wolf's body. Then she wearily shook her head. However much she hated the lying coward, she'd never be able to bring herself to finish him off, to simply skewer him to death. The soles of her feet were sticky, blood was lapping against her toes.

"What happened? Matron?", one of the other orphan children called from outside.

What now? She couldn't stay here. She listened in to her battered body. Nothing seemed to be broken though her skin was split in many places; there were bloody wounds in her head, but her legs were managing – she could stand. She was being drawn to the sea. What had helped her hand would also help the rest of her body. She limped laboriously out of the barn. Some of the orphan children were standing outside the house, having been attracted by the matron's screams.

One of the two serving maids called out: "Aross, what's been going on?"

The queen of the rats didn't respond but left the orphan-age yard. Nobody stopped her. She wanted to run. Rats always ran, but the pain in her legs and her muscles wouldn't let her. Step by step, more dragging than limping, she neared the harbour. Some figures looked at her in the semi-darkness with furrowed brows before quickly turning their heads away. People had their own worries in the old town. They probably thought she was a whore whose protector had "motivated" her, and nobody interfered in such a case. Best never to tangle with the turners and the reapers.

It took her an eternity before she reached the sea even though she hadn't taken the detour this time but the direct route to the shore. Racked with pain, she pulled her long linen dress over her head, laid it on a stone and waded up to her knees into the cold water. Subdued by the jetty, the sea only lapped the shore with small waves. Aross went in deeper, step by step, her skin was burning all over her body. She imagined she was stepping into a magic pool with tremendous healing powers. Her body was standing in flames, and despite the cold water, she felt herself to be sweating as she never had before. After a short time, the burning eased off, and she carefully washed the blood from her face, as well as her arms and legs. She could hardly recognise the wounds on her body in the semi-darkness – nevertheless, it was dawning on her that she had been lucky.

Is that how I should describe it? Lucky? Lucky that my life goes on?

"Yes, I was lucky!" she called out to the waves, making her hand into a fist while ignoring the pain in her forefinger. At that same moment something occurred to her. Something that she'd forgotten long ago because she'd wanted to forget it. She dallied in the sea. The words of Shewhoknows lapped in her mind like waves: "You bite and bite. Then I will ensure that you think of me in your hour of greatest need on the day of the thousand bites. I can only help you once, and then you are on your own. Remember everything we have spoken about."

The old woman hadn't been totally mad. How could she have known that? And what sort of protective magic had she put into effect? Crazy that the matron was dead and Aross was still alive. No longer did she want to suppress her meeting with the old woman. She rummaged around in her memory furiously. What else had Shewhoknows said? Aross waded carefully back to the shore and sat down on a rock. She wrapped her arms around her knees – she was hardly aware of her shivering and her pain, she was wallowing so much in the old woman's metaforces.

"Listen out for the witch's peal, then you'll understand that the time is right", she remembered that much, but where was the connection? And what had she said about teeth? And she'd mentioned a bone reader! Whatever that was supposed to mean.

Aross slipped her grey dress over her head with a groan. Actually, calling the tattered piece of linen a dress was being flattering, but it was all she had.

"Dear sea, thank you for your help!" she called out. Her skin was still burning a little, but she was feeling much better. She'd wash out the bloodstains on her dress tomorrow. The way things were looking, there would be a tomorrow for the rat girl. A new day she would cannon into and fight her way through. The next thing she needed was a place to sleep. The orphanage was out of the question; the town watch would be investigating the events – the matron was not a nobody after all and the circumstances of her death were suspicious. What was Grim going to tell them? Nobody would believe him that Aross had called a thousand rats to protect her against the matron.

The girl knew under which bridge most of the Hubstone vagrants slept. That's where she'd go and think over her next steps – in peace and quiet.

white and red

The day began with getting up, going to the stream, washing. Same old, same old. Mind you, there was no voice harassing him – Farin was alone with his cares.

Just don't get agitated, and think quietly, he thought to himself. Just don't wake any slumbering spirits. Just wait and see what the day brings, is my motto for today.

Uneasily at ease he sat opposite his father at the table in the cottage and chewed on a piece of old bread. "The blacksmith could forge swords from this bread."

His father looked up. "Just say, we need fresh bread, lad."

With his mouth full of spittle to soften the crust, Farin refrained from commenting further. It took a while before he managed to swallow it without breaking a tooth. An idea bubbled to the surface. "Father, where's the nearest library?"

"What? What's that?"

"A room with an awful lot of books."

"Don't be cheeky! I know what a library is, boy. But what do *you* want to do there?"

"Read books."

"What a load of crap! People don't need that. Look at me."

Oh, right. Best not say anything, Farin.

"I can't even read," wheezed the gravedigger, and even managed to sound proud as he spoke.

"Do you know the answer to my question?"

The gravedigger scratched his stubble, reminding Farin of the noises in the sawmill. "There's supposed to be a big library in Hubstone – your mother mentioned it once."

"Have you never been to Hubstone?"

"Naw, why would I bother? It's far too far away, right down south. Here will do just fine."

Oh, right. Best not say anything, Farin.

"That's enough talk, we need bread and cheese, milk from the goat farmer, and a knuckle of ham wouldn't be bad either," said the gravedigger.

That sounded very promising. Even just the sound of the words made Farin's mouth water, which also helped the bread move along down his gullet and into his stomach without causing any long-term damage.

Father untied his threadbare moneybag and laboriously rooted around in it. "Here, six coppers, that should do you."

Farin stretched out his hand and took the coins. "I'll head off now, father." A slight hesitation before he asked his next question: "Do you know what a chimera is?"

The gravedigger shook his head wearily. "What sort of questions are you asking at all?" He raised his right forefinger. "Ah! You mean a kind of a mare? Of course I know what that is! It's an old nag, like the rickety one belonging to the alderman."

"Thank you, father." His old man had tried anyway. "I'll head off, then." He jumped up, put the coins in his pocket, grabbed the old wicker basket with the old clay jug and left the hut.

The baker would be his first port of call. The wonderful smell of fresh bread in his basket should accompany him for as long as possible. Surprised at his own good mood, for which there was no logical reason, he decided not to darken today with depressing thoughts. Not even thoughts of smart-arse chimeras that might be floating around in his head.

Farin headed on the path towards Heap at his customary brisk pace, and it wasn't long before he spotted the rope-maker in the distance with his enormous shaggy dog heading towards the market. The wares he was going to peddle were in a bulgy basket that he carried on his shoulders.

Farin increased his speed and called, long before he reached them: "Growler, my old friend!"

The dog spun around, his ears pricked upwards like two little steeples, then he stormed towards the gravedigger's son, barking joyfully.

"Don't knock me over, you big mop!" he laughed.

Growler arrived and was just about to jump up at him as usual. But at the last moment he planted his forepaws into the ground, his hackles stood on end and he emitted a growl such as Farin had never heard from him. The muscles in the dog's head were tensed up, and his eyes had become so big that Farin could see their whites. A look, harder than this morning's bread, hit him forcefully. Growler arched his back, curled up his lips, and bared his impressive incisors threateningly.

Farin stood there, dumbstruck, and stared back. What was going on? The dog was pure aggression and about to attack him.

"It's only me, Growler," he said, trying to calm down the dog.

The ropemaker had stopped and turned. Of course, he noticed that something was amiss and called loudly: "Growler, come here! Now!"

Farin didn't want to provoke the dog, so he looked past him and made no further effort to greet or even to touch him. Growler growled again, then ran back to his master.

The ropemaker shrugged his shoulders, turned and continued his journey. Farin stood there for a while, rooted to the spot. His good mood had evaporated. How could that be? Downcast, he shuffled onwards. He didn't bother trying to catch up with the ropemaker. Did the animal hate him now too? He felt as though he'd lost his last remaining friend in the village – and this was, in fact, the case.

The villagers jostled and pushed their way among the stalls on the marketplace between the church and the bakery. The baker's stall, which stood directly in front of his establishment, attracted a group of children who were hoping to scavenge a few crumbs. When he was younger, Farin too had waited there wide-eyed and occasionally got a morsel by begging. Today he bought two loaves of bread, broke a little corner off one of them and tossed it towards one of the boys. The lad caught it skilfully and called out in a bright voice: "Thanks!"

He bought the goat's milk two stalls further on, where it was poured into the clay jug. A chunk of cheese changed hands too. His enjoyment of the abundance of colours, the aromas, the voices of the market criers supplanted his unpleasant experience with Growler. Peat and his cronies were horsing around at the last stall with its knives, daggers, axes, saws and whetstones. Farin remembered Peat's name, but what were the others called again? Blunt, Dull and Dense were what he had in his head. He quickly turned around. He really didn't want to tangle with them again. Too late – Peat was already pointing at him with a derisive grin. Farin pushed himself between two women who were haggling loudly with a fishmonger. They prodded at two herrings, claiming the fish were older than their grandmothers. It struck Farin, that he hadn't bartered at all – he simply paid the price the sellers had demanded. Which was probably why his father sent him to the market so rarely. Well, it wasn't so tragic when it came to bread and milk, the prices for those wares barely fluctuated anyway.

After half an hour he'd spent all his coppers, and so he left the market. He marched back towards the gravedigger's cottage with a full basket, hardly feeling the weight, his anticipation of dinner filling him with joy. At one point he held the basket directly under his nose. Aromatic bread, ham and cheese – they smelled better than any perfume.

Halfway between Hubstone and home he saw four figures standing in the middle of the road: Peat and his companions. Holy shit, they were waiting for him – there was no doubt about it. They were taking this fight-your-way-through-life far too literally – and they had just found their newest victim.

"Ah, our friend, the desecrator of bodies," said Peat to him in greeting, his attitude and voice poisonous. "You still haven't described to us how you played around with the lovely Gerlunda."

"Tee-hee," said the others as if on command.

Was he expecting an answer? Farin said nothing.

With an angry face Peat spoke accusingly: "I had to carry corpses around for a whole afternoon because of you."

"I did it too," suggested Farin.

"You can't do anything else. Didn't I promise you that you were going to pay for it?" He waved his forefinger self-importantly. "And I always keep my promises."

How could Farin respond to that? Did the four of them really want to beat him up again?

"What are those lovely things you've bought for us?" asked Peat and tried to grab the basket.

"Hands off!"

"Well, look at that skinflint!" Without warning Peat rammed his elbow into Farin's stomach. The gravedigger's son bent over double, and one of the other three took advantage of his pain-induced position to give him an almighty kick in his backside, throwing him off balance and knocking him forward. He let go of the basket as he tried to protect himself with his hands before landing on his stomach. The long one – now he remembered his name, Kaal – grabbed the basket and began unpacking the newly bought purchases. He offered the clay jug to Peat.

"How sweet," answered the alderman's son. "The scoundrel needs his milk."

Peat took the container and splashed some over Farin's head. He stretched out his long arm demonstratively and then let the jug fall to the ground – of course it smashed into a thousand pieces, and the rest of the milk splattered on the stony surface. "It fell. It slipped out of my hand."

The four thought this was hilarious.

"He's also bought us bread," said Kaal provocatively, and tossed a loaf towards Peat. He took a big bite and gobbled it noisily. "Very decent of you, gravedigger's son."

Lying on the ground, full of hate and yet with astounding calmness, Farin said: "Be careful, Peat, eat slowly or you'll only puke again."

The chewing stopped involuntarily. "What?"

Just as a few days earlier, he began kicking Farin. "Beating him up isn't enough, we have to give him a good thrashing, one he'll remember for a long time", he ascertained.

"His teeth – his pretentious teeth – we should knock a

188

few out. We'll start with the upper incisors. That way he'll remember today for the rest of his life," said Kaal, proud of his original idea.

Blunt placed a foot on his back, the others were still kicking him. Kaal bent down, dug his hand into Farin's shock of hair and yanked his head upwards. "Come on! I need a hand, then I'll treat his ivories." He sniggered.

Farin was paralysed by horror and fear. They were deadly serious. This time he wasn't going to escape with two black eyes. Pearly tears were dripping from his nose. The spilled milk hurt him just as much as the kicks to the kidneys and back.

How long are you going to put up with that, worm?

The chimera – that was all he needed!

His thoughts were screaming with rage, with hatred of himself, with scorn towards these four idiots, with feebleness, defencelessness, hopelessness.

What can I do against their superior strength? And now you too. Are there five beating me to a pulp now?

Rubbish! I'm not doing anything to damage you. Apart from asking you in this…rather tense situation…a thoroughly justifiable question. Why are you letting this happen?

What can I do against these four assailants? I don't stand a chance.

What about sobbing and begging for mercy? It chuckled in amusement. But a moment later and the voice was scornful. *These types make me sick. Leave it to me to sort this out.*

Never! Piss off!

Right, so. This will be fun because very soon they're going to smash in your teeth. Then you'll have fewer to clean tomorrow. The chimera thought for a moment. *They might smash your skull in too, and then I'll be free.*

Indeed, Peat had found a rock the size of his fist on the side of the path and pressed it into Kaal's hand.

Farin twisted around like a rabid dog, trying to free himself from their grasps. He managed to knock Peat off his feet, so that he crashed to the ground beside him. The gravedigger's son made an almighty effort to get back onto his feet. Dull aimed a kick at him, connecting his boot with Farin's head. Although he was kneeling on the ground, everything was spinning around him, dizziness and consciousness were competing with each other. Peat had leaped back up onto his feet and was even more enraged than before. All four were looming over him now, holding him down with their combined force.

"Turn him on his back", ordered Kaal.

They rolled him over, then the four men pressed his arms and legs hard against the ground. He felt as if he were in a vice.

You have to do something effective and not thrash about blindly like a little baby.

His eyes were burning, his heart was pounding, his head was spinning. Farin was close to bawling.

Close your eyes, please, I can't look on at this any longer.

This stinker in his head was even worse than Peat and Kaal combined. Another blow to the head, his senses were waning.

Let go! Not much further, just a little step. It's high time you let go.

What did the voice want from him? What was he supposed to do? What was he to let go of? He wasn't holding onto anything.

"Only the upper incisors this time, we'll deal with the lower ones at our next meeting. That's thoroughly decent of us. You have to stay still, though, otherwise I can't guarantee anything." Kaal gleefully showed him the rock in his hand. A four-voiced musical round of laughter. Kaal slowly raised his arm.

He's winding himself up now. Not much time left. Let go!

The hand with the big rock raced towards his mouth. The movement lasted little longer than the blink of an eye, but to Farin it felt like an eternity.

Let go!

Everywhere fog, everything grey. Was he falling unconscious, or was he dying? The hand with the rock was flying towards Farin's mouth. In his mind he heard his teeth cracking already.

The worst thing is, it's not only your teeth they're destroying.

At the very last moment the gravedigger's son yanked his head sideways. Kaal smashed the rock into the ground, grazing Farin's ear in the process. The mishit meant Kaal's face was now within reach. Farin's forehead flew straight upwards and smashed into the bridge of Kaal's nose. The cracking of the bone rang crisp and clear. In shock and pain, Kaal released Farin's right arm. A karate chop on Blunt's gullet ensured the gravedigger's son's left arm was freed. His enemies bent over him, furious. Still lying on his back, he grabbed Kaal's head and smashed it into Dull's. And dull, ironically, was what the collision sounded like. Dull. Head to head, a mundane sound, as if he were tapping against a gravestone with his knuckles but to greater effect. They both rolled their eyes and let go of him. Lacerated, Dull crumpled in a heap, Kaal held his nose and temple, while his blood dripped through his fingers and onto Farin's cheek. A single bound and the gravedigger's son was back on his feet. So was Peat, but Farin kicked his heel into the back of his knee, sending him crashing backwards onto the ground with a groan. Blunt was still holding onto his throat, emitting a rattling noise. A kick at his shins and he too collapsed, smashing his shoulder against the ground.

"HOW CAN THAT HAPPEN?" Kaal's face, with its smashed-in nose and lacerated temple, looked like meat on display in the market. "WHAT'S POSSESSED HIM?"

Don't tell me he's seen through us. This was followed by a demonic giggle.

Kaal threw himself furiously at the gravedigger's son, hate pulsating in his pupils. Farin remained calm. A shimmy to the left, a feint to the right, and Kaal had stumbled past him into nothingness. The gravedigger's son was already behind his opponent and ramming his knee into his back. Screaming loudly, Kaal fell forward and curled up into a ball on the ground. A shadow to his left – Farin spun and with his left arm the gravedigger's son parried a right hook from Peat, his other arm was already flying on its way. Farin feinted again and grabbed it with both hands. As if he had done it a hundred times, he raised his knee and broke Peat's twisted forearm. It cracked like a brittle branch; the screams of the man rang out even louder.

"Stop! I want to talk to you!" Farin grabbed Peat's throat with his right hand, and the screaming died down. The leader of the four wretches stared at him as if paralysed, then fear flickered in his eyes.

Farin heard himself speak: *"So, bog-nose. The sun is shining, and all is well. Which is why you see me now calm and sober and in the best of moods, but if I catch sight of you and your numbskulls one more time, I will get angry. And then all good things will come to an end."*

Never before had Farin seen such an incredulous look. A pathetic gape, first at his groaning, wheezing, bleeding cronies on the ground, then at Farin. Peat's eyeballs were bulging out of their sockets as if they wanted to flee in terror.

Farin loosened his grip. *"And, to answer your question: Of course, I had fun with Gerlunda. And I can tell you it was much more enjoyable than that time with your mother."*

How was it possible to heighten Peat's amazement even more? Dismay was dribbling from his mouth and nose.

"If you bother me just one more time, I'm going to kill you, one after the other. You'll be the first, and that's a promise." Farin raised his forefinger. *"And I always keep my promises."* He held Peat's chin. *"It doesn't matter to me what happens after that. I've nothing to lose. I'm the gravedigger's son."*

Peat's lips were quivering.

"You still owe me money for the milk and the bread."

He held out his open hand before him. Unable to move his arms, Peat's eyes looked downward and gestured to the alderman's son's belt. With a quick movement Farin opened the moneybag hanging there and took out a few coins. This dirtbag even had silverlings. He counted out four coppers for the milk, the clay jug and a loaf of bread. He put the other coins back into the moneybag and threw it down at Peat's feet. The alderman's son was holding onto his broken arm, which was hurting him horribly; he was still incapable of uttering a single word.

Farin picked up his basket serenely and threw a scornful look at the four mauled maulers. They were sobbing and bleeding to beat the band, a heap of misery, as befitted their home village.

Back to the market. He'd really had to work hard for his supper today.

Fate

Farin examined his ear with his right hand and felt a crust behind the earlobe where Kaal had caught him with the rock. Whether it was his own blood or not didn't bother him. But he certainly needed to make a detour to the stream so he could wash himself first before heading back to the market. When he knelt down at the bank of the stream, he saw his own mirror image looking back at him: smeared with blood, serious and above all, strange. Farin scooped a handful of water up to his face and rubbed it clean with both hands. All that cold water ought to wake him up.

Shit! What had happened? What on earth had he done?

Your pretty incisors nearly went astray, don't forget.

The chimera! He'd lost his self-control. Semi-conscious from the kicks to his head he had…let go and left the rest to the whoever-or-whatever-it-is-you-are.

Now sob your little heart out and feel pity for your four benefactors.

There were a few boulders lying near him. Shaking his head, Farin sat down on one of them.

Unbelievable – those four are going to kill me the next time they get a chance.

Nonsense! I know enough of their types. Only strong when they're in the majority against the so-called weaker. They'll never talk to you again – run away more like.

With fists clenched, Farin shouted: "How could that have happened? I'm not able to fight, certainly not against four."

Now you see what you have inside you! It chuckled.

He instinctively rolled his eyes so much they hurt. Chimera-sarcasm or chimera-humour? Both! "You constantly scold me and laugh at me! Tell me why you helped me at all?"

Ah come on now! I only helped myself. Without incisors you'd be mumbling until the end of your hundred years of existence – that would have driven me mad.

"Is that all?"

Because I like doing things people don't expect of me. The voice paused for only a moment. *And also because I can do it. And anyway, it's fun.*

"Lots of people in the village are going to wonder about what happened. They're going to ask questions."

So what? It doesn't bear contemplating that they might suddenly be saying: The gravedigger's son isn't the wimp we thought he was after all. It sounded as though the chimera was pausing for breath. *Forget it! I'm telling you, the four wretches won't spill the beans. Not a single word. Are they going to admit that you beat the living daylights out of all of them? Alone – one against four? And the sluggish gravedigger's son of all people! Now, come on! Start thinking like a man, start being a man.*

"How many wretches do I have to beat the living daylights out of before I am a man?"

Hm. Good question. Perhaps I've underestimated you. For the first time the voice was sounding moderately friendly and even a little contemplative.

"Yes, I admit you helped me, but I still don't feel good about it."

If I hadn't helped you, would you be feeling better now?

Whether he wanted to or not, Farin had to admit that the chimera had saved more than his teeth.

How about a thank you? That would do me for starters.

"Thank you. But that's all. I still can't stand you because this body belongs to *me* – to *me* alone. There's something sinister about you, so I think you should scarper now, preferably for ever."

Farin's episode with the ropemaker's dog fitted in with this description. Of course – Growler had sensed the change in him and had expressed what he thought of it in no uncertain terms. "Not even Growler likes you, he almost bit me – no, you. Because you're disgusting."

Dogs traditionally don't like daemons, except hellhounds, of course.

"I never know when you're being serious or when you're being sarcastic. But I definitely notice when you're being mean because you're like that all the time."

Neither of them spoke for a long time. The gurgling of the stream soothed Farin. His thoughts settled down. "Now tell me who you are."

No answer. Farin couldn't sense a presence – he was beginning to develop a feel for when the voice was moving in his spirit without saying anything, or when it had disappeared. Things were becoming weirder all the time. With the basket in his hand he stood up from the rock and headed for the market. He wanted to re-run his errands before Peat and his four friends had dragged themselves back to Heap.

The baker gave only a brief quizzical look before she sold him more bread, which he stuffed into his basket. He bought a new clay jug from the farmer with the goat's milk, and then had it filled. On his way back from Heap to the gravedigger's cottage he stopped at the exact point where the four morons had ambushed him. How had he defeated the four men using so few movements? Confused, he continued on his way with his laden basket. He just wanted to go home, no matter how dilapidated and squalid the cottage was. And apart from that he was really looking forward to the meal, for such a feast was a rare occurrence. When he arrived at the gravedigger's, he unpacked the goods, filled a cup with goat's milk and swallowed it down in deep draughts.

His father stood near him and looked at him sceptically. "What happened to your ear? And your forehead? Don't tell me you fell again?"

"Not worth talking about. I'm fine."

"Hm!" The old man took a loaf of bread and broke off a piece. "Why did it take you so long?"

"Peat and his friends held me up."

"Don't tangle with them. Just run away."

"Easier said than…"

The gravedigger roared: "LISTEN TO ME! Run away! That's the only thing that works against them!"

"Wise words. I'll do that, father."

"Good!" The old man calmed down. "I'm going to the tavern now."

Oh, right.

"It's Georig's birthday today, so it'll be on the house. He's paying for the first three rounds." The gravedigger puckered his lips in joyful anticipation of the liquid refreshments and left the cottage.

It took a while for Farin to realise he was alone. And he realised quickly that he didn't want to be alone. Should he follow his father? Peat and his cronies rarely set foot in "The Warm Beer", so that wasn't an impediment. Still, he put off the decision until later and bit heartily into the fresh bread. The cheerful chewing clearly inspired his decision-making abilities and he decided to follow his father to the tavern.

What was the point of sitting around here, thinking unpleasant thoughts about chimeras and murderous men in black?

The sign on the wall outside the tavern squeaked invitingly. Although it was still early afternoon, he could hear the sound of laughing voices before he opened the door. The grave-digger was sitting at his traditional table directly at the entrance – literally, on the margins of society. Farin's heart was sore to see the old man sitting so alone while only a couple of yards away the merrymaking was in full swing. He nodded silently to his father in greeting. He sat down opposite him.

"You didn't get a beer yet, father?"

"Look after your own beer, son."

Farin looked over at the innkeeper sourly, who was drinking and joking with the locals in the main taproom and clearly didn't give a tinker's curse for his gravedigger guests. Just as Farin was about to stand and give him a piece of his mind, Georig came over and planted two tankards of beer in front of their noses.

"Felicitations on your birthday," said father.

"Best wishes on your birthday from me too. May your beer never be cold," said Farin in congratulation.

The innkeeper considered for a moment. "Thanks, should I take the beers with me again?"

"Don't you dare!" Father smirked and held onto his tankard firmly with both hands, throwing his son a reproach-ful look. Drinking was no laughing matter for him, especially as he had drunk away most of his pride already.

Georig nodded to them both and disappeared behind the counter. The tavern was filling all the time with villagers –

both men and women. The company struck up a song, and of course it could only be "The Wise Pipe Smoker". The text wasn't wise at all, so asinine in fact that Farin had forgotten it completely. Unfortunately, the singers brought it screeching back to life.

"Our life is just a joke
Without our pipes to smoke."

Torture! It was a matter worthy of the king's clemency! He leaned back and imagined somebody else, whose lips might not only close in on his mouth but also close his ears. The door opened, and Annietta stepped in! Beaming sunshine. Farin stared at her yellow linen top. She'd tied it at her waist, highlighting her shape. A white undergarment peeked out at her feet. Her long hair tied into a plait made her look as she had years before. Like the girl Farin had rescued from the dragon. Her eyes searched the room – presumably she was looking for Blossak. Farin knew he wasn't present. His heart was hammering like the knight at the tavern door. Annietta was almost beside him at the door. At which point her eyes fell on the table of the untouchables.

He just blurted it out: "Bloss isn't here, Annietta."

She looked at him in shock. "How do you know I'm looking for him? Did he tell you we'd had a row?"

Ten thoughts, a hundred words, a thousand emotions, and ten thousand times helplessness.

I wanted her attention. And now? How should I answer her?

In order to say anything at all, he started: I...um...err." Instead of sounding manly and seductive, his voice squeaked. Instantly, he realised his contribution hadn't sounded fully convincing and so he swiftly upped the ante. "I…I haven't seen him since Pater Amen's burial."

"How do you know about us?" she whispered, coming very close to him in the process. She smelled of flowers, of womanhood, of secrecy, of seduction – even better than fresh bread.

If the man in black doesn't manage it, this woman is going to kill me, thought Farin.

He pressed his hands on his thighs to stop his shaking, there were a thousand butterflies in his stomach.

Is our worm flustered? Or even excited? It was laughing in his head. *She asked you how you know about her hanky-panky with this Blossak. You'd better answer.*

Of course – he was excited, differently to when he was in mortal danger, but certainly enough for the obnoxious chimera to make an appearance.

Farin concentrated. "Bloss and I…we're good friends. He told me everything."

Stunning answer. She'll investigate that the next time she meets Blossak, and then you'll be left standing there as a pathetic liar.

Indeed, Annietta didn't seem completely convinced. "Really? Are you sure about that?" Her eyebrows went up, her eyelashes closed once, then rose again, it felt like a slap and a caress, bowling him over.

"Err…um", said Farin, trying to sound casual.

"Should we go outside?" asked Annietta, glancing quickly at the gravedigger.

What a stroke of luck. She interpreted his taciturnity on the presence of his father, who was hearing everything although not showing much interest in the conversation.

"The two of us alone…outside?" His voice was shaking. He could hardly believe it.

She placed her hands on her hips. "Don't be afraid. I'm not going to do anything to you. And if a dragon appears, I'll defend you."

After hearing these words all his blood rushed up to his head as if on command. How could a grown man blush so deeply?

Most beloved. A glow-worm!

That was all he needed! How was he going to deal with the chimera while at the same time paying appropriate attention to Annietta?

Stand up, anyway, Farin.

Politeness had called for that long ago. Success – he managed to get up out of his chair without further embarrassment. Annietta opened the door, and Farin followed her out. Just at the right time too, because tolerating the singing required immeasurable fortitude.

"Our life is just a joke

Without our pipes to smoke."

The closing door partially dampened the racket.

"So, what did Blossak tell you?" She tapped her foot lightly.

"He…well, he didn't tell me directly. I saw you in the graveyard at Amen's burial. And…then I knew."

Annietta smiled as crookedly as the song in the tavern. "That's the way, then! And what business is it of yours?"

Now! Show interest in her. Ask her who taught her how to dance. Then, why she fought with Blossak. Tell her that her charm is beguiling you…

"Sorry! None of my business." He lowered his eyes.

Oh boy oh boy! It chuckled with laughter in his head, as if he had an attack of hiccups.

"Farin, is there anything else you want to tell me?"

Had she really said Farin? His name had never sounded so nice before.

Come on! She's giving you a second chance only she doesn't know it.

"I…I'd like to ask you out."

A bit better, but hell, worm, you're shooting for the moon with that one, sighed the voice.

Clearly Annietta was of the same opinion, for she whispered: "You…you are the gravedigger's son…"

Oh, I see, said the voice, followed by a hiccup.

Annietta looked even more beautiful perturbed. What should he do now? "I…I…" The blood collected in his head again. He could find no words, could barely breathe.

The delicacy and grace of her face would have taken any dragon's breath away. She needed no knight to save her with his sword *Windswipe*.

She clearly saw things the same way. "I can't go out with you. If my father catches me with you…" Her tone of voice sounded snippy, which didn't however take from the gentleness in her eyes. "We've been standing out here long enough. I have to go, Farin."

She turned, twisting elegantly, the movement reminding Farin of her dance at the midsummer festival. Without dignifying him with another look, she whooshed away.

What remained was a whiff of her and a whiff of lonely Farin. The sign for "The Warm Beer" above his head squeaked rhythmically in time to the snatches of song.

The voice in his head clicked its tongue. It sounded like the slapping of a flat hand on a forehead. *I can't tell you why, but she likes you. And I understand something of women. But you missed your chance.*

"Shut your trap!"

The sun sank, all hope sank, the world sank. Unable to move, Farin started reproaching himself. All the things he could have said. All the things he shouldn't have said. Five extraordinarily heavy words weighed him down like a millstone around a neck. "You are the gravedigger's son!" Still, she had called him Farin in the end.

Accept the seal on your fate, gravedigger's son.

Stuff and nonsense! Seals are there to be broken. Fate is its own most terrible enemy – it always wants to be fought against. Otherwise, everything that could happen would be fate. Just a shrug of the shoulders, an excuse of the weary, the inflexible, the cowardly. Listen to me and never bother me again with your fate!

"Fate, fate, fate", murmured Farin.

You've persuaded me, worm. Climb up on your Anvil and jump at last.

A lake of sadness and Farin was swimming in the middle of it. Masses of water were crashing above his head. Why was he *what* he was and not *who* he was? He didn't have the strength to step back into the tavern and let his father know. It took him over two hours to get back to the cottage, on account of his tired shuffling. The chimera left him alone, a peculiar day was coming to a close.

Exhausted, Farin lay on his straw mat in the corner. The moonlight shining in was as cold as this world. He closed one eye tightly – a vain attempt to make it look only half so bad. It was pointless.

Close the other eye as quickly as you can.

turnips

The first frost came in the night. It liked to slink in under cover of darkness, surprising the people in the early morning with its wrathful biting. The smell of burnt wood tickled Farin's nostrils when he awoke. Father had already lit a fire in the oven, something he only did when the cold unapologetically demanded it.

Farin shed no tears when winter broke. On the contrary, he loved it when his breath puffed forth white dragon-fire in the cold air. He loved it when the great lake froze over so that he could skate across the ice. And he was also hoping he might gain a time advantage – there was a possibility that the raven might be put off by the cold and delay his journey back to Heap. A vague hope that nevertheless gave him a vague courage.

Nobody had died in the last seven days, not even through their heart stopping. This happened from time to time when people weren't killing each other. So, there was no additional work for the gravedigger and his son. It was enough if one of them spent an hour or two a day maintaining the graves. Mostly Farin. Pay was paltry if there was any at all. In the past Pater Amen would press a few coppers from the collection into the gravedigger's hand after the Sunday sermon. At the moment there was no priest and hence no Sunday service and hence no coppers.

Money or no money, he gathered the leaves together with

a rake made from beech twigs. The graves directly behind the church and near the altar were the most desirable – or rather, the most extravagant. Pater Amen's grave was one of those final resting places, of course. He had made himself comfortable in the shadow of the church steeple. This was of no concern to the trees whatsoever. They divided their falling leaves fairly, with the help of the wind, over the whole graveyard.

Nature is incorruptible, thought Farin, so long as people don't upset it too violently.

He looked at the remaining leaves on the beech tree with a critical eye. There were less than a quarter left hanging there, red, yellow and brown among the thin branches.

I'll be raking those leaves tomorrow.

His work was done for today. He passed by Gerlunda's grave with mixed feelings. Two days after they'd transported Pater Amen from the Cleft, the alderman, his father and himself had headed off to bring the preparer of poisons back. She was unceremoniously dumped back into her grave, and the old gravedigger had shovelled it closed.

Lost in thought, Farin left the graveyard and took the path for home. He hadn't heard or seen any more of Annietta – the woman seemed as far away from him as the moon. Her whispered "you are the gravedigger's son" echoed in his ears. That said it all – good that she'd reminded him of that fact. Let her be happy with Blossak – although he hadn't caught sight of him for some time either. The days were becoming colder and darker, which was why people spent more time huddled away in their houses. The voice was right in one respect – nobody in the village had mentioned his brawl with Peat and his three fine friends yet. The monotony of the day did Farin good. His mind came to rest, which clearly meant the voice rested too. Did chimeras hibernate, like hedgehogs and squirrels?

Father had kept his word and bought peasant boots made from goatskin for them both. Had he sold the ring stolen from the priest for this purpose? More likely not, because he would have had to travel to a town far away. This dilemma bothered him more than he cared to admit. Theft was theft and always wrong. Still, he wore the shoes. Better not to find out what money father had bought them with.

The sun was shining, but the fresh wind was well and truly blowing past his ears. He thought with envy of the felt cap most of the villagers wore. He rubbed his hands together vigorously and then rubbed his ears. The warm oven in the cottage invited him, so Farin increased his speed. Warm up and eat something…and then? He didn't know – his life was tottering aimlessly along, sometimes with him, sometimes without him, sometimes passing him by. Between fulfilment of duties and boredom, between morning and evening it gurgled along like the stream running past the graveyard.

Except that the stream eventually sees the sea.

He saw four riders galloping towards him from a distance. No, three riders and another nag. There was no need for warming up by the oven, Farin could feel a sudden heat, wherever it came from, shooting through his body. Three riders! Strangers! A quick decision and he was diving into the bushes by the side of the road.

Hopefully they didn't spot me.

The strangers maintained their speed and it wasn't long before they'd reached his hiding place. It seemed they hadn't noticed him.

Strange sounds could be heard: "Mhrrmm, mhm, mhrrm!"

The next moment one of the men raised his arm. "Understood! Halt!" he called out in a high voice. The other riders brought their horses to a stop at exactly the same spot.

"Mmmh!" A man, not much taller than a child, pointed at his hiding place.

"There's someone hiding there in the bushes and it seems he doesn't want to be seen!" The speaker issued a command: "Come out of there whoever you are!"

How naïve again! They didn't spot him, my eye! First, you're taken in by appearance, then by hope. How many more times are you going to fall for things, Farin?

With a leap Farin threw himself out of the other side of the bushes and ran cross-country towards the rocky ground at the foot of the Anvil, an area impassable for horses. Once he reached there, he could shake them off.

The three men reacted quickly, yanked their horses around and galloped around the bushes after him.

"THAT MUST BE HIM!" heard Farin behind him among the thundering of horse hooves.

One of the riders was upon him within moments. Farin could see out of the corner of his eye that he was swinging an axe around over his head. They wanted to kill him.

The first rocks. Farin managed to jump with a great leap onto a rocky projection. This gave him a slight advantage as the horses were forced to veer around in an arc. He jumped at full speed from one rock to the next. His pursuers cursed loudly.

The Cleft, I have to make it to the Cleft!

He knew it like the back of his hand – the terrain offered plenty of escape routes, especially as the horses would be useless to his enemies. The entrance to the chasm was like an enormous, inviting gate to freedom. His lungs were screaming for a rest, but it was too soon for that. The men rode with great skill around the rocks and were still hot on his heels.

The panting of his breath beat out the pace of his steps. Only another hundred yards. Then his pursuers would have to dismount and could forget their horses. The sun had dried the rocks, otherwise he would surely have slipped on the smooth stone and fallen. As nimble as a mountain goat he reached the entrance to the chasm. The raven wouldn't catch him, not today.

Other rules applied in the Cleft, Farin's rules.

And I'm going to introduce them to you, you bastards. How about an avalanche of boulders as a surprise?

The walls of rock narrowed. He was almost there. Farin raced towards the saving chasm. Something hard hit him on the back of his head – a missile. He bit his tongue. The unmistakable taste of iron filled his mouth. Now he was bleeding yet again because other people wanted it, for reasons he didn't understand.

Only ten more paces to the narrowest point.

He hardly felt the stinging in his skull. His pursuer mustn't have hit him full on. Farin ran on.

Only five more paces.

He only managed three more paces before his knees buckled. He stumbled forward, the rocks spun around him – where was up, where down? He felt no pain as he hit against stone. Was that the ground at all that he had fallen on? He could only see a black hole.

"That's him! We have him!" sounded a voice triumphantly above him.

Then his hearing and feeling darkened too, Farin sank down into nothingness.

The world wobbled, shivered, rocked! And it was black and smelled of turnips. His stomach and back muscles ached and screamed for release. It took a while – a minute or a week – hard to say, before Farin understood. He was lying on his stomach, hanging across the back of a horse and they had covered his head with a rough hemp sack. Bits of earth were tickling his face. It was difficult but he was getting air, which meant he was alive. Intentional or accidental? Maybe that wasn't important as he would die shortly anyway. The human body didn't take it too well if its skull were opened and its chest folded open from the neck to the bellybutton like the shutters of a window.

Quite apart from the fact that Farin had never learned how to ride a horse, this position induced torture, especially if the horse was trotting. He hopped about and up and down in a completely uncontrolled manner on the horse's bony back, his stomach feeling as though it had been run over by a cart and four. His head too.

Hopefully, I'll lose consciousness again.

Of course, unconsciousness never came. Farin decided to strike the word "hopefully" from his vocabulary, at least for what remained of his foreseeable life.

Its place was replaced by naked fear, along with its companions: bad reproaches and good intentions.

Why didn't I flee much earlier? Fate had given me the opportunity after I'd overheard this unscrupulous man in black. The riders were coming from the gravedigger's cottage. What had they done to father? Why didn't I say something to father and warn him?

The men spurred their horses into a gallop. Farin's pains eased a little. The movements of the horse's back at the faster pace felt like a gentle rocking in comparison to the previous trotting.

Should he scream? Make them aware that he had woken up and ask them to pull the sack off his head? How naïve – in all probability they'd kill him on the spot.

The back of his head droned and pounded. No wonder – he was lying upside down and the blood was streaming in. Too much of a good thing, it was flooding his brain, he was getting dizzy.

The gravedigger's son was lying stretched out on the cold ground with his hands bound – still, at least someone had tossed a horse blanket over his body. He could sense warmth on his left side, and he could hear crackling. Farin slowly turned his head, he could see a brightness now. The three men must be sitting around a cosy fire.

"I hate the cold!" cursed the man with the high voice. "Why does our little lord always give us these jobs in the middle of winter?"

"Because he likes riding around in the summer. Just don't let him hear you calling him *little* lord. You know what his punishments are like."

"Don't remind me. If you don't tell him, he'll never know. Stump will keep his mouth shut anyway. Isn't that right, Stump?"

"Hrm."

A new voice said: "Thanks be to God! You saved our bacon by hitting the lad with the throwing axe. That chap could really run, nearly as fast as us on our galloping horses." For a while only the fire crackled. The same man asked thoughtfully: "What would have happened if you'd hit him with the sharp end?"

"Dead, what else?" said the high voice.

A shudder ran down Farin's body.

"We were supposed to capture him alive."

"Listen to me now. If I want to hit him with the blunt side, then I throw the axe so that I hit him with the blunt side."

That sounded logical and luckily it had worked out that way.

"We have him, and he's alive, and that's the main thing."

"So, no problem – he's going to reward us!"

"If only he wasn't so unpredictable…"

How could it be otherwise? Of course, the men were afraid of the man in black. The hook nose, the thin lips, the murderous eyes, there was nothing good about that guy.

"Why does he want the young gravedigger? He can't do anything."

"Yes, he can. Run away like a hare. Maybe to use him as a beater in the hunt."

"Ha-ha, as bait."

Silence for a moment.

"We'll be back in the fortress tomorrow afternoon", said the man with the high voice, breaking the silence. "We only needed four days – he'll be happy."

"He'll claim he would have done it in three."

"Hm, possibly; probably true too."

"Yup, more than likely. Cos he's the most hard-nosed dog I know. Sometimes it's scary."

"His rage spurs him on."

"Exactly. And when is ever *not* enraged?"

Farin's fear seemed to have sloshed over to the men.

"Stump, go over and check if our prisoner's woken up", said the man with the high voice. He seemed to be the leader.

Farin quickly slowed his breathing. These hombres shouldn't find out that he'd been listening in the whole time. He felt cool, stubby fingers at his neck.

"Mhmmmm," an indefinable voice called out.

"Aha, he's playing dead. Thinks he's really smart, lying there listening in. A pity the unconscious can't eat or drink. And they have to go on riding on their tummies too."

"Do you think our little friend has stolen something from our boss, and he wants to punish him?"

"Maybe. We haven't had a decent execution in the castle for yonks."

"Maybe he'll have him hanged – in this cold weather he could swing in the wind until spring before he starts to stink."

"He's stinking already."

Nobody spoke for a while. Then the hombre with the high voice asked: "What does our boss want with a grave-digger?"

"Beats me. But there's no doubt he wants him – and once he has an idea in his head…"

"Then nobody can stop him. For him there's only one court of appeal in this world."

"We'll find out soon enough what he plans to do with the gravedigger. Make sure he stays with us tonight."

What did that mean? Something rustled beside him. Out of nowhere a closed fist slammed into Farin's left temple.

He was never going to recover from this torture. Every time a hoof touched the ground the pains would shoot up his body. And on a long ride the horses did nothing else *but* touch the ground, again and again as they trotted along. Like yesterday, he was hanging across the animal's back with the most fetching turnip sack over his head. No matter how hungry he might get, he would never eat turnips again. A hellish journey of hellish torture. Awake enough to feel the pain – unconscious enough not to understand what was happening around him.

"We're nearly there," said the high voice joyfully. "I'm looking forward to a hot bath."

Voices from above, the clanking of chains, something heavy was moving, creaking, squeaking, with a lot of power. Could it really be? A drawbridge?

The horse hooves echoed loudly a few times on wood before the ground became solid again. They drew to a stop.

"Into the dungeon with him until I've found the lord of the castle."

Several strong hands grabbed Farin and pulled him off the horse. They tried getting him onto his feet, but it was useless – he buckled every time.

"That's enough!" said the high-voiced leader. Two powerful hands grabbed Farin and tossed him over a shoulder like a sheaf of corn. Somebody toted him through passageways and stairwells. Less and less light made its way through the coarse texture of the sack.

Would he ever see the sun again?

He was dropped roughly and landed with a crash on a straw-covered stone floor.

The man groaned. It was the hombre with the high voice. "The lad stinks like a boar and is as heavy as a cow. If he wants to hang 'im high, he's going to need a strong bough."

No problem – no hanging, just slicing, thought Farin.

A door banged, and metal pushed along wood.

There he was now, lying in a dungeon, far away from home, the damn turnip sack still pulled over his head, his hands bound behind his back. The straw smelled damp and musty, which had something to do with the fact that it *was* damp and musty. He could see nothing. Since when did dungeons bask in glorious sunshine?

The only thing he had was fear. He didn't want to die. Would crying be worth a shot now?

Crying is pointless.

To top it all he now had the chimera for company.

I left you alone for a moment, you were absolutely adamant about it.

"Leave me alone and stay away for ever," sobbed Farin.

That would be easy. "For ever" seems to be a quite manageable timescale in your case. It doesn't look as though you're going to live to be a hundred.

"Help me or piss off."

What's with the new tone now? All of a sudden I'm good enough to be allowed to help. My hands are bound just like yours. Oh yes — because my hands are your hands. And I can't see anything either. The sack covering our head is interfering.

"My head!"

Alright, if that makes such a big difference now and is so important to you — your head, your hands, your feet, your problems, your death.

"You're still smarter, stronger and better in every aspect then me, can't you think of anything that might help us?"

I couldn't agree more with the first part of your speech. The answer to your question in the rear end, I'll answer with a simple no, because I won't help you!

"Basically, the man in black is on your heels. Doesn't that bother you?"

Not like you.

"Because it's not you who's going to be sliced open." Farin's despair was growing. He whispered: "Oh God, I'm terrified."

Please stop calling on the gods. They're not going to support you.

"What do you mean, gods? Are there more of them?"

At least two – obviously.

"Not to me."

It's the logical explanation why God won't help, no matter how often you invoke him.

"You've lost me – are there one or two?"

There have to be two, because the one is always relying on the other to take action. Which is why neither helps in the end.

Farin quit these observations with a groan. Here he was in a dungeon arguing with the voice in his head over spiritual and secular matters.

And the chimera wouldn't give up its spiritual sagacity: *Which is why you should primarily believe in yourself in such situations, and afterwards, as far as I'm concerned, in God.*

"That's what I'll do as soon as I'm out of here."

Hm, which came first, the chicken or the egg?

The gravedigger's son's eyes welled up with tears. The agony in body and mind was wearing him out.

Let me repeat: Believe in yourself, in your abilities.

Farin bawled out: "You're disgusting! Stop laughing about it all. I am nothing, I can do nothing!"

Naïve, this compassion towards yourself, and this self-pity. You should wean yourself off these things.

If Farin had his hands free at that moment, he would have ripped off his head, chimera and all. Still, at least his rage against the sarcastic know-all helped him overcome his moment of despair. "My world consists of a turnip sack."

That makes sense. To a worm, the world consists of an apple. Keep burrowing and think outside the crate.

"You couldn't wait to help me when it came to Peat and his three henchmen. You had great fun beating them to a pulp. Why won't you do anything now?"

Sounds from outside the cell made him start. His pulse began racing. Bolts were pulled back, and the door opened with a squeak. Bootsteps neared. As he couldn't see anything, pictures of the world were painted for Farin. They were dripping with horror and blood. The man in black was bending over him with his dagger and a look of enjoyment on his face, grinning horribly and considering what he should start with — the head or the chest. The next painting showed how he was picking away with his hooked nose at Farin's entrails, like a flock of crows.

Powerful hands reached under his armpits and sat him up.

"Do it quickly," Farin wanted to say, but no sound came out of his parched mouth.

ambivalent

Vigo lay on the clay floor of the arena like a lamb to the slaughter. The champion of the peregrines loomed over him like an enthusiastic executioner preparing for the coup de grâce.

Zorrghorozza and Borghezza! Vigo is a complete idiot!

A hopeless situation and thrown like a towel in the ring. He had to address the problem – should he defend himself?

The pupils in Torem's hideous, lascivious eyes gave the game away: the principal knight of the peregrines wasn't going to be happy with a single strike, he was going to dismember the champion of the stone dragons using his enormous sword with great gusto, serve him in slices on a platter to his king. Like most people, Vigo bristled mightily at the thought of his own death.

Understandable – they didn't know what awaited them afterwards. People strove for certainty and as little change as possible. And although death was a certainty, it changed everything.

"True power determines truth, which neither of us can contend with", Torem had said. First, he had behaved as if he couldn't count to two, but then he'd started philosophizing. The giant's arrogance irritated him. Another reason to kill him.

Mock away, mortal being. Pour oil onto the fire of your own pyre. A lightning move by me will turn you to ashes.

Should he really do it? One last time? But Vigo hadn't *earned* it.

There was no time left for thinking or talking, only time for living or dying. For killing or being killed. Controlled rage, born out of heat, created the breeding ground for overwhelming power.

The two-handed sword came racing down, he rolled to the side, an unspectacular sound as the blade thudded into the empty ground. Why was Vigo holding his weapon in his left hand? He pushed his sword into his right one. A bending in his shoulder – dislocated joint. A blow with his left fist and the humerus slotted back into its socket. An incredibly painful action for a normal human, a bat of an eyelid for him. He observed his enemy with eyes narrowed.

Your soul is nothing more than black slime, a speck of dust floating in the air, fleeting as a fart, as irrelevant as a boar's breath in a bora.

Glares clashed into each other as sword and shield had done before. A light flashed across Torem's eyes, betraying a spark of irritation.

Irritation leads to doubt, and doubt breeds more doubt, and badgers self-belief.

How could it be that the already condemned, moribund, presumed-to-be-dead man was standing opposite him again with a murderous look in his eyes?

Torem was already winding up for his next deadly strike. Simple to avoid this one. One step back, half a twist left.

You'll catch a fly with your feet easier than you'll hit me.

A quick stab with the sword and he caught his opponent on his hip.

I don't know yet what I'll do, but I'll show you I can do it, mortal being.

The weapon pierced through the armour, a hand's span into the flesh.

The dismay on the faces of King Ekarius and his advisor Wineview seemed genuine. Why dismay? Their champion had just risen from the ashes, yet they both looked as if they were being plagued by toothache. The penny dropped – so that's the way of it, then. He'd studied those bearers of souls long enough so he wasn't in the least surprised by their malevolent malice anymore. Only Vigo, the naïve champion, had noticed nothing – such an inadequate shell, such an inadequate intelligence! It made him furious.

Vigo hadn't deserved it, he hadn't deserved *him*, how could the champion allow himself to be led such a merry dance? The fight, a real show, where it didn't matter what was shown, but who was shown up.

Look at your masters, Vigo. They've sold you short; they've sold themselves, and you're but a poor pawn in this fix of a game.

The mighty Vigo had disappointed him, too naïve, too presumptuous, too parochial. The faces of King Ekarius and his advisor Wineview gave the game away: they wanted to watch Vigo die. A pact of the powerful, a political game. Tarian Wineview had clearly worked this arrangement out with Grachus, the king of the Southern Kingdom on the occasion of his journey to Crossford. Offer up your own people for a life in the lap of luxury.

Should he kill Torem and thereby save Vigo? Or did pride come before the fall? The far-down, final fall.

***

Vigo was standing facing the enemy, a mere two paces away. He hardly felt the pain in his shoulder now, he could move his right arm again. He'd reckoned on that, but what next? He had let go after all…

He had to pay respect to his opponent's martial artistry, he had underestimated him. And Wineview had prepared him the wrong way too – had sent him to be destroyed out of his own self-interest. They had offered up their principal knight. His thoughts were spinning faster and faster. No wonder he was dizzy. The roar of the crowd flashed around him. He felt as if he were standing on the bridge of a sailing boat in a hurricane. He wouldn't go down without a fight. He bravely braved the storm.

Torem's flesh-wound in his hip was bleeding profusely but he didn't seem to be bothered otherwise. He swung his two-hander in circular movements behind his back in order to attack in a wide sweep – one-handed as before.

With gritted teeth Vigo turned to the left and placed his weight on his right leg. He had no choice, he had to evade the blow. Parrying was out of the question, his blade would in all probability snap. He turned on his standing leg like a dancer. The mighty weapon flew past.

He had let go after all…what was going on here?

Help me!

The blow of the two-hander deliberately missed, a feint then, enabling Torem to prepare for a follow-up. Vigo stumbled, avoiding a fall with two backward paces. Once again the two-hander was whizzing towards him, this time in a horizontal arc. He evaded this blow too with a dive. Now he lay on the ground and turned onto his back. How much longer would luck be on his side?

He had definitely let go.

Blood was streaming down Torem's leg, but the giant wasn't waning. Already he had his sword prepared for the death blow – nimble and precise in everything he did.

Once again Vigo lay on the deck of the arena and saw how his life was being ripped out of his hands. He only had a miniscule moment left to live if he didn't come up with something in double-quick time. It was too late for every thought that was flitting through his mind. He should have made an honest woman out of his beloved – Orelia was the most important woman in his life. Those traitors. Now, of all times, he turned his head towards the tribune. The scornful look from Tarian Wineview was more hurtful than any injury. Vigo, the principal knight, would die today as Vigo, the principal idiot. But it wasn't only his king and his principal advisor who had sold him short, also the soulless piece of dirt within him was allowing him to be slain.

Vigo filled his lungs, then roared at the top of his voice: "TREACHERY!!"

The acoustics in the arena strengthened his call as it echoed all around. The squelching reverberated too as the blade of the two-hander penetrated his chest. With a crunch it bored into the clay beneath him – a smooth puncture. With head bowed Vigo watched how the mighty blade practically bisected his body, it didn't hurt at all. The drop of sweat that fell on his face from Torem's forehead, on the other hand, did bother him. Disgusting.

A glance towards his king's tribune. Wineview nodded towards His Majesty. A short, self-satisfied gesture. The last gesture the principal knight of the house of the stone dragons saw in his life.

***

Boundless jubilation on the victor's side caused the arena to tremble. There was nothing the mortals like better than watching others slaughter each other for their enjoyment. As predicted, Torem prepared to hack Vigo's body into a hundred pieces. First, he wanted to separate his head from his body.

"Desist, Torem, principal knight of the peregrines." King Grachus had arisen and spread his arms out. "Vigo, the principal knight of the house of the stone dragons fought honourably. He died honourably and will be honourably laid to rest."

That much honour always makes me sick.

Torem turned his attention away from the body and walked slowly towards the tribune. He paid respect to his king with a bow and said: "Your will is my life."

"My principal knight has achieved victory. Open the gates to your new king."

Ear-splitting applause again. Most of the people on the opposite tribune cheered too. Impressive, how quickly the bearers of souls could change course, flags in the wind, weak-principled, weak-willed, weak-minded.

That's people for you. I've never seen it any other way.

The arena emptied, there was nothing left to see here. Silence fell, softly and gently as snow around him. He felt in the arms of something like peace.

Crunching steps neared him.

"Pablo, dismember the body and feed it to the dogs." Tarian Wineview, the principal intriguer, came into view.

"But sir, King Grachus mentioned an honourable burial," said one of the four servants accompanying him.

"A clever strategy to get the people on his side. Nobody will care about the loser tomorrow. King Grachus won't be here much longer, instead he'll be off on his next campaign of conquest. The new governor will be called Ekarius, and his principal advisor, Tarian Wineview. And the latter will feed you to the dogs as well if you ever contradict me again."

A clear statement. So clear that servant Pablo hunched like a hundred camels. Advisor Wineview yanked the sword out of Vigo's bent fingers, then left the venue while his henchmen organised a stretcher. They rolled Vigo's body onto it and carried him to the city gate.

"Throw the body into the dungeon, the executioner can deal with him there. I'm not dismembering him for the dogs", said Pablo.

The route went along several narrow alleyways, up steps, down steps, down more steps before the servants reached a damp smelling passageway. Pablo lit a torch of pitch before they headed deeper into the underground vault. At the end of the passage they laid him down on a hefty slab.

"Let's get out of here!" said the servants.

Soon they were gone and with them the light of the torch.

Darkness didn't bother him. Time didn't exist for him. And so he knew no waiting nor impatience. An hour or a century – what was the difference?

Noises. The door creaked open. Two women and two men stared down at Vigo's corpse.

Orelia sobbed: "It had to come to this." She tenderly closed Vigo's eyes. "Take him with you. And no noise. The bribes will be wasted if they catch us after all and feed Vigo to the dogs."

He couldn't see any more, but he heard the men groaning under the weight of the stretcher. A few minutes later and he was smelling horses; the little group came to a carriage. Vigo's corpse was pushed onto the cargo bed.

"Gerlunda and I will sit on the coach box. We'll meet tomorrow at the little church", said Orelia.

Vigo's final journey had begun.

negotiations

T he turnip-sack was yanked off Farin's head. The light of the torch seared his retinas. Blinded, he could only see three shadows. His eyes refused to adjust to the light.

Three silhouettes were looking down at him. The three men he had hidden from under the workbench in the gravedigger's?

"What have we got here, then?" somebody asked.

IT'S HIM!

Farin recognised the distinctive voice at once. Although the visit to Heap had been short, he would never forget it.

The dark outlines slowly transformed themselves into facial features. If there had been the slightest scintilla of doubt about who this person was, it vanished when not only the voice fitted, but also the appearance.

"He looks knackered. Bring him up and give him victuals and drink. Then have him bathed and freshly dressed. Then bring him to me."

Two voices murmured: "Yes, sir."

The man turned on his heels and left.

Farin was gobsmacked. It is him and it isn't him. Not the raven. He gasped. Not the man in black, not the murderer and Necorer. The knight! That's who it was! The jangling, door-from-its-hinges-bursting knight.

Don't fall unconscious again, gravedigger's son.

Farin couldn't make head nor tail of anything anymore.

Mutely, he allowed himself to be led through dark, cold passageways. Then he climbed up a few steps, obediently placing one foot after the other, and then went along a cold hallway. Concentrating hard, he managed not to stumble despite aching muscles. He was able for nothing – not true! Hadn't he learned in early childhood how to go on two legs without falling over? An archway marked the entrance to a kitchen. The room struck him as an ideal location for life after death. Bright, warm, and it smelled of bread, roast meat and spices. The best explanation for his current state of mind: he had died earlier. Only – when exactly? On the horse, or not until the dungeon? The way he had been feeling, in both places.

If you were dead, I'd know about it. Now you know why I didn't need to help you.

If my life is going to carry on being so exciting, I'll never get rid of the chimera.

They sat him down on a chair and produced a pitcher of wine and a pitcher of water.

A man with a white apron and a white cap asked: "What will it be?"

"Wha...wha...?" A thousand questions were screaming for answers.

"As you wish." The man filled his mug with water.

Why the respect? Was there somebody else sitting at the table?

Only now did Farin dare to glance furtively at the three men in his vicinity. Standing beside the white-capped man was a large fellow with a leather chest-plate, leaning against the wall in a relaxed pose. Two bright eyes sparkled in his bearded face. A noble sword-hilt protruded from his belted scabbard, his trousers were studded from top to bottom, his boots were pointed at the front. A kitchen maid stood behind a long table, kneading dough with both hands. Her plump arms were glowing up to her elbows. Behind her on the wall hung all manner of knives, spoons, ladles, skewers, and pots of all sizes.

Farin clutched the mug in both hands and lifted it shakily towards his mouth. It didn't bother him how odd he must look.

"We still have the leftovers from dinner. Wild boar," explained the cook.

A striking, high voice gave instructions: "Lisa, bring him to the washtub. And tell Markan he should bring new clothes."

Farin secretly squinted over at him. It was the leader, who together with the two other men had waylaid him and brought him here, wherever here was. Robbed and transported like a sack of turnips in a turnip sack.

"Yes, sir." The maid wiped off the rest of the dough from her fingers, washed her hands in a basin and dried them on her apron.

It wasn't death that awaited him, but a bath.

Farin had never seen such a washtub before – at least five people could fit into it at the same time. The water steamed invitingly and smelled of lavender.

"What are you waiting for? Get in!" The man, who had introduced himself as Markan, shooed him onwards.

Farin undressed gingerly – tunic, trousers, shirt, peasant boots. Then he stood there in his plain, tattered underwear and waited.

"Everything off!" The corners of the man's mouth twitched. Farin wasn't used to undressing in front of strangers. Above all, he was ashamed of the condition of his clothes. He stripped everything off quickly, threw it in a ball onto the floor and climbed over a three-step ladder into the washtub. That is to say, he tried to climb in. Holy hell! As soon as he carefully dipped his toes into the water, he felt he was standing on burning coals.

"Ouch!" he hissed. Or was it his flesh hissing in boiling water? Farin quickly pulled back his foot again.

Markan looked at him with a sardonic, sparing, sharp look, although not angrily. The man leaned over the edge and plunged his hand into the water. "Exactly right. Don't be such a ninny."

Farin made a new attempt.

No, impossible. I might as well stick my legs directly into the oven. "If we leave it until tomorrow, the water might have cooled halfway towards normal bath temperature," he suggested.

Markan stood facing him, legs apart. "Oh, *now* I know what sir has planned for you. You're going to have to work hard on refining yourself and improving yourself considerably. He had the last court jester castrated because he couldn't make him laugh." He tapped his forehead with his forefinger. "Have I ever heard our lord of the castle laugh?"

What was going on here? Nothing in his life was running normally. And what sort of a figure was he cutting here, between the devil and the deep blue sea, riding on the edge of a washtub, one leg in, and the other one on the top step of the small ladder, while plumes of hot steam swirled around ears and nose.

Stop carrying on like that! You should try swimming in the lava lake on Gorrgrinnt.

Well, that's cold comfort. He peered over at Markan helplessly, whose eyes slowly began sparkling strangely. The man went towards the exit of the bathing room and called loudly down the corridor: "Lisa, come here again. Help our young visitor into the water."

In the middle of the steam, a head – red like a tomato – appeared through the fog. In an instant Farin pulled his other foot into the tub and his legs slipped in.

"AAAaaaaaaaah!" he screamed.

"Take your time, Lisa can't hear us, she's far away in the kitchen", said Markan reassuringly and left him alone.

You deceitful son of a mountain goat, thought Farin, almost forgetting his pain. His maltreated skin burned like fire and brimstone, and he believed…yes, what actually? His body was already becoming used to the heat. Slowly he let himself slide in more deeply, the warmth now flattered his chest languorously. His skin had survived the torture on the horse better than he'd expected. For the first time in ages he relaxed his body and sighed. Nobody in Heap would believe this story.

Is the whiny worm feeling better now?

"I've ended up at the knight's not at the raven's."

Trust in your abilities, was my advice to you. You could have found that out earlier.

"Of course – the sly chimera knows everything as usual, and of course it has to be before Farin."

Listening and thinking about things helps. You didn't recognise any of the voices. Do you think the raven wouldn't come himself, but take the risk of sending out three lowbrows? Do you really think a dark cultist would say: Thanks be to God! There were certain clues. All you had to do was listen.

Farin said nothing – he'd listened to the chimera and

wanted to ponder over it for a moment. He almost fell asleep in the bathtub.

When he was finished bathing, Markan gave him new clothes: underwear, leggings, a tunic, a wide leather belt – everything without decoration but made from good material. Of his own stuff, he only put on his peasant boots and belt pouch again.

Markan led him through bare corridors into a round room with six doors. Why would anyone need six doors? There was one door at home, and it had two functions. It led into the cottage and it led out of it again. That's all you needed – anything else seemed impractical to him. Markan banged on one of the doors with a carved fire-breathing dragonhead doorknocker. Farin would have liked to admire it for longer but Markan shoved him over the threshold, and immediately they were standing in the lord of the castle's scriptorium. For this much Farin had figured out already: he was in a castle. And if that wasn't enough of an adventure to be getting along with, he was now standing directly in front of the lord of the castle. He'll answer any other questions himself, the master of the washtubs had said.

"Stay here, mole. Markan, get out!" roared the knight. The quill in his enormous hand looked small and fragile.

"That's his way of saying thanks," whispered the servant as he slipped out of the room.

The lord of the castle concentrated on his visitor: "Are you wondering why I asked you to come in?"

"Forgive me, I…I wasn't *asked* in." Farin resisted any attempt to push out his upper lip by looking serious – he always looked terribly sulky when that happened.

The knight lowered his bushy eyebrows so that they

almost covered his bright blue eyes. "So what happened?"

Was the lord of the castle able to see him anymore?

"Uh, the...men chased me as if I were a wayward cow, stunned me with a throwing axe, tied me onto a horse and transported me here. Roughly and recklessly."

"Oh, that's terrible!" Shocked to the core, the knight held his hand before his mouth. His chiselled features softened – became blurred through sheer compassion. He asked gingerly: "Do you need anything?"

"No, not that, but..."

"A leg, an eye, teeth, fingers, toes?" The knight was sounding inconsolable now.

"Eh, no."

"Did they crinkle a hair on your head?"

"Eh, well, no...not exactly."

"Yes or no!"

"No."

The eyebrows slid back upwards again, the contours of the cheekbones sharpened; "I see it like this, then: they treated you with the utmost courtesy."

I should really keep discussions like this to the minimum, thought Farin. "But...but against my will", he managed to say, and somehow it sounded as brittle as the ice on the great lake in springtime.

"Aha! That's a new point. Let's summarise: courteously, yet against your will." The knight's voice shimmered with hawkishness – he'd tossed any element of empathy over the wall and into the castle moat.

"How else can I call it if...if I'm knocked down first and then abducted. Nobody had discussed it with me."

The eyebrows pushed together. "You're a primitive, lousy mole, no more, no less." His look could freeze water.

He wasn't going to let himself be dealt with like this, not by anybody. "I might be only a simple gravedigger, but I'm neither lousy nor a mole, Sir Knight."

"You can go! GET OUT!" The eyebrows shot up and down as if they wanted to beat Farin.

"What? What do you mean? Go where?" he asked.

"What's so difficult to understand about the three words "you can go"? Get lost! Go home, to your village!" explained the knight, vexed.

"You mean, I…uh…can leave your castle…anytime?"

The broad chin of the man facing him lifted and sank twice. The feelings in Farin spun around chaotically like the leaves in the graveyard. Endless questions had raged in his head a moment ago, now words failed him.

Repeat the question three times, just to be sure.

The thunder now companioned the storm: "YOU CAN GO! Run back to your pigsty, go and delicately dig ground-breaking holes."

"My apologies, I understand, Sir Knight. You collected me most courteously and now naturally I've arrived here of my own free will. No doubt about it. Please let me know for what purpose?"

The lord of the castle's look softened somewhat – what had been steel, was now iron. He leaned back and explained, seething softly: "I'm making you an offer."

Now it's getting interesting. Relax and prick up your ears!

Farin swallowed hard: "An offer?"

"I know what I said. So you don't have to parrot me. There are enough toadies around here."

When it came to knights, or at least this knight anyway, it was a good idea to consider one's words carefully. Farin made a firm decision not to repeat anything anymore.

"I need a new squire!" said the knight.

"A new squire?"

Inside Farin's head it sighed.

Frustration froze the knight.

Farin hastily asked a question in a bid to thaw him out: "What happened to the old one?"

"Dead!"

"How?"

"Very dead."

"What do you mean?"

"Passed away, departed, kicked the bucket – you should know all about that subject."

"Uh. May I ask how…?"

"NO!" roared the knight.

Farin continued to beaver away with utmost concentration. Only skilful rhetoric worked here. He had to find out some more about his future tasks.

Ask questions, good questions, intelligent questions. It chuckled. *Ground-breaking questions.*

"Am I not too old to be trained as a squire?"

A sigh at the back of the head. *Are you not listening?*

"Too curious more like. Nobody is too old to serve. Right then – agreed?"

"Sir, I feel honoured and…well, it's just so unexpected. What made you think of me specifically?"

At last, a moderately decent question!

The brows dropped over the eyes again like clouds before the sun. "Pesky inquisitiveness is one of the twenty deadly sins."

"Pastor Amen always spoke of the seven."

"He with his dual functions treated all seven with contempt and still never knew a fraction of what I've seen and experienced. I possess at least a dozen deadly sins."

"Please help me to understand. Why did you pick out the son of a gravedigger from a one-horse village?"

The knight sighed deeply. "There are few things in this world that can still surprise me. And people not at all. But you really succeeded during my visit to the graveyard."

"What do you mean? Surely not because I can shovel like a mole?"

"If you can't work it out, then you don't belong here." The knight's rough tone reminded Farin of his father.

"Because I found all that out about the raven and Gerlunda."

"Right! There you go. It comes from observational skills and combinatorics."

That's what I meant by "trust in your abilities".

Farin looked irritated. He was used to other people's words hurting him. These words sounded like praise, they caressed and did no harm, but good.

This moment passed all too quickly for with the next breath the knight continued: "Now, forget what I've said. I hate flattery. Do you remember when we stood in front of the tavern after our meeting at the graveyard? Didn't you want to ask me to take you with me?"

Bull's eye. That was exactly what Farin had attempted to ask at his departure, but the knight hadn't permitted him.

"Yes, sir." The man was more sensitive than Farin had thought. He raised his head.

"Now you're here, squire."

"What does a squire do exactly?"

"In the first place, serve his master and learn. A good squire helps him in many ways, from pulling off boots to advice on strategy. He accompanies the knight during acts of war and carries his shield. He helps him onto the horse and, if necessary, onto the chamber pot."

Farin hardly dared to utter his thought: "Can…can a squire become a knight too, later?"

The lord of the castle rolled his eyes. His brows accompanied them. "Forget it! Fat chance of you ever becoming a knight. You can't fight, can't ride, can't hunt, can't even fart like a knight. You know neither the courtly form of address nor the courtly virtues. And to top it all, you're not nobility, you're the son of a gravedigger." He pulled his eyebrows together. "You can retrieve my corpse and decorate it, that you can do. Enough talk, squire!"

The knight really knew how to present his offer gracefully.

Farin looked around. "Where am I, Sir Knight?"

"In my castle, Stormwatch, a place of permanence, a rock in these difficult days."

"Who are you?"

"Question after question. You know who I am. A knight of our King Grachus." His tone became impatient. "Lesson one: when a knight says *enough talk*, then the discussion is coming to an end. Enlightening, isn't it?"

"Your name is Emicho and you're the second knight, am I right?"

The man hesitated, his eyes narrowed – suddenly he looked like a feline predator ready to pounce on its prey. "One of my servants may have revealed my name to you. The trifle regarding me being the second knight, on the other hand, is a well-kept secret. I hate being surprised. Out with it – how do you know?"

"The raven told me."

The knight slowly rose from his chair. Farin had forgotten how big and impressive he was. Big and impressive like a thundercloud directly over your head. Despite his confusion, and the mood swings that made thinking difficult, he noticed that there was something more behind the story of the second knight.

The lord of the castle snarled: "Let me make one thing clear: the raven didn't tell you, because then you'd be dead and couldn't tell any fairy tales, lad. How did you find out that I'm the second knight?"

Farin explained in detail how he had hidden under the workbench and overheard the discussion between the raven and his accomplices.

The lord of the castle listened, stony-faced. When Farin finished, he said: "Inviting you here to my castle has already paid off. Following on from your remarks, I'm asking myself how the raven knows the identity of the second knight. I've been spied upon for a considerable time now – but he can't know this particular detail. Accordingly, there must be a traitor within the inner circle of the king."

Farin didn't understand a word. "Of the…the king?"

Emicho sighed.

For Farin king was a word like God, like ocean, like knight, like Annietta. Something endlessly distant, unattainable.

"You will never again mention the second knight in connection with my name – is that clear?"

"Yes, sir!"

"So, you accept my offer!"

It sounded more like a command than a question. "Your squire? I…uh…feel honoured. Do I get paid something for it?"

The lord of the castle grunted. "Pshaw! Think of where you come from!" He clarified more quietly: "A roof over your head, something to eat, an apprenticeship, honourable duties, and beatings only when you've earned them – isn't that enough?"

Don't sell yourself cheap. You have to start negotiating sometime in your life. Shake your head!

Farin slowly shook his head.

The lord of the castle folded his arms. "Mole, you're hardly in a position to haggle. I say a price and it's written in stone – is that clear?"

Farin nodded.

"After a successful apprenticeship I'll give you eighteen silverlings."

If he calculated carefully, these eighteen silverlings were just about eighteen silverlings more than he earned at present.

"Agreed", he said contentedly. Then another thought struck him. "How long does the squire training take?"

The knight bared his teeth. Was he making an attempt at a grin?

"If you carry on like this – all your life."

It was a grin. A pretty pathetic one.

"Oh!" said Farin.

training

Dumbfounded, Farin departed from the scriptorium. Markan received him outside the door and brought him to a room where two servants were depositing wine barrels. He instructed one of them: "Accompany our Johnny-come-lately into his quarters. South tower, fourth room."

"As you wish, sir."

The master of the bathtubs seemed considerably higher in the pecking order than the other servants. Dog-tired and overwhelmed by the events of the last few hours, Farin trotted behind the servant. Having just escaped death by the skin of his teeth he was now a living squire. An apprentice squire, to be precise. Unease gripped him – this was all going far too fast. He had learned gravedigging. The skills of his craft would certainly not be in demand here, at least not as long as the knight was living. Two grey towers within the thick walls cast dark shadows across the castle. Wherever he looked, his new surroundings seemed colourless. Thick, cold, grey stone as far as the eye could see. Or did he feel uncomfortable because he knew nobody here? When it came to the villagers in Heap, he knew where he stood, there wasn't a single face unfamiliar to him. Although he had to be honest with himself – what use was it if the familiar faces turned away as soon as he turned up? Would he miss any of the villagers? Blossak? No. Georig? No. The alderman? No.

Maybe Growler? Even the ropemaker's dog couldn't stand him anymore ever since an unwelcome chimera had begun plaguing Farin. He listened in on himself, but felt no foreign presence, only his own grey thoughts. He was already fitting in well to his new surroundings.

Who else would he miss? He'd left *her* out of his thoughts so that he wouldn't be thinking about her – Annietta. But how could he think about not thinking about her without thinking about her?

The servant pulled up the collar of his uniform. "We're going through the little yard. If you would follow me, please."

Was the servant really talking to him? Hey, don't be pulling my leg. I'm no fine gentleman. I'm only Farin, the gravedigger's son – I'm one of you, was on the tip of his tongue.

The servant opened a chunky door into a cobbled inner yard. Cold wind whipped around the grey walls, Farin shivered. They stopped at the smaller of the two towers. Worn steps wound their way in circles upwards, they passed three doors before the servant stopped outside the fourth: "Your quarters, sir."

Once again, he was having a laugh at him by calling him sir. A doorknob, almost too big for a hand, jutted out. Farin turned it leftwards, the door opened, and he stepped into a small room, where a simple bed and a mid-sized wardrobe were squeezed in.

"Be ready tomorrow early at the sixth hour". The servant disappeared down the stairwell.

Still perplexed, Farin sat down on the bed's straw mattress. So many unanswered questions – mainly because he hadn't asked them yet. His life was constantly blindsiding him no matter what he did, and he was just watching from the side-lines. He couldn't even lay the blame on the chimera's doorstep – he alone was responsible.

He lay on his back, his arms behind his head. His stomach muscles reintroduced themselves to him – they hadn't forgotten the uncomfortable ride. Lying still, his eyes wandered. Grey, bare stone walls – what else did he expect. Rough wooden beams supported the low ceiling.

Slowly, the tensions of the previous few days eased off, his chaotic inner life began putting itself in order. And so, the naked fear of not surviving disappeared, for his new employment offered a distinct advantage: he was safe from the raven here for the time being. But another fear grew in his head – that of the new. How would he fare here? What lay in store for him? Could he fulfil the knight's expectations? Difficult to judge, as he didn't know them yet. These were his quarters now as a budding squire. He'd heard stories of boys at the royal court who had started off as pages at seven years of age, then they were squires by fifteen and became knights when they were twenty-one. How was he going to fit in here? There was something not quite right about the story of the lord of the castle and his new employment. And yet he would happily polish swords and saddle the mighty charger. Exhaustion finally drew him into a deep sleep.

Urgent hammering at the door. "Sir, you must get up. Your tasks await you."

What was that? Which sir? What tasks? Where am I?

With one hand he threw the woollen blanket off the bed. The coldness in the room surprised him. He quickly put on his new clothes, which Markan had given him yesterday after his bath. They were finished in sturdy linen; neither the leggings nor the tunic had any holes or were threadbare. Finally, he threw the fur cloak which had been hanging by a hook on the wall over his shoulders. Strange – he hadn't noticed it yesterday.

"If you would kindly follow me?"

They all spoke the same way, Farin studied the servant who collected him this morning and was leading the way – a different one to yesterday's although he wore the same uniform. He had a shambling walk and a sunken head. In the long food hall of the main house there were rows and rows of benches. Roughly thirty men had gathered for breakfast.

The servant bowed. "This is where the soldiers, the officers, the knights and their squires eat. If you would kindly fortify yourself with food and drink."

Farin didn't have to think long about that one. He thanked the servant and entered the hall. Some looked questioningly at him, then back at their opposite number. "Who's that now?" he heard, sometimes whispered, sometimes out loud.

A chap with a wide nose and a pointy chin stepped in front of him and stood there, straddle legged. "Hey, you must be Emicho's new lover-boy!"

Farin tried desperately not to look as embarrassed as he felt. He bided his time.

"There's a rumour going around you're a…gravedigger."

Well, that news had spread quickly, and both the attitude of the man and the way he had intoned "gravedigger" betrayed that this fact didn't exactly impress him.

Farin had no intention of hiding the truth. "I'm the gravedigger's son from the village of Heap."

Disgust disfigured the man's face. "I don't know what

you've fooled the lord of the castle into believing, but you're not welcome here, ditch delver."

Spittle sprayed from his mouth. Farin felt the wetness on his cheek.

Stand your ground. I'm the squire of the lord of the castle, he thought.

"I go by the name of Farin. Now that my identity has been clarified, with whom do I have the honour?" he asked in a composed voice.

"Listen to him, listen to him! His identity has been clarified. Our newbie is flattering himself that he's a flatterer. Remember my name: I am Duke Turgenson, of high-born heritage. The nephew of old King Grachus! And above the old king there is only God."

It took Farin a while to take in the words. The nephew of the king! A duke.

God help me, he thought. What have I stepped into here? What should I do now? Make a bow, bend the knee, or both?

Never stoop down before arseholes.

Oh, great. The all-knowing chimera has another great piece of advice ready just at the right moment. But it wasn't the chimera who was standing in the middle of all these strangers, being gawped at as if he were a freak – thanks to the utterances of the duke. Farin stared back – never before had he seen such a high-ranking nobleman in the flesh. The fact that the others hadn't sunk to the ground in awe calmed him down a little, and so he simply remained standing. Apart from a nobly embroidered doublet, Turgenson looked neither all-knowing nor almighty. His care-worn features betrayed unfulfilled ambitions and a permanent discontentment. And to think that Farin had always believed that the aristocracy spent the whole day smiling happily.

Now he just had to sit down – allow body and mind to digest things. Anything he was going to say at this moment was going to be wrong. "Please let me pass, sir", the gravedigger's son said to the king's nephew. He made a reasonable fist of keeping his voice sounding firm although he was shaking on the inside. The other men and boys had returned to their eating, as though he didn't exist.

Only yesterday evening he had been mouthing off about it – unknown faces becoming familiar so quickly. As the aristocrat didn't move an inch, Farin went around him, secretly searching out a free place at the dining table.

"I'm on to you, low life!" whispered Turgenson after him.

Why would a duke be bothered about a nobody like me? Grouching around the place and threatening me.

There was hardly anybody in the castle lower and less important than the gravedigger's son.

A high voice rang out beside him. "Our Johnny-come-lately is awake. Get yourself something to eat and join us, back over there by the window." The man in the studded armour disappeared in that direction.

Farin nodded in surprise. Was his kidnapper's invitation meant seriously? Friendliness or fiendishness? He decided to be particularly careful – after all, they could be pulling a fast one on him. Who knows how many of the king's relatives are gathered here?

Farin quickly picked up a plate from the side table and put a few slices of bread onto it. Several men were sitting together at the end of the hall, the man with the high voice was waving him towards them. Right then, here goes, the leader of his escort party could certainly answer a few of his questions. The two men opposite pushed closer together.

Farin looked around quickly, he was the only one looking for a seat – they had actually made room for him.

Be careful, something isn't right here.

On the table were clay mugs and jugs of water. The big man poured some out for him.

Farin sat down. "You kidna…*escorted* me from my village and brought me here."

"That's right. Bring me the mole, the gravedigger's son from Heap! That was the order." He thought for a moment. "And keep him alive. The lord of the castle added that right at the end, when we were almost across the drawbridge." He grinned. "I take it we got ourselves the right mole."

The gravedigger's son from Heap rubbed the swelling on the back of his head. "Uh, yes – actually, my name is Farin."

"That'll do at a pinch."

"You were coming from our cottage when we…uh…met. Can you please tell me what you did with my father?" he asked.

"What do you think? We asked him where his son was. And he started giving out furiously and wanted to know what that unseemly yob had done wrong this time. We left him to himself and his rage."

That sounded familiar!

"How can I get a message to him? He needs to know that I'm fine."

"Have a word with the old man about it", suggested the big man with the high voice. "By the way, my name is Drogdan. And the other two friendly members of our riding party are sitting here too. The powerful clever clogs opposite is Plaudius. And tarrying to your right is Stump. He doesn't want to reveal what his real name is. Quite possible he's forgotten it."

Having gained all this new information, Farin looked at his table companions more closely. The one beside him was sitting on a fat cushion, otherwise he'd hardly be able to see above the table's edge. The brown eyes in his round head examined him curiously. The royal crest of the peregrines decorated his chest armour. A red-faced fat man was noisily chewing on his slices of bread-and-lard on the opposite side of the table. "Nishe excurshon, jush bit cold."

Farin recognised the second voice as the third one of his travelling companions.

Should he make a complaint about how he was manhandled? He decided against it – what good would it do now? "I enjoyed it too. I had my own horse, and a fine sack protected me against the cold."

"Ha! Now you're here. Why?" The fat man beside the leader chewed questioningly.

"Our lord of the castle doesn't want to hang you high, it seems, but have you as his shield bearer. How did he come to pick you of all people, a gravedigger's son from a hamlet in the arse end of nowhere?" asked Drogdan.

"To be honest with you, I don't really know why myself. Best ask him yourself."

The man shrugged his shoulders. "Get some food and drink into you first."

There were all kinds of spreads on the tables, one of which was glowing at him in a golden-yellowy manner. Was that honey? No, it couldn't be. Sweet, sticky, succulent honey – that was to be found more rarely at home than a polite word from his father.

Before he helped himself, he had to find something else out. "Where can I wash myself? Is there a stream nearby?"

Drogdan looked at him in amazement. "Stream? There's

no stream in the castle. Water comes from a well. You'll find it in the black courtyard, you can get a bucket there."

No stream, but honey flowing instead. Farin let the latter drip down onto his bread. "What are your tasks, sir?"

"Drop the formal address. We're all the knight's men here. I'm in Stump's unit, just like Plaudius."

Farin looked at the little man to his right in amazement.

Knight Stump is our commander, the best you can get", said the fat one, his mouth half-full.

Drogdan nodded. "I agree completely."

"Hrm." Clearly Stump had no objections.

A knight doesn't have to be big, thought Farin, surprised. Everything about this man was small except for his eyes, which were still looking him up and down. Luckily, he seemed satisfied with what he saw for he smiled softly, and his pupils glinted wisely.

Farin bit off a large chunk of his bread and chewed intently. Fresh bread – he kept on gobbling, who knew how long it would stay fresh, or if he'd get any more. The highborn Turgenson pointed at him with extended forefinger from the other end of the table, at which point a whole row of men fixed their hostile eyes on him.

"This Sir Turgenson – is he really a duke and a nephew of the king?"

"Hrm," confirmed the voice beside him. The furrow on Stump's brow deepened.

Drogdan nodded too. "He is, surely. Best not to tangle with him. If he has it in for you, your life will be hell here."

Oh, right!

For a moment Farin forgot his food. How could he have hit the bull's eye like that so soon after coming into the food hall. Should he tell the others he was already on the high-born's hit list? No, that would sound like complaining; he decided to bide his time for the moment and provide as few targets as possible.

"Sir, you…uh…I mean, you said the lord of the castle wants me as shield bearer. What does that mean?"

"You should bear his shield."

"Oh, yes…and apart from that? What else is he expecting from me?"

"Too much! You can be sure of that. Damn difficult, satisfying the old man. One of the few who manages to do it regularly enough is sitting to your right."

"Hrm."

"Because he has first-class people he can always rely on," continued Drogdan, looking cheerfully at the others.

Plaudius smiled too, but Farin's stomach felt queasy.

Drogdan noticed the shadow on his face. "What's up?"

"He expects *too much*? Too much sounds considerably more than too little", he said through gritted teeth.

"He's just demanding," proffered Plaudius and bit into his bread.

"What are you particularly good at doing?" asked Drogdan.

The man didn't want to mock him, he just wanted to motivate him by reminding him of his abilities.

While Farin considered the question, the big one probed further: "What's your area of speciality?"

"Uh, I…I'm good at washing corpses."

First they exchanged looks with each other, then the three looked at him.

"Oh, right. I don't think that's the reason he brought you here. If I know my lord at all, then he doesn't give a hen's shit what his corpse is going to look like." Drogdan pulled at his earlobe.

Stump beside him said: "Hrm."

"With which weapon can you fight best?" tried Plaudius.

"I…I'm a gravedigger. I never learned to manage a sword or a bow. Only a shovel."

Drogdan tilted his head back a little, a look at Stump, a look at Plaudius, the corners of his mouth were twitching. "One-handed shovel or two-handed?" He started to roar with laughter, Plaudius exploded too.

Some of the men in the middle of the table looked over curiously.

Once again it hadn't taken him long to become the target of mockery – he, the gravedigger's son, the newbie, the no-hoper. Farin lowered his head.

Drogdan quickly became serious again and nodded encouragingly towards Farin. "No harm done. We'll sort you out. Of course, you'll have to learn how to handle weapons. Really, you're too old for that. The pages already start fighting at six with their wooden swords."

I might stand half a chance against them, thought Farin. Uncertainty grumbled again in his stomach.

I have to look on all this as an adventure. An adventure where I can learn something. If they throw me out, I'll just go back to Heap. And no-one can take away the things I'll have seen and experienced up to then.

"Right, now we have to go to the army-master and get the watch schedule for the next few days." Drogdan got up from his chair. "See you later, Farin."

Stump and Plaudius nodded at him too, and the three left the hall.

Farin continued eating his breakfast with mixed feelings. He could get used to fresh bread and honey. He also took a big gulp of water. It tasted sandy somehow, not at all like the water from his stream. The hall slowly emptied. Just as Farin was wondering what he should do, he saw Markan coming towards him.

"His lordship is only expecting you this afternoon. We'll meet again on the eighth hour in the little yard in front of your tower, then I will lead you through the castle and to the squire's training grounds."

Back in his tower-room Farin braced himself for the worst. How would he measure up to the other squires, for example in sword-fighting, never having possessed his own sword? And he would also be one of the oldest, so his presence would definitely be horrendously embarrassing for him. He leaned over the wash bowl and half-heartedly rubbed his teeth clean with his forefinger. As he did so, he glanced out the narrow window. The view was sobering, just grey wall underneath the crenelated parapet. He nervously shifted from one foot to the other.

You need to calm down and stop moaning and groaning. It's definitely more interesting here than in Heap.

"That's easy for you to say, Mr Know-it-all. And before you vanish into thin air again, tell me who you are. And what you want from me." He hadn't intended the last sentence to sound so accusatory. But he couldn't stop himself expressing his anger at the uninvited visitor in his head.

That's exactly what I mean. One minute you're boring and the next you're impetuous and emotional. A wimp. And I'm not going to tell a person like that my name.

"But I'm the person in whose head you're rattling around. You're welcome to find a better one. As long as you're here, I'm going to call you Stinker. That suits you."

Sweet! I'd probably be gone if you hadn't thrown the amulet onto the fire.

Farin groaned when he heard that. "Let's move onto my second question. What do you want from me?"

Time is irrelevant when it comes down to it — and whenever it happens, it happens. Then I'll travel back.

"Back where?"

Home of course, to a dimension beyond this pathetic Worldly Kingdom.

"And why did you come here at all?"

There was a moment's pause before the voice explained: *Call it a dare, call it curiosity, call it audacity.*

"Call it dim-witted. Now I know where the word demon comes from."

Worm, whenever you try to be funny, it goes completely wrong. Do you want an answer to your question or not?

Was it possible for a chimera to be offended?

"Spill the beans — I'm listening."

We were summoned, in the middle of a most enjoyable drinking session, by a daemonic conjuration. How me and my mates laughed when we saw the amateurish portal that appeared out of the blue. We usually ignore such pathetic conjuration attempts, but I was intrigued to see its agent on the other side. And so, I stepped through the portal and found myself in your world.

"How does that work? And what's a portal?"

Imagine it as a gateway from one place to another, a dimension gate. In those days people referred to it as a daemon gate. They're usually made up of pentagrams drawn on the ground.

"Hm, how long have you been here already?"

A blink of an eye or eight hundred years — take your pick.

Farin gave a whistle in surprise. "Eight hundred years? That's an eternity."

From a human point of view – yes.

"What's keeping you here, and don't tell me that the mighty daemon wasn't able to go home in eight hundred years."

I'll ignore your infantile mockery. Daemons are crazy about magic, and there's supposed to be magic in the Worldly Kingdom. Unfortunately, I haven't found any up until now. No sorcerers, no warlocks, no spirits. Only the mean-spirited. Present company included.

"Pshaw. And the portal that called you?"

That bespeaks my magic.

"Hm." Farin considered his next question. "How many people have you planted yourself in?"

I've lost count. If I were to be doing with writing things down, I'd write about fifty. Speaking of doing the "right" thing, squire, you'd want to get a move on – you have an appointment.

Could that really all be true? The daemon had already spent eight hundred years causing trouble. Farin definitely wanted to learn more about the thing that was afflicting him. But now he had to fulfil his duties. Duties he neither knew of nor understood. He left his little turret room to get to know a whole new world. For that he needed neither a portal nor a conjuration nor a summoning nor a daemon gate.

the castle

As arranged, Markan greeted him at the eighth hour with a friendly bow at the foot of the south tower. The gravedigger's son followed him through countless corridors, up steps, down steps until they reached a large, vaulted room, both pleasant smelling and pleasantly warm. Farin watched the hustle and bustle, wide-eyed. There were at least thirty servants performing their daily chores – maids, cooks, and skivvies peeled and chopped, cooked and baked, cleaned and scrubbed. Senior maids, head chefs and major domos barked out orders although Farin was immediately under the impression that these instructions were unnecessary – everyone seemed to know what had to be done.

"The main kitchen. Let's keep going. And now it will get nippier."

Farin really didn't want to leave the commotion. But Markan simply marched onwards and so he had no alternative but to follow him.

"Now I'll take you up to the keep; we've a great view of the complex from up there." They entered the highest tower of Castle Stormwatch. By the time they were halfway up, Farin had given up counting the steps in his head. Once they arrived at the top, he was rewarded with a view so astonishing that he barely noticed the cold wind in his ears.

Markan, his hair blowing, pointed into the distance. "As you can see, the fortress was erected on a hill. A clear view of the countryside in all directions. Which means potential enemies can be spotted from a distance."

Farin liked the view. How beautiful it must look in springtime when the trees and fields became green.

"Can I see the sea from here?" he suddenly asked.

With the corners of his mouth turned down ironically, Markan explained: "The sea is to the south, four days' journey from here. No need to fear a tidal wave or flooding here."

Farin looked at the roof of the longest building in the complex curiously.

Markan followed his gaze. "That's the great hall with the sleeping quarters. Most of the castle residents live there." He pulled up his collar. "Peeking up directly behind it is the spire of the castle chapel. Do you see it? You have a complete view of the stronghold's defensive works from here."

Farin was still gobsmacked by the view. The outer wall of the fortress was softly curved and three yards thick across. He counted four open keeps, all projecting upward from the castle wall. The embrasures around each of them offered room for twenty archers. The keeps were connected by a crenelated parapet that ran along the entire inner wall of the fortress.

"Has the castle ever been captured?"

Markan shook his head in response. "Only once, when a principal knight lost in a duel. But that was more of a handover than a conquest."

Farin's eyes opened wide in astonishment. "Principal knight! Really?" Of course, he knew the tales that had flourished concerning legendary duels to the death.

"Nine duels over three hundred years in total. And only one fight was lost. Let's hope history doesn't repeat itself."

"Is there any danger of an attack?"

"Our lord of the castle is concerned by the Necorers in the south. More and more people are joining the cult and are forsaking the old king. This movement is working its way northwards like the plague a few years ago." The subject didn't seem to please Markan, who changed to a new one. "There's still lots to see – follow me! I'll show you the castle gate now with its shield wall, the drawbridge facility and the outer ward."

They climbed down the spiral staircase again. Farin was most fascinated by the enormous drawbridge across the castle moat, which was not filled with water, unfortunately, but with the products from the privies directly above. Consequently, it stank unmercifully. Farin's nose was used to being afflicted by stenches – it didn't bother him one bit. Streams of people were entering and leaving the castle via the lowered drawbridge. The chains fixed to the far end were as thick as Farin's legs, and they led through two gaps in the castle walls to within. A horizontal pivot on the ground and an enormous winch with counterweights on the chains ensured the bridge could be hoisted rapidly.

"And, last but not least, I'll show you the font of all life."

The two entered a spacious courtyard. The fortress well was dead centre, an enormous circle with a tile-covered roof covering the perimeter of the well.

"Stormwatch is situated on a hill. The well must be very deep, mustn't it if it drops down as far as the groundwater?"

Markan seemed delighted at the question. "It took two years to complete. The workers had to dig down almost eighty yards."

When it came down to it, everything here was tall and deep, wide and long, thick and very thick. With a diameter of over three yards the well contained a very impressive hole. Here too there was hustle and bustle, servant after servant carrying their wooden pails to and fro.

"Let's go to the squires' training grounds."

Farin's mood worsened immediately but he dutifully followed Markan through dark passageways until they reached an inner courtyard full of wooden frameworks, ladders and ropes. There was no-one to be seen.

"Basically, every squire learns his craft from his knight. Which is why they're mostly scattered around the Worldly Kingdom. They only come to us for the last two months of their training so that they can clear the final hurdle. Then the castle is buzzing with people. And added to that, a special honour will be bestowed on us next spring."

"Go on, Markan."

The man clearly enjoyed his listener's thirst for knowledge. His voice became more emotional. "Our lord of the castle is going to host the grand tournament this time."

"Really?" The grand knightly tournament steeped in legend! Farin almost choked with excitement and amazement.

"For one week we will be the centre of the Worldly Kingdom. Some of the senior squires will be ceremoniously dubbed knights. And the best knights of the kingdom will compete against each other in jousting, the victor being selected in the grandest joust of the year. This grey, staid old pile has been slowly regaining its importance over the last while. We're proud that we've been granted permission to host the grand tournament on our castle meadows."

Farin asked: "Will I be allowed to watch?"

Markan looked at him in surprise. "Hm, as a squire you're not allowed to watch."

"Pity."

"As a squire you're in the middle of it. Firstly, you're by your knight's side – there's a lot to do during the competition."

That sounded exciting. "And secondly?" asked Farin.

"Secondly, you take part yourself – in the tournament of the squires. With lance and sword."

The gravedigger's son grimaced – if only he hadn't asked.

"I…I must confess, I don't know too much about my future tasks, let alone about my training."

"I never noticed." Markan grinned sympathetically. "The squires must dazzle in seven skills, just as a week has seven days. We're standing in front of the training grounds for the fourth discipline."

"Ah, and that would be?"

"Is it really that hard to see? Climbing up ladders, ropes and poles. Flexibly and fleetly. Very useful when taking a castle."

Well wasn't that just great – Farin would never have thought of something like that. Knights went into war for the king – and squires followed their knights. The war didn't care one way or another – but he'd be standing in the middle of it. Don't lose courage and look the facts straight in the eye. Trying to sound as calm as possible, he posed his next question: "What are the other six disciplines about?"

Markan looked at him, hands on his hips. "Do you know anything at all?" But then he softened when he saw Farin's perplexed face. "Apart from the obvious virtues like a firm belief and a pure heart, the squires learn to fulfil all that is required of them. First, mastery of weapon – at least sword and bow."

Farin nodded although he would really rather have shaken his head.

"Secondly, he must be able to swim and dive."

Completely insane, but he'd at least be able to manage those, he'd often gone swimming in the great lake, and it had been no problem diving down to the bottom.

"Third discipline: the squire has to know about horses and their care, not forgetting acquiring excellent riding skills."

You don't say. He was super at that too, especially on his stomach with a bag over his head. At this point he really didn't want to learn anymore about what the rest of the training involved.

Markan continued mercilessly. "Fourthly – the aforementioned climbing exercises." He pointed at the course. "Fifthly, a squire has to be in tip-top physical shape. He has to be able to wrestle, jump and run."

Farin nodded wearily. Anything about digging?

"Sixthly – he has to know the running order and rules of the tournament. He must be ready to take part in the bohort."

Bohort – laughable, no problem at all, he could bohort like no other. He just had to find out what it meant.

Suddenly Markan was quiet.

Farin agonized over whether he should risk asking about the seventh skill.

Markan chuckled before relieving him of the decision: "The last one I've yet to describe – for some it's the king of disciplines. A squire must be in possession of the best manners, be able to pay court, dance, and entertain the ladies with gallant conversation in any situation."

Hee-hee, no problem, if I think of how eloquent and sophisticated you were with Annietta in front of the tavern.

Stinker was back – chimera-scorn or not, this last discipline was the killer. He'd never grown up on or by a court. He knew nothing about the carrying-on of the nobility, and he understood ladies even less. He didn't even understand women.

What's the difference, little worm?

"When are the budding squires coming?"

"The festivities will be taking place in springtime, so the squires will be arriving here at the end of February."

He'd never learn what was demanded of him in ten years, never mind the ten weeks that he had.

Impressive, all the things I can't do!

"The knight's squires who live in the castle are here all year round of course. We can pay them a visit. Their practice exercises are beginning on the training field now."

Ouch! The only thing Farin wanted to do was lock himself into his turret room.

In the distance he could already hear screaming – screams of command, screams of pain, screams of victory. Behind the great hall and between the castle wall and the chapel was a free area where clamorous weapon training was in full swing, with quarterstaffs over two yards long. Fourteen young men were in a sweat despite the cold as they twirled their poles around and attacked each other from every direction. He imagined himself in the middle of this cudgelling crowd. They'd beat him to death in no time at all. The sounds of the massive sticks crashing into each other bespoke brutal pain. The wood creaked and groaned almost as loudly as the men. The succession of hits suggested a well-practised routine so that they didn't injure each other, but their own pole would defensively deflect an oncoming attack.

"The lads come from the upper nobility. All age groups train together, from their fourteenth year, when they are promoted from pages to squires. Those two over there…", Markan pointed at two young men, "…will be taking part in the spring."

Farin stared at the pair, dumbfounded. They were wearing simple armour made from buckskin, had no helmets, were well-proportioned and moved as flowingly as the water in the stream of Heap. "They…they're soon going to be real knights?"

"FASTER!" roared the trainer more loudly than Farin had ever heard a person roar before.

The speed of the movements accelerated further, arms and staffs were barely distinguishable.

"FASTER!!!"

Just watching was making him dizzy. With what strength and dynamism, the budding knights went about their work! He'd never learn that. He didn't want to be beaten to a pulp and ridiculed here – he could get enough of that in Heap.

"Enough for today. I'll bring you back."

Markan led him back to his tower and departed with the following: "If you have any other questions or you need anything, you'll find me across the way in the main kitchen."

"I've thought of something already. Is there a library here?"

Markan's eyebrows shot up to the top of the tower. "What business do you want there?"

"Is there one?"

"Oh, yes! But only a few know of its existence, and admittance without the permission of the lord of the castle is denied. At the very end of the great hall there's a big room with the lord of the castle's book collection. Be careful! Knight Emicho is very particular when it comes to his folios."

"Books should be read and not locked away."

"Talk to the lord of the castle about that. But bear this in mind – there is no reading contest in the great tournament, I'm pretty sure about that."

"Thanks for your guidance," said Farin in farewell, closing the door to the tower bedchamber and sinking down on the bed.

What was he doing here? So, this is what it felt like to be a fish out of water.

In the early afternoon Farin entered the lord of the castle's scriptorium. Just as the day before, the knight sat with a quill in his hand behind his desk, his eyes flitting between a folio opened before him and a sheet of paper. He paid no attention to his visitor.

Farin stood awkwardly in front of the desk and waited. And waited. He became hot. It could have been because a cosy fire crackled in the hearth. It could also have been because the disregard was annoying him. It felt as if he was at the table in "The Warm Beer" except that there at least he was allowed to sit down. Biding his time, he looked at the two bearskins on the wall. Somewhere in the Worldly Kingdom there had to be white bears.

Had an hour or a week passed by now? He couldn't stand it any longer. "Do you have to write a lot as lord of the castle?"

Emicho slowly raised his head. "Squires remain patient

until spoken to by their knight, and don't natter on uninvited in the meantime."

He should have expected something like that.

After a while the lord of the castle grunted: "The quill is mightier than the sword – many of my colleagues haven't understood that yet." Then the knight stood up, went across the scriptorium to the hearth, took the poker with its lion-shaped grip from the wall, as well as a log from the wood basket and fed the little hearth fire. Then he hung the poker back in its place and turned towards Farin.

Was he inviting him to speak now?

"Uh…I have a few questions", began Farin.

"I hate questions. I prefer answers."

"Good – that's why I'll ask, and you'll answer, please."

Farin really didn't like the vertical frown above the bridge of the knight's nose. "Apologies, but was that too impertinent?"

"Is that your first question?" The fingers of his left hand danced on top of his desk.

A reasonable conversation with Emicho could easily be added as the eighth discipline in the squire training. "Markan showed me the castle and explained a few things. Sir, I…I would gladly be your shield bearer, but I am lacking many years as a page and squire."

"So? And? Squires en*quire* to ac*quire*, they know little about skills, little about knowledge, little about experience – which is why squires need to en*quire* – which is why they're called *squires*." Both forefingers pointed at Farin. "Geddit?!"

Another Emicho characteristic – knightly wit.

"Uh…regarding the seven disciplines, I can hardly…"

"AHA!" interrupted him loudly. A thundercloud scurried across Emicho's face, the furrow over his nose deepened.

"What can you hardly?"

Be careful — the tone was that of a dragon, drawing in breath to breathe out fire.

"'Fight, for example. I can't fight."

Emicho slammed the palm of his hand flat on the desk so that it banged and whanged. "What's wrong with you, mole?"

Farin shuddered, and not on account of the slap on the desk. "What...what do you mean?" Did he know something about Stinker?

"If somebody behaves stupidly too often, then I might just take him to be stupid."

"But...how did you know?"

The knight took a little bell from the desk and jingled it. The sound was gentle and quiet, but still the door opened immediately, and a servant enquired: "Your wish, sir?"

"Bring Liam here."

"Certainly, sir."

A moment later and a man wearing battered leather armour entered the scriptorium and bowed. He was of average size, had an average face and an average voice, Farin would have taken no notice of him in an average situation.

Turning to his recalcitrant squire, Emicho said: "Shortly after my visit I put one of my spies in your village of Heap. After all, Gerlunda had lived there and died there, but more importantly...the raven turned up in your nest. Liam, tell my new squire what they say about the gravedigger's son."

"I obeyed your command and kept an eye out on the goings-on in the village. I've already reported to you about the re-appearance of Gerlunda's body and the passing of the priest. What really amazed me was an anecdote in which the gravedigger's son played the leading role. He got into a scrap with four of the villagers, strong young lads who never turned their noses up at the possibility of a fight. Quite coincidentally I was able to observe it from a distance."

"Get to the point", ordered Emicho.

"They really laid into your squire, he was already lying on the ground and it looked as if they wanted to smash his head in with a rock. Then it happened incredibly quickly – he flattened them one after another with perfectly aimed blows. I wanted to investigate this further and so I grabbed two of the attackers and questioned them independently of each other. One of them had his arm in a sling and behaved pretty stubbornly – he was so terrified of the gravedigger's son he didn't want to spill the beans at first. He changed his attitude once I'd given his broken arm intensive attention."

"Very laudable. Get to the point!" The knight's impatience echoed through the scriptorium.

Liam continued quickly: "Both confirmed the other's assessment that they just couldn't explain how he, lying stretched out on the ground, was able to defeat them with a few well-aimed blows. They'd never seen anybody fight like that before."

"That'll do for now. We'll talk in detail later, Liam. Especially, seeing as you still have to tell the gravedigger where his piece-of-art of a son has got to."

Unfortunately, when Emicho said piece-of-art it sounded more like piece-of-shit.

"Certainly, sir." Liam bowed.

"Yes, it would be nice if my father and the villagers were informed," said Farin.

"As if any one of them would miss you." While the door was closing, the knight gently dabbed the nib of the feather on the paper, and then asked in a voice that resembled his little bell: "What am I to make of Liam's story? You against four. Why do you keep hiding your light under a bushel?"

Thoroughly dumbstruck, the gravedigger's son stood there. A spy in Heap! How should he explain what happened? Should he tell of the chimera?

Oh, do, that'll be fun.

It bothered him that his idea didn't bother the voice. And so he kept his mouth shut regarding Stinker. He first wanted to find out more about the knight's attitude regarding such subjects.

"I've never fought with a sword, never mind with a lance."

"You beat them with your bare fists." The knight folded his arms. "I'm sick of you standing here and telling me what you *can't* do. Learn to do things or take a hike out of my castle."

The knight's expectations of him hadn't lessened as a result of Liam's anecdote, but Farin was under no illusion. Emicho's words usually sounded hard and gruff, but when it came down to it, he always hit the nail on the head. Something within Farin woke up from its slumber. Was it ambition? Or the yearning for appreciation? Whatever, he was now determined to be a good squire, with all the bells and whistles.

"Yes, sir, I understand." Farin summoned up courage. "Another question if you don't mind. You own a library. Could you give me permission to visit it in my free time?"

"I should have Markan's tongue cut out, he talks much too much."

"It's not his fault, I asked him about it."

"Hm…" Emicho's mouth was widening but it looked like neither a grin nor a smile. "The mole can read! What's of such burning interest to you?"

"Books, uh…"

So, books interest you in the library, then, it chuckled.

Farin continued hastily: "…about mysterious things, for example. Inexplicable phenomena…uh, superstitions and so on." He stopped himself from asking directly about daemons or chimeras. Quick-tempered and unpredictable as the knight was, Farin was prepared for all possible reactions – just not the one that followed.

"Are you pulling my leg?" whispered Emicho hoarsely, pressing the quill ever harder onto the desk until it snapped. "How do you know about my dark books?" Slowly, threateningly and with angry sparks coming from his eyes, the lord of the castle rose up.

"What?" blinked Farin, innocently.

"Only a handful of people are aware of the contents of my library, and two of them are dead already."

The subliminal aggression caused Farin's hairs to stand on end. "I don't understand…"

The lord of the castle was standing in front of him now, facing him and looming over him: "What does a mole want to do with such writings?"

Think of something quick or he'll have you beheaded.

"Gerlunda. She tried to conjure up daemons in her hut. There was a pentagram on the floor and other signs of the supernatural. After that experience I just became more curious – I think she was a…witch."

The knight stared at him stony-faced. Farin sensed through his whole body that the next instant would decide his fate. Did Emicho believe him?

Well done.

Was he hearing things or had Stinker really praised him?

With eyes piercing into him, the lord of the castle announced: "Gravedigger's son. You are a plague, but there's something about you that strikes a certain nerve. And I really mean it nicely. Although I damn well don't like being nice. And really don't like doing things I don't like doing."

Farin didn't know what he should say, and so he asked anew: "Can I use your library now?"

"I'll decide on that later." The knight sat down again, he looked less angry and more thoughtful instead. "Have you anything else urgent you have to tell me?"

His new friend Duke Turgenson immediately popped into his head, the nice king's nincompoop, no, sorry, the old king's nephew. Should he tell Emicho of the unpleasant encounter in the dining hall, or would it sound like a pitiful gripe? "No, everything is fine."

"Good! I'll give Drogdan the job of training you in the basics, he'll look after you. We'll see each other in three days again. Now go!" The lord of the castle took a new quill out of a tall glass and buried himself in his papers.

Just like the day before, Farin left the scriptorium more confused than ever, but with a clear goal in front of his eyes. He wanted to become a good squire. Everything else would then take care of itself. Seven disciplines – yes, so?

burning night

I t was pitch-black when Aross lay down under the vagrants' bridge. She felt out a few abandoned rags beside her and a torn blanket with which she covered herself without further ado. The material stank terribly of sweat but was better than nothing for keeping her warm. The covered location amplified the snoring sounds, and somewhere a man was babbling nonsense to himself. Yet the girl still fell asleep quickly, so great was her exhaustion and so necessary it was for her to recover sufficiently for her slight body to face the challenges of the following day.

She got up before dawn and disappeared towards the harbour. She deliberately avoided questions and curious glances.

On her favourite jetty in the little harbour basin she examined her face in the water by the light of the rising sun. Deep cuts on her forehead, welts on her cheeks and a blood-encrusted ear. She shrugged her shoulders – since when were rats beautiful?

The weather promised sunshine and warmth. She was glad – her dress would dry more quickly after washing. An eel fisher rowed past with his boat full of traps but showed no interest in the girl staring into the water. The balmy breeze carried angry scolding sounds across towards her. Aross stood up on tiptoes and cupped her hand over her eyes against the blinding sunrise. At the far end of the harbour where pier four began, a crowd of people were standing around something she couldn't make out. A long, bright shape was hanging from the arm of a crane. The angry cries were growing louder.

Rats don't wait and think, rats go and look.

Aross approached pier four at a leisurely pace. Firstly, her body was still aching all over, and secondly, she didn't want to attract any attention. What was swinging there in the middle of the throng of people? Her stomach rumbled. Now she recognised it. The shape turned out to be a half-naked person, hanging by its feet. Each step revealed more details. A woman. A narrow upper torso with breasts, dangling like meat on a hook. The skin shone white as goat's milk in the sun. Clearly one of the whores. Aross neared the spectacle.

She stopped dead in shock. Mattilda! Her friend from the orphanage was hanging there, dead as Wolf, dead as the matron and dead as Aross's plans to help her. A sea of blood lapped underneath the body. Somebody had cut her throat and let her bleed to death, the same way the butchers did with pigs. For the protectors Mattilda was of less value than a pig, just a piece of meat with which the reapers could celebrate their name.

It's insane, she thought, no matter where I go, everything is swimming in blood.

Aross spotted a piece of wood with writing, dangling beside the body. She couldn't read it, she was only familiar with a few letters, like "A", "R" and "O". And she knew "S" particularly well. She had to move closer in order to ask someone.

A haggard woman with an apron and bonnet was remonstrating angrily. "What a disgrace! The girl wasn't even sixteen. This whoring has to be banished from the city. It's obvious who murdered her. Disgusting!"

None of the others present responded.

"What's written on the sign?" asked Aross. She was shocked by the sound of her own voice, it sounded strange and throaty, yet calm and collected.

The woman looked her up and down. "And who are you, might I ask? Are the strumpets getting younger? Did the protectors do that to you?"

Aross felt the many looks burning into her skin like the seawater had done yesterday evening. This was exactly the kind of situation she had wanted to avoid. Some of the men from the town watch pushed their way through the crowd.

Aross explained: "No, I'm not a whore. Please tell me what's written on the sign."

"*If you don't work, you hang!*" answered the woman. "What a mess!"

Aross nodded her thanks, turned and made her way back – she had no desire to be questioned by the town watch.

Dear town watch, I'm the queen of the rats and lived in the orphanage up until now, until my little animals fed on the matron. Better not – just get out of here!

Chain Dog had made an example of Mattilda. A warning. Now his other whores would work all the harder and be more obedient. The sun was now fully visible in the sky and making a valiant effort to grant Hubstone a wonderful autumn day.

Dear sun, how do you manage to beam your light onto all this shit without having to vomit?

Aross gritted her teeth as she hurried back to the little jetty. She had to direct all her strength now to staying alive, there was nothing left for grief or melancholy. Not even for anger.

In the evening I'll collect my few supplies and my water-bottle from the hayloft, thought Aross.

And the four coppers, the rest of the money from Shewhoknows, which she had hidden in a gap under a board. And, last but not least, her beloved felt cap, hanging from a nail.

This time she wandered past the little harbour basin. A few more steps and the pier came to an end at the coast, where the waves became higher. The sharp rocks under Aross's feet turned into soft sand. She followed the beach in a southerly direction. She would spend the rest of the day in the next cove, and wash and dry her dress in peace and quiet.

She sat naked between two large rocks and drew circles in the sand with her finger. Her skin had dried after a comforting bathe in the sea. Her dress, spread out on one of the stones, was drying too. It didn't exactly look clean. In the past she'd always wished for a floral pattern on her grey orphanage dress, like the silk outer garments of the noble ladies. Aross looked sceptically at the material with its many rust-brown spots.

It's become blood-patterned now anyway.

In the meantime, the sun had begun heading determinedly for the horizon. It looked to Aross as if it were fleeing – even the sun was fed up to its back teeth by now. The girl chewed on a piece of stalk – felt it on her tongue, between her teeth and her lips. Her feet had become incredibly clean following all her swimming and walking up and down the beach. That reminded her of Grim, the tricky traitor. He'd get his just desserts sometime too – how, she didn't know yet. The wind carried melancholy sounds over to her. The two bells of the cathedral steeples played their song, sometimes one after the other, sometimes in unison. Three, two, one – three, two, one.

That didn't happen too often outside of Sunday service, which meant something unusual was pending. It couldn't be the burial of an aristocrat – it sounded too cheerful for that.

She bit the stalk in two accidentally.

Rats don't wait and think, rats go and look.

Putting her clothes on was quick. Dress pulled over head – finished. She had nothing better to be doing anyway and had to make sure to get her feet dirty again.

Aross walked the long route back to the city and with every passing step the ringing became louder. Streams of residents were drawn from all directions towards the bells, as iron filings are towards a magnet, and all the people were marching towards Hubstone Cathedral. The throngs of bodies had an eerie effect on Aross. Her body still hurt from the matron's beating. Her condition and her situation were too delicate to be moving in such a crowd. She stopped and stood, uncertain.

A little boy who was holding a man's hand walked excitedly past her.

"Father, what does the bell-ringing mean?"

"It's the witch's peal!"

Dear day, you're really hitting me with bells and whistles today. It's blow after blow, just like the ringing of the two bells.

The girl hardly noticed what she was doing as she marched onwards towards the cathedral – as if somebody had placed an invisible hand on her shoulder from behind and was pushing her forward. Her reservations were redundant – she owed it to Shewhoknows and had to find out what it all meant. She hooked up with a group of plainly dressed farmers' wives and farm hands as she neared the centre of the city of Hubstone. Nobody had taken any notice of her yet. She cursed her grey blood-patterned dress more than once because it identified her as an orphan child. A crumb of comfort – one of the farmer's wives ahead of her was also wearing grey linen. Aross went directly behind her, as if she were her daughter.

The large area in front of the cathedral stretched from the end of the old town to the upper town. Thousands of people could gather there without too much pushing and shoving, which is why it was called the large square. Gatherings such as this were rare enough – only when there were royal weddings or executions. It didn't matter much which – there were always the same spectators and there was always the same cheering.

In front of the entrance to the cathedral was a stone platform with a stake stretching upwards in the middle of a pile of wood. She almost slapped her forehead with her palm. The burning of a witch was imminent. A spectacle for the people, a welcome diversion and the proof that there was always someone who was considerably worse off than oneself.

The pealing of the bells echoed in everyone's ears. The pending execution had flushed the people out onto the square like a tidal wave. The pushing and shoving increased. Suddenly the pealing ceased, and moments later a murmur swept through the crowd. Aross couldn't see much more than backsides.

But yes, now – a man stood up on the stone platform.

Even from a distance he looked impressive in his red brocade robe with its golden, shimmering adornments. He raised his arms towards the heavens as if he wanted to touch the clouds, and there was silence.

He spoke in a powerful, mellifluous voice: "Citizens of Hubstone! Today it is deemed that a monster shall receive her just punishment. A woman who has been led astray, who has surrendered herself to the devil and has confessed her sins under questioning. A black witch who for a multitude of reasons deserves to die."

The crowd cheered at his successful introduction.

"Honest citizens of Hubstone! Over the years many sins have been confessed to me, the archbishop of our capital city of the Worldly Kingdom, the supreme head of the church – but the scandalous deeds of today are yet to be matched." He looked up into the evening skies. "Lord, thou hast put me to the test."

He sounded as though he were about to burn himself at the stake.

The archbishop's voice grew even louder. "Only few of the monster's black machinations have been proclaimed. She bewitched the swine – one hundred of them perished in our pigsties in the early autumn."

"Uuuggghhh!" clamoured the honest citizens in disgust.

"She cast an evil weather spell which bestowed upon us two months of drought, causing the cornfields to dry out."

"Booooh!" yelled the honest citizens in outrage.

"She fornicated with the devil, not just once, nay, regularly, preferring to do it on Sundays during holy mass."

"Aaaarrrgggghhhh!" shouted the honest citizens, getting even more excited.

He paused dramatically for the shock to reverberate,

before continuing: "The depraved plague-infested soul must be eradicated, the witch must be condemned to death by being burned alive and turned into ashes."

"Yeeeeesss!"

There was nothing in the world that compared to the sound of thousands of bloodthirsty people. The executioner led a black-cloaked figure to beside the bishop. Even from a distance, Aross could see straight away that it was none other than the old woman from the market.

Aross swallowed hard. Shewhoknows! She had predicted this was going to happen – although it was the first burning of a witch in Hubstone for a long time – strange! Aross had no desire to watch the execution, especially as she already knew the so-called "witch". Shewhoknows was more of a magician for the girl – after all, she'd saved Aross from certain death by beating. Also, she'd been nice to Aross and had given her a silverling.

The memory came rushing back. "Do not forget my words. My death should not be in vain." Aross closed her eyes as hard as she could so that her forehead and cheeks hurt. This couldn't be allowed to happen. No way was this woman an evil witch. Without really understanding why, Aross pushed her way forward. She forgot the wounds that cane number five had inflicted on her, pressed her way through the bodies in her effort to get close to the pyre. She felt her desire to be close to Shewhoknows. Hurry!

She kept shoving forward like a lunatic, which hardly suited somebody who was trying to avoid attracting attention. Some complained loudly in her wake, but their insults were like water off a duck's back.

She came closer and closer, only another few rows. The goodly bishop was still standing on the platform, beside him the executioner with the so-called witch, and in front of them fourteen men from the town watch were standing in a semi-circle.

"Lord, have mercy on this misguided sinner." The bishop fanned his long arms up towards the heavens again.

The sinner had no intention of looking at the slavering mob but stared fixedly at her feet.

I'm here, called out Aross in her thoughts. I can't help you, I know, it's ridiculous, but I'm here.

The bishop descended from the platform, and the men of the town watch immediately forced the people backwards with their pikes, thereby creating room. The spiritual supreme leader looked even more impressive up-close. He was around fifty years old and looked well over two yards tall with the golden-white mitre on his head. Long hair, flecked with grey, hung down to his shoulders, his chiselled face radiated power and determination. On his hands were white silk gloves which contrasted with his polished black boots.

A slight nod was enough and Shewhoknows was bound to the stake, hands behind her back. Additionally, the executioner tied shackles around her upper body and her feet. She seemed already disconnected from this world and wasn't acknowledging the activity around her. The executioner was now holding a burning brand in his right hand. He didn't beat around the bush. With a theatrical bow he ignited the pyre. The people were cheering as if each of them had been presented with a hundred gold pieces and a horse with a saddle. The wood hardly smoked – it was well dried and expertly arranged – for one thing, the spectators had to have a fantastic view, and for another, it was better if the burning person didn't choke too early because of the smoke. As the wood was piled no higher than her knees, the fire flickered only as high as her thighs. These measures too ensured longer spectator enjoyment. The heat above the flames, meanwhile, where the air was wafting glassily, was surely causing unbearable pain.

Something wasn't right, Aross couldn't figure out what it was, though. The mutterings of the spectators grew louder. Although she was standing several yards away, she could already feel the heat of the flames.

First Mattilda and now Shewhoknows – terrible! And everything in the one day, how could anyone bear it?

Some began to whistle, boos joining in too. Aross still couldn't figure out what was infuriating the people and what was irritating herself too, she was too caught up in her own feelings – a mixture of disgust, horror and bitterness. She just wanted to get away – as far away as possible. With one last look she bade farewell to Shewhoknows. At that very moment the old woman raised her head and looked deeply into Aross's eyes. She felt as if a thick rope was joining them together. Then, in the middle of the murderous heat, the woman smiled.

With furrowed brows, the bishop turned and followed her gaze. His eyes fixed on Aross. His pupils, as deep a blue as that of the sea, and at least as cold, flinched. Despite her closeness to the fire, Aross suddenly froze. Irritated, the supreme leader of the church turned his head back to the sinful monster at the stake. The flames darted more greedily, Shewhoknows's dress caught fire, her skin contracted, her hair scorched, her body carbonised – her eyes were now only black hollows, but her lips were still smiling. Aross unfroze again. The girl felt goosepimples running down her spine, and her emotions were doing crazy somersaults. It felt as if she were being stroked, it felt like a belt to the head, it felt like bathing in the sea with burning skin. Stomach, heart and head spun in unison, and against each other. The smell of burning flesh made Aross gag as though someone had stuck a finger down her throat.

"GUARDS! Bring me that girl! Now!" The bishop's words cracked through the air and yanked Aross out of her world of emotions. A long, white forefinger of satin pointed directly at her. She felt as if she were holding her head between the two cathedral bells. BONG! The strike of realisation and awakening. First, she had to scarper as quickly as possible. Two guards came towards her, one of them was already stretching out his arm greedily towards her shoulder.

"I WANT THE HUSSY!" roared the bishop, his head as red as his robe.

No, you sleazebag. Nobody catches a rat with their hands and especially not the queen of the rats. I'm also the queen of pushing, shoving and jostling.

She dropped to the ground, crawled between several legs, stood up again and pushed her slight body through gaps that weren't really there at all. In comparison to her, the soldiers of the town watch were as mobile in their armour as the city gate. It wasn't long before Aross had built up a considerable lead.

She hadn't screamed!

She shouldered a man almost twice her size aside and jumped through a gap between two women. She simple shoved another honest citizen aside.

She hadn't let out a sound.

Aross increased her lead, the crowd wasn't quite so dense, so she could flee even faster. The catcalls got louder and louder – the honest citizens weren't happy with the so-called spectacle. No pleading for mercy, no screams of pain

— the archbishop might as well have burned a sack of pinecones. Aross reached the edge of the square and disappeared into the alleyways of the old town. She was safe from the town watch for the time being.

Shewhoknows hadn't screamed in spite of unimaginable agony. Was this kind of spiritual kinship just pure chance? No! nothing was pure in this world.

Witch's peal! Burning night! Tooth of time!

Aross knew what she had to do now.

Wow! What sort of a day had she cannoned into yet again?

disappointment

arin woke up early in the morning. He lit two candles with the help of the nightlight and lying on his back he watched the light flickering on the ceiling beams of his sleeping chamber. By now he had not only become used to his little tower room, he actually liked it. Here he found peace and a certain feeling of security like a bear in his den. His little kingdom – he'd never said that about a place before. His back ached – Peesel had tossed him off her back yesterday. The day before too. Drogdan had spent two full days trying to teach him how to handle horses correctly. And as if that weren't enough, sitting on them was part of it. Farin found the results sobering. The horse bit and kicked him at every opportunity. And really enjoyed unseating him. The animal's real name was Leezel, but following his experiences, Farin called her Peesel as a mark of appreciation. This measure hadn't improved their relationship, unfortunately.

Drogdan simply shook his head and said: "I don't understand it. She's the tamest and safest nag in the stable. Should we pick out another horse for you?" He had rubbed his earlobe. "Maybe a dead one?"

"No, no", said Farin, rejecting the offer. "It would be too humiliating for me if she unseated me too."

The tame, harmless nag didn't like him. The gravedigger's son suspected that his special friend, Stinker, was behind this

– Peesel, just like Growler, sensed that something evil was slumbering within Farin. The voice hadn't been seen, or rather heard, since his visit to the scriptorium, but Farin was under no illusions, he sensed it: it was hiding in wait in the background, always ready to push its way forward in risky or totally inopportune situations, spouting its poisonous sarcasm.

Farin looked forward to his morning breakfast – it was the highlight of his day, when he sat together with Drogdan, Plaudius and Stump, and scoffed down slices of bread and honey. Duke Turgenson and his men threw him hostile looks but until now they had left him in peace. But Farin knew something was simmering there, he had a good nose for things like that.

There was a knock. "Are you awake? A message from the lord of the castle!"

Farin jumped up and opened the door. "Good morning, Markan."

The master of the bathtubs gave a friendly nod. "Knight Emicho will be looking after you personally today. Be on the training grounds near the chapel at the tenth hour."

Farin nodded with mixed feelings. Mixed – because he couldn't decide between horror and bewilderment. So, the noble knight did find time for his squire, and during weapons training of all things.

Bullshit! I have neither a weapon nor training.

Having heard this news, he found his first steps into the new day considerably harder.

First, I'll eat breakfast with Drogdan, Plaudius, Stump and honey, he said, consoling himself.

Farin appeared on the little meadow between castle wall and

chapel at the appointed time. Scattered around were dummies and targets made of straw as well as some vertical poles. There wasn't much time to look around because the fourteen young men he had already been permitted to see during his tour of the castle on the first day were also present. He saw that each squire was carrying a wooden sword and shield. They were being led by the trainer who had the most full-throated "faster" he had ever heard.

The man stood in front of him, legs apart. "I am Knight Hectorius from the house of Oaklands. The lord of the castle has given notice of your appearance today!" he roared, as though he were training the squires in the neighbouring castle.

The gravedigger's son couldn't stop himself from flinching. He nodded silently.

"Today is sword and buckler. Where's your training vest?"

"Apologies, I didn't know what to expect."

All the others were wearing stuffed armour, a padded helmet and leather gloves.

"Your own fault – then you're going to fight without additional protection. That'll be a lesson to you. I'm certain you'll never forget your armour again." He turned to face the squires. "Till – give him your sword and buckler."

A boy of fourteen or fifteen handed Farin the wooden weapons.

"Now, get yourselves into pairs. Baraldon, you start with the newbie."

A squire of his age gave a quick bow. Whether he wanted it or not, Farin's face looked to all the world like a desperate plea for help. What was going on here? This couldn't be happening – how could he survive against an opponent like that?

"Get to it!" commanded the captain beside him.

The other squires paused and stared at Farin and Baraldon. The latter raised his shield and held his sword vertically beside it. Farin copied him without thinking. The wooden sword felt like a foreign body in his hand, heavier and chunkier than he'd expected. There was no time to think of an escape, for Baraldon was already on the attack. A sidestep and a simple body swerve to the right and Baraldon had already outmanoeuvred Farin, catching him on the wrong leg. A strike from the left on his sword-arm brought tears to his eyes. And then came an unexpected blow past his shield and onto his left upper arm.

He dropped the shield more out of shock than pain. "OW!" he exclaimed. His face turned deep red, nothing could be more embarrassing, more humiliating – they'd laugh him out of court and ridicule him for weeks. Baraldon lowered his sword, Farin peered left and right, nobody was laughing, only the cold wind whistled past his ears. But the faces of the squires hurt him more than any strike of a sword. Even in his home village he'd never been showered with so much scorn, so much repudiation.

"That was obviously too difficult for our newbie. Twine, you fight him." The knight picked the buckler off the ground and pressed it back into Farin's hand.

A new fighter approached him. Shame-faced, Farin closed his eyes momentarily. The smallest in the group, a boy of twelve or younger, bowed and positioned himself in attack mode. He did his best to make his child's face seem determined and dangerous. Suddenly, the boy's features changed. His eyes widened, his cheeks became redder, he looked past Farin and knelt down on one knee. Everyone present was suddenly standing stock still, before bending their knee too, as if on command. "My Lord", they murmured in unison.

Knight Emicho nodded and positioned himself by Hectorius. The squires kept glancing at the lord of the castle, a clear indication that his presence meant something special.

"Carry on!" commanded the lord of the castle with an impassive look.

A little child is going to make mincemeat of you in front of everyone. Start – I'll help you.

Stinker was a real stinker. That was all he needed. Farin wondered what it would be like to simply die on the spot. With his heart stopping for all he cared. Fall down and curtains. But he had no time for that. Also, he wanted to be a good squire, see the sea and kiss Annietta. The boy attacked, clearly spurred on by the presence of the knight.

I'll defend myself as hard as I can!

Farin deflected the first blow from above with his shield. His response fizzled out as he fumbled with his sword in the air. The second blow hit him from the right. He should have deflected it with his sword, that became clear to him when it was far too late.

Let go! Otherwise you'll just keep getting hit, worm.

Another blow from above, Farin yanked his shield upwards. He noticed too late it had only been a feint, he already felt a sword sweep the pit of his stomach. He folded forwards, the pain taking his breath away – the sword slipped out of his sweating hand and fell to the ground.

Not the sword! It chuckled. *It's not too late yet, I can still help you. Even without the weapon we can give the lad a hiding on his backside.*

Farin shook his head while clenching his teeth. The last

thing he needed was getting help from Stinker.

False pride, worm! Let go!

"No," he whispered, yet loudly enough that everybody heard him.

At which point the lad named Twine lowered his wooden sword and stepped back into the group. That was the killer blow – Farin wasn't worth fighting against, he was dishonourable and the magnet of mockery.

The lord of the castle looked at him coldly and turned to his captain.

"Carry on with the training. Without him there – he's coming with me." He looked over at his squire with a minimum of enthusiasm.

That was it, the abrupt ending to good intentions. The knight would pour bucketfuls of scorn over him before kicking him out. After the report from his super spy Liam, Emicho must have thought he was going to have a pure fighting machine on his hands. And the truth had unfolded before him. Farin hadn't been able to withstand more than one blow – even against a child.

He trotted after the knight, every step alternating between shame and scandal. Emicho turned around – he still didn't say a word but marched towards the drawbridge. Left, right, shame, scandal.

Was he going to throw him out of the castle straight away? Farin didn't dare to ask if he could at least get his belt pouch and his cloak from the tower room. He also wanted to say goodbye to Drogdan, Plaudius and Stump – they had always been decent towards him, nicer than any other people he knew, but he didn't dare to open his mouth.

Approximately thirty shames and scandals later, just before the bridge house, Knight Emicho veered right towards the stables. Farin shuffled, head bowed, ten steps behind. Wherever the lord of the castle went, the people showed their respect by genuflecting or curtseying. They paid no heed to the moron with the bowed head in his wake. Emicho entered a stable with empty stalls. Practice swords made of oak wood hung on one of the walls, and two iron rings contained fighting sticks of varying lengths and strengths. The knight handed one of them to Farin.

"Take it in your right hand."

"I'm allowed to stay in the castle?"

Knight Emicho rolled his eyes so much his eyebrows almost followed suit. His mighty chest rose and fell like a bellows, and then he answered: "Very often it doesn't depend so much on how powerfully we can strike, but rather on how much we can take. And believe me, you certainly take the biscuit."

Very slowly Farin began to straighten up to his normal height. He carefully grasped the handle of the practice sword. This was all too much for him.

"Let's cut to the chase! Hold your weapon up!"

Amazed, Farin raised his arm.

"A knight who drops his sword is no knight. Let's start at the very beginning, with the grip. You're holding your sword like your dick, that'll never work." He stepped up to the gravedigger's son. "Your fingers closer to the cross-guard, your thumb slanting over it." Emicho bent Farin's fingers into their correct positions.

First speechless through embarrassment, now speechless through amazement at the lord of the castle's reaction after Farin's fiasco. He was clearly being given another chance. He weighed the weapon in his hand and already felt more control and confidence with this new grip. Still, Farin was under no illusions. He was years and countless training sessions behind the others when it came to the art of sword fighting. "I'll never be a good squire", he whispered.

Knight Emicho stared daggers at him. "If I hear another expression like that coming from your mouth, you'll be thrown into the shit in the castle moat – and the bridge will remain up forever as far you're concerned, understood?"

"Yes, sir."

"How am I supposed to have faith in you if you don't have faith in yourself?"

The very words out of my mouth – I'm getting to like this knight more and more with every passing day.

"Yes, sir."

"Let's talk about your pathetic *no* in the fight against the suckling. In many ways I don't give a shit about the code and the celebrated sense of honour associated with it – but we never grovel for mercy – ever."

Farin took a deep breath – his *no* during the fight had only been his rejection of the chimera's help. He breathed out again and didn't bother with a "yes, sir" or a justification.

No whining. Head high, Farin!

"Tell me one thing. What distinguishes a squire? What's the most important thing for you?" he asked bluntly.

Good question!

The knight answered without hesitation. "For me there are two things: firstly – loyalty. Absolute loyalty. I must be able to rely on you, in every situation. And believe me, I have every reason to demand it. And the second thing stems *from* that: you must always give of your best. That means, you hold onto your sword firmly, you stay concentrated in hopeless situations, and you never give up. Like in your fight with the four scoundrels in your village. Be furious at the right moment and thoughtful at the right moment, always serving the purpose. Recognising these moments is more important than the sword or the bow and arrow."

Emicho's words hit Farin like darts – little shafts of light that didn't hurt, but rather gave courage and self-confidence. A feeling of gratitude overcame him. He swallowed hard, his mouth dry. "I understand."

"I'm not so sure about that – you're still struggling too much with yourself. And your real battle is yet to begin." The knight's dark eyebrows brought out the brightness in his eyes even more.

What was the knight talking about?

There wasn't much time for thinking this over. Emicho continued: "Drogdan will train with you in this stable, and he'll keep doing that until you're able to beat one of the straw dummies in the meadow."

A silent nod.

"But don't take too long. The grand tournament will be held here in the spring – on the meadow in front of the castle. The best knights will travel from throughout the Worldly Kingdom – a great honour for the north to be allowed to host the competition. You'll be taking part in all the squire disciplines."

A silent nod.

"Another thing: your first opponent just now, Baraldon, was hoping for your position following the death of my old squire. The fact that I didn't pick him is a slap in the face for him, his father and his family. If they see now which lad I picked ahead of Baraldon Turgenson, it will be an unforgiveable vilification as far as they're concerned."

"Turgenson?"

"Exactly." The knight folded his mighty arms in front of

his chest. "Baraldon is the son of your new aristocratic friend, Duke Turgenson. I didn't want *him*, but *you*. Why the devil, God only knows."

That explained some things. Was the lord of the castle aware of everything that went on within his grey walls?

"What happened to your old squire?"

"He fell from the western watchtower – fractured skull. An accident. Maybe he'd drunk too much."

"I...won't disappoint you, sir."

"Too late, but every disappointment is a cause for hope." He thought for a moment, then continued: "Hope – a word I haven't used in a long while."

Emicho hung the two wooden swords back up on the wall. "Another thing – I give you permission to enter the library."

His heart gave a little joyful leap. "Thank you, sir. And...I promise you loyalty."

A searching look, a quick nod, then the lord of the castle turned and disappeared out the stable door.

Farin's chest felt cold and hot at the same time. His life in Castle Stormwatch was to continue and there was no threat of it becoming boring. It took a while before the grave-digger's son was able to move again. First, he went through his conversation with the lord of the castle once more in his head. This time the knight had succeeded in surprising him with his words and deeds. Emicho hadn't dropped him at the first opportunity, quite the contrary, he'd stood behind him today even though a few things had gone wrong.

Loyalty? What is that exactly? An alliance? No, not quite – Farin felt he could sense the meaning. A bond of fidelity and steadfastness. Once again, he felt embarrassment – it hadn't been him who had shown loyalty today, but the unpredictable, blustering knight, of all people.

If I prove my fidelity to him, and he notices that I'm trying to better myself in all the disciplines, then he'll stick with me in future too. That's how I'll proceed – Emicho will be proud of me.

Farin had never been so serious about anything before.

How could he help? What could he do now? One way of proving his loyalty to the lord of the castle stuck in his mind: I'll find out more about the death of his squire.

That evening Farin entered the dining hall with mixed feelings. Of course his disaster on the training ground had done the rounds, and everyone who relayed the story embellished it as they sniggered. What would people be telling in a month's time? Crying, he'd thrown his sword away, called out for his mama and been chased away by a four-year-old.

"Ah! Stand up, men, here comes the hero. An expert in his field – at pleading for mercy and pissing in his pants." Duke Turgenson laughed filthily. Most of the others present followed suit. "That he has the nerve to turn up here at all." He stood in Farin's way just as he had done the first time. "Do us all a favour and crawl back into your hole in the ground."

Duke or no duke – he couldn't put up with that. Farin took a deep breath. "Yes, I'm far from being a swordfighter, I proved that today beyond doubt. But for so long as I'm squire to the lord of the castle I'll eat my meals in this room. If it doesn't suit you to dine with me, I'm sure you can find another venue."

The laughter stopped. Turgenson went deep purple, drew his hand back to strike, then thought otherwise. "Shameless yob. Emicho may still have his protective hand over you, you waster. But I know people like you all too well – you won't last long. And what I'll do with you then, you couldn't imagine in your worst nightmare."

This high-born, spoilt shithead was trying to destroy Farin's newly awakened self-confidence. "You know nothing about my nightmares."

The gravedigger's son pushed his way past the duke and headed for the three familiar faces at the far corner by the window. Only now did Farin notice how much he was trembling.

"The reluctant squire", said Drogdan in greeting. "Would you define your appearance just now as *best not get into a scrap with the duke?*"

"What else was I supposed to do?"

Plaudius's response was decidedly tight-lipped: "Turgenson was hardly exaggerating. I heard about your heroic deeds already."

"From whom?"

"From the lord of the castle himself, among others. He said, you hold your sword like your di…"

"Did he say anything else?" blurted Farin.

Drogdan joined in. "He wants me to teach you a few ground rules of swordplay." His tone of voice made no secret of his lack of enthusiasm for this task.

With eyes lowered the gravedigger's son said: "I never learned to fight – sorry."

"I heard you dropped your sword and pleaded with the little lad not to even tap you with his wooden sword." Plaudius screwed up his nose.

"Yes, I let go of the weapon." Farin looked up and straightened his back. "Yes, I suffered a few blows. Yes, I had no chance against him. But I never gave up and no way did I beg for mercy."

Nobody said a word for a while. Farin felt Stump's eyes examining him keenly. "Hrm", said the small one, suddenly convinced, and placed a friendly hand on his shoulder.

Drogdan's cheekbones slowly relaxed. "If Stump believes you, then that's the end of the matter as far as I'm concerned."

Plaudius's features softened too. Then he grinned. "What matter?"

"Thank you, that means a lot to me! I won't disappoint you." Farin's words expressed firm conviction.

Drogdan cleared his throat. "Right then, get yourself something to eat – it's goose today."

Food and drink had been far from the gravedigger son's mind although he was sitting in the dining hall. There was no way he was going to stand up and walk through the malignant mob to where the food was being served. "I'm not hungry."

The three men looked at him sceptically.

Farin couldn't stop thinking about the dead squire. Of course, there would be more suitable opportunities, but he simply couldn't wait: "What do you know about the death of my predecessor?"

Drogdan and Plaudius looked at Stump.

"Hrm", he nodded to Drogdan in encouragement.

The latter pinched his earlobe with his right hand. "Did I understand you correctly and you want to find out more about how your predecessor died?"

"Yes, please. What was his name?"

"He was called Keimund."

"When did the accident happen?"

"Eight days ago – Emicho sent us off shortly afterwards to…collect you." Drogdan grinned for the first time that evening.

"Why are you so curious about the deceased?" Plaudius shrugged his shoulders. "Dead is dead – there's nothing you can do about it." He gnawed at the goose drumstick he was holding in his greasy fingers.

"Sadly true, and for a change, I know a lot about this particular topic. The dead often have one last story to tell."

"Aha." Plaudius licked his fingers. "I'd rather eat one last drumstick."

"How was he interred?" asked Farin.

Drogdan looked at him in surprise. "He hasn't been yet – his family should be here in five days at the latest to receive Keimund's body. He belongs to an old aristocratic family, you see, and he'll be interred in their crypt in the far south."

Farin had been hoping for something like that. Now he really had to reveal his plan. "So, you're storing his body somewhere in the castle?"

"Of course, until his relations collect him."

"Where is he?"

"Who?" asked Plaudius.

"Squire Keimund."

Drogdan responded, tight-lipped: "The body is lying deep in the dungeon in the ice hall. Even the wine freezes in its goblets down there. Why the old man took such extreme measures, I don't know."

"The colder, the better!" said Farin, delightedly. "That's really good, otherwise decomposition would have destroyed some things after eight days. Rigor mortis has dissipated in any event."

The looks on the faces around him suggested that the

men rarely spun yarns over the condition of bodies during their meals.

Without pausing for thought, the question came tumbling out: "Can you bring me to him?"

Drogdan wrinkled his nose: "Take you into the castle catacombs? Into the ice hall? To Keimund's body? Will Emicho approve?"

Plaudius stopped chewing. "Even if we wanted to, it's far from easy. The entrance to the catacombs is sealed off by the gate of bars. There are only a few keys and fewer people who can claim them as their own."

"So far, I've only been making a fool of myself, but I understand something about bodies. Give me a chance to prove myself."

Drogdan and Plaudius looked at their drumsticks, then their heads pivoted for the third time that evening to their leader.

The little man looked at Farin with intelligent, examining eyes. Eyes which could be furious at the right moment and thoughtful at the right moment.

Impressive that a small, mute man could be so successful. Shouldn't that give hope to a gravedigger's son too?

He was clearly finding it hard to reach a decision. Farin wanted to help. "Come on, Stump, please, if a person says *hrm*, then he also has to say *hrm*."

His face impassive, Sump fiddled at his belt under the table. Then he produced an object with his stumpy fingers: a long, rusty key with a multi-pronged bit. "Hrm", Stump added. It sounded like a mixture of annoyance and enjoyment.

"You have a key to the catacombs? I should have known," whispered Drogdan.

Plaudius forgot to chew.

Farin was simultaneously gripped by excitement and enthusiasm. "Thanks, Stump. Let's go then. Who's coming?"

"Now? Already? You *are* in a hurry," groaned Drogdan.

Plaudius echoed his companion, smacking his lips. "Hurrying isn't good for the stomach."

"A fifth drumstick isn't either," said Drogdan and looked at Farin.

"But before we go, eat something. Plaudius, give the little fella some of yours, then he won't have to run the gauntlet to the serving counter."

Scowling, Plaudius pushed his drumstick over to Farin, but his eyes were twinkling in a friendly manner.

The gravedigger's son devoured it ravenously. "Thanks, I'm delighted you're helping." He quickly wiped his greasy fingers on his shirtsleeve. "Don't be angry but I'm in a real hurry. Even if it's cold down there, the dead don't get any fresher." Farin looked at the others. "And his relations could be here tomorrow."

"No, they're coming from the most southerly south and will need another couple of days."

"Why are the catacombs locked and bolted?"

"They're made up of endless passageways, an enormous labyrinth haunted by the ghosts of those who couldn't find their way out", explained Drogdan.

"That doesn't scare me, that makes me more curious."

"But it does me", said Plaudius.

"Shall we all go?" Farin deliberately put the brakes on his euphoria, because although the catacombs sounded really fascinating, he didn't want to impose too much on the three men.

"Mhmm."

That surely meant "all", because both Plaudius and Drogdan nodded and stood up. Just like his master, Knight Stump was a dab hand at leaving little room for interpretation.

investigations

F or every step his companions took, Stump had to take two, which clearly presented no problem to him. He moved swiftly ahead and was greeted several times with respectful nods, and not just from the servants, but also from soldiers and officers. The little man led Plaudius, Drogdan and Farin into a bleak vault in the typical grey of Stormwatch, from where stone steps led both upwards and downwards. The passageway into the darkest recess looked particularly uncomfortable and unforgiving. A moment later and Stump was marching into it with determination – how could it be otherwise?

"Luckily I've never been banished down here," clarified Plaudius.

"There's always the last time," explained Drogdan.

"You really mean, the first time."

"No, you heard me correctly, Plaudius. Who knows if we'll ever get out of the catacombs alive? They say hosts of people have lost their way in the catacombs over the years. Their ghosts are still wandering around down there – in search of food and a way out."

"You don't really believe old wives' tales like that, do you?"

"They usually contain a grain of truth," said Drogdan, shrugging his shoulders.

They continued trudging down the crooked steps until

Stump stopped on a narrow landing. A lonely oil-lamp was smouldering in an alcove in front of them. Under it was a wicker basket with resin torches, two of which their leader pulled out, lighting one with the help of the oil-lamp. He quickly lit the second with the first torch and pressed it into Drogdan's hand.

They continued their descent into the depths of the castle catacombs. It wasn't long before the two torches were their only sources of light. They turned a corner and found themselves in a square-shaped area with two wooden benches at a table. On the wall hung an empty shelf for pikes and spears. Considerable time had settled on the simple furniture in the form of considerable dust – nobody had sat here in months. They didn't stay long either, continuing until they reached a fork. One of the two passageways defied trespassers by means of a thick grille made up of six horizontal iron rods set into the walls, which prevented anyone from entering. Their leader gestured to it with his torch.

"The gate of bars," said Plaudius.

"We have to get through it," said Drogdan. "How can we move the bars? Where's the locking mechanism?"

"Hrm."

With a deft movement Stump pushed his rusty key into an innocuous hole in the wall to his left. It clicked as the catch released. He sank the bars into the wall on the right by pushing each of them to the side, so that the four could pass through.

"A lot of effort for a corpse. How much further is it to the ice hall? I'm finding it pretty cold already," grumbled Plaudius.

At that very moment, their leader stopped and opened a

heavy wooden door to his left, revealing a chamber – the temperature dropped another few degrees. Farin thought for a moment he could hear running water, but it was only a rhythmical drip, dripping noise that reached his ears.

"Why is this narrow hole called the ice hall? It's hardly bigger than a lousy room in the south tower," declared Drogdan.

"Hm!" thought Farin, realising he sounded almost like Stump.

It was true that the four had to squeeze in together. There were two recesses in the wall in front of them, one at chest-hight, the other knee-high. A linen bundle, two yards long, lay in the upper one.

"Now what?" asked Drogdan impatiently.

"I need more light." Farin could only see a shadow in this gloomy environment.

Plaudius pulled an oil-lamp from a slot near the door. "How about this?"

"Excellent. Please keep the light on me because I have to use both hands."

While Farin took the linen covers off the body, Stump lit the oil-lamp with his torch, and Plaudius turned up the wick to make it as bright as possible. The body of the dead squire shimmered white in the flickering light, his head was covered by thin blond hair, his eye sockets gave his face an owlish look.

"That's Squire Keimund," confirmed Drogdan, tight-lipped.

"That *was* him," added Plaudius, being more specific.

Farin didn't feel helpless for a change, but completely in his element. "Pity he's been washed already – important clues might have been destroyed that way."

"What sort of clues?" Plaudius couldn't help staring at the corpse's naked feet.

Considering that eight days had passed, the body was in good condition. An exemplary corpse, thought Farin. He began his examination at the feet. Toes and legs unscathed. No bruising on either the knees or the hip bones. Farin kneaded the loose, light skin that had suffered neither haematomas nor other impacts.

"What are you doing there?" hissed Drogdan with little enthusiasm.

"Trust me." Farin was now inspecting the torso. He discovered a tattoo on the inside of his right forearm. Inconspicuous – just a circle, within it an upside-down pentagram with a flame in the middle.

"A pentacle. What does it mean?"

Farin's companions, their heads tilted forward, examined the symbol, made up of simple carved lines. They all shook their heads.

"Doesn't say anything to me," opined Drogdan. "Hurry up, I'm getting cold."

Farin nodded and turned his attention to the hands. Both undamaged – no evidence of scratches or abrasions, no broken fingers. Strange for somebody who had fallen off a tower.

Farin turned the corpse's head with his right hand. The face was no longer symmetrical, its left eye socket was lower – a sure sign that the skull had been fractured, probably in several places. Apart from that he couldn't find anything out of the ordinary – quite the contrary, the squire's facial features seemed relaxed. He then opened Keimund's jaws with both hands, as he would a wolf trap. "Shine the light on his mouth, Plaudius."

"Boy, oh boy!" was the enthusiastic response. Plaudius said no more, however, but dutifully held the oil lamp right in front of the deceased's face. Farin examined the tongue with particular care – it often offered the first clue as to cause of death. Its colour varied depending on the manner of death and the tongue always told its owner's last story: death by decrepitude or by haemorrhage or by oxygen deficiency. You just had to listen intently. Farin was interested to know if Keimund had bitten on it as he was dying.

The oral cavity looked normal, the colour of the tongue too, but a tear the width of a thumb ran from the tip upwards along the muscle. Farin carefully pushed the lower jaw up again.

"Finished?" urged Plaudius.

"The front, yes, but everything has two sides. Help me to turn him on his stomach, please."

"Oh heck – do you want me to light up his backside now?"

"Not necessary – that won't tell us anything, Plaudius," said Farin, placating him. He could see out of the corner of his eye that his three comrades were exchanging silent looks. They obviously figured he'd lost the plot – and he couldn't expect them to put up with much more.

With Drogdan's help he turned over the body so that the gravedigger could examine the back of the head. And here he found the definitive cause of the heart stopping. Two large holes in the skull were clearly visible.

"Let's concentrate on these," suggested Farin.

"Yes, I heard he fell from the tower onto his head and was dead immediately," said Drogdan.

"Bring the lamp as near as you can, Plaudius." Farin looked at the two holes carefully. The lower one consisted of a rupture with irregular wound margins. Farin regretted once again that the body had been washed already – he would have liked to have examined the haemorrhaging in more detail.

"Does the castle have its own gravedigger?"

Drogdan shook his head emphatically. "God, no, it wouldn't be worth it. Old Dannolin does it along with all his other tasks. I think he was even executioner once."

The second hole was positioned at the top of the skull, it was in the form of a square, or a trapezium to be precise. The wound margins in this case were smooth and regular. Farin probed it with his slightly bent forefinger and felt around the inside of the hole in the skullcap. With the tip of his finger he felt a thin fissure connecting the two holes. The cold cerebral matter made his finger freeze, as if he were boring into a block of ice. He ignored the cold, he was too fascinated by the manner in which the deceased told his story, offered solutions and answers to which Farin only had to find the right questions.

"What are you doing there?" asked Plaudius harshly.

"Listening – the deceased is speaking to me."

"I don't hear anything." The fat man rolled his eyes.

I'd better finish soon, Farin thought.

His companions were losing patience at the same speed as their body temperature was dropping, and their enthusiasm for this little adventure into the castle's cold catacombs had been half-hearted to start with.

"Done already!" asserted Farin. "Let's turn him back over quickly and get back into the warmth."

"The nutcase's first reasonable suggestion", praised Drogdan glancing sideways at him quickly and spinning Keimund's corpse back onto its back. "Come on, let's split!"

"Just the cerecloth." Farin gently covered the deceased with the fabric.

The way back seemed shorter to him, maybe it had something to do with their leader's quicker pace. When they reached the iron bars, Stump began to close the upper ones by pushing them towards the left wall. Plaudius helped by moving the lower ones with his frozen fingers – however, he didn't quite manage to push the last one completely back into the mechanism. It seemed that only Farin noticed, for nobody reacted – they all wanted to get back to the hearth as quickly as possible.

Why didn't Farin tell the others? He had never liked locked doors and…there was always the chance he might want to make a little trip back here again. Preferably alone. He was thin enough to be able to squeeze through the gap below.

"What did that profit us, apart from freezing my dick off?" asked Drogdan once they were back in the stairwell.

"Plenty! Really, plenty!" blurted out Farin. "What exactly, you've yet to learn – I still haven't finished my deliberations. Where can I get parchment and charcoal?"

"I'll get you what you need. Do you want to write a letter home?" asked Plaudius.

"No, I want to draw a picture."

"You're the battiest bat we've ever had up here in the castle."

Neither Drogdan nor Stump contradicted their comrade.

"Trust me. And grant me one last wish – nothing in comparison to our trip into the catacombs."

"What else?" grumbled Drogdan. "Even though the lord of the castle told us to look after you, he never suggested we should be your serfs."

"I understand that. Just show me the place where the body was found."

"Right so, but that'll be it then. Let's go to the west keep."

Having arrived there, Drogdan pointed to the cobblestones at the foot of the tower. "This is where Keimund was lying." He pointed up at a platform, just over three yards above them. "That's where he fell over the parapet to his death."

"Not very high. Was he on guard duty?"

"No, squires don't do guard duty."

"Were there witnesses?"

"No, he was on his own up there. Some people say he committed suicide." Drogdan shook his head. "But I don't believe that."

Farin carefully examined the spot where the body was found and felt the cobblestones. He could find nothing out of the ordinary, which only reinforced his suspicions.

"That's it. We're finished," said the gravedigger's son.

"We did these very unusual favours for you. Now, spit it out, why all the hullabaloo?" Drogdan looked at him provokingly.

"Have you found your clues?" asked Plaudius.

Farin whispered: "I have. And many clues point in one direction. Thanks again for your help and your belief in me. And I'll gladly repay you – please keep this to yourselves: I'm certain it wasn't an accident and definitely not suicide. Squire Keimund was murdered. And the murderer thinks he's safe and is probably living amongst us."

Suspicious, surprised and solicitous looks.

"Hrrmm!" said Stump.

The candles in the little room in the south tower burned long into the night. Farin sat on his bed, legs tucked up, and sketched. A small board served as a base for the parchment. He'd succeeded in sketching what he wanted at his first attempt. He held it in front of him with arms outstretched and examined his work from a distance. It looked completely unspectacular, but its accuracy was what pleased Farin. He drew a circle under it which contained a pentagram with a flame within it. He could hardly wait to tell the lord of the castle of his discoveries. He would ask to speak to Knight Emicho tomorrow at noon. At last he could prove he was of some use, offer his expertise and earn a bit of recognition. He thought over everything he had been considering and kept coming to the same conclusion. It took him forever to fall asleep he was so excited.

Directly after breakfast the next morning Farin made his way to the lord of the castle's scriptorium. One of the two guards standing at the closed door said: "The lord of the castle is unavailable today."

"But it's incredibly important," blurted Farin.

The man sighed: "For the last twenty years I've been dreaming of the day when somebody will turn up and say: I only have rubbishy stuff for the lord of the castle, pretty boring and less relevant than a pubic louse. Should I come back again in two weeks?"

"Oh, right. How about tomorrow?"

"His lordship will be travelling the next three days. Come back in four."

Farin turned around sullenly and went back to his tower room. Did the knight not take his squire on trips? On the other hand, swordplay training with Drogdan was beginning this afternoon – maybe that was more important to the lord of the castle. Farin knew that he was never going to be a master swordsman, but he wanted to improve as much as he could in the short time available before the tournament. No, he wanted to be even better than that! His misfortunate fight against the boy on the training meadow still gnawed at him.

Drogdan, leaning lazily against the wall, was already waiting for him in the stables. "Here, I brought you this." He handed Farin a belt with a sword in its scabbard.

"Are we not practising with wooden swords?" he blurted out fearfully.

"Listen to me! You're too old to be spending the next couple of years brandishing a kid's sword in the air. So, we're starting directly with genuine steel. And count yourself lucky if you pick up the fundamentals in the next few months."

"Yes, Drogdan," nodded Farin enthusiastically. Then he put on the belt and drew his sword. "Boy, but that's heavy." He looked at the blade with a mixture of delight and unease. Metal forged by human hands for only one purpose: to kill other people. The sword had no decorations, no blood groove, no signature – pure, functional steel, pointed at the tip and sharp on the sides. He lovingly caressed the hilt covered in thin buckskin. He tightened his fingers around it so that his knuckles became white. He would never again deliberately drop a sword.

A quick glance was enough for Drogdan. "Don't grip it too hard and cramped. Loosen your fingers, grip it a little higher and now strike and stab holes in the air. Let your hand and arm get used to the weapon. And give the sword a chance to get used to you."

Farin spent the next hour defeating countless enemies. Numerous invisible enemies, which had the advantage that he wasn't wading knee-deep in their blood and the floor of the stable still looked pretty unsplattered. Drogdan watched him impassively as he progressed with his butchering.

Following a few more victories Farin asked: "And? Drogdan? What do you think? Am I a natural talent?" Then he swung around, skewering three more spirits of the air.

"You are blessed. We just have to refine your leg positions, as well as the way you stand on your feet, the way you roll off the soles, your grip, the coordination of shoulders and arm, the correct way of swinging the weapon, the position of your torso, the way you observe, and allied to that, the way you turn your head, and of course, your arm and hip-work."

Farin stopped dead in his tracks. The spirits of the air breathed a sigh of relief. "Is there *anything* I can do well yet?"

"Of course. A lot of things, in fact. Let me think now…for example…gosh, why can't I think of anything now?"

"Very funny. I've been getting lessons in sarcasm all my life."

Drogdan gave a crooked smile. "You were positively screaming for sarcasm." He clapped his hands. "That's enough for today. I'll think up new exercises for you for tomorrow. And don't feel down. After all, you didn't do too much damage to the sword and you didn't injure yourself with the blade." He pointed his forefinger upward. "Now put the sharp, long, keen blade *very* carefully back into its scabbard."

Drogdan really knew how to cheer up gravediggers' sons.

At least he added a bit: "Take the weapon with you to your tower room – it's yours. Bring it with you to all training sessions."

"I...I thank you." Farin gave a deep bow. A sword – he owned a real sword.

After this experience Farin decided to visit the library, at least the part he was permitted to enter. What had Markan said to him during his tour of the castle on the first day: The library is in a room in the great hall.

At the end of a long, dreary corridor he arrived at a guard standing outside a panelled double door. The man blocked his way with an impressive halberd.

"Entry forbidden!"

Oh, I see.

Always the same in this stronghold. Everything grey and depressing and any time it promised to become more colourful Farin failed at a closed door with a guard in front of it.

"The lord of the castle has granted me permission to enter the library."

"Hm! Anyone can claim that. Who are you?" The man's face bristled with duteousness. Presumably it only happened once a month that someone requested permission to enter the library.

"I...I'm the lord of the castle's new squire. Farin is my name."

"Hm. I don't know you, and so I cannot grant you access." His eyes glimmered defiantly.

Farin gave it another go. "You've more than likely heard of me already. The squire who drops his sword in every training fight with toddlers and grovels for mercy."

"Well, obviously, news like that spreads like wildfire. So that's you, then!" The guard seemed mightily impressed.

"I never learned how to fight because I spent all my

childhood buried in books. My kingdom is the library, entry to which Knight Emicho, Lord of Stormwatch has specifically granted."

"I know nothing about that. Entrance denied!"

"Must I really trouble the lord of the castle to come to you? He won't be at all happy."

"Entrance denied. I'm only doing my duty."

This was typical in the grey castle. He stood there like an idiot facing the stubborn guard and would have to turn back without having achieved anything.

The soldier tilted his head slightly and then mumbled: "Alright, then. I'll let you in." His stubborn look was in stark contrast to what he'd said, but he raised the halberd so that it was vertical beside him and freed the way. "You may enter. But I'm watching you."

Surprised, Farin pushed open the heavy double doors. Get in quickly before the guard reconsiders things. But why the sudden change of heart?

He stood in a hall flooded with light from countless leaded windows through which the rays of sunshine streamed, lighting up every corner. Rows and rows of bookshelves wherever he looked, packed full of many thousands of bound sheets, folios, books both thick and thin. The racks seemed to soar into the heavens. Countless ladders enabled access to the writings in the higher spheres. Their tops were hooked onto rails enabling the ladders to be pushed effortlessly without fear of them falling over. Farin stood in front of all those towers of books, open-mouthed and wondering what he was doing here at all. Yes, mother taught him how to read, and he'd loved it. But he hadn't mastered it properly, it sometimes took him half an eternity before he comprehended the meaning of a particular word.

If he did nothing but read every day for the next forty years, how many books would he manage in the first row of shelves? A tenth? A hundredth more like.

Don't lose courage, he thought to himself. You need to concentrate and pick a selection. Find the three books that will enrich your life, answer your questions, help you to understand the world better. Oh yes – and help you get rid of the chimera.

After all, that had been his primary reason for visiting the library. Good resolution, but where should he begin? Bravely, he stepped into the first aisle, turned to his right and pulled out a book at random. The heavy leather cover without an inscription made him curious. He opened it carefully. Not one of the letters, drawn carefully in black ink, did he recognise. How could that happen? Slowly it began to dawn on him: here were books that weren't only in his own language. And the book he was holding in his hands was definitely in another – the gobbledegook only made him dizzy

Has the new bookworm of the stronghold bitten off a little more than he can chew?

You were tempting fate by thinking too much about Stinker, thought Farin, scolding himself. "I thought you only made an appearance when I was afraid?"

It can also happen when you're being asinine – in other words, just about always. Ever since you threw the amulet onto the fire I've been on standby. What you're holding in your hand is a book with instructions on how to lessen pain during menstruation. That will really change your life.

Farin looked at the black ink sceptically. "You could be telling me anything. Are you claiming that you understand the meaning of these words?"

I'm not claiming anything, I've no need to do that. It's Cartanesian, a language I speak fluently. You forget that I've been learning for the last eight hundred years.

"How many languages can you speak?"

Twenty-two.

What a pretentious stinker!

But then Farin hesitated and pursed his lips. He realised for the first time that it wasn't just a shameless, rude, unbearable lout that had made itself at home in his head, but also an unimaginably deep and dank pool of knowledge and experience. Lost in thought he pushed the book back onto its shelf, went to the next aisle, pulled out a heavy tome at head height and opened it in the middle. On the left page he saw a large gadget that looked like an instrument of torture. The explanatory letters next to it were unfamiliar too.

Condunesian, you have to read it from right to left.

"You could be telling me anything at all…" He shoved out his lower lip suspiciously.

Allow a part of your spirit to float, then let it go, and I'll prove it to you.

"You mean I should hand over control of my body to you? Never."

You did it once before already when Peat and his friends wanted to knock out your teeth.

"That was a mistake — after all, I was almost unconscious."

Hah, bookworm — it was your idea to come here. Do you want to read what you have in your hands there? Then let me…enlighten this part of your dull soul a little. Otherwise, good luck.

The realisation struck him like a thunderbolt. That was all he needed – he couldn't deny it: Stinker was right.

Farin looked at the gobbledegook in his hands again. He

held the pages further away from his eyes, the letters became a little blurry as he relaxed. What did he want? Oh, yes, to let go, float, create a space for new thoughts, new impulses, new ideas. Nothing changed, what had he expected?

The gravedigger's son decided to put the stupid tome back in its place, after all, the theme of instruments of torture didn't interest him.

"...even the tightening of the loom must be done with complete accuracy. Carpet manufacturing...figure 21: assembling the loom."

Nobody in Heap possessed a carpet, even here in the castle there were less than a handful, so why would he need...

Farin stared at the book, his eyes like burning lenses. Luckily, the old paper didn't ignite. Goose pimples rolled along his back – first up, then down. He could read it, he could understand it. With furrowed brows, the gravedigger's son looked at the title of the tome. "The Art of Carpet Weaving and the Variations between the Northern and Southern Lands." Another theme he wasn't exactly passionate about, but he understood what was written there.

"Stinker, that's...that's amazing."

Sorry? I didn't quite catch you there.

"Yes, you did. I'm not going to repeat myself." Fascinated, the gravedigger's son flicked through the old book. He never would have believed that someone from the weaving profession could have come up with such scholarship. Were there any treatises on washing corpses hidden away somewhere?

"Tell me, daemon. Explain to me all that about letting go again. And what roles do body, spirit and soul play in the proceedings?"

I'm not going to repeat myself.

"I get it, you're right. I was too stroppy just now. Explain it to me again, please."

There was a grumbling in his head, but Stinker only hesitated for a moment: *It's humans that make such a song and dance when it comes to body, spirit and soul. Let's start with the trivial: the body. That's the impractical long thing that's learned to walk on two legs, on top of which, crowning it all off, there's a balloon – far too big, ugly and round. You can't change them – humans: your body is your shell – look after it, keep it in good shape. You only have the one. Most humans are far too careless when it comes to taking care of it, which is why I was pleasantly surprised when I saw your morning teeth-cleaning ritual.*

Farin was dumbstruck.

How do you define your spirit? Herein you find the manifestation of your feelings, experiences and considerations, even beyond the limit of your own intellect. Your consciousness, your trust in yourself, your mindset, all determining the direction of your actions.

"Don't understand."

Did I really say intellect? That's because the limits of the aforementioned are pretty narrow in your case.

"I understood that and don't find it funny."

The chimera seemed to be completely in its element. *You act so that you feel as contented as possible. You strive by your actions and their consequences to keep things straightened out with yourself, in other words to bring your spirit and body into harmony.*

"Of course, yes. It's all very simple. I act as smartly as possibly. And want to feel good in the process. I always do that."

A sigh indicated to Farin that Stinker had a completely different opinion. *That could be very easy, but it isn't. Abstraction isn't your strong point. A lot of the time your behaviour is the opposite of intelligent or rational.*

"Aha – your insults are starting again."

Let me give you a simple example. Do you remember that incident in Heap when Peat and his cronies harassed you the first time?

"Harassed is a good one, the tall moron, what's his name again, made me trip over his leg."

Kaal is his name. What would have been the correct decision for body and spirit?

Profound silence! The many dogeared books around him listening intently.

Are you listening to me or have you fallen asleep? What would have been...smart?

One of the border posts in a corner of his narrowly confined intellect began to shake. Then it came, quietly and cautiously: "Run away?"

Exactly, there's still hope for you. Run away and quickly too. Your body was already injured on account of the fall, your spirit in the form of intelligence and experience made it clear to you beyond any doubt that you didn't stand a snowball's chance in hell against the four thugs. Your average daemon wouldn't give it a second thought but would flee. Vamoose, and – hey presto! And what did the clever little worm decide on – in spite of any imaginable type of reason? He stays and plants his small, bare little fist into Peat's gob. Little worm fights because he imagines he has to go through hell. And so he calls out, full of self-confidence: Come on with your punches and kicks, I'm not going to run away from you cowardly dogs, there are only four of you and you're a hundred times stronger than me.

Farin's behaviour that time *did* sound pretty gormless, coming out of the chimera's mouth. "They insulted my honour as gravedigger," he blurted angrily.

Another sigh. *Honour?* Something was shaking in Farin even though he himself wasn't shaking. *Anyway, you didn't run away. Also, so you could look at your bloody face afterwards in the stream. After eight-hundred years I still don't understand the point of that kind of behaviour.*

Although the voice didn't have its usual sarcastic and mean tone, Farin was feeling worse and worse. The daemon was shining a light on him from all sides, was turning him inside out and upside down. Any moment now and he'd be laughing at him gleefully.

This pointer on the scales, that ensures balance between body and spirit, we call the soul. According to your measurements, your soul remained unsullied during this incident. In order to define the soul, clarify this: what does your soul good when your soul is talking to you.

With surprising strength Farin said: "If I follow my instinct, if I trust my intuition, if it feels right. If it's honourable."

Hm – not bad. All that strengthens the ties between body, spirit and soul. All that results in harmony. Only the thing regarding honour is something that people play fast and loose with all too often.

"Honour is important!" insisted Farin.

Stinker felt provoked. *Honour is a pennon in the wind. Honour is a matter of opinion. Your enemy kills you. Honourable. What is true honour then? People claim they have to search out honour. Rubbish! Honour comes to you of its own free will. It finds you if you've earned it. But we're digressing.*

"And what do you want from me now?" asked Farin, more harshly than he'd intended. The fact that Stinker of all things was mouthing off about honour and harmony was almost too much to bear.

I'm interested in this unreasonable needle in the weighing scales. The soul is the most magical thing I've found in the human kingdom so far. I would have died of boredom long ago in your world without this phenomenon. But it's the soul that brings the unexpected to light again and again. And yours is pure and strong.

The words came across greedily.

"That sounds comprehensible. I think I can use some of that for myself. The only thing disturbing my harmonious trinity is a sarcastic chimera rampaging around inside my head, uninvited."

Wimpish little worm, you understand nothing. You're a long way from equanimity, concordance and balance. You're neither focussed, nor do you possess a reasonable measure of self-awareness. You're lacking in aggression, decisiveness and tenacity. I can help you compensate for your deficits to achieve psychological balance. But for that you have to let me in. The chimera snorted impatiently. *You've just done it, you've opened a tiny window into your dusty spirit, through which I can slip in and enable you to read in foreign languages. That's more than your God ever did for you.*

Farin mechanically pushed the book on carpet weaving back in its place. "Hm! I have a goal I'm following with determination. I want to be a good squire!"

Well, then!

"Now I have to get a move on, I don't know how much more time the guard will allow me in the library. How do I orientate myself among all this book chaos?

The shelves are colour coded. On the south wall is a board with explanations. I think you'll find the really interesting works at the back of the library.

Only now did Farin notice the big boards left and right. The various subject areas such as history, geography, arithmetic, philosophy, natural history and crafts were given individual colours which could be found again on little signs at the tops of the shelves. He'd accidentally landed in the crafts section. Was he interested in any of the other themes? No sign of demonology, anyway.

He was about to move on when…wait – history. Farin wanted to find out more about Castle Stormwatch. He looked for the white markings and found two long shelves with books about architecture, lost kingdoms, battles and wars, old and new constructions. When he got to the end, several crimson tomes drew his attention. A quick look confirmed that the books were written in his language.

"Time's up. I'm locking the library now." Tap, tap, tap. The sound of the halberd on the tiled floor echoed loudly and clearly. Farin concluded his excursion into the world of the written word by stuffing the first volume under his tunic. He wanted to read it in peace later in the tower room.

"Thank you", he said to the guard as he left the library. Luckily, the man took no notice of his fat, literate stomach.

the dress

I t was around midnight when Aross scaled the graveyard wall. The crumbling mortar between the large stones was a perfect fit for her small toes. This was where the aristocracy buried their dead, entrance to the riffraff strictly forbidden.

Bans never bothered rats.

The detour had been necessary as she'd spotted two soldiers of the town watch on the large square doing their rounds between the cathedral and the place of execution.

Crouched, she flitted her way between the graves and crypts. She stopped at a fresh grave mound and rubbed dark earth onto her forehead, cheeks, chin and throat. Arms and feet received the same treatment too. Now she resembled her shadow. She reached the front of the cathedral without further difficulties and examined the scene. The large square lay in darkness. On her right and towards the upper town, lanterns burned every hundred paces all the way up to the royal palace. Thirty yards in front of the cathedral entrance, the remaining embers of the pyre cast the surrounding area in a diffuse circle of light. The two guards were standing a few yards in front of the enormous double doors and were looking straight at the remains of the fire. The soldier closer to her looked just like a horse that was standing and sleeping. The other seemed to fit into the image by occasionally shaking himself and snorting.

Shit, thought Aross. Embers and guards made the matter much more complicated. Do they always stand here? Are they guarding the entrance to the cathedral or the execution platform?

The girl had no idea – after all, she never hung around the large square in the middle of the night. The eager crescent of the moon splashed light here and there. She thought about her situation – sometimes thinking helped even if nothing struck you. A big cloud pushed its way in front of the moon. That seemed to Aross to be a sign, and so she decided to take advantage of the opportunity. It was hardly going to get any darker. All rats were grey – not only during the night. She crept towards the embers, which were still radiating enormous heat, in a roundabout manner. The ice-cold cobbles were becoming warmer and warmer.

A voice echoed across the square. Aross remained motionless, pressed to the ground, her heart beating wildly in her breast.

"Have you nodded off again, Fredder?"

"Uh…? Um…noooo. Not at all."

"That's alright then," said the other guard, with a touch of malice in his voice.

Shit and more shit! Now they were both awake.

The girl waited another while and threw a concerned look up to the heavens. The cloud cover was thinning and threatening to separate – the moon wasn't going to hide her for much longer.

Using her forearms, the girl pushed herself across the square and closer to the platform. Only another few yards and she could hide herself behind it. Success! Two steps led up the stone platform. She cautiously looked over the top ledge. Good that she'd rubbed her face with earth, so it wouldn't reflect the embers like a red Chinese lantern.

Where had Shewhoknows been standing? Aross couldn't make it out exactly, now that the wooden stake was missing. Of course – the fire had also reduced it to ashes. Ashes everywhere. Fire was an equaliser. Enough heat and everything turned into grey flakes. The girl raised her head, the embers were drying out her eyes, burning her brows, at least that's what it felt like. She couldn't see a single bone, never mind the skull. Instead, she spotted glowing, oval rings. The iron shackles with which the old woman had been tied to the stake. That's exactly where she must have stood. And that's where she'd died, for reasons Aross couldn't understand. She didn't believe one word of the spurious tittle-tattle about weather magic nor the nonsense about hanky-panky with the devil.

She hadn't anticipated this being so difficult. Even if the light of the embers was quite weak, it still created shadows. Long shadows that sometimes moved. In spite of this danger and the increasing heat, Aross crept closer to the shackles.

"There's something moving over there in the pyre, Fred-der."

"Uh...? Um...noooo. Not at all."

"Wake up, you idiot. I'm telling you, there's something there."

"Uaah!" A loud yawn. "Sure – the witch is still living and is about to walk home as if nothing at all happened." The man craned his neck. "I can't see anything."

"I'll go have a look." The chainmail rattled lightly as the guard on the left marched closer, pike extended. He took his job damn seriously.

Aross narrowed her eyes to protect them from the heat, and in desperation searched the embers and ashes one last time. The earth on her face stretched on her skin. Nothing! She could do no more, now she had to scarper as quickly as possible. A bright point attracted her attention, a little away from the shackles, something small and shiny. Aross didn't hesitate for a second but grabbed it. Ashes burned her fingers, the hot object bit into her palm, but she gripped it as hard as she had gripped Shewhoknows's silverling that time.

"In the name of the King, come down! What are you looking for up there?"

Aross was already on her feet, made one leap down the two steps and ran as she had never run before, diagonally across the large square, away from the heat, away from the guard, away from the fear. She heard rattling steps behind her that slowly died away. A quick glance over her shoulder showed her the guard had given up. Good that chainmail boots and fast running didn't exactly go hand in hand.

The girl reached the narrow alleyways of the old town. Only now did her heartbeat slow down. Her closed hand which held the object hurt, but she took no notice. She knew where she would spend the night – she headed back to the place she had headed back to a thousand times before – the orphanage.

She was surprised by a new sensation when the dark silhouette of her old home came into view. She felt no sense of belonging, no sense of security or familiarity, but was filled with mistrust and suspicion. She crept closer, saw nothing out of the ordinary, everybody was long since in bed. In spite of her anxiety, she yawned. She absolutely needed a place to sleep. She tiptoed into the old barn. It smelled musty and her toes sank into the damp ground.

Oh yes, all that blood, she thought.

The haystack, the old ladder to the hayloft, the pitchfork against the wall, a few sleeping hens – everything as she remembered it. Only Wolf was missing from the corner.

She quietly climbed the ladder and slipped through the hatch, closed it behind her and crept into the deep straw. Only now did she open her hand. There was the knickknack that Shewhoknows had spoken of. A molar. Her molar! Her memento of the old woman, that was all that was left of her. What a world!

Forgive me, Shewhoknows. But you really wanted me to collect it. The witch's tooth! The tooth of time? Whatever it was supposed to mean, whatever it was supposed to be good for. The girl realised with contentment that she had paid her debt to the old woman. Weary, she curled up in the straw. Exhaustion led her into a dreamless sleep.

Voices!

Aross's eyes opened wide. She was lying in the hayloft in the orphanage barn, and the sun was already high in the sky. Two men were talking a short distance away in the yard.

One of the kitchen maids came out of the house and stuttered a few obsequious phrases. "Your Excellency" was one of them.

Aross crept across the straw as quietly as she could, ready for another wild flight across the roof. Steps approached, she held her breath. She could see nothing – she didn't dare to stick her head out of the hole in the roof. She did the only thing that was open to her for the moment – she eavesdropped.

One of the men explained: "It happened in the old barn. Rats tore the orphanage matron to pieces. I've never seen such a mutilated body in all my livelong days."

"I want to take a look in the barn, captain," said a mellif-luous voice.

Dammit, what did *he* want here?

The door opened and Aross pressed her eye to a gap between the floorboards. The Archbishop of Hubstone was standing directly under her and looking all around him.

The maid said eagerly: "The matron was lying here, under the ladder. Everything was full of blood and the rats..."

"Spare me your drivel!" said the bishop, cutting her off. "Just answer my questions."

"My apologies, Your Excellency."

"I'm looking for a girl. Fifteen years old at most. Small, ugly, grubby. Short, slime-coloured hair, scratched face. She was at the witch burning yesterday and was wearing a dress from this orphanage."

"All the children were here, sir."

"Apparently, not everyone. I could of course have all your fingernails pulled out to help you remember", suggested the bishop.

"Please, sir...only one girl is missing, but she's been gone two days already. Aross is her name – it can only be her."

"Aross? Strange name. What's her story?"

"The matron was giving her a beating when the rats appeared."

"Where is this Aross?"

"Sir, I don't know. She ran off and hasn't appeared since."

"You're not exactly helpful. Do you at least know what happened here?"

"I'm sorry...I only helped to move the bodies, Your Excellency."

"What do you mean, bodies? Who else died apart from the matron?"

"The dog, Wolf. Aross stabbed him to death, there in the corner, with the pitchfork."

"You're talking about a moronic mutt? Why did she do that?"

"Sir…we can't explain it. To be honest, the girl really liked the dog and was always nice to him."

More marching steps echoed across the yard. Aross reckoned there had to be at least ten men standing before the barn. Things were getting better and better. Or worse and worse.

Dear day, hardly do I open my eyes, but you have the first surprise ready for me. I could really begin to believe you have something against me. I really need air, she thought. Oh yes – don't forget to breathe.

The sharp voice of a soldier cut the air: "Your Excellency! Here is a man who wishes to speak to you. A matter of great urgency, he claims."

"Very well. I'll deal with him."

The maid interrupted by whining: "Sir, I've said everything. May I go now?"

This was clearly going too far for His Excellency, the archbishop.

"People always have something to hide. What do you think, captain?"

"Uh…I follow orders and leave the thinking to others."

"Very good! Take the stupid cow away. Get everything she knows about Aross out of her. When she arrived in the orphanage, where she comes from, what she likes to eat, who her friends are…everything! Skin her alive or do whatever with her, then she won't forget anything."

"No...sir...mercy. I have done nothing, sir. I'll tell you everything! I beg you, don't take me away!"

"Shut your trap!" The bishop's voice trembled with fury. Aross could sense through the ceiling how dangerous and unpredictable the man was. "Take her away!" he ordered. "Captain, wait outside."

"As you command."

Aross heard the stamping of boots once again. The captain left the barn and the town watch led the maid across the yard. The poor thing whined and wailed, there was the sound of a slap, then she was silent.

The bishop closed the door, leaving himself and the newcomer alone in the barn below. The latter was standing so far to the left that Aross couldn't see him through the little gap.

The bishop snapped at him in a lowered voice: "You do realise that you should only come and see me in the most urgent of cases. I'm a very busy man."

"Who says this isn't an urgent case?" the stranger sounded throaty and sinister. He clicked his tongue quietly. "But let's leave that for the moment, we'd need more time than the few minutes we have. What brings you to this...establishment?"

Aross thought she was hearing things. How could he be talking like this to the godlike archbishop?

"A girl called Aross lives in this orphanage. This much is obvious: the mistress of the dark arts we burned at the stake yesterday was in league with the girl."

"Mistress of the dark arts? Is that your term for the evil witch?" it wheezed, unimpressed. "I arrived just in time to experience your performance. The old woman stole the show from you. Ah well, there won't be a second performance with the same cast."

A cold shiver ran up the girl's spine. The voice was swimming in scorn and malevolence. Such wickedness was unfolding only a few inches away from her this morning – such an honour!

"She was anything but evil and anything but a witch. But she was becoming a problem and a danger to our plans. The boss wanted her to burn. Or do you believe that nonsense about screwing the devil?"

"Of course not, but that's not the point. The main thing is – the people believe it."

The bishop let out a malicious laugh. "Don't you worry about that. I decide what our honest citizens believe."

"Of course! One reason I like you so much," whispered the voice. "Why was the witch so dangerous?"

"She knew all about the Necorers. An obscure woman with extraordinary abilities. She sailed here from over the ocean with Redbeard."

"On the Barbarossa? Amazing! But I wanted to discuss another problem with you. I'm just back from Heap. The gravedigger's son has left the village."

"How is that possible?" the bishop groaned. "If you hadn't slit open the priest there lengthwise, we'd have got all the information we needed."

"You see I have no difficulty in slaughtering a man of the cloth – just for fun."

Aross shivered. She found the man sinister. Also, her bladder was very full.

"Are you trying to threaten me?" The archbishop was indignant now. He certainly wasn't used to anything like this.

"I'm not *trying* to, I *am*. You should have told me about this Gerlunda much earlier. Now it's going to be much more hassle finding her," he whispered.

"What about the village alderman? Didn't you want to take him in hand too?" asked the bishop. He clearly didn't want the argument to intensify.

"I'll leave him in peace for the time being. We've rocked the boat enough already, so we'll concentrate on the most likely thing. My instinct tells me: The gravedigger's son has it and that's why he disappeared from the village."

"Where could he be hiding?"

"His father absolutely didn't want to tell me. A tough nut, I had to cut off a few body parts before he eventually spilled the beans."

His wheezy chuckle as he spoke caused a fearful shiver to run down Aross's back. She would never have believed a person could be capable of such malicious whispering.

"You'll never believe it, but the gravedigger's son is staying in Castle Stormwatch in the company of our good friend Emicho and is being trained as a squire. Nothing slips past the boss."

"That's incredible! Who would believe it?" said the bishop in amazement. "Does Emicho suspect anything?"

"I don't know. We have a plan for getting rid of the troublesome knight once and for all. And we're going to need your help. The grand tournament will take place right on his doorstep next year – the perfect opportunity. The boss has also instructed our informers in the castle. It won't be long before we know what the gravedigger's son is up to."

Aross didn't understand a single word of the conversation. She thought about Shewhoknows, who sailed over the ocean with Redbeard. Whatever that meant.

The man certainly didn't seem to be overflowing with respect for His Excellency, the archbishop of Hubstone.

Aross could feel every muscle in her body, she was lying in such a cramped position on the rough planks and squinting through the gap. Added to that she was dying for a piss. Maybe onto the archbishop's head?

Seeing as God's representative in the Worldly Kingdom was paying a visit, a prayer had to be uttered: Please go away, just please go away. Amen.

She really shouldn't have appealed to heaven and certainly not with those words, for now the bishop was looking up towards the ceiling. Their eyes met.

He can't possibly see me, the gap is too small, and anyway I'm lying in darkness, Aross tried to reassure herself. It was getting hot, almost as hot as the previous evening on the platform.

The bishop yanked open the barndoor: "Captain, where does the ladder lead to?"

"Up to a little hayloft, nothing special, I've searched it already."

"I'm going to check it out myself", decided the bishop.

Aross regretted her prayer, it had only made everything worse. Her legs were twitching, she had to flee.

The sound of cracking wood stopped her.

"For Christ's sake! The damn rungs are half rotten."

The God-fearing man abandoned his attempt to scale the ladder.

A rustling sound. A flying, clucking hen.

"Where did the rats come from so suddenly, and since when have they ganged up to attack people?" asked the bishop, more to himself than to his companions. "My instinct tells me, it has something to do with that girl called Aross. So, bring the hussy to me."

"We'll catch her," assured the captain.

"What's the story with the only witness – Grim?"

"It was clearly too much for him when the rats made mincemeat of the matron. He fainted. He knows no more than what he's told us already. What should we do with him?"

The bishop clarified the matter callously. "The rabble really revolt me. String him up or cut his throat."

"He claims he can deliver Aross to us if we let him go. Nobody knows her as well as he does." The captain's voice suggested he believed Grim.

"The little shitbag is unimportant. Well then, if he helps to find the hussy, let him go. We can string him up afterwards anyway. Come on, I want to have a look in the orphanage."

The men left the barn. For a fleeting moment Aross caught a glimpse of the creepy whisperer. A chalk-white hooked nose peeked out from under a black cape. The mouth consisted of a thin line, no lips. He followed the others out the door.

The girl in the hayloft was alone once more and continued to shiver for a time.

What have I landed myself in now?

The sounds outside suggested that the men had entered the orphanage. Aross carefully stuck her head out through the hole in the roof. The town watch was no longer to be seen; the yard was completely deserted.

She needed to get away from here as fast as possible before anybody decided to check out the loft.

At the very back under the straw was her water bottle with its leather strap. She hung it around her neck. She took her felt cap from its hook and put it on her head. She left the coins where they were; it would make too much of a racket were she to loosen the board and would take too long if she didn't want to risk peeing in her dress. And the tooth? Where should she put that? Stupid question, where did teeth belong? She stuck it in her mouth like a sweet. A bitter, ashen taste spread out on her tongue. If she swallowed it by mistake, it would turn up again, anyway. Main thing was, she had both hands free for climbing. Off she went, through the hole in the roof shingles and over the ledge to the beech tree. She made her way, hand over hand, along the bough, down onto the ground. The entrance door to the orphanage remained closed, nobody seemed to have noticed the girl. She ran – just get away from here.

Aross gathered herself together, leaning against a wall in one of the laneways. It took a while for her breathing to normalise. God's supreme servant was a despicable misanthrope – that much was clear. She didn't want to know all the things he did in the name of the Lord – on no account must he catch her. His visitor, the hoarse whisperer, sounded at least as dangerous. And the mendacious meanie Grim really believed he could hunt her down?

The first thing she needed to do was to get another dress or dye her old one. The children of the orphanage were, of course, strictly forbidden from doing either of those things. But she wasn't a child of the orphanage anymore. Aross realised she was free now, free from serving at table, free from orphanage rules, free from the matron.

Now I'll be making my own rules. The first thing I'll do is get myself a dress from one of the clotheslines in the upper town.

People seemed to be looking at her more than was usual. When she touched her face, she understood why – much of the graveyard clay was still sticking to it. It wasn't far to the well in the old town. Using both hands she washed the dirt from her skin with the yellowed water. She had to learn to be as inconspicuous as possible. The upper town was teeming with clotheslines, hanging between the houses. Mostly airily high, but that wouldn't present too much of a difficulty to Aross.

Everything was clean as a whistle here compared to the old town, and it even smelled half-way decent. No wonder – the canals ran under the ground and flowed downward. The one thing the Uptowners had to spare for the slums was the shit from the sewers.

Her cap pulled low over her face, Aross climbed two steps at a time in spite of her short legs. The long steps led up the hill to the royal castle. She didn't want to run for too long, so halfway up she veered left and walked through the narrow streets with a face that suggested she was on a very important errand. Her timing was perfect, the women had spent the morning washing clothes and hanging them up in the sunshine. The lines ran every which way, from balconies to hooks, from windows to metal loops.

What a choice: shirts, socks, legwear, underwear and dresses dripping everywhere. Preferably long-sleeved, after all, winter was coming, although it was rarely really cold in Hubstone, thankfully. It gets really cold up north, a kitchen maid had explained one time. So cold that the water became hard as iron. Aross hadn't believed such nonsense, of course. How was that supposed to happen?

A clothesline in a side street attracted her attention. Three linen dresses hung across the alley just over three yards high. They were all roughly her size; she liked the middle one best, brown with nice long sleeves. A man approached her, she looked down at the ground – all innocence – he ambled past her without giving her a second look. Aross quickly glanced over her shoulder, the man disappeared around a corner. A quick look ahead – not a sinner to be seen. She scaled up the house wall on the left, child's play, first up the railing beside the front door, next onto the porch roof over the entrance, and now there was only another yard before grabbing the dress. And then, instead of tossing them a coin in payment, she would simply turn tail and run!

With one foot balanced on the ledge, she stretched her fingers forward. Only two widths of a thumb. Her forefinger was already touching the material. Then two arms were grabbing her under her armpits and pulling her through an open window into the house.

"YOU THIEF! Think you can steal my washing, do you? You're in for a sound thrashing and then I'll hand you over to the town watch – let's see what *they* do to you."

Aross went pale with fright – she'd completely overlooked the open window on the second floor. A fat woman, two heads taller than Aross, was holding onto her tightly. She could grip even harder than Grim.

"What were you thinking of, girl?" Two beady eyes flashed angrily at her. Two powerful arms were shaking her.

"Eh-eh-eh-eh, uh-uh-uh-uh…"

The woman stopped her vigorous shaking.

"Has the cat got your tongue? What's wrong with you?"

"Aaahh, iiih, uhht." Aross's mouth was clattering.

"Don't think you can fool *me*! You're not going to get away from *me*."

She dragged Aross by the arm to the door, turned a large key and stuck it in her apron. She quickly walked to the window and closed it, not forgetting to bolt it.

"You look agile. Now you won't be able to escape until I'm done with you and call the town watch."

Aross instinctively remembered the beatings she'd suffered at the hands of the matron. She couldn't help searching the walls for canes.

"Sit over there!" barked the woman, gripping Aross firmly, dragging her to a chair and pushing her down on it.

Aross had walked right into the rattrap – not cheese, but clothing to catch her.

Still, now that everything was barricaded, the woman let go of her. "What have you got in your mouth?"

Aross didn't react.

The fat woman's cheeks went pink with anger. "Take it out, now!"

Reluctantly, the girl took the tooth out of her mouth. The woman looked in disbelief at her hand. Arms akimbo, she looked Aross up and down. "So that's what rotten, impudent girl thieves look like."

Aross still couldn't think of what she should say. She could think of nothing else but escape, but the wherewithal still failed her.

"What sort of a minx are you? Are you so hungry you have to suck on a tooth?"

"I…I don't know."

"When I look at you like that…totally scrawny, your ribs are showing through your dress." She examined Aross again, rubbed the material on her collar between her thumb and forefinger. "That's nothing but a rag," she sighed and frowned.

The woman sat down on an armchair directly opposite Aross. "Your grey dress. Are you from the orphanage?"

If she admitted it, the fat woman really would hand her

over to the town watch. It was getting more and more dangerous for Aross. Her only option was to fight. Her eyes darted left, then right. Maybe she'd find something she could hit hard with.

The woman leaned forward and yanked the cap off Aross's head. "And your face looks a mess."

Would the old dear please stop telling me what I know already? Is she going to give me a beating now or not?

The woman stared silently at Aross, the anger in her beady eyes evaporated. Her pink expression suggested several scenarios struggling with each other. Then she let out a peculiar groan, stood up, went to the window and leaned out of it.

Aross sat on her chair and thought furiously. The idea of fleeing felt like a cold shower – didn't appeal to Aross at all. No, not one little bit.

I'll take a run-up and shove the fat one out onto the street below.

The woman stood on her tiptoes and leaned further out of the window. Aross stood up, her poisonous stare fixed on the bum in the window. What other option was there if she wanted to save her own skin? The town watch would bring her straight to the bishop, that unscrupulous misanthrope. Torture, burning at the stake, hanged up by her feet and slit open like Mattilda – terrifying pictures flashed across the girl's mind.

Do it, Aross. Now or never!

"Which of the three dresses did you want to steal?" asked the fat woman in a friendly voice. "I'll give it to you as a present."

Never!

Gobsmacked, Aross sank back onto the chair. What did

she mean by that? What did the woman want from her? She surely had some trick up her sleeve.

Aross let her chance of escape pass by. The fat woman turned around, holding all three dresses in her hands. "Which do you like best?"

"I…uh…the…the brown one," stammered Aross.

"Stand up then."

She hesitantly got to her feet. The fat woman held the dress in front of Aross's body.

"Yes, fits quite well, maybe a little long, but you're still growing. It's practically dry. Why don't you try it on?"

Aross stood there, dumbfounded. That must have been a joke. Aross was a pathetic thief, that was beyond doubt. Friendliness and presents weren't part of the deal.

"Come on, then! We'll throw away that rag. Unless you really want to hold onto it."

Stunned beyond belief, Aross barely managed a shake of her head before pulling off her orphan dress. She still didn't know what to make of it all.

"Dear, oh dear, you really are nothing more than skin and bones." The fat woman held her hand in front of her mouth in horror. "And…who beat you like that?"

The signs of cane number five still shimmered impressively in green and blue – never mind the welts and encrusted wounds.

"Heavens, that's near enough to an execution. Did they catch you trying to steal the royal crown?" She said it with a friendly smile.

Suddenly something struck Aross, something that rarely played a role in her life – the truth. "I…I know, it sounds funny. But I'm innocent and in spite of that I was severely beaten."

"Hm. Come on now, slip into your new dress."

She helped Aross pull on the brown dress. The material was thicker and felt comfortable to the touch.

"Better already, child. If you like, I'll give you something to eat too."

Aross was completely at a loss. Was there anything more disarming than friendliness and kindness, especially when it came so unexpectedly? The terrible events of the past few days swooped hither and yon in her head like the seagulls in the harbour. The loss of Wolf, the terrible execution of Shewhoknows, Mattilda's death, her hatred for Grim and Chain Dog. A lonely waif, surrounded by catastrophes, fighting her way through the cesspool, being hunted down by the most powerful man in the city, the archbishop. Everything was collapsing in on her at the same time, pressing down on her tiny shoulders. But that wasn't all. Aross sobbed quietly so that only she could hear it. Then the tears rolled down her cheeks, she couldn't remember the last time she'd cried – but now, the time had come. The woman stretched out her arms and pulled the girl gently to her chest. The same hands that had only a moment ago grabbed her angrily and pulled her through the window and into the house were now stroking her back. An unbelievable feeling.

"What's the matter, child? Everything is alright, you can keep the dress and can go whenever you want to."

The silent tears were in full flow now. The fat woman's apron was becoming damp. Something else was causing her to sob which was enough to make you weep. A deep sense of shame and a guilty conscience! Hadn't she only just toyed with the idea of pushing the woman out of the window? Had the violence, corruption and depravity rubbed off on her to such a degree that she could no longer tell the difference between right and wrong?

"I…I, sorry. Thank…thank you. Thank you so much."

It was taking Aross a while to calm down.

Rats don't cry!

The new, long, brown sleeves were perfect for wiping away tears. At the last moment Aross managed to stop herself from heartily blowing her nose into one of them too. As if able to read minds, the woman produced a handkerchief before the girl's nose, dug the key out of her apron and opened the door.

"Well child, do you want something to eat before your go?" she asked.

Aross nodded, dried off her tears and nose with the handkerchief and followed the woman down the stairs and into a large living room. Only now was she really taking in her surroundings. On the walls hung pictures with people on them. Who could paint so wonderfully? The dark, polished furniture gleamed at her. Warm, soft carpets were spread out on the floor.

Her hostess placed a basket with bread and a plate with cheese, clarified butter and blood sausage on the table. "If you prefer something sweet, I have cherry jam as well." She pointed at a row of fruit jars on a shelf.

"No-one has ever been so friendly towards me," murmured Aross.

"Then isn't it about time!" The fat woman turned around and dabbed her face with a corner of her apron.

Aross placed the tooth on the table.

The woman only barely flinched. She pointed to Aross's breastbone. "There's a little inside pocket here in your dress. You can put…", she pointed at the tooth, "…that in there."

Surprised, Aross peered into her neckline. Amazing! Well,

that was practical. She quickly hid the tooth in the little pocket and immediately began to feast on the food.

"Oh dear, we left your cap lying upstairs. You sit there and I'll fetch it."

Aross opened her mouth wide and bit into the fresh bread. The woman trudged up the stairs. The girl's eyes were amazed by the beautiful furnishings, especially the cabinet with its dresser opposite her. She'd never seen such plates before, made from a white material with golden rims. She loved the painted cups hanging over them, each with pairs of handles. In a small cast-iron bowl was a pile of silver coins, and even a golden thaler among them.

The second bite tasted even better than the first. Aross still couldn't believe her luck. The fat woman came down the stairs and pressed the old felt cap on Aross's head. "I can't say it's nice", she commented.

"I'm not either, which is why it suits me," said Aross, chomping noisily.

"Oh, come on now, who says things like that?"

If she were to be honest, she could answer – none other than the archbishop of this great city would say such a thing.

But Aross decided to hold back on the honesty, she was used to doing that anyway. "Oh, it doesn't matter." She concentrated on her bread and butter.

After a quarter of an hour she felt full. She'd devoured three slices of bread, each as thick as a thumb. Aross stood up, went over to the woman and hugged her. Her arms were nowhere near long enough to embrace her completely. "Thank you again. I'm sorry I was going to steal your dress."

"Don't worry about it. Theft is never a good idea. If you're caught, they'll chop off your hand." The woman gently pinched her cheek. "Good luck on you travels."

Aross left the house in the knowledge that politeness, understanding and kindness were also to be found in the world. A warm and comforting feeling. Only even rarer than a decent meal, unfortunately.

Dear day, you've won again – it isn't often you bring me to tears.

alone in the catacombs

Would you have a few candles for me?" Farin asked the quartermaster.

"Certainly, sir." The man pressed a bound bundle of eight candles made from mutton tallow into his hand. "Why didn't you send a servant?"

The gravedigger's son shrugged his shoulders. "Thank you very much."

To be perfectly honest, he was quite capable of wiping his own backside and didn't need anyone's assistance, but he wasn't able to say that to the man. Instead, he gave a friendly nod before returning into his little tower room.

He spent a part of the night reading with great diligence. The candles were very smoky and stank a lot, but they in no way dimmed his thirst for knowledge. He wanted to learn quickly and surprise others, especially, if he were honest with himself, the knight. It would mean a lot to him if Emicho had a good opinion of him. His new life presented a unique opportunity. He wanted to become a good squire, but without forgetting his roots as a gravedigger.

In the tome with the leather binding he found three removeable maps of the immediate area as well as two architectural drawings of Castle Stormwatch. The depiction of the catacombs fascinated Farin above all else. In the map he saw a bird's eye view of a labyrinth of passageways, rooms and doors. With his finger on the parchment he tried to figure out the route he had followed with Stump, Plaudius and Drogdan towards the ice hall. That turned out to be unexpectedly difficult as the map presented an endless number of routes. Farin finally recognised the fork with the gate of bars and could recreate Stump's route. His fingernail tapped on a narrow chamber. That had to be the ice hall, where Keimund's corpse was being preserved. He turned the map around and mulled over it. Yes, there was no other alternative. But there was one small problem that bothered him. The four of them had only barely fitted into the little room with its two recesses. The little room had seemed to him like a bare stone wardrobe, whereas when he looked at the map, no matter which way he turned it, he saw the delineation of a narrow *second* door. A passageway directly behind it wound its way towards further rooms, considerably larger than the ice hall.

And where, if you please, could that second door in that narrow hole have possibly been? Only a narrow gap, if anything, could possibly have fitted, and one that somebody must have walled up. Inexplicable. Maybe there was a secret passage, or the map was inaccurate.

Farin couldn't help shaking his head. The discrepancy between the sketch and his memory was making him fidgety. Curiosity was niggling at him and was giving him no peace. A thought was circling his mind like a vulture above a cadaver.

Should I really go into the catacombs again? On my own?

The lower iron bar wasn't fully engaged, a one-off opportunity to risk it without Stump's key. This oversight would be noticed at the latest by the time the deceased Squire Keimund's relatives arrived. The thought made him sad. How joyless the long journey from the south to Castle

Stormwatch must be, whose only purpose was to receive the body of their son? And how would they then take the terrible news that their child had been murdered?

I'll risk it, decided Farin.

He stood up, slipped on his fur coat, carefully rolled up the map of the catacombs, put it under his belt and left his little room.

Hey, worm – you surprise me.

"Hey, Stinker. It's late, go to bed."

Do you not want to know why you surprise me?

"I suspect you don't care what I want – you're going to tell me anyway."

Well deduced, little one! Here we go – you're generally distinguished by your lack of drive and tendency to boredom so that the wind blows you in front of it like a collection of dry leaves. And now? No normal person would descend alone into these gloomy vaults. But be my guest, let me not hold you up.

"I'm not normal – I'm the gravedigger's son."

Aha!

If only that buffoon would drop his arrogant chuckling.

None of the servants were out and about in the castle at night, and most of the guards recognised him as the lord of the castle's new, battle-shy squire, and so he was allowed to move freely. With only the occasional torch burning on the walls of the hallways and corridors the castle was mostly in darkness and shadow. Where it wasn't dark or shadowy, blackness reigned. That didn't matter to Farin. Black was his stock-in-trade – the colour of mourning, the colour of last respects. He found himself sooner than expected in the bare vault with its stairs leading in all directions. The gravedigger's son grabbed a torch and stepped into the passageway leading to the darkest recesses. Down the crooked steps, and after a short time he was standing in front of the horizontal iron bars. Yes, the bottom one wasn't engaged which was why he could push it into the wall on the right.

Now we'll see if I can fit under it. Plaudius certainly wouldn't have stood a chance of squeezing through.

He lay down like a lizard, pressed his chin on the cold stone floor and pushed his way under the lowest bar. The thick collar of his fur coat got caught at first before finally disengaging and slipping through. He quickly got back onto his feet on the other side and walked down the long corridor. Shouldn't the heavy wooden door to the ice hall be here on the left soon? The light of his torch being so weak, he almost walked past it. He opened the door and this time he was all alone in the little room – if he didn't include Squire Keimund. The body lay just where they had left it – in the upper recess. Farin pulled the map out from his belt and unrolled it. A passageway on the right side was supposed to lead to further domains of the catacombs. The wall was no more than a yard wide and it had no opening leading onwards. He meticulously examined the fixed stone, pressing and tapping on every block, every crack, every joint and still could find nothing out of the ordinary. The stupid drawing was telling lies. Why would another passageway lead from this room, of all rooms, which was hardly bigger than a privy? Irritated by his lack of success, Farin stooped down and crept along the floor – massive stones, wherever he looked. He held his torch at the lower recess, nothing noticeable there either. What in God's name was he doing here at all? He could have been lying comfortably in his bed ages ago. He could think of no answer to his question except to crawl into the recess and lie down in there. When the coldness of the stone began to permeate through his fur coat, he pulled up his legs, preparing to stand up again. His left arm accidentally banged against the wall, which surprisingly gave way. What looked like stone turned out to be nothing more than a board, plastered in grey, which Farin could easily dislodge. His torch nearly slipped out of his hand while he scrabbled through the hole – luckily, it hadn't gone out. Now he found himself at the start of a low, narrow passageway which slowly became wider and higher as he crawled along. It continued on, slightly staggered, under the ice hall. The map hadn't indicated differences in elevation. What a piece of luck that he'd arrived here! Continuing to crawl along, Farin reached another passageway, where he was able to straighten up.

The gravedigger's son curiously followed the sharp bend to the left. The circle of light emanating from his torch revealed doors on both sides. The first one had a crude lock on it, the one opposite was ajar. He kicked it right open and shone his torch inside. He couldn't believe his eyes: an expansive open chamber opened up before him. Peculiar signs and runes embellishing the walls. Everything in rusty red – or was it blood red? There was a bookcase against one wall with a dozen books, beside it a lectern with a tome opened on it. The floor was decorated on opposite ends with two delicately drawn pentagrams. In the corners were candles as thick as arms, and within the pentagrams were various herbs, such as marjoram and parsley.

Cunning chimera piped up: *Typical incantation chamber, as people like to furnish them. Step into the first pentagram, recite your incantation fluently and flawlessly, and the being called is torn out of their kingdom and forced to appear in the second pentagram. Which is why daemons are stinky and endeavour to kill the conjuror. A small gap in the pentagram and they can attack.*

Knight Emicho surely knew about this room, especially as the books had to belong to him. Maybe he had installed the secret chamber himself. Farin's brave new world had come crashing down around him already. Was it all just lies and deception? Why was the knight practising melancholy occultism in the catacombs? The pentagrams spoke for themselves. How else could this layout be explained? The lord of the castle was clearly dabbling in the convocation of daemons, evils spirits and creatures of the dark. And he had been carrying on to Farin as if the Necorers and the man in black were his deadly enemies.

No, not Emicho. That can't be true.

He was plagued by doubts, but he was too tired to argue. Who else was involved in this? Were they all in cahoots together? The whole morass made him sick, hypocrisy and lies made him sick. Emicho's words echoed in his ears: "Loyalty is important to me. Absolute loyalty. I have to be able to rely on you, in every situation." The knight expected loyalty only in his direction, the rest was just a sham. Definitely no respect towards a gravedigger's son, he was petty livestock at best, and they, as everyone knew, just produced shit when it came down to it.

Don't get all worked up about it – maybe there's a simple explanation.

The disappointment of being disappointed in Emicho was eating away at something inside him. A bit of his body or spirit or even a bit of his soul? Maybe a little bit of each – Farin couldn't tell.

He might as well look at the tome. Numerous artefacts and insignias full of black magic were depicted on the two opened pages, which – combined with human sacrifice – would appeal to any summoned-up daemons. Farin turned over the leaf. A circle with an upside-down pentagram and a flame caught his eye.

"Like on the squire."

The symbol of the unutterable.

"What? You know its meaning? Why are you only telling me now?"

Did you ask me before?

Farin swallowed his anger. "Who is the unutterable? Did the man in black not mention his name in our yard?"

I don't like talking about him. There are many reasons why. If he's really in the Necorers' service, it will get awkward. Strangely for Stinker, he sounded unusually concerned.

"So he really does exist? Is he a daemon?"

Yes, indeed.

"Why is he called that? Because it's dangerous to utter his name?"

Rubbish, he'd love that. But his name is long and difficult.

"And what sort of thing does this daemon do?"

Fire!

Farin was tearing his hair out. "Do they call you the unbearable? You're hiding something from me. What's this daemon all about?"

He's an arsehole. A damn dangerous arsehole. I don't want to talk about him.

"Hm. Then tell me something about all this bullshit here." Farin gestured to the pentagrams and the tome.

Fundamentally, the modus operandi practised in this chamber is amateurish, because only daemons belonging to the most primitive categories can be invoked. But finding this in Emicho's cellar surprises me too.

Farin's disappointment in Emicho weighed heavily on him. He was also overcome by cold and weariness, and his thirst for action had burst like a bubble. He just wanted to get out of there, so he turned and left the oval chamber. A look at the map told him that the passage led to another room which connected to the great hall. He hurried along the bare corridor, ignoring other doors before climbing a steep, narrow set of stairs. He really had to keep going – his torch was going to burn out soon, he noticed with concern.

What had Drogdan stated: "The ghosts of many are wandering around the catacombs, never having found their way out."

Stuff and nonsense! I haven't seen any ghosts yet.

"And I haven't seen a way out."

Well, I can manage for several months without food or drink.

"Good for you, Stinker."

A strange wooden wall emerged ahead in the dim light of the torch. He couldn't make out individual planks, an enormous chunk was blocking his way. Dead end. A perplexing dead end. Farin kept the wall lit with one hand, he felt along it with his other one. On the very right he touched a lever, roughly the size of a dagger. Without considering it for more than a moment – in truth he had nothing to lose – he pressed it down firmly. A click, and a hand's span away from it a narrow door opened. Farin slipped through and found himself standing in a familiar room – the knight's scriptorium.

Shit, shit, shit! If any final proof were needed, here it was. Who apart from Emicho could get from here easily and quickly to his dark, secret place?

The scriptorium was unlocked, no guard to be seen. Farin, cold and tired, shuffled back to his tower room. Emicho would be back from his travels tomorrow and Farin could confront him with the facts. Hard to know how the knight would react. Probably quickly and easily, by taking him out of circulation pronto. Would the lord of the castle show any interest at all in Farin's findings regarding Squire Keimund? Farin had promised Emicho he would be loyal. He wanted to stick to his pledge, but his feeling of loyalty towards his lord and master was being severely tested.

loyalty

F ollowing a sleepless night, the gravedigger's son stood before the lord of the castle's scriptorium the next morning, waiting to be admitted. His head was steaming with rage. The sentry looked at him sceptically, he seemed to sense the young man's feelings and the urgent questions that weighed heavily on Farin's heart. The carved fire-breathing dragon head on the door seemed to be laughing at him.

"His Lordship will speak to you now!" The sentry gestured Farin to come forward.

And about time! The gravedigger's son pulled the door open forcefully and stepped in. Knight Emicho was standing by the fireplace, staring into the flames. Farin couldn't replicate its warmth – he wondered if he should come straight to the point, regarding his discoveries in the catacombs. How about a friendly "what are you getting up to down in your catacombs, Sir Dark Knight?"

The lord of the castle looked away from the flames and turned to his squire. "How did you get on over the last three days?"

His heart pounding, Farin took a deep breath. Fury, disappointment and horror were screaming for assuagement. It had to come out! "Sir, I...I don't understand it!" he croaked. "I...found the parchments in the catacombs. And the conjuration spells and the books about the rituals and the relevant insignias for black magic. Why? It's only the daemon conjurers from the cult of the Necorers who do that, the ones you hate so much."

Well, you're certainly not mincing your words.

The knight's bushy eyebrows pushed themselves in front of his face like a mask. He stood there stony-faced and looked at his obstreperous squire.

Emicho asked in a cold voice: "Anything else? Well, spit it out!" He turned back to the fireplace and added a log as if he didn't have a care in the world. He used the poker to push it into position.

Farin gasped for breath like a fish out of water. Had Emicho not heard him? Why was the knight not responding and defending himself? He could allay Farin's fears, say that everything was a big mistake, give explanations for all that crap in the catacombs – that's what Farin had been secretly hoping for. But the man remained silent regarding the allegations – wasn't that practically a confession? No – a small bit of him still refused to believe his master was guilty.

"Please tell me it isn't what it looks like", pleaded Farin.

"It seems you've been sniffing around in the catacombs behind my back", said Emicho, going on the attack. The knight was using a diversionary tactic. The gravedigger's son was slowly coming to the conclusion that the lord of the castle was one of the Necorers. Nothing could be worse. And just as that realisation struck him, it became worse. Much worse! The realisation hit him between the eyes, which were as wide as saucers. No doubt at all!

Outrageous! NO! Not that too!

For the gravedigger's son, his nice new world of castles and squires had collapsed like a house of cards, once and for all. Farin shivered as he visualised the full consequences of what was happening. His lips were prickling, he was pressing them together so firmly. He couldn't and wouldn't serve a brutal criminal any longer, he would rather die.

As if spellbound, he stared at the object in the knight's hand – he was incapable of any other reaction. How naïve could he possibly have been? In his mind, he pictured his life coming to an end. At least he'd managed to reach the age of eighteen.

Without betraying his true feelings, he asked in a firm voice: "Should I turn around so you can slay me just as slyly as you slew your squire, Keimund? You're holding the relevant weapon in your hand."

If he thought he'd break down the knight's reserve this way, he was sorely disappointed. What next?

Emicho approached Farin deliberately. He lifted the hand holding the poker in a threatening manner. Then he stretched out his long arm, caught the back of one of the visitor chairs with the poker's spike, and pulled it directly in front of Farin's feet. "Sit!" he ordered. The knight calmly sat down behind his writing desk again.

"Firstly – no matter what happens, no matter how much you feel yourself to be in the right, never talk to me like that when other people are present. I would have already killed you after your first groundless accusation!"

So now he was trying another tactic! Farin could hardly breathe. "There's nobody else here!" he choked. "You're…you're a murderer!"

"Every knight is a murderer," said Emicho, airily. "Tell me, Farin, from the village of Heap, what makes you think I slew the squire?"

Is this false knight planning on talking his way out of it and making me look like an idiot? Naïve and ignorant of the world, perhaps, but not stupid.

Farin spoke in a grave voice: "I examined Keimund's body and the place where it was found. He had no idea he was about to be killed. Quite the contrary. He suffered a blow to the back of the head, completely unexpectedly, which made him bite his tongue. It was a tall person, judging by the angle of impact. There are numerous clues. Nobody falls from a fortified tower to his death with such a peaceful facial expression, especially without the abrasions on hands, elbows or knees appropriate to such a fall. Not unless a fireplace implement with a trapezoid-shaped spike was driven into his brain through the back of his head before-hand. The deep hole in the squire's skull comes from your poker, the other one from the impact with the ground after he was already dead. The margins of the wound tell their own story. Keimund was carried onto the fortified tower and thrown from it. Did you do it yourself or get one of your henchmen to do the dirty work?" Farin swallowed hard after speaking; his admiration for the knight had been trans-formed into bitter disappointment.

Emicho turned the poker over with his right hand and examined all sides as if he were looking at it for the first time. Then he stood up and hung it back with the other fireplace instruments. With a furrow over his bushy eyebrows he turned to face Farin. "I really don't like your tone at all! But in view of the present circumstances, I'll overlook it for now. Regarding your question – I never leave such inconveniences to my vassals. I hauled him up the tower myself and tossed him down."

Farin could do nothing but close his eyes. He had refused until the very end to believe these misdeeds had taken place in spite of all the evidence, but now the knight had admitted it, willingly and audaciously – and clearly without a hint of a bad conscience. He seemed to be very sure of himself. Would Farin be his next victim?

You truly are a bone reader. Now just calm down and bide your time.

"Who else knows about your...deductions?" asked Emicho.

"Nobody!" spat Farin into the room. With that he'd sealed his fate. The knight could get him out of the way just as he had Keimund, and no one would be any the wiser.

"So, the first person you've presented these deadly-serious allegations to is me?" He lowered his brows. "I don't need to kill you myself – one word from me and you'll be strung up. Just like that. Nobody in this castle will ask for a reason." Emicho's voice grew sharper. "And unlike Keimund with his influential aristocratic family in the south, no cock will crow for you, either here or in Heap."

Farin was becoming overwhelmed by emotions but he looked at Emicho fixedly. "I made you a promise. That's the reason why I came to you. Nobody is aware of my line of reasoning. The only thing I told Plaudius, Drogdan and Stump was that I believed it was murder, nothing more."

"And after all these...revelations, you really dare to come here? To the root of all evil, to the dastardly murderer and traitor? What a naïve, starry-eyed idealist you are."

Was the knight mocking him now, or what was he up to? Farin lowered his head.

Emicho asked: "What promise do you mean?"

Farin lifted his head. "Loyalty, I promised you loyalty."

The knight scratched his broad chin. "You are a remark-able young man. I feel justified in having chosen you to be my squire. One, who has an awful lot to learn, but who nevertheless brings extraordinary potential with him." His voice grew sharper. "Boy, before you accuse me any further, I'll explain to you my version of the story." Emicho leaned back and folded his arms behind his head. "Didn't you tell me yourself how much the raven already knows about me?"

"All that about the second knight?"

Emicho nodded. "How does information like that seep out? Quite obvious – the raven slipped a spy into my inner circle. A traitor who reported to him regularly about what was happening in Castle Stormwatch, and especially about all the things the lord of the castle was planning. This spy's name was Keimund. He shamelessly exploited his trusted position as squire and betrayed his master at every possible opportunity." The knight slammed his large fist on his chest. "Me it was, he betrayed! I have many good reasons why I couldn't blow his cover and have him executed. I absolutely have to avoid a scandal involving his influential aristocratic family at this point in time. I had no option but to kill him and make his death seem like an accident. Do you now understand my desire to find a squire I can trust unreservedly?"

Farin sat on the chair, stiff and silent although turmoil was churning inside him.

"As to your snooping around in the catacombs, we'll come to that later. I'll only say this much: in contrast to the Necorers, I am not an idolater of devils. On the contrary, these people are my bitter enemies. I've been hunting them down ever since I learned to think and to fight. Because I hate the cult of the evil, because I hate daemons and devils, because I hate human sacrifice. My library and the newly set-up incantation chamber in the catacombs serve only one purpose: learn everything about your enemy. In order to fight it, I must know what charlatanry is, what phantasms are, what bloody reality is. I'm a daemon hunter, and my knowledge and my experience provide me with the necessary equipment."

"Daemon hunter?" A deep, dry swallow followed. Farin didn't know what was happening.

Daemon hunter! He doesn't really believe in daemons, does he? Tsk!

"I've good reasons for that." Emicho's eyes blazed angrily. "The most important is this one: my father was double-crossed by a daemon and killed. I'm going to avenge him."

Uhhh?

The knight slammed the flat of his hand on the desk. "The raven is after the same miscreant. But they don't want to kill him but use him for themselves. He can give them and their followers power. This daemon is as evil as he is mighty. He can determine the fate of whole nations."

Ehhh!?

Farin didn't understand a single word anymore, especially as the chimera's disconcerting reactions were confusing things further. Stinker usually knew everything beforehand, and better.

"What can the daemon do?"

"Let's start with the simple things: make a principal knight unbeatable."

The gravedigger's son needed to digest the new information first. To win time, he asked: "What exactly happened to your father?"

"I never got to know him. The daemon killed him when my mother, Orelia, was pregnant with me."

Zorrghorozza and Borghezzza! I'm getting a faint but flimsy flicker of understanding. Don't say the wrong thing now.

The chimera had never sounded like that before. What

was happening here? The latest developments were really beginning to wear Farin out. He was dizzy – it felt as if his brain was hanging from a piece of string and someone was swinging it from side to side. Stinker had left him alone with all his doubts the whole time, and now he was rattling around and cursing in his head in a rather unhelpful manner.

"Have I answered my squire to his satisfaction? Now for *my* questions!" He leaned forward. "How did you gain access to the ice hall? After all, the gate of bars is blocking the way."

"I persuaded Stump to show me the dead squire. Because I wanted to help."

The knight nodded. "And then?"

The gravedigger's son eagerly told of his solo action during the night, of how he had forced his way below the bars and discovered the secret in the lower recess, because a passageway had been drawn in the map from the library.

"That's where I came out then." Farin pointed at the wall beside the fireplace – no door was visible from this side.

The knight's eyebrows wandered higher and higher as he listened. "There are few people that idiotic as to wander down there all alone. You are an unusual fellow, Farin. I accept you intended well."

The knight stood up, placed both hands on the writing desk and leaned forward. His brows dropped like the executioner's axe, and his voice sounded just as sharp. "The crucial question is this: Do you believe me? Because your further loyalty depends on the answer."

Only now did Farin notice that a heavy weight had been lifted from his shoulders. The knight's explanations, simple as they were, sounded plausible. He raised his eyes and looked Emicho straight in the eyes. "Yes! Forgive me...I'm sorry that I doubted you."

"I'm sorry too, squire! But you redeemed yourself by coming to me straight away." The lord of the castle sat down again.

You're so sweet, the two of you. A smacking kissing sound in Farin's head. But suddenly Stinker's head sounded urgent. *Now ask him who his father was.*

"Farin, I demand that you come to me first next time – before you turn everything upside down in my castle."

"Yes, sir!" It was the first time that the knight had addressed him as Farin. "Who...who was your father, sir?"

"You should distinguish yourself through unfailing loyalty to me, not through unfailing curiosity."

"I...uh, I'm sorry, but the double-crossing of your father still bothers me."

Emicho thrust his chin a little forward. Just as the gravedigger's son thought the knight wasn't going to answer the question, he spoke: "It happened over thirty years ago. His name was Vigo. He was by profession principal knight and made the mistake of trusting his king, King Ekarius of the house of the stone dragons. And he counted on the daemon in his body."

Borghezza and Zorrghorozza! Now I know why the knight seemed so familiar to me from the start. He's part of me. Stinker even sounded a little proud.

"And the daemon betrayed him in the end. I'll get my revenge", thundered the knight with furious determination.

Farin suppressed a swallow. "And how exactly are you going to get your revenge on the daemon?"

"As soon as I've found him, I'll kill him. He's looking for a human to be his host, like a parasite. There are suitable rituals that will destroy him for ever."

"And what happens to the host?"

"He dies, while the daemon is being driven out. Nobody survives such torture."

Right, then!

Oh well, tough luck, little fella.

"Now that we've answered the most important questions, I have to turn to other matters. I'll deal with Stump later. How could he possibly use his key to give some obscure squire a guided tour of the catacombs?"

"Please, sir, be angry at me, not at Stump. When it comes down to it, it was the lord of the castle's squire that put the pressure on. He could see that I was only trying to help."

Emicho pulled a face. With a lot of imagination, you could interpret it as a smile.

"Scram now, squire!"

"I'll be practising swordsmanship with Drogdan this afternoon. Please let me know if there's anything I can do for you." Farin bowed.

Emicho nodded and turned to the stack of papers on his desk.

It was incredible. All the cares that had been persecuting him before he entered the scriptorium had vanished into thin air. In their stead other burdens had jumped spectacularly on his shoulders and were weighing him down like a saddle with lead weights attached. A daemon hunter was after none other than Stinker. The damned chimera was putting his life in danger. It owed him an explanation.

jumping for joy

Aross had returned to her little cove south of Hubstone with a full stomach and a rare feeling of contentment. She stood on the sand between the cliffs and watched the setting sun. She had just bathed and was wearing her new long-sleeved dress with its inner pocket in which the tooth snugly rested. How were things to continue? The town watch was on her heels. The mendacious Grim would be looking for her too, she could even imagine he might know one or two of her favourite spots and could become a danger to her. After all, they'd been living in close proximity to each other all these years. That bastard was to blame for everything – how could he stab poor Wolf to death and then claim it had been Aross?

And now he wants to turn me in. Well, he'll have to catch me first. He's going to live to regret that he made an enemy out of me.

The girl reached into her dress and pulled out the tooth. Lost in thought she held it between her thumb and forefinger and turned it over and back. What was its significance? What was it good for? Whatever its purpose, it was a memento of the woman whose incredible rat-magic had saved her life. Pictures from her past flashed before her eyes. A jumble, colourful and grey, sparkling and dull, loud and quiet. A crazy world. She thought of the orphanage, the barn, the hayloft. The things that had happened there.

Her eyes moved away from her hands and up to the heavens above. And another picture presented itself to her. First befogged, then it gradually cleared. A perception – more than a conjecture, more than a daydream – a veritable nightmare. Grim was lying on top of her and holding her in his iron grip until the archbishop's men arrived and took her away. That couldn't be! Her dread transformed into determination.

As the sun sank behind the horizon, she made her way to the orphanage – she wanted to finally collect her coppers. She kept an eye out for the town watch as she went along and also for a place where she could watch the orphanage from a distance before daylight disappeared completely. It didn't take long to find a suitable spot, and the girl trudged up some steps. She didn't get up very far as the building had collapsed two years earlier. Not to worry, the view was just right. No soldiers, no town watch, nothing out of the ordinary around the orphanage, she saw to her satisfaction.

She waited until midnight, then slipped through the old town to her one-time home. She quietly opened the barn door, crept inside and closed it behind her. The hens were either sleeping or ignoring her. The girl saw the broken rungs of the ladder. A pity – it would have been just fine if the rotten bishop had broken his neck. She yawned. Poor as she was, she couldn't afford to be tired – she still had work to do.

Exhausted, Aross clambered up the ladder. She knew exactly which rungs would hold firm. She gently opened the trapdoor, scrabbled through and closed it behind her. On her knees, she pushed the straw aside and prised up the board under which the coins were hidden. The nails didn't hold properly anymore, but the wood still squeaked pitifully when she lifted the board.

Oh wow, she'd never noticed it being that loud before.

For a moment she listened intently to the night, as she used to do with the big shells on the beach, but nobody in the vicinity seemed to have heard anything. Reassured, she stuck the coins in her pocket, spread out the straw and lay down. That was good. Her legs were stretched out over the trapdoor, so she would wake up if anyone tried to open it.

Sounds woke her. The beech tree was rustling, or rather, whoever was climbing the tree. Getting up there wasn't easy as the lower branches were quite high up. Aross quietly opened the trapdoor and placed her feet on the top rung. She hesitated and listened to the roof area. The wind was blowing, but apart from that, nothing but silence. Had she only dreamed it? No, careful steps on the shingles told her a different story. The roof beams groaned, and a shadow appeared in the hole above her head. The face that belonged to it peered down at her.

"Hello, Aross," said Grim quietly. "You shouldn't have come here. But you're stupid and easy to predict. They'll give me a reward if I take you to the town watch. They promised me five silverlings." He bared his teeth. "But first I want to hurt you – really hard."

Aross held onto the rails of the ladder anxiously. "Think about it carefully, Grim. Do you really want to cross swords with Aross Slimefoot?"

The boy gave an amused snort. "Yes, sure. I'm bigger, stronger and faster than you. You won't get away from me."

"You're just meaner than me."

"Hee-hee." Grim accepted the praise. Then he tilted his head. "The soldiers arrested and threatened me because of you. I'm going to beat you up just for that. Tell me why the captain fancies you so much."

"No idea. Tell me how you could stab the poor old dog to death and then spread lies about me."

"It was very easy and lots of fun. And I'd do it again." He gave a smug smile.

"You're aware, aren't you, somewhere deep inside yourself, that you really are a disgusting pig," said Aross.

"You don't say. Pity my plan didn't work. The matron would have beaten you to death..." His voice groaned with barely suppressed rage, "...if the rats hadn't turned up."

"And it was so horrible that little Grim fainted." Aross chuckled gleefully. An adult chuckle.

"Now you're going to pay for it." Grim's mouth and eyes became sadistic looking.

"I could have done something to you while you were helplessly lying there. I didn't, though."

"Exactly. You didn't. Because you're stupid."

"Then do the clever thing yourself and leave me in peace."

"I'm going to show you!" Like a predator he darted through the hole and onto the floor of the loft. He landed on all fours, ready to spring on his victim.

At that same moment Aross pushed herself powerfully off the ladder and took an enormous jump. She had pushed herself too far in her hurry and so only one leg landed on the soft hay, the other on the hard ground. A stab of pain went through her foot. Grim's filthy, victorious laugh pained her even more. She pulled herself up with a groan.

"I have you, rat", he hissed.

She had to hand it to Grim, she'd underestimated him — he was almost as limber and agile as she was. He sprang through the trapdoor in an elegant movement and jumped down to her. It reminded her of their last fight, only this time Aross was standing below and Grim was flying down from above. Even if the girl could make it to the door, she'd never have the time to open it.

Grim landed on the haystack. A dreadful crunching sound followed by an even more dreadful groan as the prongs of the pitchfork dug into his chest. Skewered like a sausage, he jutted out over the hay with his feet jerking.

He looked at Aross in disbelief. "You...put...the fork...in...here?"

Aross nodded at him. "And, because I'm stupid, the wrong way around."

She had warned him. She'd given the little shit another chance even after everything. She'd worked at it for over an hour during the night, making sure the prongs of the pitchfork faced upwards like a candlestick, before covering it over with the hay.

Grim wheezed, blood came streaming out of his mouth. He looked down at his chest in disbelief, the prongs had probably broken his spine. His eyeballs were bulging in their sockets.

She said matter-of-factly: "The manure fork for the shit-head. Our fight ends here, Grim. You've lost. My war goes on."

No answer.

Aross felt nothing. She knew she ought to be feeling rage or horror because this person had forced her to take such extreme measures. And because of his monstrous villainy, and because she hated the bishop's and Chain Dog's guts. But she felt nothing. Her mind and her heart were cold, cold as the water in the north, which was hard as iron if what the girl had said was true.

Chain Dog, I'm going to bite you next, thought Aross. Maybe tomorrow, maybe in a week, maybe in a year. But I'm going to get you.

She knew she was finished with the place for once and for all. She'd never come here again – never again did she want to see the orphanage with its murderous henhouse. This place was swimming in blood. She stooped down to get her cap, which had fallen off during her jump, and she put it on her head. One of the hens clearly thought Aross had provided the coop with a new perch, because it fluttered up onto Grim's shoulder and made itself at home.

Aross Slimefoot, queen of the rats, opened the barndoor for the last time in her life. In comparison to her, Grim was an altar boy. She turned back to face him. "Now you know how Wolf felt. Die well!"

power

The day hustled along and Drogdan harried Farin in the stables. Accomplished swordplay was proving to be much more difficult than he'd imagined. His teacher had revealed himself to be a mind reader – no matter what Farin tried, Drogdan's sword was always at the ready, fending off every attack. Farin was padded from head to toe, his teacher on the other hand had foregone a training vest or any other form of protection.

"You're never going to hit me," he'd said with an encouraging grin – and up until now, unfortunately, he'd been proven right.

Let me take control for a minute. I'll only batter him with the side of the sword, promise. Next time he'll roll himself into a carpet with his head pulled in before he tackles you.

When would Stinker finally get the message that Farin wasn't going to do that? The gravedigger's son had to learn how to handle a sword himself, he didn't want to be depending on a daemon. Wasn't the story of Vigo a warning? Interesting that Stinker had so suddenly reappeared again now. Immediately following Farin's insightful meeting with Emicho, the gravedigger's son had really wanted to question the chimera on numerous points, or more specifically, to confront him. But he had, until this moment, prudently hidden himself away.

Didn't hide myself away, I was considering.

Right then. He was considering. Farin rolled his eyes. "Is that something stinky?"

"Where's your head, squire? You're in the middle of a fight so keep moving. You can think about things when you're dead." Drogdan glared at him. "The squire competitions will take place every morning during the grand tournament. Don't you dare disgrace our house! We are the stone dragons and our tradition is to present the best fighters!"

His words were effective; from then on Farin concentrated on the work in hand. Several sword sequences rained down on Drogdan's blade.

"The day you get me into a sweat, I'll buy you a beer. And if you hit me, a whole barrel. You have to show more variation in your striking, your attacks are too predictable."

With a dastardly circling of his weapon and a strike against the cross guard, Drogdan forced the sword with a jolt out of Farin's hand, which landed after making an elegant arc in the dung. Still, at least it managed to neatly split a horse turd in the process.

"How many times do I have to tell you: never drop your sword!"

Ashamed and frustrated, Farin picked up his sword. "Am I making any strides at all?"

"Of course, lots! You're always unbeatable when the lessons are over. We're finished for today – you can walk away now…making great strides."

"I don't think that's funny."

"But I do", grinned Drogdan.

Farin visited the library again in the early evening. The guard in front of the door recognised him from a distance and gave him a friendly nod. "Ah, the well-read young squire. Step inside." He raised his halberd to attention and even opened the door.

"Thank you very much," said the gravedigger's son, joyfully.

First, he climbed up the ladder and put the crimson tome back in its place. A thirst for knowledge such as he'd never felt before possessed him. He walked through the aisles, concentrating intently. He'd internalised the knight's colour coding, which was why he was all the more surprised when he reached the last row of books. Here were only uncategorised books, and it was quickly clear to him why. These works consisted purely of books on demonology, witchcraft and black magic.

He gingerly leafed through a weighty tome with dark leather binding until he reached the middle section where he found numerous drawings of horned, scaly daemonic faces.

Disgusting drawings!

"Is that what you look like, Stinker?"

Nonsense! That's how humans, in their unfathomable naivety, imagine us. I'm much uglier.

"Oh, right."

A familiar sign drew Farin's attention. With furrowed brows he looked at the circle with the upside-down pentagram and the flame. The book wasn't written in his language, which was why he understood neither the title nor the description.

"The symbol of the unutterable again. Can you help me?"

No answer and no stirring either. Anytime it concerned the unutterable, the daemon got petulant.

"Stinker? Don't be hiding yourself!"

Do you think Stinker is the correct form of address if you want something from me, treacherous worm?

"Yes, as long as you rankle me by calling me worm. And, anyway, you still haven't told me your real name." Farin paused: "What do you mean, treacherous worm? You can talk! Just explain to me what that talk about treachery and this King Ecki…uh… all means."

Why can you not remember any names? King Ekarius!

"Stop going off the point! What does it all mean?"

Since when do I have to explain myself to a worm? Pshaw! I don't have to explain myself to anybody. You asked Emicho in a most underhand way how you could get rid of me.

Stinker really did sound miffed. Enough to drive you up the wall. Whose wall, though?

"Listen to me, chimera. Have I ever made any secret of my desire to get rid of you? You're a big problem for me, and there's nobody I can talk to about it."

That would be a waste of time anyway. A quarter of the people couldn't give a shit about your problems, and the other three-quarters are delighted you have them.

"You're just mean and nasty as per usual!"

And you're a thankless, legless, spineless slimy crawler.

"Say worm, it's faster. And now, help me with the book."

Haven't you noticed I'm offended?

"Let's clear that up later. Can you…", Farin took a deep breath, "…read this book?"

Pshaw! And now the bookworm comes crawling up to me and wants help in reading.

"Do daemons have a heart?"

Well, obviously!

"Then give it a kick and help me."

Hm.

"We talk about everything when it's only us in the tower room."

Hm.

"Please."

Hm. Let go, you know how it works.

Farin positioned himself behind one of the two lecterns in the central aisle, placed the tome on top of it and relaxed. He let his thoughts circle, his spirit float, felt something enveloping him and leading him carefully through a wall of fog.

"The unutterable – prince of fire and chaos", he read aloud. Again, the gravedigger's son was astounded at his miraculous ability to suddenly read and understand the strange language.

That's Cartanesian. Some of the highest category daemons are described in that language.

"Do the Necorers believe in the daemon princes as in a god?"

Worse! You've no idea what you're letting yourself in for.

"What do you mean? The unutterable really seems to be frightening you."

Ha! Wait until you meet him.

The gravedigger's son buried himself deeper into the tome. The misdeeds of the fire princes were described in the following pages – nothing for those of a weak disposition. Chaos meant intrigues, coup d'états, torture, blood. Suddenly Farin spun around. The library guard had tiptoed up to him quietly, was standing close behind. And shoved his halberd with force into Farin's torso. Or tried to.

Farin spun to the side with superhuman speed so that the point slid past and the barbed hook merely tore his shirt. His left arm shot out and grasped the shaft of the weapon. With a simple flick of his wrist he snapped the thick oak wood as if it were no more than a rotten branch. The iron head clattered to the floor – the attacker was now holding no more than the broken shaft in his hand.

"What?" That was all the guard could say, the surprise written all over his face – Farin didn't need Stinker's help to read that. The man quickly regained his composure, reached to his belt and drew out a long dagger. He held it in front of him, ready to attack.

"You must die!" growled the guard.

Immediately he lunged forward, aiming to thrust his weapon into Farin's heart. A shimmy to the right, a light-ning-fast spin to the left. The attacker was highly trained, he didn't fall for the dummy. He instinctively turned his dagger so that the blade slid across Farin's chest. Shirt and skin gaped open.

Farin didn't feel the pain. He heard himself say: *"I'm going to get angry soon."*

His hand grabbed his attacker's right wrist, as he had grabbed the halberd-shaft before. *"Let go!"*

The attacker didn't obey.

Farin increased the pressure. *"Drop the dagger!"*

The wrist cracked three or four times – like opening a walnut. The pain convulsed his face, the veins on his temples bulged, but the guard refused to drop the dagger. His left hand reached into his boot and pulled out a knife.

A thundering voice: *"Now I'm furious!"*

A turn, a powerful jerk, a crunch, a scream. Farin was paralysed by his horror at himself. His hand was still holding on to the wrist, only neither the arm nor the chainmail sleeve was attached to the attacker's body anymore. An enormous hole gaped from the guard's left shoulder. Farin had ripped the arm from the shoulder joint with incredible force, like petals from a daisy.

"He loves me not", he ascertained loudly. Or was it the monster inside him, who had just saved his life?

The gravedigger's son casually tossed the arm on the ground. It slid along the floor for a yard, leaving a bloody smear on the parquet. The fingers were still clasping the grip of the dagger.

Learn from his example. He doesn't drop his weapon.

The attacker's remaining arm was losing power. Farin grabbed the knife and plunged it vertically through the chainmail and into his stomach. The man staggered, torn sinews and muscles were dangling from his shoulder, then he collapsed. He rolled around on the floor in his own blood.

The gravedigger's son went down on his knee. *"Why did you attack me? Who is your employer?"*

The attacker's eyes were bloodshot.

"Who sent you?"

"I serve…the fire. You're all going to…burn." His pupils fractured. His head slumped sideways.

Farin stared, dumbstruck, at the dead man. It took forever before he could avert his eyes. It seemed to him like an awakening. An awakening from a nightmare. He was standing in the library, his chest was burning. The cut wasn't deep, he had suffered no other injuries. He had miraculously survived the treacherous attack. And he realised now as he stood there in shock that the miracle's name was Stinker. It was a lucky coincidence that the daemon was controlling his body at the moment of attack.

It took a while before Farin could speak again: "He wanted to kill me! Just stab me to death in the back! Why?" He whispered as he trembled. "I should have been the person lying there. You saved me!"

Oh, come on! Why would I help you? It was just reflexes.

"If it was just reflexes, I wouldn't need to be thanking you." Farin thought for a moment. "What sort of a mission was he on? Bad luck that he's dead. Now we can't interrogate him."

Farin bent down to the corpse and exposed the left forearm. Nothing unusual there.

You don't have to examine him – I know what he died of.

Nauseated, Farin looked over at the other arm, which lay three yards away on the floor. It had to be done. He went over and looked carefully at the limb. He found it on the inner side of the forearm: an upside-down pentagram with a flame in the middle, surrounded by a circle.

"That's what I suspected. The same tattoo as on Squire Keimund."

That's not a tattoo. Farin's ears pricked up. Stinker's voice sounded unusually anxious.

"It's deep in his skin. What else can it be?"

A stigma. A stigma of the unutterable. That's how he indoctrinates petty-minded beings like humans. To put it simply: the guard who wanted to kill you was controlled remotely.

The gravedigger's son went ashen faced. He didn't want to believe it, but he'd only just lived through it. He asked in bewilderment: "Can he do that with everyone?"

No, he only controls those on whom he personally branded the stigma earlier.

"This is getting worse and worse! Well, I have to report to Emicho. How am I going to explain the condition of the body?"

He picked the head of the halberd up and smashed it at hip height against the wood of the nearest bookcase.

What's that supposed to mean?

"Do you want to explain to Emicho how the fight went?"

For the second time that day Farin headed off to report certain events to the lord of the castle.

Emicho looked down at the corpse and shook his head. "Clemens was the soldier's name. He's been in my service for two years and was considered a first-rate fighter. How did you manage to defeat him?"

"I noticed just in time that somebody was creeping up behind me and was able to throw myself to the floor at the right moment."

The knight gave a sceptical look and asked: "And why does it look like a slaughterhouse in here?" He gestured to the wrenched-off arm and the slashed stomach.

"Incredible luck. The man lunged forward with the halberd and the spike got stuck in the shelving. That broke the weapon and his arm tore away."

I've rarely heard such a pathetic explanation.

The knight's face suggested that Stinker wasn't the only one with that opinion.

"Then I grabbed his dagger and stabbed him. It was horrible."

"Hm!" Emicho examined the shelf. "Ah, here!" The bright spot in the wood was clearly visible. He bent down to the top of the halberd and picked it up by the shaft. "Top quality oak! Just snapped through. Stuck to the shelf. You *were* unbelievably lucky, Farin."

Emicho scratched his stubble. "Incredible." He paused for a moment, then asked: "Did Clemens say anything else?"

"Only: 'I serve the fire. You're all going to burn'."

"The Necorers' poison is spreading throughout the

Worldly Kingdom. Misguided fanatics. Whole villages have been obliterated in the east already because they rejected the principles of these people. Let's keep this story to ourselves. I'll only tell Stump – he's one of the few people I trust in the castle." The knight didn't seem to be completely convinced by this version of the story – except, he didn't have any better explanation for the ripped-off arm and the broken weapon.

"Yes, sir!" Farin sensed that he didn't belong to the trusted few.

The truth is just too far-fetched for anybody's imagination, thanks be to God, thought Farin. I'll tell Emicho about the unutterable when the time is right.

Don't say thanks be to God. That's not fair – he had nothing to do with it.

Late that evening a young man sat on his bed in the tower room and talked to himself nervously.

"Do you think Emicho accepted my version of the fight?"

Not entirely. But then even with a lot of imagination he couldn't think of any alternative version of events.

"I start shaking whenever I think back to the library. You were pretty angry."

Ah sure, that was nothing. First anger comes, then rage, and the last one is frenzy – that's when I become unpleasant.

"Oh, right." Farin would rather not experience the daemon when he was in a frenzy.

You have all the prerequisites. And I'll bring the rest.

"To do what?"

To achieve something in your little life. To perform feats that nobody else can.

Farin shrugged his shoulders. Even if it was true, did he want to?

"I had a regular routine in Heap before you came on the scene."

Stinker gave a daemonic groan. *Yes, plenty of routine and little life.*

"Hm!"

Exactly – hm! I'd never have been able to defeat the guard without your bodily prerequisites. A little additional strength, speed and technique, combined with will and determination, and we'll both be having a lot of fun.

"I'm afraid Clemens didn't have any fun today."

He attacked you from behind. You did well for a squire.

"Yes, it's only a pity ripping off arms isn't one of the squire disciplines." Farin didn't really mean it to sound as sarcastic as it did.

You don't understand! I signify powwwer.

Farin's head vibrated. "Doesn't matter."

Idiot! Power turns a worm into a...DRAGON! And I make the difference! In the library today you were a dragon.

Farin really didn't know what to say to that. Stinker had an answer for everything – no, not for everything. This morning at Emicho's the chimera had been a stammering mess.

"Let's go back to this morning. Tell me what happened that time. Why does Emicho think you betrayed his father?"

That surprised me as well. I was inside Vigo for many years, the principal knight of the stone dragons. Who do you think helped him be so successful? I stood by him during every trial by combat.

"Except for the last time."

Humans are mortal. Vigo had become too arrogant. Smug and comfortable, he was relying on me completely.

"And that was a mistake!"

That was his mistake – I am an evil daemon – neither guardian angel nor do-gooder.

"Aha! Why did you save me in the library? You could have allowed the worm to die – just as you did Vigo."

Stinker paused, then he grunted: *Daemons are unpredictable.*

"Which is exactly why I want to be rid of you and not rely on you."

Which makes you different to all my previous hosts.

"What's that supposed to mean?"

You do unusual things.

"Such as?"

Stinker sighed pitifully. *The completely whacky care you take of your teeth, and every morning at that.*

"Oh, you mean that."

What did you think? You hardly think I'm going to praise you!

"Pft! You said I was different. So, how?"

Once the other hosts had realised what I can make happen, they wanted me to be performing miracles constantly. But you bristle against the idea with every sinew in your body.

"I don't want that. I want to be me."

Pft!

The discussion was threatening to lead nowhere. And so Farin asked: "So you didn't help Vigo, and that's why he had to die?"

He lost in an honourable duel against the other principal knight. I stayed out of it, that was all – after all his opponent didn't have a daemon on his side either.

"Hm. But Vigo was relying on your help. You could have remained loyal to him."

This constant waffle about loyalty. There are two sides to that too, a worm especially should know that. When the going gets tough, loyalty demands that you switch off reason and conscience.

"I don't understand what you mean."

Hellfire and damnation! Imagine Emicho commands that his loyal retainer Drogdan be killed. How does the loyal Farin react then?

"I…I wouldn't do it. If he commanded me to do something like that, then I wouldn't serve him anymore. He won't do anything like that."

Worm-eaten argument! And if he claims that Duke Turgenson belongs to the cult of the Necorers and must be killed? What then?

"I…I don't know."

Where are the borders? You condemned the lord of the castle rashly. So don't even think of trying to make my life hell.

"That's something else. You're a parasite and don't belong in my head."

I saved your life only a few short hours ago. And I didn't seek you out. Or did somebody force you to steal the amulet, to carry it around your neck for days on end and then to even throw it onto the fire to seal our pact?

"Hm. The last part was a mistake, but we're not making any progress here. Fate has brought us together. It can certainly separate us again."

I really don't know how, without the gravedigger's son sustaining long-lasting damage. Hee-hee, you heard Emicho.

Farin rolled his eyes. "Back to the duel. Vigo lost, which means he was killed. What happened next?"

Orelia bribed the jailkeeper so she could get to Vigo's body before it was dismembered and fed to the dogs. He was buried two days later in a secret location. When his body was laid out the evening before the interment the amulet appeared on his chest. As you yourself experienced first-hand, it's the medium I can slip into in this world when I'm not in a person. At that very moment Vigo's beloved Orelia turned away with eyes filled with tears and left the church. Her lady-in-waiting noticed the piece of jewellery on the dead man's chest, and she took it. Stole it, to be exact.

"Orelia is Emicho's mother and was pregnant with him when Vigo died."

That's the way it must have been. I was in Vigo's loins when Emicho was conceived.

"Should he call you *daddy* then?"

Funny, little squire. He wants to kill me, forgotten already?

"And the light-fingered lady-in-waiting…did she happen to be called Gerlunda?"

You're beginning to be uncanny. Yes, that was her name. The thieving, fraudulent human being.

"Who later moved to the pretty village of Heap."

You've hit the nail on the head.

"Did you hide in Gerlunda from that time on?"

Time is of no importance to me. Still, I don't like remembering the old witch. Because of me she scored your symbol of God into her chest almost every day. As if that could possibly help, but she couldn't stand me.

"I don't understand at all." Farin considered for a few moments. "Do you have something to do with witchcraft?"

No! That too is nothing but a misconception which has cost many human women their lives. That suspicion came about when some crazies believed that the devil was having carnal knowledge of girls and women. It all kicked off with countless witch trials and your traditional slandering and insinuations.

"They say that the daemons are responsible for all the evil in this world."

There are daemons and there are daemons. People need to shovel all that blame at somebody's door. And it's the simplest thing in the world to point at a non-material being. The more people get together, the worse. You manage to place the blame for the polluting of the air, the poisoning of the water, the destruction of the forests, and the predominance of pestilences and illnesses firmly on the shoulders of daemons. Don't get me started on how you behave towards each other.

"Pater Amen always preached that the devil created the seven deadly sins," recalled Farin.

Stinker snorted: *Sure, of course. Pride, avarice, envy, wrath, lust, gluttony and sloth are all inventions of mine. It has nothing to do with humans at all. You have to distinguish between the stories of the fallen angels who were banished from Paradise because they foreswore the divine order, and the genuine daemons from other dimensions. You humans like mixing up things that you have no real understanding of.*

"Now I'm mixed up."

I'm clearly demanding too much of you.

Farin didn't let himself be provoked. "Whichever way you or I look at it, I am the squire of a daemon hunter who is hunting down and wants to kill the very daemon who is floating around in my head. I don't believe it!"

Emicho is carrying my blood. No wonder he's so great.

Farin groaned but decided not to comment. "And the cult of the Necorers with its dark, unutterable other daemon is hunting me down because he wants you."

That's the nub of it.

"What do we do now?"

We? Did you really say we? That's the first step in the right direction.

"More a mistake, really."

Oh, right. Worms don't take steps, they have neither legs, nor feet nor backbone.

"Stinker, you're nothing but a daemonic idiot."

Hee-hee, you're nothing but a human half-wit.

"I really want to be a good squire. How are we going to carry on?"

As before! When it comes down to it, the two of us are at the source, searching for an idea that will help us both. Stinker paused for a moment, then came out with another suggestion: *Alternatively, you could ride back to the Anvil and jump into the ravine.*

The suggestion made Farin smile.

This chimera really is full of shit. Whatever's going to happen next?

THE END

The adventures of Farin, Stinker and Aross continue in
The Gravedigger's Son and the Waif Girl, Volume 2

Thank you very much for reading this book. If you enjoyed it, please leave a short rating/review at Amazon. As I am an independent author with no backing of a publisher, every positive comment helps to convince others, to read my novels.

Sam Feuerbach

Printed in Great Britain
by Amazon